P9-AQZ-955

Beneath and Beyond

The Hidden City

by

Claudette Cleveland

Strategic Book Group

Copyright © 2011 Claudette Cleveland.

All rights reserved.

No part of this book may be reproduced or transmitted in any form or by any means, graphic, electronic, or mechanical, including photocopying, recording, taping, or by any information storage retrieval system, without the permission, in writing, of the publisher.

Strategic Book Group
P.O. Box 333
Durham CT 06422
www.StrategicBookClub.com

ISBN: 978-1-61204-242-8
Library of Congress Catalogue Card Number: TXu 1-636-245

Contents

Chapter 1   Althea in Mexico 1

Chapter 2   Tashi in Tibet 6

Chapter 3   Childhood Memories 12

Chapter 4   The Legend Continues 15

Chapter 5   The Next Day 19

Chapter 6   The Next Episode 24

Chapter 7   Morning 28

Chapter 8   Village Center 31

Chapter 9   The Next Night 34

Chapter 10 Solana 47

Chapter 11 Berry Collecting 55

Chapter 12 The Story Continues 65

Chapter 13 The Harvest 79

Chapter 14 The Tall White Being Speaks: 82

Chapter 15 The Story Continues 85

Chapter 16 Mauri Moves to the Central Building 87

Chapter 17   The Next Day in Tashi's Village 91

Chapter 18   Mother Begins 94

Chapter 19   The Next Night in Tashi's Home 103

Chapter 20   The Abbot 107

Chapter 21   The Reading 113

Chapter 22   The Story Resumes 115

Chapter 23   Tashi Learns and Grows Up 119

Chapter 24   An Unusual Event 130

Chapter 25   Mauri's Secret Cave 132

Chapter 26   Pãka Tells His Dream 141

Chapter 27   The Next Morning 148

Chapter 28   Another day in the Hidden City 167

Chapter 29   A Unique Movie 181

Chapter 30   Tashi Meets with His Teacher a Second Time 188

Chapter 31   In the Park 192

Chapter 32   Another Day in the Hidden City 203

Chapter 33   The Group of Thirteen 206

Chapter 34   The Dream 208

Chapter 35   Back in the Cave 215

Chapter 36   The Homecoming and Celebration 218

Chapter 37   Dawn of the Next Morning 222

Chapter 38   Mother and Tashi Return to the Village 246

Chapter 39   Tashi Hides in His Cave 250

Chapter 40   Bashur Visits the Cave 254

Chapter 41   Tashi Walks Toward His Village 257

Chapter 42   Back to the Present................................. 260

Chapter 43   The End of Mother's Story........................... 262

Chapter 44   Pa'as's Mission Begins.............................. 269

Chapter 45   Hasue Meets with a Familiar Teacher 273

Chapter 46   Hasue Leaves His Home and His Village 276

Chapter 47   Hasue Begins His Journey............................ 278

Chapter 48   Back to the Present................................. 282

Chapter 49   Althea and Tashi Meet Again 288

Chapter 50   Tashi and Althea Get Married 297

Chapter 51   At the Inn.. 302

Chapter 52   Tashi Arrives in America............................ 312

Chapter 1

Althea in Mexico

The fair-skinned, blue-eyed American tourist stopped dead in her tracks. She could not take another step, as though an invisible wall stood before her. She was confused. What could cause her to be suddenly nauseous and dizzy? It was hot, but not unbearably so. Besides, she loved the hot weather. She had traveled to this city of ruins with a friend from Nuevo Laredo, Mexico, but her friend had gone off with her boyfriend to explore. She sat alone unable to move.

An overwhelming feeling of sadness engulfed her. It became so intense that she struggled to hold back the tears behind her sun-glassed eyes. Sadness and depression were so profound that she felt she could not walk another step. She found a large platform rock to sit on. *Maybe I am hungry,* she thought. Sometimes she suffered similar symptoms from low blood sugar. How could it be, though? She had just eaten a very high-protein breakfast not more than an hour before. Having no other explanation for her debilitation, she rummaged through her backpack and found a protein bar, which was rather mashed but still tightly wrapped in its foil cover. She nibbled on it.

As she sat gazing out over crowds of tourists wearing necklaces of Japanese cameras, the scene changed before her eyes. A deafening silence came over the whole area as though everyone stopped talking at once. She heard the soft crunch of hundreds of feet disturbing pebbles and clumps of grass as they moved across the ground. She closed her eyes. This was not the first time she had gotten a mental vision that she consciously could not explain, but she'd never felt the emotion she had on this day—not an emotion that completely incapacitated her.

She opened her eyes to take a drink of the bottled water she had bought from a wandering entrepreneur. The vision did not change even with her eyes wide open. The sunny bright day turned to night as she gazed at the hundreds of rather short, brown bodies walking toward the large pyramid at the center of the plaza of Teotihuacán, an ancient city outside of Mexico City.

Every few feet someone carried what appeared to be a flaming stick, which caused a blue and orange glow that bounced above the dark-haired heads of the marchers, whose eyes were focused straight ahead with an eerie trance-like gaze.

The pace of this solemn mass of bodies proceeded at a snail's pace. They walked so close together that even though there were hundreds of individuals, they took on the look of a single dark shape slowly flowing down the corridor. The beings at the front of the procession stood apart from this mass of humanity.

The wave of marchers were close enough to her by now that even in the darkness, she could make out some of the features of the one tall being at the very front of the procession and the ten other tall white beings immediately behind him. The oil lamp sticks, which were carried on either side of him, reflected on the leader's long white body. He glanced her way. She saw his cobalt blue eyes, and felt as though they would bore a hole in her. This being, with apparently human emotions, had eyes that were swimming in a pool of liquid, which occasionally overflowed onto his angular face.

His sadness penetrated her core. Overwhelmed by her feeling, she froze in place momentarily. She felt herself rise and walk along the edge of the procession opposite him. So strong was his magnetism that it was as though she was being pulled forward by some invisible force field.

She again looked over in his direction. He carried a rod of some sort. The shimmering tip of the rod reflected the various colors of the burning lamps. It was a magnificent clear crystal. The rod itself glowed golden along its approximately twelve-inch spine, which accommodated an array of multi-shaped colored gemstones. Not being an expert, she could only guess, but there appeared to be a ruby, an emerald, a sapphire, and an amethyst, as well as three other different colored stones. The seven gems, not including the crystal on the tip, gave off a particular aura or colored ray, which mingled with the white and golden aura of its bearer.

So bright stood this tall, white being that even in the semidarkness, she couldn't take her eyes off him. His energy pulled her along his path. The more she focused on the golden rod, the more hypnotic it became. The tremendously sharp intuitive pains in her stomach occasionally overshadowed the ache in her heart, pains she had only previously experienced prior to an emotionally, traumatic event.

Closer and closer the processional came to the central pyramid. The sky turned from a black-blue to a dull gray. The stars disappeared as though someone pulled their chains, extinguishing their illumination one by one.

At the center of the plaza the leading tall being made a right angle turn and headed toward the towering sun pyramid. The short, dark-haired masses stopped at the pyramid's base and stood still. A tense feeling of anticipation grew as eleven tall beings and she ascended the steps of the pyramid. About halfway up, ten of the beings stopped, turned, and faced the crowd. The tall one carrying the rod and she continued to climb toward the top. The sky lightened more with each ascending step. Finally, at the very top, the tall white one turned and faced the silent crowd below. All eyes were upon him, heads tilted back for a clearer view. The majestic tall being's eyes were focused on the eastern horizon in anticipation of the rising sun.

An inner knowing told her that according to the custom followed for generations on this summer solstice day, he would lead the people in a religious or spiritual ceremony, which began as the first rays of the sun showed themselves. After many prayers and rituals, this head priest would give the prophecies and spiritual guidance to his spiritual followers as he received the sacred words from the "gods."

She knew from her studies that solstice in Latin means the sun stands still. Up to the day of the solstice, the sun rises higher and higher in the noon sky, but on that day it appears to stand still or not visibly rise. The summer solstice was normally a joyous time of the year for these people, for it represented the onset of a warm growing period. Everything that had been planted in the spring was flourishing. Also, the first full moon of June is called the Honey Moon because it is the time for harvesting honey from the hives, a much sought-after commodity. So as not to compete with the union of the gods and goddesses, which was thought to occur in May, human weddings or unions were celebrated in June. They were celebrated with drinks sweetened with the new honey, which the ancients believed encouraged love and fertility.

On that hot steamy day at the Teotihuacán ruins, the female American tourist found herself at the top of the sun pyramid not remembering how she got there. Physically and emotionally exhausted, she painstakingly climbed down the narrow steps and literally crawled to the outside perimeter of the ancient city where her physical stamina quickly restored itself. The farther away from the ancient city she got, the more her energy returned to normal. Even her breathing, which had been labored, returned to a normal rhythm.

* * *

Bashur still remembered sitting in his spacecraft gazing down at all the fire and smoke camouflaging what once had been a loving and harmonious settlement nestled along a rise beside the fast-moving pure water of a river. It had been his project from the beginning. How the earth had changed in this twenty-first century since its early development when he was first sent here on assignment from his home planet, Araphius. When the catastrophic events started on earth, he was transferred to Uranus to await his next assignment. From there he orchestrated many of the developments that were to be built and rebuilt in this galaxy. One such development was a colony he had built on a site now called Teotihuacán near Mexico City.

He had designated one of his fellow beings as his assistant to live in this new colony on earth. He and eleven others were to live among the natives and help them build the new mountain city similar to his earlier colonization of what is now call Machu Picchu, Peru. The new appointee would be the head priest of the recently created colony in Mexico. The new Mayan colony from its origin had the same spiritual atmosphere as Central City of Lemuria, a continent in the Pacific. A tear came to his eyes as he clearly recalled his protégée's last walk up the main avenue. How appropriate it is, Bashur thought that they now refer to that main avenue as the avenue of the dead.

This same protégée walked the earth now as a human woman. She had visited the ruins of her past assignment and remembered.

Bashur had again been assigned to earth. Many times he had sent representatives to walk among the people of earth in an attempt to teach the oneness. Each time, the earthlings destroyed the representative's human body. However, he hoped for a different outcome for his newest assignment. He personally was to prepare a boy for the upcoming shift in the earth's energy. This time Bashur would remain on earth throughout the shift and take an even more assertive roll in the transition.

Chapter Two

Tashi in Tibet

With the summer sun warming his back, Tashi, now a young man, stood at the edge of Lake Yamdrok-Tso, the turquoise lake in southern Tibet, his mind wandering back in time. What stories this turquoise body of water could tell. His reminiscent thoughts, he knew, were prompted by the fact that he had just helped his mother's soul cross over and had seen her body taken to the sky burial sight. As he sat by the softly lapping waters, he remembered the many nights he had sat at her knee, listening to her tell the ancient legends that had been passed down through the generations.

As he watched the sunlight dance on the surface of the magical lake, he swore he heard his mother's voice telling the ancient tales again, as though she had experienced them herself through the eyes of Mauri, a young girl of the ancient Motherland. Remembering his mother's far away look and emotional expressions, he wondered if maybe it was true that she had actually experienced them in some other lifetime.

Sitting on a rock next to the lake, Tashi gazed out into the distance at the snow-capped mountains. In his dream-like state his mother's voice became stronger and louder, as though he were that little boy again sitting at her knee, hanging on her every word.

Mother always started the legendary stories the same way. She began by setting the scene in colorful detail. His favorite tale came to mind as he watched the gentle ripples of the lake. He had never grown tired of hearing it again and again. Hypnotized by the lake, he heard her begin.

6

The land was flat and the plants shimmered like an emerald coat interwoven with rubies, amethysts, diamonds, and other natural gems. The people lived in clusters then, called villages today. They lived in complete harmony with the land and the animals.

Mother spoke as though she told the story from her own experiences.

I lived with my parents and two brothers. The climate was constant with little deviation and just enough rainfall, never too little or too much, but just enough to satisfy the thirst of the human and animal inhabitants, as well as that of the abundant plant life. We never lacked crystal clear drinking water.

Our lessons began at an early age. The teachers encouraged us to talk to the animals, plants, and trees as though they, too, were members of the village and family. Our formal education began at about the age of three. Once a month a priest from Central City of the Motherland visited our village in order to give us a special lesson. The rest of the time, the village spiritual leader instructed us, testing us on the application of the Central City priest's lessons. Each of these lessons had to be mastered before we were allowed to go on to the next. I remember I would sometimes get the symbols confused, at which time one of my bird companions would let out the loudest shrill letting me know I had made a mistake during my practice.

My father spent hours drilling me by having me repeatedly draw each symbol on the ground with a stick. The memories of watching him erase my drawings with his large foot when they were not perfect will never leave me. It wasn't that I was slow; it's just that my mind would wander. During the repetitious drawing, I was aware of pictures of people, places, and things drifting through my mind. As a small child, I found the mental pictures far more interesting than the current lesson drill. These mental pictures were often accompanied by voices talking as though they spoke to me personally. Later, I described the visions and dialogue to my mother, especially the visions I did not understand, which, because of my young age, encompassed most of them.

My mother told my father about some of my more dramatic visions. He later asked me to describe them to him in more detail. Frequently, he became pensively silent after one of my more elaborate descriptions.

When the visions started coming more frequently and clearly, he arranged for a private session with the Central City priest during one of his monthly visits. The priest encouraged me to continue to let the voices and pictures come through. He gave my father instructions for exercises to help me bring the visions through even clearer. They wanted me to be able to bring them forth at will. This was a lot more fun than repeatedly drawing symbols in the dirt.

I remember one of my visions had moving images. As I watched the pictures in my mind, our village came to life as it did on a normal morning. The sun shone. The people of the village gardened, cleaned, and prepared food. Without warning, the ground began to tremble. The bottom of my small bare feet tickled, causing me to giggle as Mother Earth gently shook. As I gazed at the sky toward the dawn, I noticed that a cloud of dense smoke created a gray veil that muted the first morning rays of Father Sun. *What kind of cook fire could be large enough to do that?* I thought. I asked a nearby adult about it. I received no answer, only an alarmed expression.

As the day went on, the cloud of smoke with its highlights of red sparks came closer to our village. By late afternoon the wind had brought the cloud creeping, not unlike a cat on silent paws, into our village itself. Everyone in the village started coughing and covering their noses and mouths. The red sparks burned our skin as they floated out of the cloud and bit our skin like pesky mosquitoes.

With focused determination our parents swiftly ushered us inside our dwellings. The stronger men of the village filled clay containers and woven baskets with water and poured it on rooftops before the sparks found food enough in the grasses of the roofs to become a grownup fire. The mothers of the village were told to gather and pack foods and essentials because evacuation might be necessary.

My mental vision was so real it was as though I were actually living it as I repeated it to my father and the chief, who had joined him shortly after I started describing my mental pictures. I actually coughed as the cloud enveloped me in the vision. Only a few days later my vision became a reality.

Just like in my visions, I peeked through the woven grass-door covering of our dwelling even though they told me to stay back from any openings. Being an extremely curious child, I gazed through the peek-hole and saw the men running back and forth, bringing containers of water from the nearby stream in an effort to keep ahead of the insatiable hunger of the fires. Even my young mind could see that the fires were like bears just awakened from their winter fast. Everything was prey to their appetites. Some of the men fell to the ground gasping for clean air when the cloud strangled them. Some of the women helped those on the ground by putting a wet cloth over their noses and assisting them into a dwelling free of the cloud.

After a brief rest and a clearing of their air passages, the men returned outside into the cloud and resumed their firemen duties. I did not understand the gravity of the moment, but I felt and saw that the cloud and the fire were not going to be stopped or satisfied.

Mother finished the last of the packing as Father entered and announced that we must leave—quickly. He told her that, along with our village of about thirty people and other nearby villages, we were to head northwest toward the moving water. Mother delegated a bundle to each of us to carry, one appropriate to our size and strength. Being the smallest, mine was the lightest but was bulky for my slight frame.

Without much delay we, along with the other families of the village, started walking toward the northwest. After about an hour, even my light bundle became heavy. A few people leading the migration decided that we would take a rest, allowing the slower ones and latecomers to catch up with the pack. My little legs and arms welcomed the rest. Most of us children considered the events themselves an exciting adventure. However, there was no gaiety in the adult's actions or words, as they whispered among themselves. By the expressions on their faces they considered the situation serious and grave.

After a short time, the whole group, even the latecomers, was together, and we pressed onward. Looking back toward the direction from which we had traveled, we saw an even thicker and denser cloud. The fires consumed all in their path. Some of the treetops resembled ceremonial torches, but much larger and more majestically bright.

9

The trembling of the earth, which before only tickled my feet, was now shaking my entire body to the point that I found it difficult for my small stature to walk without falling. Carrying the oversized pack made it even more difficult to remain upright and move ahead. Progress was slow. When I did fall, I was immediately pulled to my feet and dragged along by the arm by a nearby adult."

Mother paused a moment and then continued as though she had to take a moment to make certain she was remembering the catastrophic event correctly with every detail.

We walked for hours. Because of the veil of smoke over the sun, darkness came early. The elders sent one of the young men of our migrating village ahead to find a suitable campsite. He returned, announcing that a short distance farther was a clear area next to a wide stream. We would be safe there, he said, in case the fire took a turn or caught up with us. Also, it would give the refugee villagers an opportunity to replenish their water supply as well as wash away the soot and ashes that had accumulated on their bodies.

As the young man predicted, shortly we arrived at the chosen campsite. Mother had packed much dried food, so from the pack she took ground-up tapa root and mixed it with stream water, making it into a sticky porridge. She placed a portion of the porridge on an elder leaf for each of us, which my brother had gathered at her request. Someone found berries growing along the stream, and when mixed with the porridge, they made what could have been a rather bland meal a bit more flavorful. The berries, vigorously stirred into the gray colored porridge, turned it into a pink and quite appealing dish. I started to eat, but I almost fell asleep halfway through the meal. For as small a child as I was, it had been a long, physically and emotionally exhausting day. The excitement I felt at the beginning of the journey had worn off after the first two hours of continuous walking.

The pack I carried contained our finely woven sleeping mats. Woven from stripped grasses, each mat had its own specific color and design so that everyone knew which one was his or hers. Mine had a large eight-pointed star in the center, which had been bleached to a brilliant white. The ever-trembling earth lulled me, and my exhausted body fell into a deep sleep in a matter of minutes. Mother covered me with a warm blanket made from spun milk-pod cotton. Had I been able to stay awake, I would have heard and participated in the meditation led by our priest, as well as the harmonious chanting performed by all the refugees. Meditation was considered an essential ritual in our everyday lives. The priest taught, as they were taught by the tall white beings of the Central City, that meditating brought clarity to the mind and rejuvenation to the human body.

Father Sun never did show himself the next morning, but the dawn turned the obsidian black night into a hazy gray. Mother had already prepared our morning meal, which consisted of some of the same porridge, and berries we had eaten the night before, as well as a strip of dried fish. My father had gathered several cattail stalks, growing along the banks of the stream. He stripped them, giving us chunks of their sweet soft center. We were told to eat quickly for we had a long day's walk before we reached the big moving water.

We walked the entire day with only a few breaks. Just when I thought I could not take another step, someone in the lead shouted, 'Moana,' the sea. This gave everyone including myself the needed adrenal surge to continue on. I felt a quickening in my step, which for my short legs felt like running. I had never seen this water they called Moana, but had heard many stories about it. What would it look like? What would it smell like? What would it feel like? My curiosity took control of me. My excitement gave me the boost of energy to continue at the accelerated speed the group was moving.

Chapter Three

Childhood Memories

Tashi's mother always stopped the nightly stories or myths at a major high point of the adventure, making him yearn for the climax of the nightly tale, and declaring that she would continue another night. Almost since early childhood, Tashi knew the stories verbatim, yet each time while laying in his bed waiting for sleep, he'd visualize his mother as a child in that night's epic tale. That night he endeavored to see her as a child playing on the beach. He had never seen an ocean or a beach, so he only imagined what they looked like from his mother's nightly descriptions. Like most people in that region of Tibet, he had never been beyond the Himalayan Mountains where his small village was located.

With his eyes closed on the verge of sleep, Tashi smelled the smoke in the atmosphere and on his body, as his mother had described in that night's episode. He never tired of hearing his mother's stories, for each time she would add something new. He looked forward to the continuing sagas with intense excitement. As the highlights of that evening's segment played like a film in his head, his body relaxed and he surrendered to sleep.

The following day Tashi went about his routine chores. Carrying an empty pouch made from the skin of a mountain sheep, he started toward the meadow where the yaks were grazing. Gathering the yak dung was an everyday duty, but especially during the warmer months when the yaks ate more and thus produced more dung. After his pouch was full, he took the dung home where his sister and he formed it into round, uniform patties. The moist patties were stuck in neat rows on the sunlit side of their stucco-covered clay-block house to dry. The more patties they stored, the more assured the family would be of having ample heat and cooking fuel during the colder months. His mother often sent him to the meadow several times a day during the spring and summer months when the dung was so abundant. In the tundra region of Tibet in which he lived, wood or other fuel was not readily available.

It was also his job to check on the herd, to make certain all were well. He always took his slingshot with him, as did all the mountain herders in Tibet. It was uncommon to spot a wolf lurking on the perimeter of the herd waiting for vulnerable prey, but it occasionally happened. He had already killed two attacking wolves at the young age of ten. He had become quite accurate with the leather sling his father had made for him. Since the first day his father and uncle taught him how to use it, it felt like a natural weapon in his hands.

He received his first sling on his eighth birthday. The memory of seeing his father's smile out of the corner of his eye, then seeing that same smile turn to a grimace as Tashi shot Mother's prize rooster, killing it instantly, still sent a chill up his spine. He was not certain whether the grimace was for the rooster or for himself. One thing was for certain, Mother's wrath would be directed to both he and his father when he handed her the majestic kill to clean.

Out of duty, Father reprimanded him and delivered a lecture on respecting the sling as a deadly weapon and on honoring all life. He reiterated many times that a sling was not a toy, making certain that he talked loud enough for Mother to hear. The rest of that disturbing day, Tashi busied himself with various chores, making sure to maintain a wide berth of Mother until she had time to calm down after the rooster incident.

At dinner, Father, who talked about everything else but the menu, which of course was rooster, led the conversation. Tashi had difficulty looking at, much less eating, the prized victim of his carelessness. He took a double helping of the barley cakes and yak cheese. Two full cups of the goat's milk soothed the emptiness in his stomach.

After the dinner dishes were cleared and cleaned, it was time for the next chapter in the story Mother had started the night before. With the evening yak butter candle lighted, everyone gathered around Mother in anticipation.

Mother sat with her eyes shut in silence for what seemed like an eternity. Only the occasional crackling from the candle was heard.

Chapter Four

The Legend Continues

An air of mystery as well as tension rippled up and down the beach as more and more village refugees arrived to establish a camp at the edge of the moving waters. Except for our odd meals, we children found those days on the beach fun and exciting, oblivious to the real danger that was creeping closer and closer toward our encampment. We stood at the moving water's edge and dared each wave to slap us. It became a game we played for hours as we dug our heels into the sand even deeper when we saw the seventh wave start to come roaring toward us. Like a lion warns its prey before the attack, the wave's roar grew in volume as its force became more intense, until finally it hit us with its full might. Some of the bigger children withstood its forceful push and remained standing, but being smaller than most, I more often than not tumbled off my feet as the wave attempted to capture me and pull me out to its deep and mysterious domain. Frequently one of the older children saved me from such a kidnapping, my body being the medium in this tug of war game.

Repeatedly, the moving water delivered a gift as a wave tumbled the prize onto the shore beside our feet. One such gift, a prickly star, landed in front of me as I stood daring the seventh wave. Once, a large white disk with inscribed writing on it rolled up, my legs stopping its movement long enough for me to pick it up. I took it to my mother for her to interpret the somewhat familiar but strange symbols. She told me it was written in the language of the gods and that she didn't know what it said. I tucked it away among my meager belongings so I could ask the priest teacher at my first opportunity. Sometimes rocks that were as light as air came floating in on the top of a wave.

That month our makeshift village on the shore was for the most part fun and frolicking, at least for the children. The adults, however, worked intensely and demonstrated little gaiety. The men, busy using sharpened stones from sunrise to sunset, downed mammoth trees that were broader around than I was tall. Later they hollowed them into boats that would serve as transportation.

I sometimes heard the adults talking of the dangerous journey that we would take in those boats. The journey was to take us to freedom from the dangers of Mother Earth's wrath, to a land on the other side of the moving water. Each day we children strained our eyes trying to catch a glimpse of this land that was supposed to be across the moving water. We never did actually see it, although sometimes our eyes played tricks on us and we thought that we saw the mirage of this mysterious place, but when we blinked, the land image faded with the mist of a wave. We knew our imaginations were playing a game with us.

One day when the boats looked as though they were near completion, I saw my mother heating and stirring a gummy substance until it was thin and runny. From the smell of it I hoped that it was not our dinner. I was relieved when my father applied several coats of the boiling brew to the wood surface of a boat, inside and out.

Almost every day, we children gathered armloads of tall grasses and reeds from the nearby lagoons. The older women of each refugee village sat in circles weaving watertight baskets from the mountains of grasses we deposited before them. When we asked why they were making so many, they told us that they would be needed for the journey. Racks with colorful fish speared by the older boys were drying near the fires. Other racks had berries and cut up root vegetables laid out in an orderly fashion so that the dry heat of the fire could extract the moisture. The temporary villages up and down the shore were a hubbub of activity from morning until night.

Every night, hazy beacons of light flickered up and down the shore as the villages' central fires glowed. Songs of thanksgiving were sung around each campfire. Even though the words of the songs from each village were slightly different, the overall sound created a harmonious melody like an orchestra of instruments playing different notes but the same song. Every night I was lulled to sleep by their melodious tones combining with the percussion of the crashing ocean waves.

Throughout the month as the earth's rumble intensified, preparations for the journey continued at an intense pace. The water baskets were filled, the food baskets were brimming with the dried morsels, and the boats were finished and tested for their sea worthiness. We were told that our journey would begin at sunrise even though we had not seen the sun since we had fled from our villages over a month ago.

At first light each of the boats was loaded with supplies. We ate what would be our last hot meal for a long time. The moment arrived to board the loaded crafts. We children were placed in the center and deepest part of the boats. Next, on either side of us were the women. The men took their stations on both ends, paddles in hand. Finally the day had come to depart across the waves. We would never return to our beloved Motherland, which was burning and slowly sinking into the sea.

The men in the back of the boat pushed the boats into the moving waters. In our family boat rode my father and his brothers and their two sons, along with my mother, my aunt, my brothers, and myself. Our journey to the mysterious land across the water began as the men jumped into the boat and started to paddle. I detected a tear or two escaping from the watery eyes of many of the adults as our boat journeyed farther and farther from the shore.

I broke the silence by asking Mother how Father and the other men knew which way to steer the boats. She pointed to the sky. My eyes searched through the haze until I saw them, three bright lights the color of berries, which made the shape of a triangle. I knew they were not normal stars but since no other information was volunteered, I squelched the questions in my mind. As the hours and days of our voyage passed, the three bright lights were always present. At night when I looked up, their brightness was even greater.

One day I asked Mother if the bright lights were the same as the white star people, that we saw dancing in the velvet sky every night in our village. Her answer only created more questions. She said, 'They are the gods of the white star people.'

Often during the journey, I glanced up to assure myself that the gods were still there, still directing. Every time the now familiar triangle came into my sight, I felt a cocoon of warmth envelope me, giving me the same feeling I had when I had received mental visions in the village.

Tashi's mother stopped speaking. They knew they would hear no more that night. After a few minutes of silence, she opened her eyes and, in what they perceived as a slightly different voice, told them it was time for bed. They knew it would not help to plead for another episode, so in silence, they climbed the ladder to their beds.

Chapter Five

The Next Day

Tashi awoke, not to the familiar crow of his mother's prized rooster, which he had silenced the day before with a reckless zing of his slingshot, but instead to the redundant thud of the butter churn. In his slightly dreamy state, he visualized his grandmother sitting before the churn, raising and lowering the rod that would eventually turn the yak milk into a lump of creamy butter. With each thud of the beater hitting the bottom of the churn, he could taste the fresh butter that would be stirred into his barley porridge.

The butter-making also told him that it was the day of the month when his family took various offerings to the monastery, which was a two-hour walk from their village. Tashi rose from his sleeping mat and climbed down the ladder into the central room of the house. His mother stood stirring the breakfast barley porridge. The burning sandalwood and juniper incense created a haze that made everything appear as though it was not solid but a part of a dream. The pack that had been readied for the four-hour journey to and from the monastery was sitting next to the doorway.

Tashi's sister, Yeshe, was not far behind him coming down the ladder. Everyone took their places at the table, and Father gave thanks for the abundance. They ate barley cakes and barley porridge called tsampa. Grandma finished the butter and wrapped it in a cloth, tied with a band woven with the family design as well as the eternal knot, a Tibetan symbol of the unity of all things and the illusory character of time.

Without much delay after breakfast, the family walked down the road toward the monastery. The road paralleled the stream that flowed into the turquoise lake, the same lake where Tashi, the man, now sat reminiscing. At the edge of the lake, led by father, they paid homage to the lake gods. Tashi had never seen the gods of the lake. He had only heard tales of their miraculous ability to rise from the lake's center to high above the mountains until they appeared as a star. Then later, as the legend was told, they would reenter the lake without even causing a ripple on its surface. He envied those who had actually witnessed these events.

Father performed the lake prayer ritual, part of which was consuming a small snack of barley cakes and a cup of buttermilk. This act was thought to ensure continued abundance. Afterward, the family started the assent up the mountain to the monastery on a well-established pilgrim's path. At some points the path narrowed so that it necessitated walking in single file, since the wall of the mountain bordered one side and a drop of several hundred feet bordered the other side. The day was bright with sunlight, which warmed their faces even though the air grew cooler and thinner as they continued the trek up the mountain.

The travelers saw the monastery from the path. It appeared to be a small toy building from their position at the bottom of the mountain. The higher they walked, the larger and more colorful the view of the monastery became as its many colorful poles of prayer flags came into focus. The sun glistened on the golden Dharma wheel, symbolizing the auspiciousness of the turning of the precious wheel of Buddha's doctrine flanked by the two golden deer, representing Buddha's first teachings in Deer Park. The legend is that so wondrous and peaceful was the Buddha's appearance that even the animals came to listen.

The statues were like a beacon for them as they journeyed closer and closer toward their destination. Along the path a raven announced to the creatures of the mountain the family's arrival. They stopped at one turn on the path and walked out onto a large boulder from which they viewed the entire valley. Standing there, they heard the song of the mountains being sung in harmony with the tinkling of the bells securely fastened around the necks of yaks grazing in the valley below. They never questioned the source of the songs for they knew that the beloved saint, Milarepa, could be heard throughout the land if their hearts and ears were open to his melodic spiritual messages.

Tashi had always been especially fascinated with the many myths and legends of the most famous Tibetan yogi, Milarepa. As he recalled, Milarepa was a southern Tibetan whose early existence was a simple yet prosperous life in the high snow-clad tableland in the Himalayan Mountains until a greedy uncle, who at the death of Milarepa's father, ousted him, his mother, and his sister, leaving them to live a sub-standard lifestyle.

Furious, Milarepa's mother, knowing of her son's natural gifts for magic, entered him into a monastery known for its teaching of black magic. Milarepa was a star pupil, so when he graduated, his mother coerced him to revenge the uncle's wrongdoing by bringing their confiscated house down during his cousin's wedding, killing many. Influenced by his mother's hate, he performed many devastating acts of black magic until one day he met a lama who convinced him that his gifts used to harm others were also self-destructive.

Under the guidance of master teachers, he spent the rest of his life making amends for his wrongdoings and striving to reach nirvana, the ultimate stage of spirituality.

Choosing the life of a yogi, he traveled among the nomads throughout Tibet on his spiritual journey. He became an icon for the teachings of Buddha, spreading his messages through his lyrical songs. Even today Milarepa's song could be heard sung in many nomad camps.

* * *

No matter how many times Tashi walked through the gates of the plaza of the monastery, he never failed to feel a tingle that enveloped his whole being. This day was no different. Some peddlers had stationed themselves just inside the gates with their array of goods spread before them. The family walked by them and the many beggars with their outstretched, cupped hands. Near the entrance to the monastery, Father, Mother, and Grandmother turned each of the large brass prayer wheels clockwise while chanting the mantra, "Om Mani Padme Hum," Tibetan for hail to the jewel of the lotus. As the large drum whirled around, their prayers were sent to the universe.

They began chanting as they joined the processional of spiritual pilgrims, which ultimately ended at the feet of the jewel-studded statue of their beloved bohista, the Buddha of Compassion. Tashi knew that this was only a statue of the enlightened one, an incarnation of selflessness, virtue, and wisdom, but when he prostrated himself before it, energy surged through him. He could not explain the euphoric feeling he had in its presence.

The floor of the monastery was cool to his knees and body as he genuflected before the statue of Buddha. He heard bells somewhere in the monastery. Their high-pitched tones seemed to pierce his soul until he felt his very core was resonating with them. After a while he arose, leaving the offering of yak butter at the base of the Buddha, which was illuminated by the light of the hundreds of yak butter candles.

As he circumvented the room, statues of the enlightened ones with their bright blue eyes and uplifted hands showing him the triangle with a star etched at the center of their palm, seemed to become alive to him. Even in the dim light their illuminated blue eyes followed him wherever he was in the room.

It was usually after one of his visits to the monastery that he felt an overwhelming envy for his step-brother who had been chosen to become a monk and had left for his servitude at the age of seven. It was expected that each family relinquish one of their sons, usually the oldest, in service to the lamas. His brother qualified.

He had not seen him since Tashi was six years old, but he could still remember the day Jetsen left, escorted to his new home by Tashi's father. He was living and studying in a monastery at least three days away. A traveling yogi who knew their family sometimes brought them word of his well-being. Tashi barely knew his stepbrother, for as the years went by his memory of him faded. Among his other studies, Jetsen was also learning the martial arts, a specialty of the particular monastery in which he was studying.

Only on the monthly monastery visits would Tashi think of his stepbrother. Just after being in the energy of this immense Buddha icon, Tashi felt the envy of not being able to bask in that kind of powerful energy on a daily basis. His envious feeling always dissipated on the walk home as he came closer and closer to his beloved village where his friends and familiar surroundings awaited him. He wondered how his stepbrother could not miss the view of Yamdrok-Tso, the turquoise lake, or the celebration after the fall barley harvest or most of all, his mother's nightly stories.

It was dusk when the returning pilgrims' village came into view. Without any prodding, everyone in the family went their separate ways to do their individual evening tasks that were a necessary routine. As the tasks were completed, one by one each of them came into the house where the aromas of a cooking supper permeated the room. After rinsing some of the travel dust off with the water in a bowl sitting next to the door, they sat down at the already set table.

Tonight was a special one for they were to have yak butter tea. From one of the peddlers at the monastery, Father had traded some fine specimens of turquoise and coral for several blocks of black tea from China. Since he could remember, Tashi was always looking for the gemstones found in the mountains, which were a valuable bartering tool for the prized black tea.

After dinner Tashi and his family sat in anticipation of mother's next episode of the nightly story, staring dreamily at the last lingering embers of the evening's cook fire, as Mother readied herself. The yak butter candles were lit and mother took her storyteller position in front of them with the dying embers behind her creating the impression of a halo as the light of the embers back lighted her aura. When her eyes closed and she fell silent, they knew the next episode was about to begin.

Chapter Six

The Next Episode

Mother begins.

The days and nights in the boats on the moving waters were too many for my young mind to count. Finally, the day came when our canoes slid onto a strange shore. Although the sand was the same as that of Lemuria, the Motherland, the atmosphere and terrain beyond the sand were quite different. The men hopped out and pulled the crafts onto the sandy land. Our legs felt as though they were made of willow branches as we stepped onto the shore. We had not put our weight on them for a very long time. Our parents laughed as we tried to manipulate one foot in front of the other on legs that refused to stiffen enough to hold the rest of our bodies erect.

After everyone was ashore, we gathered together to give thanks for our safe voyage and to ask for guidance in this new and strange land. The leaders of the various villages led the thanksgiving prayer. A special prayer of gratitude was given for our safe arrival to the new land to which the 'gods' above had escorted us.

We made our camp on the beach near the edge of the forest. For the first time in a long time we were able to see the night sky and the white star people. The berry colored triangle had disappeared as soon as our canoes rode onto the shore. The air was clear and did not burn our nostrils as it had in our motherland, and throughout most of the voyage. The moon created sparkling crystals on the moving water's surface, which resembled tiny dancing fairies, as were described in our myths. There was an air of hopefulness among the people, and yet, I also sensed an undercurrent of anxiety, a fear of the unknown.

The next morning as the sun peeked its head up above the horizon, a representative from every village gathered for a meeting around a central fire. While they were meeting, the Central City priest, Kanaloa, led us in meditation and breathing exercises. Afterward, he and our local chief started assigning duties to every person. Even the youngest and the smallest, whoever could walk, were given a job to perform. Our best hunters were sent into the forest to hunt for meat. Others were sent with the water baskets to replenish our drinking water. The younger women were sent searching for fruits, nuts, and roots. The boys became the wood gatherers.

My job, as one of the smaller ones, was to accompany the grandmothers as they walked along the shore collecting clams, mussels, and other such edible life forms that had washed up during the night. No one complained, for all the chores were for the purpose of a grand festival that evening to celebrate our safe journey. I had been a part of many festivals in our village in the Motherland, but this would be the first one in this strange land that was to be our new home.

The anticipation of the celebration created a circus-like atmosphere. We children ran up and down the shore from one village grouping to another. Our nostrils took in the scents of new as well as familiar foods as they lay cooking near each village's central fire.

As the day went on, the various groups wandered back into camp with their bounty. Everywhere I looked there were baskets of delectable foods, some of which I had never seen before. The Central City priest was sitting by the fire putting holes in a strange hollow stalk he called bamboo. He heated a hardwood branch about the size of his small finger in the fire, and then pierced it immediately into the hollow stalk. He repeated this until a clean hole appeared on one side of the stalk. Every once in a while he blew through the stalk. With each breath a different set of tones rang through the air. He continued boring holes until he was satisfied with the range of octaves of the tones that his breath created by blowing through the hollow bamboo tube and covering the various holes with his fingers.

25

On this first day in the new land, as the sun was swallowed by the moving water and everyone had returned to their temporary camp, the baskets of food were set out on long woven mats. Various types of meat and fowl were cooking over and around the fires. Our stomachs growled as the juices fell into the coals hissing and releasing a gamut of appetite-alluring aromas.

When the sun was completely consumed by the moving water, the priest blew through the hollow bamboo stalk. Clear tones permeated the air. Various parts of my body tingled and resonated with each new tone as he put a finger over one hole after another and blew. This continued until my body was tingling from head to toe. The priest then gave thanks to 'All that Is.' He said other words, which were lost on me, because my stomach's voice was far louder than his words or chants. Loud shouts bellowed from everyone in unison indicating that the eating could begin, not too soon for my stomach. Our hollowed out wooden bowls were filled to the brim. Throughout the meal everyone joyously chattered. The future, although unknown, seemed ever brighter during this celebration of good fortune and thanks.

After everyone had had his or her fill and the remaining food was safely stored, we all found a spot around the newly replenished central fire. A huge turned up log was set on one side of the fire creating a stage-like seat for the priest from Central City. On this special night in our new land, he was going to tell the story of how Central City of the Motherland was established. We were told to remember every detail and to retell the story over and over again to our children and our children's children. The glories and spirit of our ancestors, he told us, must never be forgotten. He said this would help us later to understand who and what we are.

At that point the priest closed his eyes and went silent. His only movements were the slight quiver of his lips and eyelids. The rest of his body did not even twitch. Except for the roar of the moving water and the crackle of the fire, the silence was deafening. Our eyes were glued to him in anticipation.

Much to Tashi's regret, Mother stopped the nightly story just before the priest on the beach began and said she would continue the next night. Although she often stopped her nightly story right before something exciting was going to happen, Tashi could not resist begging her to go on. As always, her reply was, "If you're so anxious to know the rest of the story, tell your dream spirits to tell you more while you sleep."

Sometimes Tashi did ask the dream spirits and thus had dreams that continued the story, but he was never quite certain that his dreams were the true story, at least not until the next night when his mother continued. Sometimes his version was similar and sometimes it had several differences. Even so, tonight he would contact his dream spirits, he thought.

Chapter Seven

Morning

The following morning Tashi awoke to what he thought would be a typical day in southern Tibet. As he lay in his bed a moment, replaying his dream, he heard a strange voice coming from the opening in the floor, which led down to the main room of their house. It was a male voice. He listened closely but could not figure out any of the words.

Curiosity overcame him, so he quickly pulled on his leggings and shirt and rapidly climbed down the ladder. No one looked his way as he ducked out the door to relieve his bladder. As he came back in he noticed for the first time that there were two men present even though he had heard only one voice.

Tashi's mother greeted him and told the two men that this was her son Tashi who was now ten. Mother turned to Tashi and explained, "These two men are visiting from Lhasa and have been commissioned to start a school in our village so that the children can learn to read and write in Tibetan as well as in Chinese." Tashi's village had never had a school before. Any structured teaching came through the area priest or lama and it consisted of religious symbols taught through rote and mantras.

The taller of the two men explained that the needed teaching materials and the teacher would be provided if the village would agree to build the physical school building, as well as provide room and board for the teacher who would be sent from Lhasa. At the request of this man, a village meeting was scheduled for that evening so that the proposition could be discussed and agreed or disagreed upon by the village populace.

It would take the cooperation of the whole village for the school to succeed. Not only would the school have to be built, but the parents of the school-age children would have to rearrange their daily routines so that the children were freed from some of their chores in order to attend classes on a regular basis.

The representatives from Lhasa asked for Mother and Father's cooperation in arranging the meeting. Mother was one of the few people in the village who had some limited ability to read and write. When Mother was a child, she had an aunt who had lived with her family a few months every year. This aunt was a nun and had been taught to read and write at the nunnery. Being quick of mind and yearning for new worlds to be open to her, Mother begged her aunt to teach her to read and write during her yearly visits.

Hearing of her previous experience, the men from Lhasa thought Mother would be an enthusiastic supporter of their proposition and rightfully so. The people of the village were somewhat leery of change and often resistant to it. However, when Mother spoke, people listened. She had a mystical way of saying just the right words to put people at ease. They trusted and respected her. Hardly a day went by when someone was not in the house getting personal counseling of one kind or another.

Mother was also the village healer. She knew what herbs were needed if someone was ill. She had remedies for even serious illnesses. Often she used a set of thorns that she would stick into the ill person at certain places on their bodies. The long thorns never seemed to hurt or draw blood from her patients, yet afterward the patients appeared to be better and often recovered quickly to total wellness.

Sometimes the same patient returned to have the thorns stuck into his or her body three days in a row. Tashi's house was always a hub of activity. Tashi's grandmother often helped with the treatments. She could frequently be seen cooking some kind of smelly concoction she called a poultice. Once Tashi saw a man with a black sticky mixture spread all over his injured arm. He actually left with it on his arm. When he came back several days later to have the poultice removed, his arm was totally healed.

Those who came for a healing always left some gift as a symbol of gratitude in exchange for the healing. Mother never refused the gift for she knew the exchange was necessary if the healing was going to be effective. By the village standards, Tashi's family was considered quite wealthy, but Mother never let on that this was so. She knew her special knowledge was a gift to be used and shared.

Having a taste of education herself and hungering for more all her life, she was very excited about the proposition the Lhasa men were presenting. She had tried to teach Tashi and his sister what she knew, but too often found that her knowledge was inadequate. The prospect of her children learning to read and write fluently created a glow around her that was almost blinding.

Father and Tashi went from house to house announcing the meeting that was scheduled for that evening after dinner. They asked villagers to meet at dusk before the mountains swallowed the sun, near the well in the center of the village.

Chapter Eight

Village Center

T he villagers gathered at dusk. The central plaza was noisy with chatter. There was a festive atmosphere for very few strangers except for when an occasional yogi or Sherpa visited their village, and certainly not someone from the sacred city of Lhasa. Mother and Father escorted the strangers to the platform around the well. Mother raised her hand, and the chatter died down until there was absolute silence with the exception of the quiet whimpering of a baby. She introduced the two men from Lhasa and briefly stated why they were there. As expected, a murmur spread through the circle of villagers. The idea of a school was quite a foreign one in this remote village of Tibet. Mother raised her hand, and again the people quieted.

The tall man explained to the crowd why he was there and reiterated the details of the proposition. He introduced the shorter man, Pasang-la, who had not, as yet, uttered a word. He further detailed, "If the village agrees to the proposition, Pasang-la will be the first teacher until someone from your village is trained enough to do the teaching. The schooling will benefit the children in our rapidly changing country. Being able to read and write, at least in Tibetan, will certainly help bring the village as well as the country into the twenty-first century."

There was no mention of learning other languages at that time. Mother had advised the men that the idea of foreign languages might be a bit radical for the villagers presently. They, too, had decided that a foreign language, especially Chinese, might prove to be a bit too extreme to discuss at an open meeting, knowing of the volatile resentment against Tibet's newest conquerors.

After the men completed their well-prepared presentation, Mother gave her views, which of course were all favorable to the proposition. Father joined her and explained ways to fulfill the physical obligations of building the school and housing the teacher. Mother and he volunteered to build an additional room onto their house to accommodate the teacher.

She explained, "If everyone provided one evening meal a month for the teacher, it will not be a hardship on anyone." Many heads nodded in agreement. Mother did have the gift of persuasion.

The Lhasa men and Tashi's parents, feeling they had explained enough, asked if there were any questions. Some hands started waving in the air.

A man in the back asked, "Do all the children have to attend the school? At what ages do they need to be to attend?"

One dissenter raised the question, "How are the chores to get done if all the children are sitting in school all day? Which is most important for their well being, food for their stomachs or food for their minds?"

Another asked, "How are the sheep to be brought down from the mountains, if the boys are not available? It takes at least five long days."

These and other questions were answered to what seemed to be everyone's satisfaction. Mother asked each household to have one member indicate whether they agreed with or opposed the proposition. Only two or three families of the more than the fifty present were hesitant to agree, but ultimately they too agreed with only a few reservations, which they were told would be worked out later.

Father, who had been silent, spoke, "If all the men will meet with me after the meeting, we can discuss the building plans. With everyone's cooperation, we can have the school built in only one month."

Tashi was excited and a bit nervous about what it would be like to be in such a structured atmosphere. He loved the outdoors in and around his village during all the seasons. Being outdoors and alone gave him the freedom to dream freely without interruption. It had become a special part of his life. He wondered if he would still have that freedom if he were in school all day.

The mountain began swallowing the sun and the families dispersed to their individual homes. Mother smiled from ear to ear. Tashi rather selfishly hoped that the strangers, who were staying the night at their house, would not interfere with the nightly story. He overheard Mother offering the men sweetened barley cakes and yak butter tea. He hoped the offer included some of the treat for his sister and him.

As Tashi had feared, the nightly story was postponed until the following night, but he did enjoy the special treat. Mother said that because the Lhasa men had details to discuss with Father and she before they left the next morning, the storytelling would be postponed.

Chapter Nine

The Next Night

The men left the next morning, and Tashi's day was more like a normal day in southern Tibet. He did his chores as usual, as well as some small duties his father had requested of him because his father was busy organizing materials for the new school and for the additional room in their house.

After dinner, the family gathered by the fireplace waiting for Mother to start the evening's episode of the story.

Mother, as Mauri, started the evening story where she had left off. The Central City priest was about to tell the history and legend of the Motherland, Lemuria.

Everyone was gathered around the priest who sat on an overturned log. His eyes were shut. When he opened his eyes an exaggerated exhale of breath was heard throughout the gathered refugees as though all were holding their breath in anticipation of the priest's words. Everyone silently hung onto each of his words. Contented with a full stomach, I found my mind traveling in and out of a dream state. As he talked, my mental visions started to take form. It was not until I was much older that I fully understood my visions on that memorable night. The priest began.

Deep below the sea laid the remnants of an advanced civilization. In its prime, its buildings were a sparkling white. The fertile growth of the sea has now obscured the land's physical shape, but its Light, its glorious spiritual white glow, shines forever. In its day the main city of beehive-like buildings housed some of the greatest beings to ever walk the earth.

These great beings, many of them from afar, beyond the farthest star we can see, taught the people the meaning of true trust in the universe. They taught them it was not necessary to struggle, for God never intended them to be at odds with each other or the elements of the earth. They taught them to understand that all their primal needs were met when they were one with all that is.

Their body, mind and spirit lived in complete harmony within their physical houses. These highly evolved teachers showed the people how to meld all three so as to operate as a total spiritual human.

The priest stopped for a moment as though listening to someone. He then said he had a message from a special teacher. In a different voice than his own, he spoke the following in a singsong rhythm.

> The buildings of Lemuria were made of stone
> Around a central city they formed a cone
> Most of the officials worked and resided in buildings
>   of white
> They were of a color that matched their Light
> On the roofs were layers of gold
> On the columns the stories were told
> All was abundant nobody lacked
> Until later on when cities were sacked
> This only happened when the originals left the land
> Then out of the sky came another band
> There was no love within their heart
> For control and greed the people did part
> Race against race they soon did pit
> Until the whole empire was then split

Their influence was felt from tribe to tribe
For all the officials they did bribe
They used their magic to get their way
They created much fear in order to sway
Among themselves they began to fight
For each thought the other wrong, they right
Soon one group waged war against another
Like brother pitted against brother
Their weapons were technologically advanced
Destruction prevailed, the people's spirit lanced
On another planet not far from the earth
A similar situation was taking birth
The conflict escalated and that planet imploded
Large pieces of it on the earth exploded
The continent of Lemuria its ultimate target
Much as a nuclear reaction when the earth it met
Explosions were seen from far away
The gods were angry many would say
The explosion so strong that the earth then shook
Causing the gases within the earth to cook
Soon the earth bubbled like a pot
And Lemuria slipped down into the empty slot
Far beneath the sea are the remains
Of a culture that believed in no pains, no strains
Every now and again a piece of Lemuria does arise
But from what or where it came, no one can surmise
The spirit of Lemuria will rise again
It will help you to remember where you have been
With love we do send these historical tales
For more information talk with the whales

The priest paused again, then in a different tone of voice, the following message was given.

Telepathy was the way they talked

Their energy was not balked
They taught what it was like to believe
In the power of nature and it to receive
All over the globe they sent their belief
And when it was needed they sent relief
They taught of course that God was the source
And with God's help they had great force
They gave the people eight virtues with which to live
    their life
In all eight directions there was no strife
Not all understood the white beings that were tall
So under dark power they did thus fall
No accident was the sinking of Mu
There was evil at work at that time, too
Ra was a symbol on which to set sight
It brought them hope when dim the Light

After a few moments of silence the priest began again. The old priest from Central City, Kanaloa, gazed out at his listeners who were waiting in silent anticipation.

Let me start at the beginning so that you will better understand how we got to where we are now, on this beach with no homeland to return to.

In the beginning, the people on this planet, sometimes called earth or terra, were divided into small extended family groups whose whole existence was centered on their primal needs of food and shelter. The life span of these early people was on the average twenty to twenty-five years. They lived much like the animals lived. They migrated from one area to another in order to obtain food. They weren't friendly to other family groups when they encountered them and thought nothing of killing them and using them for food. Occasionally they captured a young female from one of the rival families and used her for breeding in order to increase the family's size.

With this statement, there was an exclamatory sigh from the priest's extremely attentive audience.

One night, a bright light was seen in the sky by one of the family groups who were camping in a wooded area. It was a larger and brighter light than any of the skylights they had ever seen before. It appeared to be coming closer and closer to the land. As was the custom, Pana-pololei, the head of the family, and his brother, Ikarka-loa, took up their weapons, which were primarily long spears of hard wood, painstakingly sharpened to a deadly point. With several of these spears in hand, they headed toward where they thought the light had entered the trees.

The light had apparently landed a short distance from the camp. As the chosen protectors and best hunters of the family, they hid themselves in the shadows of the trees as they walked closer to the landing area. Needless to say in their primitive existence they had never seen such a sight as they witnessed that night.

Sitting before them in a meadow was a large round structure that had blinking lights all around it. It had the roar of a thousand lions. It was so loud, in fact, that Pana-pololei and Ikarka-loa covered their ears. After what seemed an eternity to them, the roaring stopped. The disk started to crack open and huge animal-like beings, like they had never seen before, exited. These animal-like beings had huge round heads and small pointed feet. Their tails were long and thin and connected one to another. Their skin was light and reflected the lights of the round, disk-like cave from which they were descending. They moved as though walking on air and when one turned, they all turned. Their backs spit fire the color of lightning after it has struck a tree.

As they moved, Pana-pololei and Ikarka-loa could hear a swishing noise like a circular wind disturbing the dry leaves of a tree. On their breasts was a design, which glistened in the light cast from their blinking cave. The outside of the design was the shape of a hollow sun. Inside the hollow sun shape were three glistening stones, two at the top across from one another and one below between the top ones. Each stone was connected with a line, which formed an inverted triangle within the circle. Pana-pololei thought these beings must be a large relative to the small singing sparrow bird that had a similar inverted triangle design on its breast. Pana-pololei's family often encountered these small birds when they were camped near a seed meadow. Related though they must be, Pana-pololei thought, these peculiar animals certainly did not have the same sweet song as the sparrows.

As the swishing animals came closer, the fear in Pana-pololei and his brother rose as they readied their weapons in order to defend themselves. It was true, they were out numbered, but both knew they had successfully overcome greater odds in the past. The two had proven many times before that they were very skillful hunters. The noisy animals were now within ten feet of them, but had made no movement to attack.

Pana-pololei determined that it was to their advantage to strike the first blow, so he threw his pointed stick. He watched anxiously, willing his spear to find its target, but it suddenly stopped in mid-air, veered abruptly to the right of its target, and grounded itself in the grasses.

Ikarka-loa's thrown spear followed the same course. Another spear was thrown and another and another until all the brothers' weapons were sticking out of the ground to the far right of their target. Bewildered, Pana-pololei and his brother saw no recourse other than retreat. They turned and ran toward their home camp. They must warn the family of the large loud animals with their god-like magical powers. They felt no wind divert the direction of the spear, a magic of the gods with which they were more familiar.

Back in camp, Pana-pololei rallied the family into a defensive formation. Everyone except the smallest of children took up a weapon. The family could hear the noise coming closer. Then something beyond belief happened. A bright beam of light came from above and surrounded Pana-pololei's thirteen-year-old daughter. Another surrounded his brother's daughter, and yet another surrounded his wife's young sister. The beams were so bright that everyone was momentarily blinded.

When they regained their sight, the beams of light and the young women were gone. They stood there in silence, frozen in place. The swishing noise had ceased. There was no evidence that anything unusual had taken place, except for the absence of three of their family members. The whole incident seemed like a dream or more accurately a nightmare.

Frustrated and confused, the entire camp remained on alert all night. Pana-pololei thought, but did not express his worries. *How could they possibly defend themselves against such vigorous beasts? Could they be gods?*

By the time the sun showed itself above the trees, the family had decided that the best defense was to get as far away from these beasts as they could. They gathered their meager belongings and headed in the opposite direction of where the blinking lights had first been spotted. They traveled from sunup to sundown until they felt assured that enough distance was between them and the beasts.

Many sunrises later, the tribal family was camped by a stream, when one of the lookouts spotted three small figures walking in the center of the shallow stream toward the camp. The family was called to alert. As the figures came closer, the member of the family with the keenest sight recognized the figures as the three young women, who had been mysteriously captured by the mysterious beasts.

Pana-pololei ran to meet them, weapons in hand in case it was a trap. The trio was alone. He escorted them into camp. All were happy, but puzzled about how three women could have escaped from such powerful foes. In turn they questioned the three at great length with little result. The three remembered nothing except finding themselves suddenly at the edge of the stream within sight of their lost families.

Since no apparent harm had come to them and the continuous questioning gave no new information, the family put the incident behind them and gradually fell back into their normal routine, which was basically survival, something they understood and could deal with quite well.

Months went by and it was apparent that the three women were with child, which was not unusual as the women were ripe for such an event, and since their return had mated with some of the males in the tribe. The day of birthing finally came, and the family was joyous for these meant three additions to their clan. They had lost two older members four months prior, which made the triple event even more exciting, since it meant that the family would actually grow by one.

The births were not easy for the new mothers, but within five days two girls and a boy were born. Pana-pololei's wife's sister was the first one to give birth. The newborn was a big, healthy boy, whose head was covered with a crop of thick black hair. His eyes were dark and deep-set. The family was elated. This meant another hunter and warrior.

A larger than normal female baby was born to Ikarka-loa's daughter the following day. She was born bald with no more hair on her head than a covering of light fuzz. Her eyes were the color of the sky when a storm was approaching, a deep blue-gray. This birth caused much gossip to circulate among the family, for it was the custom of these people to sacrifice the malformed babies to the Earth Mother.

The malformed babies were anointed with the juice of the blue berries and put on a raft made of sticks that was placed in a moving stream. They believed that ultimately Earth Mother swallowed the misfit. They felt that as a result of this gift Earth Mother would be generous and kind to the family by sending them many more babies that were perfect.

The baby girl was being made ready for the sacrifice when Kahala, Pana-pololei's daughter, gave birth to her baby, also a girl. She was the largest of the three. Her birth brought gasps from the family when they saw her for the first time. She, too, was born covered with a head of only light fuzz. When her eyelids opened two pools of intense cobalt blue stared back at her viewers.

As the infant looked into the eyes of the various family members, they felt as though her eyes were boring a hole through them to their very soul. The common reaction was an involuntary step back and a gasp. As a few examined her body, they saw that she had six fingers and a second toe that was much longer than all the rest. Her feet were pointed, not square like the rest of the family.

That evening, the family gathered to decide the fate of the newest born. Many were fearful that the Earth Mother was angry with the family. Otherwise what was the meaning of this monster that had been born into their family? Should she, too, be sacrificed to the Mother? Then again, they feared that this baby was so deformed that Earth Mother would be insulted by the gift and direct her wrath even more at their tribe.

Around the evening fire the members of the family expressed their opinions and fears. One woman worried that the vicious animals with the shiny skin had cast an evil spell on the family.

While this meeting was taking place, the subject of the meeting, the newborn 'monster,' was laying under a ledge at the entrance to the cave, which was the tribal family's current shelter. Simultaneous with the mentioning of the vicious strange-skinned animals, a bright beam of light came near the cave resting on the abnormal new baby. The family sat frozen with fear. As suddenly as the beam came it disappeared, and so did the newborn.

They sat motionless in silence long after the beam left. Mothers clung to their children and huddled closer together. Finally when it was apparent that it was only the newborn monster that the blinking birds wanted, Pana-pololei spoke. "The family must leave at dawn and travel as far away as possible, to a place where these monsters can not harm us or steal more of our people."

Even as he said this, he knew from deep inside of himself that distance would not protect them from the perplexing intruders' mysterious wraths, but he had no other solution. The calm authority with which he spoke these words seemed to ease the mass fear that was mounting in the huddled group.

At dawn the tribal family gathered their belongings and retreated in the opposite direction from whence the beam had appeared. The family traveled at an uncommonly fast speed and did not stop until they felt certain enough distance had been put between them and the location of the nightmarish event.

Dozens of cycles passed before the terror of that night had faded enough from their minds so that when eventually their migration brought them back close to the location of the original encounter with the odd birds, only a vague recall of the event was active in their memories.

Pana-pololei was now growing old by the family's standards, but he was still strong of mind, though his body had not the strength it once did. A younger man was now the chief hunter for the people. Only on the more gentle hunts did Pana-pololei participate.

The family had camped early in the day by the stream. The new campsite was abundant with game and vegetables for food. The grandmother healer needed to replenish her special herbal potions, so several of the children gathered herbs with her as they walked along the wet area. When she pointed to a specific plant, the children picked the part of the plant that she designated. Sometimes she wanted only the leaves or berries. Other times she wanted the root. Whatever the case, she insisted that the children leave part of the plant, or in some cases all of several plants, so that the area was never stripped clean of the specimen. This assured that the valuable herb would continue to grow and always be available for their future needs.

The hunters were readying themselves with their weapons to start on a hunt. As Pana-pololei sat sharpening the point of a wooden spear, his mind wandered back many years to when he had last sat along this stream's bank. While his mind reminisced, the memory of that frightful night came bubbling up from a corner of his sub-conscience where he had hidden it so his fear of helplessness could not torment him. The memory had only occasionally surfaced in his dreams over the many intervening years.

Pana-pololei had lived longer than most anyone had in his family. He had seen many harvest seasons pass. He had outlived even his daughter, whose eyes never regained their sparkle after the birth and abduction of her baby.

The hunters were chattering as they meandered back into camp with their bounty. The hunt had been successful. The women prepared the meat, while the older women were scraping and stretching the skins for later use. They would work on them throughout their stay at this campsite, until the hides were soft and supple. A fire was made that would continue to burn during the entire time the family was camped there in order to dry the skins as well as smoke the meat.

Pana-pololei listened closely to the bragging of the hunters. They expressed no unusual sightings or events. Maybe he could finally and at last put that twelve-year-old nightmare to rest.

Through the next six days, the camp's activities were fairly normal and routine. The nightly fires were filled with laughter and singing. It was on the seventh night of their encampment that strange sounds were heard, all being eerily familiar sounds to the older members of the family. The sounds pierced them as though a pointed reed were being pushed into their ears.

Then his dreaded nightmare came to life all over again: a bright light was seen in the sky, growing brighter as it came closer to the surface of the earth. The tribal family sat paralyzed by its intense brightness. Many of the younger members had never seen such a sight. They were more awestruck than frightened.

Those who were older found themselves shaking with terror as old memories awakened.

The tension was great when Pana-pololei's nephew, who was born the year after the tribe's last encounter with the bright light, reached for his weapons and rallied the two other young warriors to follow him to investigate the possible threat. Pana-pololei got to his feet, reliving the events of long ago in his mind and body. He was going with them. They objected, but he overruled their objections.

It took them little time to make their way through the forest toward the landing place of the bright light, for it was not far away. Hiding, as before, in the shadows of the trees, Pana-pololei saw the same round bird with its flashing lights. He and the young warriors watched as its mouth opened and a young woman, taller than any of his people, walked out of the thunderous craft. Her hair was light, and as the glow from the shimmering bird's lights reflected in her eyes, Pana-pololei could see they were the color of a summer sky.

All four of the hunters stood frozen as the lanky female made her way toward them. Pana-pololei sensed a familiarity about her, and the memory of his daughter became a clear picture in his mind.

The tall woman was nearly to their hiding place when one of the hunters raised his spear.

Pana-pololei shouted, "NO!"

The hunters froze in place for what they were sure would have been a lethal throw. The woman was directly in front of them now. She looked into Pana-pololei's eyes and embraced him. A shiver ran up his back and tears streamed down his cheeks. The touch of her body to his melted away any fear or remorse he was carrying.

The young hunters stood motionless, their mouths agape. The tall female stood about a head taller than Pana-pololei. Words were spoken between the two, but the young hunters could not understand their meaning. After what seemed like an

45

eternity, the woman took Pana-pololei's hand, and they walked toward the camp. Behind them they heard a roar as the thunderous bird coughed fire and rose into the dark sky from which it had descended.

As the three hunters and the tall female entered into the glow of the campsite's fire, a chorus of gasps went up from the family. Many covered their eyes as the penetrating radiance from the eyes of the female by Pana-pololei's side made it impossible for them to look at her for any length of time.

After the initial shock at the sight of the tall female, the tribe's fear was replaced with hypnotic attention, the group listened while she told her story, their eyes glued to her radiance and their ears hearing only her melodious words.

Chapter Ten

Solana

Tashi's mother continues her story.
The priest then began to tell the story through the eyes of Pana-pololei's granddaughter, who is telling her story to her newly found family.

I am called Solana. From my earliest recollection I was pampered, and all my needs were met. Throughout my life my food and environment were closely regulated. There were many like me so I had many childhood friends. We were taught numerous ideas that will seem strange to you, such as beliefs about nature and God. Our bodies were constantly checked and monitored by a medicine person.

At the time of my coming into womanhood, I was segregated from the rest. Then a seed was implanted in me. At the end of the gestation period, I bore a baby. My baby was taken from me to be cared for by them, the clan of flashing birds you saw, grandfather.

Solana turned her eyes toward her escort into the camp. Involuntary gasps came from her mesmerized audience.

Shortly after that they said I could go back to my first family if I wanted to. Although I do not recognize or remember any of you, something inside me longed for your closeness. It was as though I needed to find my true home. If you allow me to stay,

I am to teach you all the miracles I have learned while growing up with the white bird people.

With this statement her audience fell silent. She waited in anticipation for a response from the family.

In the twelve years of her absence, Pana-pololei's descendent had matured into a tall, straight-backed young woman. Her long hair was the color of the sun, and her skin had a pale peach glow, not ruddy like that of her grandfather's. When she brought her hands up to gester as she spoke, the clan could not help but stare at her six fingers. They also noticed she was not barefooted but wore pointed shoes, which reflected the flames of the fire.

After a long silence Pana-pololei spoke. "I have no doubt that this young woman is my granddaughter, Solana as she is called, who was taken from us as a baby. She has come to us like a miracle. Look in her eyes and feel the love and warmth. It is the same love and joy that her mother, my daughter, had before that fateful night when her baby was taken from her and her heart slowly broke. Now her child has returned and like a star she shines bright. I wish to know all she has learned, but it must be up to the whole tribal family whether we accept her among us.

One of the elder women found the courage to respond to Pana-pololei's plea. She asked if the elders of the family could be left alone to discuss the matter. She told Pana-pololei and his granddaughter go to a nearby cave until the tribe had come to a decision. Pana-pololei and Solana agreed.

Solana was anxious to learn all about her birth mother and her family. She was somewhat saddened when Pana-pololei told her that her mother had died, but she hoped being with her grandfather now would help mend both their hearts. Taking a few provisions, they started for the cave.

The elders of the family discussed the proposition nearly all night. After a brief rest, a vote was taken. Only a few of the older people of the tribe were hesitant to accept Pana-pololei's long lost granddaughter into the tribal family. They had no doubt that this woman was the "monster" that Pana-pololei's daughter had bore over twelve years ago, for her facial features were identical to her mother's, with the exception of her hair and eye color and of course her strange six fingers.

They wondered if it was a trick. By taking her back, were they putting the safety of the family in jeopardy? Would she attract more beams of light from the sky to take more of their babies?

The elders called the young people to the meeting. It was their future offspring that would be at risk. The young people proved to be more daring, not having actually experienced the abductions. They convinced the elders to allow her to be a member of the tribe on a trial basis. After all, what could one female do to their family who had such able warriors? They assured the elders that she would be watched closely.

The priest paused, then continued in yet another tone of voice.

Throughout the Motherland, representatives who were born with the thunderous, cave-like birds were sent back to their original earth families and the teaching began.

Solana taught her family about different things to eat. She taught them about magic potions and stressed cleanliness. She also encouraged them to build a permanent settlement as well as to cooperate with the other families rather than fight them. She emphasized the benefits of breeding with mates outside their own family. As a result of her teachings being put into practice, the life span of the people increased with each generation. Although primitive at first, permanent housing and villages were built. Certain members of the tribe that exhibited the aptitude for it were taught new and strange healing techniques. The children were put in classes at an early age, where they were taught to expand beyond their earthly awareness and to love all people, even those outside their immediate family.

Once during each season, Solana disappeared for a period of time. At that time, the bright star appeared during the night, and a beam of light enveloped her. Like magic she was gone.

49

After about a moon's time she appeared again from the same beam. At first this event frightened the tribe, but when she returned each time with no apparent ill fate having occurred to her or the family, they accepted it as a routine happening.

After each disappearance, she had new concepts to teach. Also, each time she came back from one of her disappearances, she looked younger. She didn't age like the rest of her earthly tribe. She performed so many good deeds for her family members that she was gradually raised in status to almost that of a deity serving as a counselor for all.

Often when the family visited other tribes, she met someone like herself. Their common experience and knowledge was a remedy for their loneliness. To have someone like herself to talk to was a joyous occasion for Solana. She loved her family and the work that the tall ones had taught her to do, but it set her apart from the rest of the tribe. She could honestly say that she had no friends within her own family whom she could talk with, woman-to-woman.

Her earthly tribal family grew and the settlement became larger and larger. Frequently someone from another settlement joined Solana's tribe for the purpose of mating with one of the females in exchange for one of the males mating with one of the other settlement's females.

All fighting ceased. Little by little the entire Motherland became a land of blissful settlements. The comings and goings of the round flashing birds were met with joy, and they too were considered to be of a god-like stature. Often the night skies were filled with a kaleidoscope of blinking colored lights.

The population of the land grew as people lived longer and reproduced more abundantly. Under Solana's guidance and those in the shiny birds, her tribe's skills improved and eventually more elaborate buildings were erected. One settlement was given special attention, and the building was on an even grandeur scale. This grandiose place was referred to as the Central City.

One or two young people were chosen from all the other settlements to live in the Central City on the continent of Lemuria. There, the tall white beings from the shinny birds held classes for all the representatives. After the classes were completed, each of these specially trained students was sent back to their ancestral settlement for the specific task of telling stories of the great city and of sharing the teaching they had acquired.

The priest paused for a while and gazed out toward the sea for a meditative moment.

Tashi's mother continued.

It was as though he had left our presence and traveled to a memory in his own life. A veil of sadness fell over him, and a single tear gathered at the corner of his eye. After a deep breath, resembling a sigh, he continued.

The People took pilgrimages to the Central City from all over the continent and occasionally some came from other continents. The mere act of walking inside the perimeter of the boundary of the glorious city brought lightness to their souls that could never be forgotten.

The Central City was a busy city. There was much activity, but even with the hustle and bustle of its daily activity, there was a peacefulness that was unlike that anywhere else in the land. Never were angry words spoken, and no one would think of doing harm to another.

In this majestic hub, the sun glistened on the roofs of pearly white buildings; melodious bells rang as though the symphony of God was performing. At its center a huge crystal cast rays of colors outward over the city, creating a rainbow arch over its many avenues.

There was a lightness of heart in everyone. Many of the tall ones walked throughout the city and appeared as though they were walking on clouds. So light was their step that their feet, although they could not be seen, seemed to barely touch the ground. Looking into their eyes was like gazing through the windows of God.

Those fortunate enough to have one of the tall ones touch them, described the touch like a fire starting at the base of their spines and continuing up to the very top of their heads until they were certain they were flying right off the earth. Every cell in their body vibrated with energy. Aches, pains, and negative thoughts or doubts instantly left them, replaced by a peacefulness that was literally indescribable.

As these words from the priest spread out over the refugees on the beach, a soft gentle sigh came from each of them. The priest continued.

Many laboratory buildings existed in the Central City. An enormous dome-shaped building with a transparent roof housed experimental plant life. Enough food and vegetables were grown in this building to easily feed the massive and ever-increasing population of the city.

Another towering building was a beehive of activity, focused entirely on healing techniques. Within its confines were rooms devoted solely to herbal cures. Other rooms were designed so that as you lay on the pads within an enclosed pod, certain tones resonated through your body. Yet, in other rooms, beams of specific colors penetrated any area of your body that was ailing or out of balance.

Within this same building were large classrooms filled with students learning various techniques and principles of healing, including vibrational healing. A cluster of rooms was set aside for energy surgery. Baths filled with hot steaming mineral and herbal salt water and medicinal aromas that penetrated every cell in the body were housed in an area connected to the back of the healing center. The charged water of these baths often stung the nostrils as the aroma was breathed into the body, leaving a tingly feeling on the skin as it seeped into the pores.

On the perimeter of the bathing rooms were small cubicles that were so filled with steam that the ceiling and walls were wet and droplets sizzled as they let go of the ceiling and fell into the red-hot coals below. The steam room's moist heat enveloped the body, permitting the mind to escape the physical body and find a place of clarity and truth.

All who lived in or visited the Central City were allowed the use of any of its healing facilities. People, old and young, from far and near, came for healing and rejuvenation of their mind, body, and spirit. Those who came with crippling diseases walked again, tall and straight. All the participants at the healing center looked and felt younger than their earthly years. The blind saw again. The deaf heard again. Those who felt despair found a sense of well-being and hope.

Another sigh was heard from the gathered refugees, Tashi's mother said.

In this magical city, there were multilevel buildings, which looked like beehives. They housed student representatives from the villages. These students were chosen to partake in a comprehensive study in order to become priests or spiritual leaders and teachers. Sometimes the study took twenty-two seasons or more to complete.

The purpose to this rigorous study was to raise the frequency of the energy vibrations of each of the students. Just as the light air you breathe vibrates at a higher speed than the heavy rock you sit on, the energy of the love feeling is lighter and vibrates at a higher rate than does the fear feeling. The tall white beings' energy vibrated at a higher rate than ours, which is the reason they were often invisible to our lower vibrational human eyes. Striving to rid us of human fears was our ultimate and most difficult task.

There were twelve degrees of accomplishment, and each

degree was represented by a certain color. The level or degree at which each was studying was represented in the band of color on his or her tunic. As the students mastered certain skills and knowledge, they wore a different color band on their robes. Every color is a different vibration. As their skills increased and their vibrations rose, they were given a color band that correlated to their vibrational level. Some spent years in one color before advancing to a higher vibration color. Still, others, after achieving a certain level of accomplishment, decided to remain at that level and return to their villages. If one left the academy of learning, a new student from the same village was chosen through testing to take his or her place.

Very few students became masters, which was denoted by a band of gold on their tunic. The criterion for that degree was extremely difficult to attain, and mastership among earthlings was extremely rare. Those in the final stages of seeking the gold degree spent most of their time cloistered alone with their master teachers. The tall white ones at the learning center were grand master teachers.

I took notice of the color of the band on the old priest's robe, and wondered what level he had accomplished, Mauri thought. A brilliant violet the color of amethyst bordered his loosely fitted attire. An amethyst stone was over his third eye set into a beautifully decorated headband. Why didn't he wear the gold band of the highest master priest? I wondered if his studies had ceased when the rumbling began and the Central City sank into the depths of the sea. I was surprised that no one at the gathering inquired about this and decided that it may not be proper for me to ask about it right now.

The story-telling had ended for the night. It had been a longer session than the usual so without debate, Tashi and his sister rose and climbed the stairs to their beds. Mother never moved or uttered another word to them. It was as though her mind and her spirit were somewhere else.

In the silence Tashi lay in his bed, enjoying the scenes that played in his head. There were visions of a far away land that existed long ago, an ancient time not forgotten because of generations of storytelling.

Chapter Eleven

Berry Collecting

The next morning, Tashi heard the familiar sound of a distant rooster announcing the dawn of another day in his beloved small village nestled in the Himalayas. The visions from the previous night's story had continued in his dreams. Images of the magical Central City were still alive in his mind when he heard the well-known sounds below him as the household stirred to begin the day. Throughout the morning Tashi could not stop the visions from entertaining his mind. Who were these tall white people of Lemuria? Where did they come from? Where were they now?

He finished his early morning chores still in his dream state. At breakfast, Mother announced that Tashi was to travel to the nearby mountains to collect berries and seeds. She had already prepared sacks for the medicinal bounty and had packed a midday snack. Slinging the sacks onto his shoulder, Tashi left the village to start the climb up the mountain.

Part way up the mountain, he felt an uncontrollable desire to visit his secret cave, which he had discovered on one of his previous berry-collecting journeys. Anxious to get there, he began walking faster than usual, collecting various berries and seeds at a remarkable speed as he ascended the mountain. His mother had taught him which berries and seeds were edible and which were not, but could still be used in some of her healing potions. As he gathered them, he was careful to make sure they were put in separate sacks, for certain ones could contaminate the others.

Today was a good day for gathering. His sacks were more than half full in a short time, and Tashi felt pleased with his accomplishment. It was nearly midday, and he was only a slight distance from his secret cave. He elected to treat himself to his snack in his hideaway.

Tashi's cave was located on the side of the mountain. Bramble and bushes hid its entrance, and you would only be able to spot it if you knew where it was. He had discovered it one day when, while collecting leaves and berries, an animal disappeared behind the bushes and did not come out. Curious, he crawled under the brush and discovered the entrance to the cave.

Tashi descended down a narrow rock ledge on the side of the mountain. Farther below was the river. He pushed away some of the bramble and crawled into the cave. Just enough light filtered through the overgrowth at its entrance to dimly light the interior. The cavern inside was about four feet wide by eight feet deep and approximately six feet in height.

Tashi entered the cave cautiously, making certain no person or thing had claimed it since his last visit. Other than the sound of a few tiny scurrying feet, which he determined were probably pack rats, the cave was empty.

He loved his little cave. He felt comforted in its quiet interior with only the roar of the river below to remind him that there was an outside world. He unloaded the sacks from his shoulders and rummaged through the one that contained the snack.

As he munched on the bits of yak cheese and barley cake, visions from his dreams of Lemuria became clearer in his mind. They became so clear, in fact, it felt almost as though he were walking the avenues of Central City himself.

As he nibbled and dreamed of the paradise city, the cave unexpectedly lit up with a bright blue-white light. At first he was confused, thinking it was only a part of his dream, because this same bright light had appeared to him in his dreams right before he awoke in the morning.

The light in the cave started to condense and take a somewhat human form, while a warm and overwhelming feeling of peace cloaked him. Standing before him was a man clad in only a shift-like robe. What skin

56

he could detect was very fair, almost white, not the reddish brown complexion of his people. When this fair man looked at Tashi, he saw that his eyes were the color of the sky, only more vibrant. The tall being took a position opposite Tashi and sat down. Tashi could hear his own heart rapidly beating with anticipation and was surprised by his own lack of fear in the tall white being's presence.

After a moment or two the being spoke yet he saw no mouth. His words were almost hypnotic. Tashi sat fixed in place as he listened to the words float through his mind.

> A child of the stars, you've come from afar
> To this planet of green to heal the scar
> A teacher of teachers will be your trade
> Your words will stay, though you may fade
> A slayer of dragons, you wield your sword
> Any fear your prey, through its heart you bored
> Yes, dear one, you have again come to this land
> Remember your past and then take a stand

When the last words of the being were absorbed, the shrill call of a raven rang through the cave's opening. Like in his dreams, the image of the radiating being faded.

The entire encounter seemed to have taken only a few minutes. At first, Tashi thought he had simply fallen asleep and had dreamed the entire event, but it had seemed so real. His mind ran rampant with speculation. For a time, he sat rationalizing, trying to find a logical explanation for what he had experienced. Then, out of the corner of his eye, he spotted something shiny reflecting the dim light of the cave. He reached to pick it up, wondering why he had not seen it before.

The object was a small silver disk with an upside down triangle in its center. On each point of the triangle was a stone. Holding the disk so that a light ray from the cave's entrance illuminated its surface, Tashi saw that the stones were the color of the turquoise stone that was so prevalent in the Himalayas. He could not imagine where this finely-crafted silver piece came from. It was unlike any of the pendants he had seen crafted by people in his village and unlike any of the medallions he had seen in the marketplaces.

Tashi picked up a few strands of the tough mountain grasses the pack rats were using in their nest and wove a necklace on which he hung the disk. Tying on the pendant with a knot in the ends of the grass cord, he put it over his head. When the disk fell to his chest and lay over his heart, a feeling of lightness came over him. Leaving a bit of his uneaten barley cake for the pack rats in exchange for the strands of grass, Tashi gathered his sacks and exited the cave, making certain its entrance was again concealed with bramble.

The sun was quite close to the top of the mountains in the west. He could not believe it was late in the day. It seemed like only minutes had passed since he had first entered the cave. The thoughts in his mind raced as he concluded that he must have fallen asleep. He felt exceptionally rested. Ideas flooded his mind as his hand went to the disk lying on his heart. One part of him wanted to believe that the whole experience had been real, but a more timid part of him wanted to dismiss it as a dream.

A gust of chilly air brought his combating mind back into the present. It was getting late, and he still had more berries and seeds to collect. He knew he must hurry if he was to get home before the sun was completely swallowed by the mountains. There would be no moon tonight, and when night possessed the land, it was easy to become confused and lose one's sense of direction. Only the most experienced herders safely navigated mountain travel at night.

Tashi climbed up the cliff to the path, which curved down the mountain. He made haste in descending to the valley, stopping only occasionally to add berries and seeds to his sacks. He was on the outskirts of his village when the ravenous mountain peak ate the last sliver of the sun.

As he approached his house, his eyes glanced at the disk on his chest. He quickly hid the circular pendant behind his shirt. He was not ready to explain how he had acquired the disk, especially since it was not even clear in his own mind. It would be his secret for the present. When the time was right he would share his experience and show the disk to his mother, alone. She seemed to understand his visions and was sympathetic to his daydreaming, unlike his father who discouraged it.

Tashi entered the house and, in silence, placed his sacks on the table. Grandmother emptied them, sorting the various seeds and berries into separate containers. No one made a comment about the lateness of his arrival. His mother's only greeting was to tell him to wash for dinner.

However, the grass string and the circular impression under his shirt had not been missed her keen eye, but she felt this was not the time for a confrontation. The chatter and bustle of preparing the evening meal took precedence over everything else. It gave Tashi a sense of relief not to be the center of interest and not to have to answer questions concerning his day's activities.

After the dinner table was cleared and readied for the morning, mother situated herself in her usual storytelling position, closing her eyes and remaining silent for several minutes. During the silence, Tashi found his hand going to his chest, and as his hand caressed the circular disk, a sudden gush of heat encompassed his head.

His mother continued her story.

The refugees on the beach slowly rose from their position in the circle around the priest from the Central City. The recitation of the legend by the priest was at an end for the night. All drifted to their sleeping palettes. Only the roar of the moving water was heard, as though everyone was lost in the silence of his or her own mind.

As dawn lifted the veil of the inky sky with a wash of pearly gray, Lemuria's immigrants awakened, not only to the roar of the water, but to a persistent gale-like wind that took their breath as they spoke their first words of the morning to their loved ones.

Anything lying loose was sent into the air by the wind's swirling fingers reaching out over the beach. Without a word, everyone retrieved the airborne objects and stowed them securely in sacks, protecting them from the greedy wind. They put the sacks behind rocks and trees where the beach met the forest.

Each family found a small clearing in which to set up a new camp, protected by the forest sentries. The rain that was carried in the grip of the wind filtered through openings in the foliage roof of the forest. The morning fires sputtered as frequent drops landed on red coals. All the immigrants remained gathered, huddled closely together around their individual family fires until the storm subsided.

In order to pass the time and take their minds off the bellow of the storm, each small group sang songs with words that were lyrical legends of their family's existence. The overall resonance coming from the forest resembled that of the birds in the spring, all simultaneously telling their tales of the winter they had just completed.

After the storm gave up its fury, one by one the families slowly walked out of their protected sanctuaries to view what the furor of the storm had done to their campsite. They found the beach speckled with debris of all shapes and sizes. Everyone assumed the job of gathering the usable gifts from the tempest. Driftwood, to be used for firewood, was stacked in piles to dry in the sun. Many of the edible shellfish and other fish, which were stranded on the beach when the waters receded, were gathered and put in buckets of water to keep them fresh until they could be cooked or dried. Ropes of seaweed were wound around a log until baskets could be woven from their tough cord. With the efforts of everyone doing their part, the beach soon appeared as it had before the storm and the sea had delivered her gifts.

Miraculously, no one was injured so there was almost a feeling of jubilation among the people. They resolved that it was safer to make the forest camps their permanent living quarters rather than to move back onto the beach. However, they did establish a circle with a fire at its center on the beach as a common ritual and gathering place for all the individual tribes. They positioned it toward the midpoint of all the tribal camps. At this site council meetings would be held as well as celebrations. It would be a place where all gathered to hear of the myths and legends from the Central City priest.

So abundant was the bounty on the beach after the storm that the evening meal started to resemble that of a festival. A member of each tribe worked diligently, building a huge fire where the shellfish could be put in boiling bags to cook. Plate-sized leaves were gathered and staked next to the fire. Fresh water was brought to the fire's edge. Fish that were found on the shore were speared with a common stick and strung over the fire to roast. Each fish was wrapped in a blanket of spinach leaves so as to keep the valuable oils of the fish from escaping.

Close to sunset, three men blew the signal for gathering with white conch shell horns. The members of all the tribes assembled in the central gathering location on the beach. After the sharing of food and a meditation led by one of the tribal leaders, the priest from the Central City took his position near the hearty fire. He elevated himself slightly on an upturned log so all could see him as he continued his telling of the legend of Central City.

The priest closed his eyes. Those close to him heard a slight murmuring, chant-like sound coming from him. Those in the back could only see his lips quivering. After a bit, when all was silent and only the roar and lapping of the sea and the crackling of the fire could be heard, the priest opened his eyes and began speaking.

Although learning in Central City was measured in degrees, no one was considered or judged to be better than another. The color and vibrational system was merely a way to divide the students into group levels of accomplishment so that more students, who far outnumbered the tall ones, could be more effectively taught. The twelve degrees and their representative colors were: first degree (black); second degree (red); third degree (brown); fourth degree (orange); fifth degree (yellow); sixth degree (sea foam green); seventh degree (emerald green); eighth degree (sky blue); ninth degree (lapis blue); tenth degree (violet); eleventh degree (white); and twelfth degree (gold). Each degree correlated to a stone or metal both in color and vibration. How these levels were arrived at, I do not know. The tall ones determined the structural levels for us and only they knew their origin. It was not important for us to know.

The influence of the tall ones and their teachings grew and grew. Peace and love reigned throughout Mu, the Motherland. Many people came from other universes and settled in this land or in one of its outposts. Still peace and harmony was prevalent.

Mu grew beyond its continental borders. No one was turned away. A new continent in another ocean was settled and, in the beginning, was directly influenced by Central City. Representatives from this other continent were allowed to enter the student program. As the earthlings' spirituality became stronger, the tall ones taught us more technical skills. These technical skills were like miracles to us.

Thousands of years passed with little to no turmoil. The word of a place where people lived in peace and abundance became known throughout the universes. The earth was known as a new frontier where a society could make a new beginning. The reasons for leaving their home planets and settling on earth were as numerous as the planets themselves. For whatever reasons the immigrants were brought to the green planet, they were seldom disappointed.

Sometime during this great migration of extra-terrestrials, a group of renegade Pleiadians took up residency on this eastern continent from Mu. Being of relatively low spiritual evolution, but extremely technically skilled, their primary goal was to gain power. This sought-after power increased through the energy work they performed on those around them. Masters at biological engineering, they experimented on the inhabitants of nearby communities. Implants were placed in all but twelve of the earthlings' strains of DNA, debilitating the other strains. The implants made it possible for the power hungry renegades to control these unsuspecting human guinea pigs' thinking and actions.

They were like slaves, since only their ability to exist on the three-dimensional plane was kept active. Noting this, the tall ones warned the renegades that they were disobeying universal law, God's law, but so great was their need for power that the renegades disregarded the warning. Slowly more and more groups of people came under their mandate, until the renegade's power reached the fringes of the actual Motherland itself.

The loving atmosphere of Lemuria was slowly deteriorating, as these separatist people infiltrated the populace by working on the outlying borders of Mu, slowly creeping toward Central City itself. Since the dogma of the tall ones was anti-violence, their only defense was to continue teaching love and equality in God's eyes and oneness. Despite the tall one's diligent efforts, the renegades were gaining in power as more and more of them came from the Pleiades. Warfare, under their influence, was prevalent and encouraged, tribe against tribe, father against son. Loving and innocent people were killed because they would not abide by the anarchical rules of the renegades and their followers. Sophisticated weapons were introduced, which could extinguish whole areas with the push of a button. Still, Central City continued to exist seemingly protected by an invisible shield.

After thousands of years of this deterioration, the renegades were helped in their cause by an event on yet another planet that many of their kind had infiltrated from. There were many struggles on this other planet, which was in the earth's solar system and was the closest planet to the earth at that time. It eventually exploded from all the negative energy, creating a tremendous shake up within the solar system, especially on the planet earth.

The earth's axis tilted, causing dry areas to become wet, hot areas to become cold, and so on. The planet's plates shifted, inducing earthquakes, volcanic eruptions, and whole masses of earth to buckle up or sink deep into the sea. The earth's landmass became smaller as the rising seas replaced it. The earth was becoming more blue than green.

Many lives were lost. Miraculously, many who were more spiritually evolved and more tuned into the energies of the tall white beings escaped death, just as you special people are doing now. Led by the tall ones from above, we and others are finding refuge on other parts of the earth that were not affected by the mass destruction. Some refugees in other places have even gone deep into the earth itself. Still, other, more evolved beings, are evacuating from the earth's surface totally. The flashing birds are taking them to a planet that is in the beginning stages of being populated.

Dear ones, you are special people who have been led by the tall white beings to a safe place. You have been entrusted with the task of rebuilding this planet in the spirit of the Motherland. Let us learn from these events and never forget the lessons of the tall ones. It is we who will assure that the spirit of Lemuria and it glorious Central City will rise again.

You must tell your children, and they must tell their children, and on and on, the legends of this glorious spirit. You must never let this spirit die. It must live long after our human lives end on this planet. The tall white beings will be here for us when it is necessary, but will not take an active part in our lives or the activities of this planet while the lower vibration beings are in power. The time will come for the tall white ones to take action, but this will not happen until there is another shift in the planet's energy.

The priest closed his eyes and went silent. No one spoke for what seemed an eternity. Then one of the tribal leaders rose and helped the priest down from the log. Another leader rose and said 'Amen,' indicating it was time for everyone to return to his or her individual camps.

This was the end of Mother's storytelling for the night. Without a word, Tashi and his sister climbed the ladder to their beds. He thought, as he readied for sleep, that his dreams would surely be full after such a moving story. He was not disappointed.

Chapter Twelve

The Story Continues

The next day was routine for Tashi. After he finished his chores, he and the other boys in the village helped with the building of the new schoolhouse. The day passed rapidly but without any extraordinary events. Supper was completed and mother took her usual storytelling position.

Following a brief silence, Mother began.

After several months of adjusting and settling, the twelve refugee tribes on the beach decided to hold a council meeting in their new land with a chief from each tribe being present as that tribe's representative. The priest from Central City presided over the so-called board of Elders. Their task was to set the policies for the people in this new land, assuring that all doctrine was for everyone's higher good. Any procedures had to benefit everyone equally. No tribe was considered more important than another.

Because of his divine connection and training in Central City, the priest had the power to make the final decision if the board was divided on a certain policy. In the old Central City a board of Master Priests, the tall white beings, were the decision-makers, but since there was only one Central City priest among the refugees, he would have the deciding vote. I should clarify that some of the priests of the Motherland were women, but the one who had escaped the holocaust via the sea from the Motherland was male. The tall white beings, which were the teachers, practiced no discrimination toward either human gender, for they were androgynous. Whoever was ready to learn had the opportunity, regardless of their physical gender. It was the Pleiadian renegades, the separatists, who promoted sexual bigotry.

Then Mother added her own editorial comment. "I understand that it is this same bigotry that is prevalent today in our Tibetan lama system as well as other religious orders. However, these early refugees of the Motherland were still influenced by the tall one's teaching.

The elders of the refugees met. This first Grand Council decided to establish a united colony on the shores of the new land. They worked out the details of the responsibilities of each tribe to the higher good of the colony. The physical conditions were first on the agenda. Housing of sorts was to be erected with the materials at hand. Food caches were to be established in each tribal community, making one person from each tribe in charge of maintaining them as well as delegating the gathers, fishermen, planters, and hunters.

A principal healer from each tribe was in charge of erecting a healing center containing any herbs and healing supplies needed. They also met with the chief healer of each tribe for the purpose of sharing methods and supplies. Some of the previous supplies were not available in this new environment, although many were introduced again through plantings in a common herbal greenhouse garden.

Each tribe was responsible for developing that tribe's special talents, and a method of trading and sharing took place. The same procedures that were practiced when Central City reined were being re-established in this new and strange land.

At this first meeting of the elders it was decided that they would meet on a regular basis, that being four times evenly spaced during each moon. Any tribe could ask for a special meeting to be called by petitioning to the priest who then set the time and place.

The weather cooperated with the refugees during their first week of organizing a new orderly civilization. It was mild with no dramatic events to distract the people from arranging their new lives. Great progress was reported at the following Grand Council meeting. At this productive second meeting plans for a Central building were discussed.

The elders chose a central location. Architects and builders from each tribe worked under the direction of the priest to construct a building that was big enough to house all the people for the ceremonies and festivals. It would also be used as a teaching center and training center for prospective new tribal priests. The elders agreed to send one building engineer and one architect to meet with the priest in one moon in order to determine the plans for the construction.

During the construction era, the priest gathered everyone on the beach for several nights of telling the stories of the Motherland. On one such night, each tribe arrived at the central place carrying extra baskets of food to be shared. After a sharing of both food and tribal news, all the refugees settled in a spot where each could see and hear the priest. The priest took his position on an elevated log stool, closed his eyes, and a hushed silence crawled over the gatherers.

Tonight we will talk of the tall ones, the masters who were the builders of one of the most spiritually advanced civilizations that Earth has ever seen, and will probably never see again for hundreds of thousands of years. The tall ones are a race of people from a planet far beyond the sun. Although they are very technically advanced, they are also very spiritually evolved. They came to this relatively new planet through orders from the Intergalactic Council of Elders, from whom they received all their commands directly.

Their vibrations, the speed at which the cells of their body vibrate, are so high that they do not possess a visible three-dimensional body as you and I do. As time went on they were able to adjust their vibrations so the people of Earth could see an image or form representing their energy bodies. From the beginning, they spoke to us through our minds. Because it was difficult to maintain the lower visual vibration for any length of time, they came and went frequently in their shiny birds. The vehicles were necessary only for the transportation of those with the tall ones who were not so highly evolved, but yet had to contend with bodies.

After hundreds of thousands of years a new species of earth people evolved from the tall ones' shared DNA as well as from their teachings. It was a species that could live in a human body and walk among the people. The new species had special powers unlike the original inhabitants of Earth. Because they were more spiritually evolved and lighter, they substantially raised the vibrations, the rate at which energy moves, of this planet and its people.

One of the tall ones was what we might call the chief or director. We knew him as Bashur. Very seldom would he show himself on the planet but all knew of his existence. He commanded from the Mother ship, which we occasionally saw far up in the sky on a clear night. Some of the members of his crew were our teachers. Although these crew members were still very highly evolved, they were not of the vibrational degree that Bashur was. Part of the unfolding evolvement of these crew members involved teaching us and the other natives on the earth.

Eventually, in order to communicate, these first teachers devised a set of symbols and sounds that all people could understand. For instance, the circle always represented the Source or "All That Is." We earthlings now apply our sun as a symbol for the Source because it is our most powerful circle and it brings life to everything on Earth, as does God. The cross was another symbol the teachers introduced, indicating the four directions on the earth. The triangle with the point at the top indicated energy sent from the Source to us. The triangle with the point at the bottom indicated the Source within us returning that energy as it connected to the one above.

The spiral as seen in the flower of the fern that grew abundantly in the Motherland, was a symbol showing us that our souls or essences are eternal, or that life is infinite, never beginning and never ending. These were the primary symbols although many more were introduced as time went on.

The number three was the magical number for the civilization called Mu. It represented our uniqueness of being a combination of body, mind, and spirit that comes together as one and connected to the Source as one. That is why our chants and higher teachings are always done in threes. There are many more symbols I could talk about, but for right now we will go on with the story.

The tall ones were responsible for technical knowledge as well as spiritual knowledge, but the two were always taught as one. The technical advancements always had a high spiritual purpose. The schools in Central City were open to everyone. Everyone could apply, but only certain people were chosen to be participants in the arduous training that could eventually lead to their becoming master teachers themselves.

Not everyone had the aptitude or vibration level to be a student, so each village leader held a screening for potential applicants twice a year. Basically the screening assured the priest that that applicant's vibrations were high enough so the applicant would not be harmed or even killed by the high energy involved in the lessons or the high vibrations of the teachers themselves.

Safety for the applicant was the main reason the screening had to be done. If the applicant was too low in vibration, his human molecular structure was stressed to the point where he could even die from too much exposure to the evolved white beings. I have actually witnessed one such case.

Another such case involved an influential man from one of the outposts that had been sent to Central City for lessons. After being there for a number of days, his ego took over and dominated his soul. He became abusive physically and verbally to his fellow students, thinking himself better than the others. During one of the lessons, while one of the tall ones was speaking and chanting, he started to involuntarily shake until he was thrashing about on the floor. He was removed from the room and taken to the healing center where he received help in balancing his molecular structure and energy field. He then was sent back to his village. He simply was not ready for the lessons from the tall ones.

As the priest described the man, his attentive audience, like a well-practiced chorus, nodded their heads and vocalized their ahs, explained Mother.

> The technical knowledge that was taught in Central City academy was to be kept secret because if a lower vibrational being obtained some of it without the spiritual background, this knowledge could conceivably be used in harming others or themselves. The knowledge was also guarded because if only part of the truth was known, it was more detrimental than if none of the truth was known.
>
> The tall ones gave to all the people eight basic rules to live by. These were the first steps in becoming healthy, more spiritual beings.
>
> These rules or universal laws were never written, but were to be memorized by all. By the time a child was two or three, they were to know all the universal laws at least at a primal level. We now call them our taboos.
>
> The first rule is that there is only one source of energy from which all comes. It comes to us with no conditions attached. Its energy, which is the highest vibration, creates and sustains all life on earth but is not human, animal, or plant itself.
>
> The second rule is that a special time is to be set aside to connect with the source and bring its power more strongly within you. This is especially important since the connection can sometimes atrophy in humans, causing both physical and spiritual deficiency.
>
> The third rule is that each person's mother and father be respected, for they represent the perfect human marriage of the male and female within you.
>
> The fourth rule is to honor all life because you are a part of that life. We are all one.

Tashi's thoughts went immediately to the reckless act of killing his mother's rooster with his new slingshot and the emotional pain he felt afterwards. It was as though part of him had died with it. Could that be what this rule means?

> The fifth rule is to sow your seeds and fertilize your fields with higher intent so that the purist of harvests may occur. This includes the discriminatory planting of human seeds that are fertilized with the source energy.
> The sixth rule is to let people gather their own earthly goods for themselves. The universe provides ample abundance for all. You need only seek and you shall have.
> The seventh rule is to be truthful in all words and let each speak of and be responsible for his acts.
> The eighth rule is that all things are available to all people and jealousy or envy of other's possessions and attributes blocks a person from ever obtaining that for which he is jealous or envious.

Mother hesitated and Tashi could detect a change in the tone of her voice as she continued the story.

> The priest stopped telling the legend of the Motherland for the night with the promise that more stories would be told in the future. He emphasized again that they should know and remember their history, and that it was up to them to share it with all those who came after them.
> You remember the little girl, Mauri, who had gotten the vision of the catastrophic event on Mu before the exodus. Mauri was put into the care of her grandmother because there was so much activity every day that her mother or father could not properly watch her."

Mother continued now in the voice of Mauri.

> I helped my grandmother gather the berries, leaves, and roots. Some days we boiled concoctions of them and stored them in treated skin bags that we had brought with us. She taught me to weave

baskets and mats from the leaves of the trees that looked like hands waving when the wind blew.

Several people came to Grandmother complaining of stomach cramps and the inability to hold their food. Grandmother took a small piece of the yellow ginger root from a plant, ground it into a powder and steeped it in water. The ailing people were told to drink the smelly tea. Later some of the people returned to tell grandmother that their cramps and other symptoms had disappeared.

My visions continued to come during this time of construction, but there was no one available to talk to about them. Everyone was busy from sunrise to sunset with the various chores it took to build a whole new city of villages. A number of men from each tribe were chosen to help build the central meeting area. The remainder of each tribe set about building more permanent housing in their respective villages.

In the center of each tribe's establishment, underground channels lined with rock were dug connecting the fresh water from the nearby stream to a collection station in the circle of the houses. Although some of the women helped with the construction, most were kept busy making fishnets, pounding the soaked soft bark of a tree that grew only along the stream's edge into flat pliable sheets for clothing, as well as collecting and storing edible foods. After a month or two the settlements were fairly well established. It was then that a general meeting at the central place was called. The priest presided.

Mother paused in her storytelling and her whole persona changed as the priest in the story started to tell the tale.

This meeting was called specifically to discuss the schooling of our people. I intend to follow the guidelines of our forefathers in choosing those who are ready for this schooling. A screening has been set up similar to that which was in Central City. Each tribe will send those who they sense are ready to learn to the Central House. To start with we ask that each tribe send only five applicants whom they surmise to be of the highest vibration. Then I will call on the Holiest of Holy to screen them. If for some reason they do not pass the screening, the tribe may send replacements until three to five students represent each tribe.

The priest waited a moment while a murmur swept through the crowd.

'The day after tomorrow at sunrise the chosen three to five from each tribe will gather in the Central House. One by one I will call each for the screening into the Holiest of Holies sacred room, a room that is pure with high vibrational energy. One week from today we will announce those who will begin their education in this new land.'

As though overwhelmed by the previous proclamation, the priest fell silent, as did his audience, for what seemed like an eternity to me.

Mother said, continuing the story in the voice of Mauri.

Slowly, one by one the leader of each tribe stood beside the priest. Each in turn announced a tribal meeting to be held at their water source in the center of their individual settlements. After all had made their announcement, the refugees returned to their homes.

Like swarms of bees, each group of villagers took the path back to their settlement, buzzing among themselves of the recent announcement.

Again Mother's tone changed, almost as though she was a small blurry-eyed child waking the next morning in a primitive village near a beach.

Excitement filled the air of our village as everyone gathered at the central water source of the settlement. The chief of our tribe rose up onto a log so he could be seen and heard by all.

He began. 'The priest has instructed each chief as to how the five applicants will be chosen. Each applicant must speak the language, which eliminates babies and the smallest of children. They must be agile in body, which eliminates the old people who have stiffened, for certain physical feats will be required for this first group of students. The remainder of our village will meet at my house.'

Myself, along with my mother, father, brother, and other qualified members of the village gathered around the chief's house. I had no idea what to expect, although I did not feel nervous. My mother held my hand assuredly. One by one they filed into the village chief's house. After a brief time they came out not speaking a word to the crowd who were waiting their turn. Soon it was my turn to go in, alone. I sat down in front of the chief.

The chief started by asking me about my dreams. "Can you remember them and what were they like?"

I told him about a few of my more unusual ones. He asked, 'Do you ever have visions while you are awake?'

Of course I responded with a yes, telling him of the vision I had received right before our exodus to this new land. Then he asked me, "Tell me, have you ever seen or heard any spirit beings or invisible friends?"

In my naïve, child-like way I described the glowing spirits who talked to me on occasion. Without further comment, I was then excused and the next person was called in.

I thought the questions were silly. Didn't everyone have a spirit being to help him or her? I knew most people dreamed because I had often heard them laughing about their dreams, especially after a celebration. The interviews continued throughout most of the morning until everyone waiting was questioned. The chief was alone during most of the early afternoon. Chanting could be heard coming from his house.

The tribe busied itself with the normal chores of collecting fruits, vegetables, and wood for the evening meal. I continued helping my grandmother sort the various leaves, barks, roots, and berries she had collected while I was being interviewed. After the evening meal, the chief exited his house and stood before his tribe's people, as they gathered around the evening central fire. A respectful silence swept over the group.

"The spirit has talked to me and helped me in this task of deciding who will be the first members of our tribe to be schooled by the priest in this new land," he said. "This carries quite a responsibility, for you who are chosen will be representatives of our tribe. The Great Spirit has helped me choose five people and two alternates who will go in the place of any one of the first five who the priest decides is not yet ready."

He called off the names. My name was called first. My body shook with anxiety. What if I could not remember all the symbols? My mind went back to the time before the upheaval when I had had difficulty concentrating on my sand drawing. As a result of my day dreaming, I failed to hear anything said beyond that point. My grandmother put her arm around me and I calmed down.

"These five people will meet with the priest at first light tomorrow for further screening. The two alternates will stay close to our settlement in case the priest calls for them," the chief announced.

That night I had a difficult time going to sleep. When I finally did, my sleep was filled with dreams. Many times during the night I awoke confused as to whether I had dreamed the event or if it was really something that had happened or was going to happen. In one dream I saw myself in a cape made of feathers. I was older then but I knew it was I. I was sitting before a large group speaking to them. I could not hear what was being said, but when I strained to hear I awoke.

Finally, after a very restless night, my mother awakened me at first light. With the other four chosen ones, I proceeded to the Central House where the priest was waiting for us.

After all the chosen ones were gathered in a circle, the priest led a meditation. I found myself relaxing, and after the chanting by the priest, I felt the familiar euphoria or light feeling that always engulfed me during meditation or chanting. I loved feeling like this. The pictures in my head became so vivid and clear, not like the dreams, which were misty and often vague.

One by one each person present was called into the private room of the priest. After each came back out they joined the circle and continued meditating with the rest of the group. However, two of the original chosen did not join the circle again, but left the Central building. Not long afterward, two new candidates entered and joined the circle of waiting applicants.

Soon it would be my turn to enter the private holy room. I could feel it. I tried to remain calm by breathing the way the priest in the Motherland had taught me. It helped. Then I heard my name called.

As I entered the room, an energy force encased me. It felt as though a warm blanket of fleece was draped around my body. The room was exceptionally warm, and was filled with a haze of smoke, which smelled like a smoldering sandalwood tree. It was dark but for the two flames which caused shadows to dance on the ceiling and walls of this windowless interior.

I silently studied the priest, who was sitting on the floor, motionless with his legs intertwined. His elbows rested on his knees, hands up, with the first finger and thumb pressing against one another. His head was slightly down, and his eyes were gently closed with only an occasional twitch of an eyelid to indicate he was not a statue. I patiently waited for what seemed like an eternity, trying to keep my body still even though my mind raced with thoughts and images. I felt a pressure at the back of my head as though someone or something was pressing on it.

Just when I thought I could no longer remain still, the priest opened his eyes and greeted me. His soft and soothing voice put me at ease immediately.

"You have been chosen for the final screening necessary to become a student of the sacred knowledge. Do you agree to do this screening?" I heard the priest gently ask, while I felt his gaze looking directly through my eyes into my very soul.

In a meek voice, I responded with a yes, understanding neither what it meant to be screened nor what the sacred knowledge could be. I only knew that my tribe was depending on me doing my best as one of their representatives.

The priest continued. "Mauri, describe to me in as much detail as you can, what you see behind me."

I took a deep breath, and started describing everything I saw sitting on a platform behind and slightly above the priest's head.

I began speaking in a voice that was not that of a seven-year-old child. "On two sides of the bowl are similar figures that look like a bird, an animal, and a man. There are bright-colored stones imbedded in each. The eyes are the color of the sky. Between each set of eyes is a dark blue sapphire. Each wears a crown the color of the setting sun, and on its highest point is the largest amethyst that I've ever seen. On the chest of each figure is an emerald as bright as the summer grass. Each of their stomachs holds a stone as yellow as the white trees' fall leaves. In each abdomen is set a stone the orange color of the tongues of a fire. Below that one is a red stone the color of my blood when I cut myself. Each figure has six fingers on each hand and a triangle shape in the center of the palm. Around each of their necks is a silver disk that shines like the moon on a quiet lake. In the center of the circular disk is an upside down triangle with circles at their points the color of the green-blue rocks found on the Motherland. It is almost like the necklace you and the other teachers wear around your necks."

At that point I paused. The priest took me by the hand and led me to within inches of the bowl and figures I had been describing. He asked me to look inside the bowl. At first I thought it was a trick question when the priest asked me to tell him what I saw.

After several hesitating moments, I finally responded with, "All I see is a flame with seven tongues, each a different color. Above it is a white ball of mist.' I sheepishly added, 'That is all I see."

The priest responded, "Now, Mauri, close your eyes and place your hands on the bowl. Tell me what you hear."

At first I could only hear a high-pitched tone in my ear. Then I took a deep breath and the tone started to become words. "I hear the bowl telling me that I am to fear no evil, for the Great Spirit is with me. It is also telling me that I come from the stars, and that I am ready to start my journey in experiencing what it is like to be an earthling as a spiritual being. All that I learn I will teach to other earthlings, although not all will be ready to listen. I am a teacher of teachers."

As the last of the words left my mouth, I fell to my knees, my arms moving forward, and my forehead touching the cool floor. The priest stood over me for a while, and then helped me to my feet. He escorted me to a nearby mat and gave me a grain cake with berries spread on top. With each bite, my eyes became more focused until finally I looked at the priest and asked in a normal child-like voice, "Did I pass?"

A smile grew on the priest's face as he said, "Yes, you did, my dear little one. Mauri, only those who are ready are able to see the covenant behind me. You not only saw it, but you also saw details that I was not able to see until I had had years of study. The bowl, you called it, is on another dimension. It is of a much higher vibration than our human dimension. You may go back to your settlement and rest. Tell your parents I will come tomorrow morning to speak with them. And Mauri, at this time, we ask you to not tell anyone what we did in the sacred room. There are others who have not yet had their turn with the screening test."

I took the path to my village. The first to see me was my mother, who was weaving a lidded basket. She set the basket aside and welcomed me home. "How did you do, dear? Can you tell me what happened?"

"I passed, Mother," I responded as I hugged my mother. "I can't tell you everything. The priest told me not to speak of what happened, but he told me to tell you that he wishes to speak to you and Father tomorrow morning. He told me to rest today and drink lots of water."

Mother wanted to ask more questions but knew it would only put pressure on me, so instead she gave me some water from the basket and rolled out her mat so I could lie down. Then she left the house to search for Father. He was in the forest nearby sharpening fishing spears that he had made the day before. She relayed the little bit of information I had given her. He had wanted to know right away the results of my screening. For a long time, Father had known that there was something strange and wonderful about me, his daughter.

Tashi's mother closed her eyes, and he knew the evening story was at an end. As he started to climb the ladder to his bed, his hand went to his chest and found the necklace he had found in the cave. Could this be like the necklace that Mauri saw in the story? He still wasn't sure he should as yet reveal his find to his parents, for then he would have to explain the hours he had spent in his secret cave. He didn't feel ready to share his special secret.

Chapter Thirteen

The Harvest

Tashi's village was bustling with activity. The time of harvesting the barley was upon them. Preparations were made. Large cloths on which the barley was dumped and shaken to separate the grain from the shaft were mended. Extra baskets were made to hold the grain. There would be no idle hands in the village that week.

Everyone was busy from sunrise to sunset. The men were already in the field cutting the grain and tying it into bundles. Stalks of the bundled barley were encircling the area where the large cloths were spread out. The women stationed themselves around the perimeter of the cloth.

It was Tashi's job, just like other Tibetan boys his age, to cut the heads from the stalks of barley and put them on the cloth. The women shook the cloth until the grain loosened and collected under the shaft. As the contents on the cloth were tossed into the air, the lighter shafts were carried away by the constant Tibetan wind.

The young girls raked away the larger shaft and bundled it. Some would be put into the clay bricks that were made for building. The rest would be valuable feed for the livestock when winter set in. They scooped the pure barley grain into large baskets. When a basket was full, two of the larger, stronger boys carried it into the village storage building.

The whole area resembled a dust storm. Everything in and around the village had a coating of fine dust. To ease their breathing in the thin mountain air, the harvesters wore a cloth mask that was kept damp.

Even then, at the day's end, their nostrils were coated inside with the dust.

As the sun went behind the mountains, they returned to their homes. They removed their clothing and left it outside the house. They hung it on poles so that the mountain's evening breezes would blow most of the dust from them. The clothing was not washed until the harvest was completed. The rest of the evening was simple: dinner and sleep.

It had been an exceptionally abundant crop that year, so the harvest took close to two weeks instead of the normal one to complete. A gratitude harvest celebration was to take place at its completion. Some of the older women busied themselves making various foods for the celebration banquet. The celebration commenced for three days.

They gave homage and thanks to the spiritual guardians of the grain, the wind, the rain, and other various god-like helpers of this abundance. On the third day, the village priest presided over a special ritual giving thanks to God and the Buddha. A ritual of barley tea, barley cakes, and the specially made barley beer, called chang, were consumed. At the closing of the celebrations at twilight, the area lama gathered everyone and led them in a chant that lasted for about an hour. At the sundown ceremony, the lama gave the prophecies for the coming months. These predictions included weather reports and planting schedules with some spiritual guidance thrown in.

That year in Tashi's village, the opening of the school was also celebrated during harvest, because the teacher from Lhasa arrived in the middle of it. Tashi's parents established the teacher in the room they had added to their house. The village officially welcomed him during the third day of the celebration. When asked to speak, he announced that school would begin three days after the celebration was completed. He said that he, in the meantime, would unpack the schoolbooks and materials, and asked if anyone wanted to help him. Several volunteered.

Everything in the village settled down the day after the celebration, and the chores that had been neglected during it were caught up. Tashi's grandmother decided that, since he would soon be in school, another gathering trip to the mountains for leaves, berries, and roots should be taken right away.

Again equipped with a snack pack and empty skin bags, he started out for the path up the mountain. The berries were bountiful. It had been a good year for growing things, so he knew he would fill his sack quickly. His step quickened when he realized that there would be time for another visit to his secret cave. The mysterious necklace that he had acquired on his last visit became warm as his hand caressed it. He had not told anyone about it, not even his mother.

Tashi arrived at the entrance to his cave and pulled away the dry bushes concealing it. He entered and stood for a moment to let his eyes adjust to the semi-darkness. The small stream of light from its opening to the outside world allowed Tashi to see that only the nest of the pack rats had changed position, and that nothing or anyone else was sharing the cave with him this day.

Tashi thought about his previous visit as he ate the barley cake Mother had packed in his pack. His hand caressed the circle disk around his neck. He found himself growing very weary as he chewed the last bits of the cake. Almost beyond his control, his eyes closed. As though on cue, a bright light appeared behind his closed eyelids. The entire cave warmed as though bathed in warm sunlight, although the sun could never reach its inner chamber. His eyes slowly opened, and the bright light took the shape of a somewhat human form. He could hear the same tones of music, which he had heard before, as the form came closer to him. For some reason he felt no fear, only peace. As he gazed at the being, he heard words in his head.

Chapter Fourteen

The Tall White Being Speaks:

W*e meet again. You shall be the teacher of teachers. You shall teach the sacred knowledge to those who are ready to learn as your mother has, and as her father did, and as his mother did, and so on. Very soon you will start your training. Your mother will decide when it will begin. You have been chosen through the reincarnation agreement to be instrumental in keeping the spirit of Lemuria alive. Your other incarnations as a priest will soon be remembered. Your initiation as a spiritual teacher is about to commence. The disk you wear has been activated and is now dissolving the veils of those past memories."*

Soft and soothing musical notes resonated in the cave as melodic words were heard through his mind.

From beyond the sun you did arrive
In a shiny bird sent to teach their spirit to revive
Now again your skills and knowledge are needed
For the spirit of Mu will again be heeded
Your stories will be told both near and far
Reminding the souls of the eight-pointed star
The origins of Earthlings will help them to see
A golden time when their spirits were free
Words of hope will flow from your pen
They will vibrate the core of both women and men

Again we will meet, for it has begun
Again you will bask in a golden sun.

With the being's last words and the musical tones still vibrating in his head, Tashi's eyes again closed.

He found himself waking to the scratching of little claws on his knapsack. He shooed away the busy pack rats with his hand, but his mind was still trying to comprehend what he had just witnessed. Gathering his belongings, he exited the cave and realized only then that the mountain was close to swallowing the sun. It had seemed that he was in the cave for only a short time. How could the whole afternoon have gone by?

As he scurried down the mountain path, he rationalized that he must have fallen asleep. What other explanation could there be? Yet bits and pieces of the tall being and the song flashed through his mind's eye as he rapidly made his way to his village. He noticed it had grown quite dark now, but strangely enough he had no trouble seeing his way home. It was as though someone or something was lighting his way.

A few houses from his home he met his father. He was carrying a light. He noticed that the worried look on his face turned to relief as Tashi called to him. How was he going to explain his lateness? To his surprise, his father never asked. As they entered his home, Tashi was met with a warm smile from his mother. He wanted so much to share what had happened to him, but it was still so strange to him, and he wasn't certain he could explain it to someone who had not been there. Besides, he would then have to confess about the time he had spent in his secret cave. He knew he was not ready to divulge that.

Tashi unloaded the bags of berries, leaves, and roots. His grandmother looked very pleased. "You have done well, Tashi. The bounty you have collected will help many ailing people," she told him, as she gave him a hug.

His mother diverted the attention away from Tashi by instructing everyone to sit down to dinner. Tashi was confused about why he was not reprehended for being late, but chose not to broach the subject, which might have made it necessary for him to invent some feeble excuse.

After dinner Mother took her usual storytelling position.

Chapter Fifteen

The Story Continues

Tashi's mother started in the voice of Mauri.

That next morning in my village, the priest arrived at my home quite early. My mother and father were ready for him. Feeling flutters in my stomach as the anticipated meeting neared, I wondered whether I would be allowed to listen or if it was grown-up talk. Somewhere deep inside me I knew that after today my life would take a different direction, but I could not even conceive in my wildest imagination what it would be. During the night I had been awakened many times with various visions for which I did not understand the meaning.

The priest was welcomed into our dwelling. Mother had prepared a tea from some special mint leaves and a piece of ginger root. He asked me to wait outside a few moments until I was called. I exited the dwelling and sat outside next to my grandmother, who was sorting some herbs and grinding some seeds. Without much enthusiasm, I helped her sort a small bag of seeds.

My mind raced with the possibilities of what was happening inside the house. I felt them talking about me. The other villagers seemed as curious as I was. They made excuses for passing my house and stopping to chat with Grandmother, but no one asked about the purpose of the priest's visit. That was not considered polite.

Finally, my father's head showed through the opening of our home. Without a word he motioned me to come in.

The priest, Mother, and Father were drinking tea and chatting about the weather when I entered the house. Mother asked me to take a seat next to her. Father opened the conversation by telling me that the priest had explained my participation in the screening that had taken place the day before.

The priest spoke to me directly. "Mauri, every so often the Great Spirit, All That Is, sends someone to the Earth as a teacher for all. During meditation I have been told you are one of these teachers. I have also been told that I am to guide you to better understand the marvelous gifts you have brought with you to this planet. It is for this reason I have asked your parents to allow you to live in the Central Building so that you might give all your energy to preparing for the time when you will be the spiritual leader and keeper of the sacred knowledge for all the people on earth."

I sat silent, not fully understanding the ramifications of all the priest was saying. When asked if I had any questions, I quietly asked, "Will I get to see my family ever?"

The priest smiled. "Yes, of course you will, but your duties will not be to the family, but of a higher order. In other words, Mauri, your time will be spent developing and practicing for the leadership position you will assume when you are ready. Your parents have agreed to this arrangement and were not surprised when I told them your unique insights. Now, do you have any other questions?"

"I guess not," I said, as a small tear formed in my eye. I didn't know why I felt so happy but also sad. I almost felt as empty as I felt when I had not eaten in a long time.

I listened silently as the arrangements for the move to the Central Building were discussed. The move was to take place in three days, after the priest had completed the rest of the screening for the schooling of the others from the various tribal families.

Chapter Sixteen

Mauri Moves to the Central Building

I gathered what few personal belongings I had, which consisted of a few articles of clothing, a sleeping mat, and a child's collection of favorite stones.

Tashi's mother continued.

My father walked me to the Central Building where the priest met us. He showed me the room where I would live adjacent to the large central meeting hall. It was a small, simple room with a small opening high on the wall where light and ventilation entered.

My father laid my satchel of belongings near my sleeping mat, which he unrolled. He gave me a long hug and told me he loved me. His eyes were misty as he turned and left for home.

The priest broke the emotionally filled silence by inviting me to have some root tea and a grain cake with him in the meditation room. I nodded my head yes, afraid to let my voice reveal my anxiety. He served me a bowl of tea and a cake, and then sat down opposite me.

He started the conversation with, "Mauri, I think right now we just need to get to know one another better. Tell me how you feel about all these changes in your young life."

"Well," I began slowly, "I'm a little bit afraid."

"What scares you the most?"

"I'm afraid I won't be able to remember all the symbols. Before the shaking, fire, and flood in the Motherland, I daydreamed instead of practicing drawing the symbols. My father and the tribal priest scolded me for it."

"You will soon have no difficulty remembering those symbols and others. Your ability to daydream is part of the reason you are here. I will do my best to answer your questions and teach you how to use those daydreams to teach others how to live the sacred knowledge of universal love. I know this sounds very complicated right now, but I assure you, my job is to help you to have fun learning and remembering who you really are. Mauri, you have been chosen for an important job, but enjoying it is very important, too. Finish your tea and cake and we will take a walk to a special place I want to share with you."

When I finished my snack and the bowls were put up, the priest took me by the hand. He led me out of the Central Building and into a forest. We walked along a path until we came to what appeared to be a wall of green bushes. He pushed aside one of the bushes and revealed a small opening. From his pack he took out an oil lamp, which he lit by striking a flint against a rock. With the lamp lighting the dark entrance, we walked inside. It was a space, which seemed to have been carved out of gray rock. The light danced off the variegated shades of the smooth gray wall and ceiling. He directed me to sit on a mound of dried grasses, which acted as a cushion, giving me comfort as well as protection against the cold stone floor. He took a position on another mound of grasses opposite me.

After a moment he began speaking. "Mauri, the Great Spirit has given you some very special gifts. I have meditated on what my part in your development of these gifts is. The guidance I have received is that I am to direct you to become comfortable with your channel to the universal knowledge. I am to help you rid yourself of any fears or doubts that might occur as you develop these special gifts."

I, just eight years old, sat taking in every word as the priest tried to explain my future responsibilities without causing me any undue anxiety. Putting into his own words what he had only just learned from his master teachers so that a small child could understand was a challenge. He closed his eyes before he continued, hoping he would receive the right words to explain his part in my growth as a prophet.

While he was still trying to gather the words in his mind, I took his hand, and in a gentle voice that seemed to be older than my years, said, "I know that I have been chosen to lead my people during this time of tremendous change in our lives. I am young in age but my soul is old. Our spiritual bodies must be very strong in the coming times. If fear rules, we shall cease to exist as a people. Your assistance in helping me to understand the messages I receive and protecting me from those who react to them out of fear is as important a task as the one I have been chosen to do."

Tears were rolling down the priest's cheeks as he sat paralyzed with the overwhelming love streaming from me, a small but powerful child whose aura took on a golden glow. He wondered why he had not noticed my power while he was still in the Motherland. Had he been too absorbed in his own importance as the spiritual leader from the Central City? Had he been bigoted that a descendant of these common village people could not possibly have the spiritual insights that he as a trained priest from Central City had? How very humble I, a gentle little girl, made him feel. He wiped his eyes and let them meet mine. A blanket of warm love engulfed him, setting his body tingling.

In a voice that was more of that of an eight-year old, I asked, "What do I need to do first in order to prepare for this responsibility?"

The nervous impatience of a small child, whose mind working in a literal manner, was speaking to him now. The priest answered, "This cave is your special place where you can come to be alone when you feel confused by what is happening to you or around you. It is a place of safety where you can come to meditate or just be alone. No one will be allowed to enter this cave except me, and only if you give me permission."

I sat, looking up at him, not really sure I understood what he meant.

He saw the confusion in my eyes, so he tried to simplify what my development process entailed. He thought a minute and decided that explaining only one task would leave me less frightened. After all, this had come about rather suddenly. One day I was an eight-year-old helping my grandmother sort herbs, and the next day I was told I would be responsible for the spiritual well-being of an entire people. Such a drastic change might even overwhelm a master teacher. He, himself, was rather unnerved by even his small part.

"Mauri, the first lesson we will work on is your meditation skill, going deeper into that silent place within, so that the pictures you receive will be clearer. Each day we will spend time together just meditating. Then you can share any insights or pictures you see in your mind with me. We will also spend time talking about any dreams you have. With my humble abilities I will help you to understand the words and the pictures. You must feel free to ask questions, no matter how silly you might think they are, for no question is unimportant."

"Now, little one, let us go back to the Central Building and make your room more comfortable. This afternoon the students from the various villages will come for their first lesson. In addition to our private time together, you will attend the lessons with the other students."

I thought for a moment, and then voiced my mental question. "Will I have to know all the symbols and be able to write them in the sand? I always had a hard time remembering them."

The priest smiled. "We will learn them while playing a game. Do not worry, little one. You will find learning them fun."

The priest and I walked out into the bright sunlight, putting the bush back so as to camouflage the entrance to the cave from the path. We were both silent as we followed the subtle trail, which ended at the back entrance to the Central Building. It had been a good discussion for our first encounter. We needed to get to know and be at ease with each other, the priest thought. This had been a good beginning.

Mother's eyes closed and her head went down. The storytelling was completed for the night.

Chapter Seventeen

The Next Day in Tashi's Village

Tashi had had vivid dreams that night. He kept replaying the story that Mother had told mixed with the vision he had gotten in his secret cave. He knew he needed to speak to Mother about the symbol around his neck as well as the rhymed message he had received, but this was the first day of the new school. She was busy making certain the teacher from Lhasa had everything he needed.

The teacher had eaten earlier and had already left for the schoolhouse by the time Tashi had finished his morning chores. After breakfast he and his sister left for the school. He was a bit anxious about what to expect, but Mother assured them that they would love learning.

The first thing that the teacher, Pasang-la, did was to lead them in mediation and prayer before he assigned the students seats according to their sizes and ages. Since most everyone present had not had any formal teaching, and only knew some of the basics of reading and writing, everyone was on the same academic level. The teacher handed out a pad of paper and pencil to everyone. A blackboard on which his name was written was in the front of the small room. He asked each student to tell him his or her name, which he then wrote on the board below his.

Everyone was instructed to copy the letters of his or her name onto their pad of paper. It felt awkward to Tashi to hold the pencil, much less make it do what he wanted it to do. The teacher was very patient and eventually with much practice by all, the papers had a rather crude writing on them somewhat resembling the writings on the board.

The introduction to writing was followed by a chorus-like recitation of the different letters of the alphabet as Pasang-la wrote them on the board one by one. Over and over again like a chant they repeated each letter of the alphabet as he pointed to it.

This recitation continued for some time. Next, the numbers were written on the board and recited until everyone was in unison. After a lunch snack all the students copied everything that had been written on the board onto their pad of paper as exactly as his or her dexterity and skills allowed.

In the afternoon, all the students gathered in a circle and the teacher took one of his many books from the shelf and read a chapter about the history of Tibet. Tashi found this the most interesting part of the day's schooling. He could almost picture the events as the teacher read.

After he read several chapters, Pasang-la unrolled a large map and held it up against the wall. It had various colored shapes and lines of blue, which, he later told them, were rivers. Tashi was surprised to see how small Tibet was in relation to other countries of the world. He had been told that China was big, but had no idea that it was so very much larger than so many other countries. When Mr. Pasang-la finished explaining the map, having them repeat the names of some of the important countries, he told them to take home their pads and write one whole page of his or her name, as well as one page each of all the letters and numbers. He instructed them to bring the pads to school everyday.

With a wave of his hand, all fifteen of them bounded for their individual homes, anxious to share their new knowledge—although they knew the sharing would be postponed by the afternoon chores awaiting most of them.

Tashi's mother and father wanted to hear all about the events of the first day of school. Tashi let his sister tell most of it. He only filled in the parts that she forgot to tell. The history story that had been read, as she told it, was different than what he remembered, but of course his sister was only six years old so her perspective was quite different.

While dinner was being prepared, Mother instructed Tashi and his sister to do the practice sheets that the teacher had asked them to complete. Mother could not resist occasionally leaving her cooking to glance over their shoulder. She so wanted her children to be educated. Even before the school was established in the village, Mother tutored her children in some of the basic writing skills that her aunt, the nun, had taught her.

When dinner and cleanup was completed, Mother assumed her storytelling position. Tashi had been afraid that she might skip storytelling because of the extra time that their schoolwork had taken up. He was delighted when she sat before them with her eyes closed.

Chapter Eighteen

Mother Begins

The first night in my new dwelling was strange. I was accustomed to people nearby. I wasn't afraid, just a little anxious. In my home I could always hear the comforting breathing or the snores of my grandmother if I awakened during the night. Now, when I awoke during the night there was silence, except for the song of the wind and the distant lapping of the sea.

The following morning I met the priest in a small cooking room, where we ate some porridge and tea. While we were eating, the priest explained the planned events of my first day at the Central Building. He explained that soon the other students would arrive in the big room and the classes would begin.

By the time we had finished our food, many of the other students were nervously milling around in the big room. The priest and I joined them. The priest seated himself on one side of the room and told me to take a seat next to him. He directed the rest of the students to sit forming a circle around the room. When everyone was seated and settled, the priest began. He asked each student to give his or her name and the name of his or her family tribe.

Introductions completed, the priest explained to the students that they had been chosen as representatives of their tribes in order to attend the schooling similar to the process that had been practiced in the Motherland and that eventually they would share their learning with their own tribes. He said that he would tell them when and how to do so. However, before that time, they were not to talk about the lessons to anyone outside that room. He explained that it was important that each of them totally understood the lesson material before they shared it so as to prevent misinformation or incomplete information from being passed on.

The priest stated, "You are to meet at the Central Building each day unless I tell you otherwise. A great amount of your time will be spent in meditation, for only at deep levels of consciousness will you fully understand the teaching." With that being said he led us into a meditation.

I found it difficult to keep my mind from racing. So many questions arose. The harder I tried to quiet my mind, the more questions raced to its surface. Finally the repetitious beat on the small drum by the priest helped me to focus my thoughts enough so that I could relax. The smell of the burning sandalwood became keener, and a rainbow of colors waved before my closed eyes.

Abruptly, I felt a slight jerk and all was black. As I entered the blackness, a wave of peace enveloped me. I was enjoying the peaceful emptiness when a series of vivid colored pictures flooded into my inner vision. At first I could not decide whether they were dreams or something taking place in my real life. I chose not to worry about it and just enjoy the array of colorful mental images.

After what seemed like a very short period, but was actually over an hour, from somewhere far away, I heard the priest telling me to come back into the room and into the present. With a snap and a jerk in my body, I became disoriented as I opened my eyes and saw a circle of faces staring at me. At first, they seemed unfamiliar to me. However, within a few minutes my stupor left and I recognized the group and the surroundings. I looked at the priest, who laid his hand gently on my shoulder and with a smile on his face said, "Welcome back, little one."

I felt a bit uneasy receiving the unsolicited attention. The priest broke the students' silent gazes when he started talking. He asked everyone to pick up the pointed stick that lay in front of him or her. With it he asked us to draw a symbol in the sand floor just as he drew it. He started at the top and drew a line straight down, followed by a line crossing the up-and-down line. Both lines were exactly the same length.

Everyone started scratching in the sand. Some drew lines that were curved or wiggled. Others had lines that were different lengths. The priest patiently told us to smooth out the sand and draw another until we felt it was the same as his. Satisfied with our progress, he showed us another symbol, which was a line drawn starting at the top and curving around until it met itself, forming a shape like that of the sun. Some students found this one more difficult to draw. Most of their drawn shapes were lopsided or the line did not meet at the top. Many attempts were made before each felt he had drawn the symbol close enough to that of the priest's to be acceptable.

After the priest was pleased that everyone had been able to reproduce the two symbols with ease, he asked us to lay down our sticks and stare at the symbols until in our minds we heard the symbol's meaning. After a while the priest went from person to person and asked what meaning they had heard. Some were confused and not sure we heard anything, but were encouraged by the priest to not be shy and just state the first thoughts that had come to our minds.

Finally it was my turn to talk. I was certain I did not have the 'right' answers for mine were different than the other students. I was urged again by the priest to state whatever it was that I had heard.

I took a deep breath and in a quiet little voice said, "I heard that this symbol, the cross, represents the directions that all energy flows." I had heard more but was too timid to speak it. "The circle represents the source like the sun that activates or gives life to everything including us, but it is even more powerful than the sun."

The priest smiled with delight and thought what a miraculous jewel this little one was. She was certainly something special, and to think he had the job of helping her to develop. He prayed he had been prepared enough by the masters from the Central City to do the task justice.

He picked up his stick and drew another cross on top of the first cross, but slightly tilted it, creating a wheel with eight spikes. He instructed everyone to copy it. After which he told them, "The first cross represents the four directions that God sends universal energy to us. The second cross represents the four elements by which that energy comes to us: fire, wind, water, and earth."

By the time everyone was able to duplicate the symbol, the sun was low on the horizon. He told us to spend time practicing drawing the symbols by ourselves in our villages, and to meditate on their meaning, bringing our new insights to class. All, except me, were excused to go back to their individual villages.

If these classes had been held in the Central City, we would have gone to a building that housed all the beginning students. The priest thought, *Would there ever be another city as grand and with as much loving energy as what the Central City of the Motherland had had?* Involuntarily, a tear formed in his eye every time he remembered the catastrophic events that had taken his beloved Motherland.

The responsibility of continuing the teachings of that magnificent civilization weighed heavily upon his shoulders. He had heard that the inhabitants of the Motherland had fled in all directions. Insights had come to him that a group was establishing a city far east of the Motherland in a place called Atlantis. He had also heard that it was greatly influenced by those who put much emphasis on the technical or physical aspects of life, having the spiritual aspects of life secondary and sometimes not acknowledging spirituality at all. He could not imagine how this way of life would continue to work for any length of time, since the physical always followed the spiritual. He could only imagine that in time such a way of life would result in another earthly disaster.

He excused me to my room where he instructed me to rest and meditate until the evening meal. That night we would have our usual discussion as well as a study session of the night sky. The priest thought this was a great deal of information for a small child, but he felt some urgency to give me as much as I could possibly handle. There was something very special about me, obviously a true descendant of the tall ones with those bright, cobalt blue eyes, not like those of my tribal peers. He couldn't help but ask himself why he had been chosen as my teacher. With all their power, why had not one of the tall ones taken me in order to train me themselves? He decided to meditate on these

97

questions so as to ease his anxiety about this responsibility that was apparently his.

A kind and gentle older widowed woman from one of the villages, named Koha, was chosen to live in the Central Building. Her children were grown and she had no major responsibility to her tribe. Her tasks were to prepare the meals in addition to being a female confidant to me. Koha was also to share her vast knowledge of the plants and animals, particularly their uses for medicinal purposes. The priest thought that I would feel more at ease discussing some of my earthly questions with a woman rather than with him. The priest had lost his wife when a tree fell on her during the catastrophic events in the Motherland.

Koha was introduced to me at the evening meal. He excused himself so as to let us get to know each other before he and I had our first lesson of the sky. While enjoying the evening meal, Koha and I took an instant liking to each other. It was almost as though we had known each other all our lives. The priest never ceased to be amazed at the intricate wonders of the Great Spirit. He immediately saw my tension ease when Koha lightly touched my shoulder with a love pat.

He ate his food in his private chambers and thoroughly enjoyed it. Cooking was never one of his strong points, besides being limited by the time he had for such tasks. Each village had contributed various utensils and food as well as artifacts to make the living quarters in the Central Building more comfortable. The particular symbol designs of each village were evident on the baskets, clay containers, and woven mats that were scattered about the Central Building. Several of the villages had given tools whose handles were carvings of their animal totems—animals they were particularly close to on a spirit level. All these things were given with a great deal of love, which made the atmosphere of the Central Building extremely inviting and soothing. The weekly meetings of all the refugees were very inspirational in this loving setting.

The classes continued year after year. New students were screened and chosen each year. Everyone was encouraged to learn at his or her own speed. Some learned very quickly while others took longer to master specific knowledge. No one was judged if they did not proceed as rapidly as their classmates through the courses set up by the priest.

Mauri's skills and perceptions grew far more than any of her original classmates' abilities, but of course the priest knew this would be the case. This shy little girl was to do great things for her people. He knew that at some point her skills and esoteric knowledge would surpass even his. The priest hoped his ego could remain in place when this took place.

One of my classmates, a boy named Pãka, was also very quick with his studies. He and I became intimate friends. He was near my age, so we related on that level to each other as well. Often when we were to do individual study and meditation, we accompanied one another to a quiet place in the forest to meditate and study together. When free time was available, we played the symbol game together.

Over the years we connected mind to mind. He was literally my only close childhood friend. My metaphysical abilities often put distance between the other students and myself. My insights intimidated most of the people in this newly established community near the moving waters.

The priest had noticed the growing affection between the two of us and approved. He hoped that one day it would not prove to be a problem. Pãka's eyes were not the cobalt blue of mine, but they were not the dark brown of most of the people either. They were more of an emerald green. His hair, too, was lighter than most, but not as light as mine, which day by day was becoming closer to the color of the sun. He was also a good head taller than the rest of the boys his age.

Even when we two were not together we knew what the other was doing and thinking. One day while walking alone in the forest, Pãka entangled his ankle in some briar and was unable to get out. I felt his pain and sent help for him. Mentally I knew exactly where he was trapped and directed the rescue party to him. Yes, it was, indeed, a special relationship, which grew closer and closer each day as we met at the Central Building for our schooling.

We were both very quick with any of the metaphysical exercises and experienced much fun in challenging each other. The academic studies, such as the study of the stars and the earth elements, took more concentration for me, as well as did remembering the names given to the constellations and plant life. Sometimes I called them by a name that had never been mentioned, but when spoken had a familiar ring to Pãka and the priest. The symbols also were difficult for me to copy exactly as the priest drew them. Mine nearly always had a slight variation.

When a meaning for the symbols was asked of me, I gave a definition that no one had ever heard before, but which my teacher and I both found more logically correct. My private sessions with the priest helped me to accept all these differences. He explained to me that I had insight deeper than most of the students, and that they were not yet ready for the higher-vibration information that I was receiving—information that more than likely came from a dimension higher in vibration than that of the earth's third dimension.

As I grew older I learned to accept the fact that I was unique, but somewhere deep inside me I yearned to be a part of the group. Except for Pãka, Koha, the housekeeper, and the priest, most people kept a comfortable distance between themselves and myself.

The time for me to understand all the physical, emotional, mental, and spiritual aspects of transforming from a girl to a woman was close at hand. Koha, who became my surrogate mother, made a special effort to help me to understand the tremendous changes taking place in my body. Having grown up in a protected atmosphere with little interchange with my female peers, these physical changes confused me. When I had my first monthly cycle, I found myself filled with anxiety, and yet also a peacefulness that I had never before felt. As I became accustomed to my new physical self, I found that my intuition became even keener. Other more subtle changes were also apparent. Things that had interested me before seemed silly now.

One day while I was meditating in my secret cave, a bright light came into the chamber. As I gazed at the light it took the form of that of a tall white being. It was surrounded with an aura of iridescent blue light, the same color as its eyes. I saw long fingers on each wispy arm as the being came into focus. Thinking at first that my eyes were playing tricks on me, I then saw that the fingers numbered six on each arm. In my mind I heard words coming from the being. The words were like a song being sung with tones of music in the background. I sat motionless, engulfed in the light as the musical words came through me.

Over the hill
Over the dale
Lead the way
You will not fail
A child of great worth
You will come to bear
For all people
He will feel a deep care
A hidden city
Will welcome your grace
At last you will claim
Your rightful place

Even after the cave became silent and the bright light dimmed, I found it difficult to move. I wasn't sure I fully understood the message the being told me, or maybe I just didn't want to understand it. If I understood it I would have to admit that it was true, and that meant my world as well as my people's world was about to change drastically. Since the flight from the Motherland, it had taken many years to bring order back to the people. Even then when the ground sometimes shook, the people gathered together in fear so as to calm and assure one another.

Finally, when the bright blue-white light that filled the interior of the cave dissipated and the thought words ceased, I stood. I needed to talk to the priest about my vision, but this one had been like no other vision I had ever experienced. Today's occurrence appeared to be really happening and not just in a dream or a vision. The tall white being was physically standing next to me in the cave. This unusual event needed to be digested before I talked to anyone about it, even the priest.

During the evening meal on the day of my vision in the cave, the priest noticed a different glow to my aura. He knew something special had taken place. He opened the door to me sharing it with him. "Mauri, you may start to have some unusual events that you may not be able to understand, but when that happens and you are ready to talk about them, I am available." That's all he could say. He knew that the next move had to be mine. During meditation he had been given explicit instructions not to interfere with my acceptance of my new spiritual openings

I did not respond to his invitation to share. I just was not sure of how I would explain what had taken place. I thought that in a couple of days I would go back to the cave, and maybe during meditation I would be able to understand the message more fully so that I could share it. Often messages of this type were more metaphoric than literal. I wanted to make certain my interpretation was not my ego at work. So many new things had taken place lately that my confidence in my insights had waned slightly.

That night I had especially vivid dreams. They were lucid as though I was actually living them right now in the present. I awoke the next morning nearly as tired as when I had gone to bed. I felt like I had not slept a wink. Thank goodness the only thing scheduled that day was playing the symbol game with Pãka. The other students were to be tested on some skills that Pãka and I had long ago mastered.

Pãka and I laid out the twenty-two smooth, round stones, with the image side facing down. The symbolic images were the same as the ones that the priest had taught to the students. We carefully rolled out a cloth made from the pounding of roots on which a large eight-pointed star was drawn. A circle connected the eight points. I picked my first stone on which was drawn a circle. I placed it in the middle of the star. Today my message through the stones would be of a universal nature since the circle represented God or All That Is. I continued choosing stones until there was one on each point. After meditating on the spread of stones, Pãka told me their meanings in relationship to my life, depending on how they were placed on the cloth. After that, Pãka chose stones and I gave my interruption of their meaning.

When Mother ended the telling of the game, she closed her eyes, a sign that the storytelling had ended for the night.

Chapter Nineteen

The Next Night in Tashi's Home

The next night after dinner, Mother closed her eyes, signifying that the story would continue when she opened them again. She began.

One day during our daily discussions the priest asked me if I had ever had a dream at night or during a meditation about being spoken to by tall white beings with cobalt blue eyes. I hesitantly answered yes. With suppressed anxiety, he asked me to tell him about the encounters.

Surprised that he used the plural, I started by telling him about the first time when I was in the cave and had received the rhymed message from a tall white being with six fingers. I wasn't certain I was ready to share the second encounter where I was given the strange but beautiful pendant.

He made no comment other than to ask if I had had any other experiences with them. I nodded my head as I put my hand to my chest. After a few minutes of silence I told the priest of my second encounter.

Another day when I was in the secret cave meditating, the bright blue-white light again filled its interior. When I opened my eyes, standing before me was a very tall being, sparkling white in color. He looked transparent as though I could put my hand right through him. By his energy I could tell that he was the same one who had come to me before. He said he had a gift for me and a message to help me to understand who I was.

The priest asked me if I could remember, and if so, to tell him what the second message was.

"The being told me that you could help me to fully understand its meaning."

"Why have you not told me of this before?"

"I thought I was just dreaming, and yet he left me this symbolic gift," I said, pulling the pendant from its hidden place.

I told the priest about my latest encounter and the message that came with the circular disk. During meditation, like before, the cave filled with a blinding, bright light. Soon the light took the shape of a human. A warm wave of energy enveloped me, and although my ears only heard the most soothing music, I knew in my mind that he was speaking to me. Every word was clear. He told me he had a message that would help me to understand why I was different from the rest of my people. He explained that I was from one of their seeds and had been sent to help Earth and its people shift into a new age. He explained that our planet is going through and will continue to go through major changes. He explained that with my special abilities I would help my people to dispel their fear when more catastrophic changes occur.

I asked him if the sinking of the Motherland was one of these changes, and he told me that it was one of the more dramatic physical ones, but the more important changes would come in the consciousness of the people who survived the physical disasters. He warned me that there are forces at work, which want to take advantage of these upheavals for their own selfish benefits, by instilling fear in people and lowering the vibration of their energy as a method of control.

I asked him how a person such as me could make any difference. He told me that my ability to channel the pure love energy enables me to teach those who are willing to listen. This powerful energy, as I share it, is so powerful that it will overcome any fear that a person may be harboring. In my presence this channeled light will brighten all the shadows created by fear.

The tall white being sang the following song. I thought I would not be able to remember it, but it continuously sings in my head.

I sang the song for the priest.

Ommmmmmm sing to the sky of your grace
Ommmmmmm feel the light of the sun warm your face
Ommmmmmm let the power of the earth through
    your feet
Ommmmmmm feel the pulse of the universe in your
    heartbeat
Ommmmmmm see the twinkle of the stars as they shine
    from above
Ommmmmmm feel the warmth in your soul as you fill it
    with love

"What happened when he finished singing the song?" The priest asked, taking my hand, as he looked deep into my vibrant blue eyes.

"After the song and the music ended, the bright light in the cave faded. I closed my eyes thinking I must have been dreaming or had astral traveled in my mind to some strange place. When I opened my eyes this was laying beside me."

I put my hand under my robe and pulled out the round shiny silver disk with the upside down triangle in the middle. On each point of the triangle was a turquoise stone. I waited for the priest's reaction. As I gazed into his eyes, I saw tears forming until his eyes could hold them no longer. As the salty droplets flowed down his cheeks, his mouth moved, but he could not find his voice. So touched was I with this unprecedented show of emotion, that I gently wiped away the beads of tears from his crevassed face.

At last, the priest gained some composure and hugged me, mumbling some words that sounded like "You have come, thank God." He bowed his head in silence, as did I.

After what seemed like a suspension of time, both the priest and I opened our eyes. The priest broke the silence. "I have been instructed by my spirit guides to help you understand your life's purpose as a

105

teacher. I will humbly assist you in any way that I can."

He thought, but did not express to me, that he had actually received a message that he was to be available whenever I needed his help in the near future. They had told him in the message that very soon a huge responsibility was to be bestowed upon me. His spirit guide said that one of the tall white beings would be the bearer of this information to me. At this time, he thought, he need not add to the burdens of this young woman by elaborating on the rest of the message he had received.

"Now, dear one, I think this calls for some special treats and celebration," he said in an enthusiastic voice and with a smile on his face in an effort to break the serious tension of the discussion. He summoned Koha to prepare a special tea and some honey grain cake. The priest and I asked Pãka to join us, for he, too, was to be an important player in the upcoming scenario, and according to the messages the Priest had been receiving he would continue to be so in the future, even after the priest had left the earth's plane.

Chapter Twenty

The Abbot

As Tashi's mother's eyes opened she spoke in a tone different from that of her storytelling voice. "Tashi, tomorrow we will go to the monastery, you and me. We will have a special audience with the Abbot. We will depart immediately after the morning meal, so put on your traveling clothes when you get dressed in the morning."

Tashi curbed his first inclination to ask her all sorts of questions. Something inside of him said that he should rein his quizzical mind. As he went to his sleeping mat, his mind was filled with mixed emotions of excitement for the adventure as well as anxiety for its unknown purpose.

The morning broke the darkness after what seemed to be a longer than normal night. Tashi had laid awake tossing and turning. He was more tired now than when he had gone to bed. When he finally did doze off, he had dreamed vividly. All he could remember of his dreams were bits and pieces, which made no sense to him now.

Without much delay, Tashi and his mother started for the path through the valley and up the mountain to the monastery that housed the Abbot. Mother chatted idly about various observations in nature along the path. When they came to the rest spot where Tashi had heard the music and song on his family's prior pilgrimages, they stopped for a snack. It was Mother who spoke first. "Tashi, do you hear the music?"

"Yes, Mother, I do."

"Have you always heard the music? Do you hear anything else?"

"As long as I can remember I have heard the music every time we have come past this spot, but it has gotten louder and clearer more recently. Last time we came this way I also heard singing. Oh, Mother, it was full of love. I thought it was my imagination, as Father calls it. I was afraid to mention it for fear of being ridiculed for daydreaming."

"I have always heard the music of the mountains, too, Tashi," Mother said. "We must never stop listening to the songs. We have been chosen to share these loving words with all who are willing to listen, but we must not be upset with those who are not yet ready to receive their inherent wisdom. The Abbot will meet with you, for it is time for you to understand how you will share these teachings with all humans. This meeting today will be the first of many."

"I don't understand. What could I, a boy, share with all humans? Why would they listen to what I have to say? I have only just recently started school."

"You will see your future unfold and be shown your path when you are ready. Too much information will only overwhelm you during this preparatory time. You must trust that your future is divinely guided. Now, let us hurry. The Abbot will be waiting."

Mother and Tashi arrived at the monastery and were escorted to the Abbot. They had brought the white silk kotta scarves, which was a traditional honoring ritual in Tibet. The scarves were long and finely woven. The Abbot, in turn, welcomed them with a blessed kotta scarf. He had tea and small cakes served to refresh them after their long walk. Tashi noticed that the cakes were sweeter than any cakes he had ever tasted. He could have eaten all of them, but refrained so as not to receive a glare from his mother.

The Abbot began the meeting by asking Mother if she would leave Tashi and him alone. He told her that a visiting Tibetan nun would like to chat with her. Mother excused herself and followed the monk who escorted her to the quarters of the nun.

"Tashi, I have received information during meditation that it is time to help you to understand some of the happenings that are taking place in your life," the Abbot began. "We will start with your cave visits. Please tell me in as much detail as you can remember everything that

108

happened when you visited your cave as well as any feelings you felt there."

At first, Tashi was taken aback. He had told no one about the cave. It had been his secret. He had heard that some people had this kind of sight but he had, to his knowledge, never met any one of them. It was a bit frightening to think that someone could know his secrets. The gentleness and slight smile of the Abbot put Tashi at ease, so he began telling him about his secret cave.

He went on to tell him about the tall white being that had visited him in the cave. After he described the being, he pulled out from under his shirt the round metal disk that had been mysteriously left for him. Tashi recited the rhymed message that was sung to him and the music that accompanied the rhymed message. With the last tone of the song still hanging in the air, he fell silent in anticipation of the Abbot's reaction to his story, which in the retelling seemed like a dream tale.

"That is very interesting, Tashi. Have you had any other unusual experiences or strange dreams you can tell me about?"

Tashi thought a moment and then began. "Sometimes I have dreams that feel as though they are really happening to me. When Mother told us of the sinking of the Motherland, I dreamed I was one of the refugees from that long-ago time. I just thought it was my imagination working at night, because of just having heard the story, but the dreams seemed so real."

"They were real, Tashi. How would you feel if I told you that you lived another life during that time, but as a female with the special gift of sight? This sight came to you back then as well as now because of your genetic heritage to one of the tall ones. The tall white beings were referred to in other cultures as giants, gods, or angels. They came from a universe that was much more advanced on all levels, mentally, physically, and spiritually. They have been on this planet since man first inhabited it and are here now to help us evolve as spiritual human beings.

"There have been others here from other universes but they were not spiritually evolved, and so their reasons for being here were not of a higher spiritual intent. Sometimes their motivation was greed and want of power. These lesser spiritually evolved star people were superior to the earthlings, mentally and physically. In the past they have been responsible for much destruction as well as the altering of the human DNA for their own selfish purposes.

"Many times the tall ones have intervened on behalf of the human race to thwart some of the greedy invaders' vicious actions. You have been chosen by the tall ones as an ambassador in human form to help to prepare the human race for the massive changes about to happen again on this planet. For your own safety, you will be taught certain things that to most will seem incomprehensible. I have received guidance that I am to help you to prepare for this task."

Tashi sat dumbfounded, but somewhere inside him all that the Abbot was saying rang true. It actually gave credence to a lot of the feelings of not belonging or feeling different from the rest of his people.

"Does this mean I am to become a monk?" Tashi asked.

"No, your earthly assignment will be fulfilled more effectively if you are associated with no organized religion or belief system, for you will be teaching disciples from every culture, not just Tibetans or Buddhists. In fact, there will be a time when you will not even claim Tibet as your home, but we will speak of that later."

The Abbot gave Tashi a few moments to absorb what he had said, then continued, "My spiritual teachers have told me the first thing you and I are to work on are the ancient sacred symbols and their meaning. I am the current custodian of the original copy of an ancient game that was used to help the students learn in the Motherland."

The Abbot rose and retrieved the game from a cabinet. It was wrapped in a faded cloth that's original color appeared to have been of bluish-green or turquoise. He set the game between him and Tashi and proceeded to unwrap it. "We will play one round together right now, so that you may understand its purpose."

Tashi watched as the Abbot pulled out a leather bag filled with oval flat stones with a symbol drawn on each one. The stones were a smooth, pure white, and cool to the touch like clear lake water. He guessed that there were about two-dozen stones. Tashi soon learned that they actually numbered twenty-two. The Abbot continued revealing the contents of the game as he unwrapped a brittle cloth with drawings on it and laid it out in front of them. He laid each of the stone's image face down in a shallow wooden box. Next he unwrapped a parchment book that had twenty-two pages, not counting the cover, all sewn together with pieces of sinew. Tashi held his breath when he noticed that the cover of the book had the image of his necklace drawn on it.

When the contents of the game were laid in place, the Abbot explained, "This particular game is an exact copy of the original one given to the ancient ancestors by the tall white beings. Some special monks had copied it many centuries before. My teacher at the monastery handed it down to me to keep until the next custodian of this knowledge was sent to me. Tashi, you are that person. Let me show you how this game is used or played. It is designed to help you and anyone who plays it to better understand many things about himself and his future."

Tashi sat on a cushion next to the Abbot. The bark paper, with a white surface that had browned with the ages, was smoothed out on the low table in front of them. The Abbot placed small pebbles on each corner to hold it flat. In the middle of the parchment was a white star with eight points. Above four of the points were the drawn symbols of the four directions, north, south, east, and west. Above the other four points was the symbol for the four elements, air, water, earth, and fire. Around all those was a circle with twelve evenly spaced rays extending out from it. Each ray was a different color, faded but still a recognizable color.

The Abbot pointed to the box of the flat stones. "Chose one of the stones. Ask for an indicator of what guidance you need to be shown about an issue in your life at this time. You might possibly want to ask for guidance in your preparation toward fulfilling your destiny."

Tashi chose a stone and placed it in the center of the star where the Abbot directed it be placed. On the face of the stone was a symbol that was a circle. Tashi was then told to select a stone for each of the points representing the four directions and to place them on those points. Next the Abbot told him to select four more stones and place them on the points representing the four elements.

On the bark paper, off to the side were spaces where four more stones were to be placed. They made a straight vertical line starting at the bottom. Above the last space was a circle with a dot in the middle. The Abbot told Tashi to chose a stone for the bottom space. This represented where he was on his path concerning the issue in his near past. The second space represented insights on where he was at the present. The third space represented where he would be if the guided path were followed. The fourth space indicated his final destiny if his life's contract were completed. Tashi put all his chosen stones in place.

The Abbot carefully handed Tashi the book of parchment in which the meaning of the symbols was explained, one symbol and its explanation for each page.

"Tashi, remember the question for which you sought guidance because all the meanings will apply to that question."

Tashi repeated his original question out loud. "Will I always be living in my village?" Tashi asked this remembering the message that the tall white beings had given him.

The Abbot looked up in the book the page about the symbol Tashi had chosen for the center of the star and read the explanation aloud.

Chapter Twenty-One

The Reading

In the center, as your question or issue you have chosen the symbol, circle. This reading has to do with your spiritual aspects of this lifetime."

Tashi had chosen another stone with the symbol, which represented a mountain range. It was placed on the first point of the star, or the east position. "Tashi, this shows where you are at this moment. This is the location where the insight into your spiritual self and higher purpose will be revealed to you."

Tashi continued choosing stones, inscribed with symbols of the ancients and the Abbot continued explaining their meaning in relationship to Tashi's future spiritual experiences. When the stone for the eighth star point was chosen and turned over, the Abbot drew in an exaggerated breath. The image on the stone was the upside down triangle with the circle around it. On each point was a small turquoise circle.

Regaining his composure, the Abbot described its meaning to the best of his ability, although he knew this was beyond his realm of expertise. "Tashi, this represents the body, mind, and spirit totally connected by the universal love to create a pure spiritual human." The Abbot ended there and could not look at Tashi for fear he would lose his emotional composure.

Somehow, Tashi knew not to ask for further explanation from this man. He knew the answers would come at a time when he was ready to better understand the meaning of this reading. He thanked the Abbot for the prophecy and bowed his head, honoring the Abbot's religious position.

While the Abbot wrapped the game in the faded cloth, just as it had been carefully wrapped for ages, Tashi thought about the meanings of the symbols. He felt a stirring in the pit of his stomach as though something was growing within him. It didn't feel bad, just disconcerting. He laughingly thought to himself that it must feel similar when a woman is carrying a child within. It's uncomfortable, yet there is an excitement as well as anxiousness about the new creation that will soon be born.

The Abbot interrupted his philosophic daydreaming when he spoke. "Tashi, you will take into your care this ancient game and work with it until you 'remember' all of the beneficial symbols that will open the doors to your soul's memory of who you really are. Once a month come to the monastery for a day or two and I will share with you any knowledge I possess about what you are unsure of. This preparation for your true work is very important. Take this notebook and write down any questions that arise. In your development it is also wise to journal on a daily basis, especially as new situations present themselves to you. Bring those writings to each of our visits."

Tashi agreed, feeling overwhelmed with all that had occurred but at the same time feeling as though a great weight had been lifted from him. Strange things had been taking place in his life and he was somewhat scared and annoyed because he did not understand their meaning.

The walk home for Tashi and his mother was rather quiet. Any conversation was centered on various observations in nature. By the time they arrived at the outskirts of the village, it was nearly dark. Grandmother had dinner ready to put on the table. Mother chatted during dinner about her visit with the nun, although the true reason for their meeting was not revealed to the rest of the family.

After dinner and when the evening chores had been completed, Mother took her usual position as the storyteller.

Chapter Twenty-Two

The Story Resumes

I continued to study with the priest. I also worked with the various medicine men and women in each of the tribal families. I assisted the priest in ceremony rituals such as the equinoxes and the solstices, as well as other minor celebrations. The years went by and soon it was time for me to learn about womanhood, for I had become a full-grown woman myself. I assisted in the birthing houses until I was certain of the spiritual procedures.

One day the now-old priest summoned me to his private chambers. Lying on a mat in the room was one of the men from one of the farther settlements. Every few minutes the man's body jerked uncontrollably and mutterings angrily spieled from him. My eyes grew larger as I watched this poor soul obviously wrestle with some inner demon.

On seeing me the old priest looked up and summoned me to his side. "Mauri, this man has been brought to us by his family. At various unpredictable times he suddenly goes into a rage of anger and attacks what or whoever is near. When this takes place his voice changes and his eyes take on a red hue. I feel this man has a very angry entity attached to his spirit. It shows itself in his body when he is humanly the weakest. With your assistance and that of our spirit guides, we will detach this angry demonic entity from this man."

I had met my spirit guides through meditation and trusted them to direct me in this feat. Even though I had assisted the priest in a detachment, I had never experienced one that was so violent and so imbedded within the person. Mostly, the inflicted people had a deceased love one attached to their energy and thus lost in that world between life on earth and the Light. The situation with this man was different. There was evilness about this entity.

"What was your first reaction when you came into the room, Mauri?" asked the priest.

"The scent is that of a dead animal that has lain in the hot sun for days. It makes me a bit nauseous. I also hear a soul screaming for help. Of course, I notice the black aura of the man lying on the mat. I feel a blanket of protection around me so I suspect that some danger to me is present."

"Very good, Mauri. You are ready to do this. If you had felt any fear at all, I would not permit you to assist in this detachment, for you would be in extreme personal danger of having it attach to your soul. Since you did not we will begin. Quiet yourself and connect with your divine self. Ask for divine assistant in freeing this man of this demon and of disposing of this heavy, low-vibration energy by flooding it with the high vibrational Light of love."

Both the priest and I were quiet for a long time until we had reached a level of consciousness where only our higher selves were present. As we were traveling to that place of emptiness a huge crow flew into our consciousness. He paused in front of our third eyes long enough to tell us that he would lead us to the void, or that place of transition where there was All There Is. After a period of mental blackness, every color of the rainbow rippled into our third eyes. The color faded and we saw the image of the man lying on the mat.

As we two channeled the pure love energy into him, an angry red being started thrashing about in the tormented man. It roared and sent flames of red energy from his crown chakra. We simultaneously saw Light beings holding golden ropes come close to the possessed man. I recognized both the beings as two of the spirit guides whom I regularly talked to in meditation.

The priest and I continued sending the pure love, or God energy, to the victim as the demonic energy emerged out of the man's crown chakra, the energy vortex where there was a soft spot as a baby. The dark energy continued to thrash about even more as though fighting for its life. When enough of the demonic energy was out, one of the Light beings tied the golden rope around it. It became even more violently active in a last attempt to retain its power. With the golden rope securely wrapped around it, the Light beings detached the rest of it from its home in the man, while all the time wrapping more rope around it, until it was totally encased in the golden strands.

Unexpectedly, something peculiar took place. Something the priest or I had never witnessed before. Out of the bond up demon, tentacles sprouted, which were connected to other humans. The two detachers recognized some of these humans, as their images became clearer in their inter-dimensional vision. The Light beings pulled the strong heavy energies from the other affected people. More Light beings came into service with more golden rope. Eventually the original and largest demon and its clones were bond in gold and herded toward an exceedingly bright light. As they traveled toward the Light, we saw that the herds of bond demons started to shrivel until the entire herd was no more than small mounds of dust, which were then brushed into an opening in the Light.

As the Light Beings disappeared I saw the color blue, like that of the sky, come into my third eye's view. It moved over my head as though I was flying through a cloudless sky. Peacefulness seeped through and around me that I had never experienced before, at least to this degree. A loving voice sent the following words through my mind. *Yeah, as you walk through the valley of the shadow of death, fear no evil for I am always with you.* The words were said with such love, and so penetrated me to the very essence of my soul, that I could not hold back the tears of joy. I felt an overwhelming sense of humility as well as gratitude to have been honored to experience such a beautiful and rewarding event.

The tears were still streaming down my cheeks when I opened my eyes and saw the priest looking at me. "Are you all right, Mauri?" he asked, also overwhelmed with the magnitude of the event.

I could only nod my head yes. After a few moments of silence, the priest arose and walked over to the man still lying on the mat, apparently asleep. He placed his hand on his forehead and quietly instructed the man to open his eyes. The man did so and was confused about why he was lying on a mat in the special chambers of the priest. Reading his thoughts, the priest briefly explained in a simplified version what had taken place. He informed him that he would no longer hear the strange voices or do things that would harm him or others. The priest instructed him to return in about seven days or sooner if he felt anything unusual or heard any voice telling him to say or do anything violent or harmful. The man agreed to do so. With that understood, the priest kissed his forehead and ushered him from the Central Building.

When the old priest came back to his chambers, he found me staring at the wall as though in a trance. My aura was as gold as the sun on the sparkling rocks that were found by the gatherers. My glow illuminated the entire room. What a special soul she is, thought the priest; however, he certainly did not envy my tasks ahead. He needed to increase my studies and insist on me taking over more of the spiritual responsibilities. He knew his days remaining on the earth plane were not many.

The man, who had the attachment, met with the priest and me several more times during the following months, but he seemed to be only himself now without any heavy energy influence.

Mother lowered her head, and Tashi knew that the story was over for the night. It had been a long and emotional day.

Chapter Twenty-Three

Tashi Learns and Grows Up

Tashi continued to learn, both from the village teacher and from his monthly visits to the monastery. The Abbot could not always explain all the strange things that were happening to him. While conversing, even though no words were spoken, Tashi would answer the Abbot's questions. On several occasions Tashi stood and exited the study room for the daily chanting session before the gong was sounded. At those times the Abbot made no effort to stop him. He had a difficult time believing that someone who was not trained for years in the monastery performed such tasks and was totally unaware of its uniqueness.

The Abbot did what he could for Tashi by introducing some of the yogi posture positions for deeper meditation and other exercises to aid him in going to a deeper altered state, but found that his student took the proper positions without being shown. Part of Tashi's studies included lessons on the human chakra system, the energy vortexes. He found it amazing that from the start Tashi could see the location and color of each of the primary chakras.

The Abbot spent one entire session explaining and demonstrating how to astral travel to other places. He explained that with his mind, he could travel to another place as though he was there in the flesh, often without anyone seeing him for his human body would remain where it was. Tashi felt guilty when he astral traveled into people's rooms and listened to their conversations. He asked the Abbot about the ethics of eavesdropping.

Not knowing quite how to answer this, the Abbot justified it by saying, "There are no secrets or hidden knowledge. It is accessible to everyone who seeks it."

Tashi wasn't certain this was an answer to his question, but decided that to pursue it would be in vain. Even though he did not always receive answers from the Abbot to his incessant questions, Tashi felt it better to be able to share his visions and dreams with someone who did not think that he was crazy in the head.

His mother freely discussed some of her knowledge and healing abilities with him. He and she practiced prophesizing some afternoons when they both had spare time and as a result, Tashi's third eye continued to open. Some days he became confused about whether his prophecies were now or in the future. With more practice the confusion subsided and he could feel the difference in the energy coming through him.

The Abbot helped a great deal with that part of his development. A prophet himself, he was able to explain that on another realm all events were concurring simultaneously. He suggested that during meditation if he looked at his own lifeline and what was happening right now, he could tell if what he was seeing had already happened or was going to happen in the future. Tashi found this very confusing, and he told the Abbot so.

"Ask your spirit guides to show or tell you when you are in the past, present, or future until you can sense for yourself the difference in the energy," the Abbot explained, not knowing how such an abstract concept as "no time" could be put into words.

Tashi grew from a wiry ten-year-old to a tall strong young man of eighteen. He was quite handsome in a mysterious way. Many of the local girls tried desperately to win his attention, but it seemed that Tashi showed no favoritism toward any particular one, which made them even more assertive in their efforts.

Through his developmental years, Tashi made many trips to his special cave. The tall white being was a frequent visitor. Each visit brought with it a rhymed message. Some of the messages were cryptic and not clear to Tashi until weeks or even months later. So as not to forget even a single word of them, he started writing them down in his journal. Some of the messages were for all of mankind, while others were guidance explicitly for Tashi, giving insights and understanding to whatever he was involved with at the time. Through his mind he found he could carry on an actual conversation with the beings. They never grew impatient with his constant questioning, and sometimes they even found a bit of humor in them.

He was nearing his nineteenth birthday when his visit to the cave brought a surprise event, which left Tashi somewhat confused. Arriving at the cave in the morning, he took his normal meditative position. Partway through the meditation two of the tall white beings appeared. The whole cave took on an iridescent blue-white glow. One of the beings was holding a white egg shape that glowed brightly. He began speaking through Tashi's mind.

"Tashi, the time has arrived for you to receive this egg. It is an egg of knowledge. With it more doors will open to your memories of who you were as well as who you are now. Before long you will go into the world and share this forgotten knowledge with the masses. Take this egg and use it wisely. Remember, too, that we are always available to answer your questions and to give you guidance, no matter where you are. This is a cooperative task. We all have our part, and yet we are all one."

Tashi took the glowing white egg and immediately felt a flutter in his heart. Tears rolled down his cheeks, and no matter how hard he tried to hold them back they continued to fall in streams. He felt so overwhelmed with a peace and love that he knew if he tried to explain this feeling to anyone, words could not encapsulate it.

As Tashi held the egg, the iridescent blue-white glow faded from the cave. He sat in a meditative yogi position for a while longer thanking the beings for the gift as well as thanking God and the Buddha within. He left the cave in a dream state and walked down the mountain. While still in a dream state, he was confronted by a neighbor as he neared his village. At first Tashi just stared into his eyes. He could not understand or hear what was being said.

His body jerked back into the human third dimension to find that the villager was touching and shaking him. The first words he comprehended when his stupor lifted were, "Are you all right, Tashi? What's wrong with you?" Suddenly his vision became clear and he recognized the man.

"Yes, I am fine. I must have been daydreaming," Tashi said in defense of his stupor.

"Tashi, I was told to stay at the entrance of the village to wait for you. Your mother wants you to go to the house of Pila immediately upon your return. Let us hurry."

"What is wrong? Is mother all right?"

"Yes, it's Pila's wife. All I know is that your mother was summoned when Pila's wife started threatening people with a knife."

Tashi asked no more questions and started running to the house of Pila. There he found his mother leaning over Pila's wife who was lying on a mat on the floor. The wife's hands were bound for her own and other's protection.

"What is it, Mother?" Tashi asked as he entered the house without knocking.

"Pila's wife went berserk and threatened to do away with her husband and her baby, who was born only a week ago."

Tashi could not believe what he was hearing. This normally quiet and demure lady had turned into a monster almost overnight. Mother had given her some of the valerian root and she was quietly resting, although every so often her body jerked and her arms and legs attempted to fling about. Even the binding was not strong enough to stop her involuntary and violent actions.

"My spirit guides are telling me that you know what to do, Tashi, and can help this lady. This sort of thing is beyond my abilities as a healer," his mother said.

"Me?" was all Tashi could manage.

"Yes, you, Tashi. Take sometime to meditate and ask for guidance. I will keep her sedated until you are ready." While talking to Tashi, Mother gave Pila's wife even more of the valerian potion.

Tashi went alone to a quiet room to meditate. Soon one of his spirit guides appeared. He heard the words in his mind. "*Tashi, this women has a dark force attached to her. It attached to her body and mind when she suffered complications and pain during childbirth. You must expel it from her or it will do much harm to her as well as to others around her."*

Tashi shouted out loud. "But what can I do? I know nothing!"

With a smile in his words the being said, *"Now, you know everything. We will be with you. Just follow our instruction. Tashi, you have done this before. Just let the white egg stimulate your memory cells."*

After a few moments, Tashi felt a calmness wrap itself around him. Music and the "Om" sound were being chanted to the tones. To light some sandalwood sage in her room was the next instruction he received through his mind. He went back into the room where his mother was still sitting next to the crazed woman.

"Light some sandalwood and sage incense," he instructed Pila. "Several sticks. If you don't have enough, send someone to our house to get more."

The woman's husband immediately set about fulfilling the instructions.

Tashi's mother looked into the eyes of her son and smiled. She knew his guides were with him. "What would you like me to do?"

"I am told, Mother, you are to fill yourself with as much Light and Love as you can and let it overflow and fill the room."

Tashi asked the others in the room to step outside and told them he would call them when he was finished. Like frightened children those present made their exit.

Tashi took himself into trance mediation and asked that his spirit guides help and protect his mother and him. The deeper he went into meditation the clearer it became to him that something was tormenting and controlling this defenseless woman. He sat motionless and watched the spirit guides wrap Pila's wife in the White Light. Suddenly a blackish entity raised its ugly head out of the crown chakra of the woman. As the White Light engulfed the entity, it literally fought for its life thrashing, with all its strength, taking on a red hue as its anger intensified. Slowly, the guides pulled the entity from the woman. As part of the dark entity rose from her, the guides bound it with a glimmering gold lasso. The more persistently it fought, the more it exposed itself from its hidden home within the woman's soul and the more the guides bound it even tighter with the golden rope.

When the last of the creature was free from the woman, something strange and unexpected happened. Tashi witnessed one of its long tentacles pulling another person who had entered his third eye's sight. He recognized the person attached to the other end of the tentacle as the midwife whose job it was to assist in most of the childbirths in the village. It was obvious to Tashi that this creature, too, had affected her, and now possibly one of its clones was attached. Two more spirit guides came into action and pulled the clone from the midwife and bound it immediately with the golden rope. Like yak herders, the guides herded the two dark entities into the Light.

The villager's wife lay still in an exhausted yet peaceful lump on the mat. Her muscles were relaxed, and her head did not thrash as it had before the detachment.

Tashi came out of his trance and walked to the window. As he gazed out at the familiar terrain and focused on his beloved mountains, his mind replayed the day's events. During the detachments, after the creatures were roped, tied, and taken into the Light by the spirit guides, a soft sky-blue color came into his inter-dimensional vision. The words that he had heard in his head at that time still resonated through his mind: *Though as you walk through the valley of the shadow of death, I will always be with you.*

Those comforting words reminded Tashi of an episode in his mother's nightly story in which Mauri had heard similar words after a similar detachment experience. A tear trickled down his cheek, drawing an irregular line on his face through the day's collection of Himalayan dust. Whatever his purpose was in this lifetime, he knew he was not alone. Even as a child he felt the presence of someone or something that was far more powerful than his human energy.

The chatter and commotion behind him broke Tashi's spell. The woman was awake, and her relatives and friends were now gathered around her. Tashi walked to the smiling, but groggy, new mother and gently pushed the well-wishers aside. He quietly spoke to the woman. "How do you feel?"

"I don't understand what happened to me. Everything is foggy. Was I dreaming? Where is my husband, my baby? Why are all these people here?" The woman was confused. Tashi asked everyone to leave again so he could talk to her alone.

Everyone had reluctantly been ushered outside again. Tashi, in a calm voice, explained what had happened to her and why. His first description of the dark entity frightened her, but as Tashi explained and assured her that she would no longer have to fear the creature's return, she became more relaxed and tranquil. He told her he would check on her on a regular basis for the next few weeks. This seemed to put her mind at ease even more. He asked that her husband and baby be brought back to her. As the three reunited in hugs, Tashi and his mother left, leaving the three to the joyous reunion.

Tashi knew that there was one more person he had to check on before going home. He asked his mother if she would accompany him to the house of the village midwife. She agreed without question. They walked to the other side of the village where this special healer lived in a small but tidy house. As they were welcomed and ushered into the house, Tashi noticed numerous rows of small potted plants with various herbs peeking their heads through the soil. On a shelf on one wall were clay pots filled with colorful dried seeds, leaves, and powders, with botanical names scratched on them.

Mother asked the midwife to sit so that her son could talk to her. Tashi told her what had transpired when the entity attached. Quietly, she listened with only an occasional nod of her head. He asked her if she had any questions. She had one.

"How can I prevent this sort of thing from happening again? Although I didn't even feel the energy enter me, I did feel it when it left. I suddenly felt very sick to my stomach, to the extreme that I actually threw up some vile green matter. Although shaken, afterwards, I felt a lot lighter. Thank you for explaining what had happened to me."

"I was only an instrument in a greater plan, but on their and my behalf, you are very welcome. As far as what you can do to prevent this sort of thing from happening again, we will work with you and teach you certain precautions I have been shown by my spirit guides. I will notify you tomorrow about when we will start the lessons." Tashi's words seemed to excite as well as calm the midwife.

She looked at him with adoration. What a special young man, this once gangly baby had become.

Suddenly feeling the letdown that seemed to evidently come after such an immensely uplifting and rewarding experience, Tashi and his mother returned to their home. A simple dinner was waiting for them. His sister had prepared some barley soup that was warming near the fire. Yak milk was poured, and Tashi and his mother silently consumed the much-appreciated food.

By the time the last of the dinner was eaten, it was well into the night, so shortly afterward, the entire household retired to their individual sleeping quarters. There would be no storytelling tonight. Tashi heard a murmur from his parent's room. His mother was probably telling his father the events that had transpired. He knew from the past that they often talked after the rest of the household was presumably asleep. It was really their only time alone. He lay there staring into the darkness as lonely little tears found their way to his pillow. He wondered what more could be in store for him. His whole life, lately, seemed a dream. Only the tickle of his tears brought him back to physical reality.

Sometime during the night, Tashi awoke, or at least he thought he was awake. Standing before him at the end of his sleeping mat was a tall white being. He appeared to be the same being that had come to him in the cave and had given him the necklace with the inverted triangle on it. Tashi sat up, almost paralyzed by the brilliant light emoting from the being. Its cobalt blue eyes held his attention captive. A message came through his mind. Again it was in rhymed form with a melodious rhythm.

To the east you shall find your way
A healer of the spirit will be your forte
Skills of the past will come into being
Remember the time when the norm was seeing
On another dimension you will taste from the cup
Love is the nourishment on which to sup

Rest well our gentle one for soon you'll venture out
The words of the masters to all you will tout

As the last words of this message rang through his mind, the vision of a large bowl-like object took form behind the being. Tashi leaned to look closer, and found he was rising to his knees, then to his feet. The strange bowl had a magnetic pull on him. On one level he knew he had never seen it before, yet on another level it seemed extremely familiar. He peered into the top of the bowl and saw the seven flames with the seven colors. He remembered seeing this before, but where? Nothing so grand had ever been in their village and he was certain he had not seen it in any of the monasteries. Maybe it was from one of Mother's stories. Questions flooded into his mind, and he felt a warm vapor engulf him. The answers were given to him in his thoughts.

"The bowl is familiar to you because in one of your lives on earth, the master teacher showed you this symbolic edifice because of your spiritual evolvement. Only souls whose vibrations are high enough to see in the higher realms can see it. Its symbols contain the secrets to the universe. You will understand those secrets and learn their application when you are ready. Don't let your human impatience take control."

When the tall being finished transmitting the answers to most of Tashi's questions, he disappeared as rapidly as he had appeared. Tashi continued standing on his mat, frozen in place, mentally dazed. Slowly his body crumbled to the mat and he fell fast asleep.

When Tashi's eyes next opened, the sun was well above the horizon. He could not believe he had slept so long without anyone arousing him. Still a bit dazed, he remembered what had happened during the night. His conscious mind rationalized that he had dreamed the extraordinary events. However, a part of Tashi's mind was beginning to think that the explanation of a great many of the current events were beyond his logical human mind.

Coming to no conclusions, Tashi rose, dressed, and climbed down the ladder. Mother was working with some recently spun yak yarn, putting it on a spool, which was to be woven later into cloth for wearing apparel. Garments woven from the hair of the yak were greatly prized. Without raising her head from her task, Mother greeted Tashi with "Good morning." Then she added, "Did you sleep well?"

"Very well, Mother," Tashi answered. "I had the most unusual dream. It must have been because I was extra tired." Tashi did not want to relate the white being's appearance or its message until he had time to digest it himself.

Mother looked up at her son and with a loving smile said, "Perhaps you should explain your dream to the Abbot when next you see him."

"I think I should write down its details so I don't forget. The Abbot suggested I keep a log. Even now some of the details are fading from my memory."

Tashi took the pad of paper on which he was journaling all his experiences and questions and added everything he could remember about his recent dream. He also included a description of the actual events of the night before with the village lady and his probable explanation for it all. Possibly the Abbot could shed some light on the why of it. He planned to make the trip up to the monastery at the end of the week.

The rest of Tashi's day was filled with light chores and a meeting with the village lady he had helped the night before. They conferred for about an hour. While he was talking with her, the same familiar warm vapor that he had felt many times before enveloped him. He found gentle and loving words flowing from his mouth. The words flowed without his thinking about what he was saying. As he touched the woman's shoulder, tears streamed down her cheeks and a smile came to her face.

Tashi explained to the woman, "Some of the strong herbs given to you during the birthing along with your fear for your baby and your own safety created a hole in your energy field. When this happens, the dark forces have an open door in which to enter."

"Will it come back if I have another child? We so wanted another."

"I will teach the midwife methods of preventing this so that you or anyone else need not fear."

Pila's wife thanked him and handed him a small statue made of yak butter that she had carved and decorated. He took the gift and left the woman sitting quietly, peacefully feeding her newborn at her breast.

His next stop was the house of the midwife. On entering he found her busy filling jars and baskets with newly gathered seeds and leaves. "Your energy appears to be bright and clean," he reassured her.

Without waiting for him to complete his statement, she blurted her questions as though they had been laying in wait for him the moment he appeared.

"But why was I affected by this dark force, Tashi? I had not taken any consciousness altering herbs and my body is strong," said the midwife, perplexed by the whole ordeal and yet a bit afraid that it might happen again.

"You are a healer and a caretaker. While you were working with Pila's wife, you felt empathy for her pain and struggle. This empathy caused your protective energy to weaken, creating an easy penetration of the clone of the entity from the dark. In the future make certain you feel only compassion and no sympathy or empathy for your patients. By practicing this, your soul will remain fully protected and clear of any negative forces. The healing energy you channel will become even more powerful. So powerful, in fact, that it may ward off any dark forces from possessing your patients as well."

"That makes sense. Why did I not think of it myself? How can I show my gratitude for what you have done for me, Tashi?"

"Help others to dispel of their fears. This will be the best thanks I can receive," Tashi said, still letting the words flow through him from their mysterious source.

The midwife took a jar off the shelf and poured some of its contents into a small animal skin bag and presented it to Tashi. "This is a very special herb. Whenever you feel your physical body is depleted and you cannot rest it, swallow a pinch of this. Use it only in an emergency."

Without further explanation or discussion, Tashi thanked her for the small bag and exited the house.

Chapter Twenty-Four

An Unusual Event

The day passed quietly and without much drama. The conversation at dinner centered on mundane happenings in the village. There was also some talk of political activities that were taking place in Lhasa. Horror stories had been told to them recently by a group of nomads who had camped on the outskirts of the village; stories of mass executions of political decadents by the Chinese government.

Although political activities had been rather quiet in Lhasa since the aftermath of the Dalai Lama's escape to India many years before, there were rumors that filtered to his village by nomads and travelers that there was an underground conspiracy group organizing to take back Tibet from the Chinese and reinstate the Dalai Lama. Tashi considered the rumors only to be wishful thinking.

The Chinese had been in control of Tibet for all of his young life. For him, co-existing under Chinese rule was a way of life. In his remote Himalayan village, there was little evidence of change except for the circulating stories. He knew that he was probably too young to fully comprehend the conflict of philosophy between the two cultures.

It had been years since Tashi had first heard the story of Mauri and her refugee cohorts, but as was suggested by the ancient priest, the story was repeated again and again. Each time Mother told it, parts were added or changed ever so slightly. He never tired of hearing it. After dinner Mother took her usual storytelling position. The nightly story began, with Mother telling Mauri's story through her voice.

I took on more and more responsibility for the spiritual guidance of the refugees of Lemuria. The school grew as more potential initiates were brought into it. When everyone reached the age where they could talk fluently, the priest and I tested them. If they passed, they became students.

Some of the original students had become advanced enough to begin teaching on a limited basis in their own individual tribes. The most advanced students of each tribe were made the tribal spiritual teachers. They were put in charge of the weekly tribal rituals, meditations, and other matters having to do with their tribe's spirituality. These tribal spiritual teachers met with me and the old priest on a regular basis, in order to discuss specific problems or general teachings. Even though we were teachers, our own learning never ended. Various techniques were taught to them, and they were encouraged to continue to raise their own energy's vibration. Those who attained the tribal teaching positions were extremely dedicated to their spiritual growth as well as in facilitating the growth of their own tribe as a whole.

I made frequent visits to the original cave as well as to another cave I had been led to by my spirit guides. Not even the priest knew the location of the second cave. During my meditations at my secret cave I received many prophecies, some of which I shared with the people, while others were strictly for my own personal growth and guidance. On one such trip to my secret cave an especially unusual event took place.

Chapter Twenty-Five

Mauri's Secret Cave

Mother's voice took on a different inflection as she started to tell the following segment of the story, still through Mauri's voice.

I awoke one morning and felt restless. No duties were scheduled for me that day, at least none of any urgency. After having some tea and dried fish, I felt compelled to make a visit to my secret cave. When I felt this restlessness in the past, I found that some meditating at my special cave helped to release some of my pent up anxiety and gain mental clarity of the cause of the unrest. It had been a while since I had last made a journey to my cave and spent some alone time there. The demands on my time had become increasingly greater as the old priest relinquished more of his spiritual duties to me. I packed a snack and alerted the priest that I would be gone most of the day.

Some of my unrest abated as I came closer to the growth of saplings and shrubs, which concealed the cave's opening in the side of the wall along the river. As I parted the growth to enter, I thought, *Maybe today, I will explore more of the cave.* I had really only been in the large front cavern. I intuitively knew that there was a great deal more of the cave beyond it. Growing along the river was a particular type of dry plant whose pod burned slowly and served as lamps. I gathered an armful of them and carried them into the cave with me.

Laying them down I dug through my pack for the flint to light one of the natural torches. Holding a lit torch in front of me, I began my cave exploration. Beyond the large cavity at the opening, the cave narrowed, both in width and height, to just below my height, causing me to bend to avoid bumping my head on the ceiling. The width was narrow enough for me to touch its damp sides with my elbows if I even slightly extended them.

As I walked along its smooth damp floor, I had the sensation that I was walking downhill. I heard absolute silence except for a rhythmic drip and the occasional sound of a scurrying rodent who had perhaps established a home in this refuge beneath the earth's surface. My skin told me that the temperature was cool but not cold. Even though there were no apparent openings to the outside world there was a movement of air within the tunnel.

I had no idea how far I had walked, but not once did I feel fear or have the desire to turn around and return to the familiar outside environment. It was as though something greater than I was drawing me into the depths of the earth.

As my mind wandered from one subject to another, I was brought back into the present by a roaring noise, reminding me of the roaring sound of the moving sea as it crept toward the shore. A high-pitched tone pierced my ears, causing my free hand to involuntarily cover one ear for its protection from the unfamiliar shrill. It was then I noticed that the temperature in the cave had changed. Instead of a constant coolness, I felt a humid movement of air.

A slight fear of the unknown rose in me, but my feet kept moving forward. As I rounded a corner in the tunnel, the cave became higher and wider. Walking further around another turn, I found myself in an enormous, brightly lit, open room. In its center stood a towering clear object, which looked like an overgrown crystal, and was similar in shape to the crystal at the tip of the priest's energy wand.

I stood momentarily paralyzed in the presence of the overpoweringly beautiful crystal, until movement in the shadows to my right diverted my attention. My eyes followed the movement, and coming out of the shadows I saw a small being dressed in a brown robe with an attached pointed hood obscuring most of his face. Immediately behind him was another small being that looked exactly like him, only the second one was rolling a large egg, larger even than the small monk-like being. Behind him came an identical being with another identical egg. Then another egg came, and another, and another. Without taking notice of me, they rolled the eggs around the large crystal in a continuous movement, never stopping or even pausing. I sensed that they knew I was there. As they passed me, they acknowledged me with a nod as though they knew who I was and had expected me. Their circling, egg-rolling work continued without hesitation.

I stood mesmerized by their focus on their task. From behind me I felt a rush of warm air, followed by a bright light. I turned around to see the tallest glowing white being with the brightest blue eyes I had ever seen. It was even taller and brighter than the being that had come to me during meditation in the other cave. I felt the same warm loving energy envelope me that I had felt before, but much more intense.

As before, I heard his thoughts as though he was actually talking out loud to me. He assured me that no harm would come to me and instructed me to follow him. He explained through the mental connection that the time had come for me to be shown something special. He told me it would help me to understand who I really was and why I possessed extraordinary abilities that were beyond those of my fellow humans and spiritual students, and even beyond my own human teacher, the priest.

I laid down the torches I had been carrying and followed the tall white being. He led me through another tunnel, which opened up into yet another even larger room occupied by more very tall white beings. In the center of the room was a high platform, large enough to lie on. The being I was following told me through my thoughts that I was to lay on the platform. For some unexplainable reason, I felt no fear of harm from the tall beings.

As I lay silently on the platform, I unexpectedly found myself in a field filled with flowers that gave off the most pleasant aroma. Lured by their perfume, I saw myself going from petal to petal smelling each one's individual fragrance. I felt myself becoming intoxicated with the incense of their aroma. If this was a dream, I never wanted to awaken.

Almost reluctantly, I felt myself being lifted out of the field and placed back onto the platform. As I opened my eyes, I saw that only the first tall being was still present in the room. I sat up with my legs dangling over the side of the platform.

Again he spoke to me through my thoughts. Your human body has been altered in a very loving way. You will bear the fruits of this alteration in about nine moons.

I listened without questioning. For some reason all that he said felt right to me, almost as though I knew what was going to happen even though my logical mind told me I did not.

The tall one helped me down from the platform, at which time I noticed he had six fingers instead of the usual five. I also noticed that they were especially long, longer than any fingers I had ever seen. He heard my thought and responded to my mental inquiry. *Six fingers are a characteristic of our advanced, spiritually evolved society. You, too, were born with six fingers on each hand, but your grandmother cut off the extra fingers the day you were born, so that you would appear to be like the rest of your species.*

I sat there stunned. I had always wondered why I had a small knob on the side of each of my hands. No one ever spoke of them so I never asked, but something in the back of my mind informed me that the knobs were not an accident of nature. One day, I thought, I would discover why they were on my hands but not on anyone else's hands in the tribe. The revelation of their origin left me stunned. This was a mammoth amount of information for me to grasp all at once. I wondered what the field of flowers was. Was that only a dream? No answer came.

The tall being mentally instructed me to follow him back to the crystal room. Still feeling somewhat hypnotized, I did as I was told. In the crystal room, one of the small brown beings approached me and handed me a white egg. Even though the egg appeared larger than I was as the small monk-like figure rolled it, when laid in my hand it became the size of a bird egg. It felt like a ball of cotton from a reed plant, not dense like a normal egg. I looked at the tall being, my face showing my puzzlement.

Perceiving my perplexity, the tall being explained to me that the egg was a symbol of knowledge and that as I meditated with it, ancient knowledge and wisdom would be revealed to me. Only those who could tune into a higher dimension than the heavy earthly third dimension could see the egg. He told me to leave the torches. He explained that until I learned to create my own light, he would lead me to the entrance of the cave and out into the earthly sunlight.

Magically, I discovered myself standing alone in the woods with a beam of sunlight warming my head. I searched my mind to remember all the events that had just taken place. I remembered being given an egg, but where was it? Was that only my imagination? No, I was sure I had been given a white egg, an egg of knowledge and wisdom, they had said, but where was it?

Slowly, I walked back to the settlement, reliving all I thought had happened that day in my secret cave. When self-doubt surfaced, I found myself massaging the knob on one of my hands. I just couldn't have made all that up. Even then in my mind, it was too clear and vivid to have been just my imagination.

I was still reliving the cave events and searching for a logical explanation when I heard a shout as I approached the edge of the Central Building. Tse Tse, one of the young boys from the same village as Pãka, my childhood friend since my first class at the Central Building, met me with panic in his eyes. 'What is it, Tse Tse?' I asked, taking him by the shoulders in an attempt to calm him.

"Pãka has been seriously hurt. Come!"

"Slow down. Where is he now?"

"In our village. The priest is with him. He told me to seek you and to take you there as soon as I found you," Tse Tse blurted without taking a breath.

"Wait here. I will get my healing bag," I said as I bolted into the Central Building.

Within minutes I was at Tse Tse's side again, and we headed for his village. I tried to get more information from him as we ran through the forest, but his words were fragmented and often lost to the wind. The few words I did catch were "wild pig," "gored," and "blood." Tse Tse led me to the house of the village healer. Once inside, I gasped as I saw my dearest friend lying there in a pool of blood, a poultice of ground Echinacea root pressed to the wound by leaves held to his body with sinew ties. The poultice covered his entire right side, but I could see a stream of blood oozing from the edges. The village healer made room for me next to his limp body.

I removed the leaf pack and poultice to reveal the wound. About a two-inch hole was ripped into Pāka's side. I quickly put the leaf pack back as I silently asked for divine assistance. I laid my hands over the pack and immediately Pāka's body twitched. A green glow encircled his weak body. For what seemed to the viewers like an eternity, I held my hands over the wound. As though receiving information from a mysterious source, I lifted my hands and at the same time removed the pack.

The bleeding had stopped. Taking a deep breath of relief, I asked the healer to bring me some Uva Ursi leaves to apply to the wound to draw out any impurities in order to prevent infection from setting in, as well as to keep the bleeding subsided. The healer quickly retrieved the dried herbal antibiotic from one of her many jars of herbs and potions and handed the leaves to me.

I also instructed the healer to bring cool water and moss for compresses to keep Pāka's fever from overtaking him and causing convulsions. I took some ground bayberry root bark from my bag and mixed it with some water. I carefully trickled some of this potion down his throat. As I rose and walked toward the door, I told the village healer to continue to apply the cool compresses to his forehead and the back of his neck. I had suddenly felt the need for some fresh air, hoping it would help me to center. My legs were struggling to support me.

The priest, who had preceded me to the village sensed my emotional strife. "Are you all right, Mauri?" The priest asked once we were out of hearing distance to the others inside the house.

Tears came to my eyes as my adrenaline surge started to subside. "Yes, I will be all right. How did this happen? Pāka is one of the most perceptive people in our settlement. Why did he not anticipate this danger coming to him?"

"It was not Pāka the wild boar was attacking. It was the youngest child of the Wehi family. Upon seeing the boar coming for her, Pāka dove in front of the charging animal. Instead of goring the toddler, the animal's horn went into Pãka's side. The child's father had grabbed a spear and stuck it through the boar's heart and lung, but not before it had buried its horn in Pãka. The animal died instantaneously. Two of the other villagers removed the animal's horn from Pãka's side and carried him into the healer's house. I knew Pãka was hanging onto life with a thin line when I arrived. That's why I sent Tse Tse to find you. Your powers have become stronger and stronger, and I knew Pãka would need a miracle to survive. A miracle I was told by my spirit guides only you could perform."

Our conversation was interrupted when one of the village women brought us some tea and cakes. We thanked the Good Samaritan, and sipped and ate the much-welcomed refreshments.

With a dazed, glassine in my eyes, I said, "Pãka will live but it will be a long recovery. He just must live. I love him as a woman loves a man. More than anyone, I want to be with him."

With a smile on his face the priest responded. "You will, dear one, you will, but now we must focus all the universal energy we are capable of channeling to him. His life force is very weak."

I nodded my head in agreement. As I nibbled on my cake, I felt something inside me stir as though heaviness had just been released when I heard myself announce to the world my love for this man. I had been suppressing my true feelings, afraid to admit even to myself that I had such earthly yearnings. It felt good to get them out into the open, or at least somewhat out in the open. I knew my confession would not go beyond the priest without my permission. For several years now, he had been my confidant when I needed to talk about something that was confusing or troubling me. The trust between us had grown greater and greater with each passing year.

I was determined not to leave Pãka's side until I was sure he was out of danger. The village healer and I took turns watching him through the crucial next several days. The priest told me he would go back to the Central Building and send me some of my things with one of the students. He hugged me as I thanked him for his kindness and concern. As he left, I went back to Pãka's side and took over the job of applying compresses. I told the village healer to get some food and rest. "It will be a long couple of days and we must keep our own energies high."

When I was alone with the unconscious Pāka, the tears started to trickle from the corners of my eyes. I felt my mind connect with his. Mentally, I spoke to him. 'Oh, Pāka, there is so much I've wanted to tell you.'

'I love you, too,' I heard his mind answer. As I looked down at him I thought I saw a slight upturn at the corner of his mouth.

For the next three days Pāka lay unconscious in the village healer's house. On the fourth night, just as dawn was yawning to its awakening, Pāka's body started to stir. I was sitting close to him with my eyes closed, but was not asleep. The movement caused me to open my eyes in time to see his body stirring. His eyelids started to flicker. I spoke. "Pāka, this is Mauri. Are you awake?"

His cracked lips started to move but no sound came from them. I took a leaf and filled it with water. I put it to his lips and let the drops dribble into his parched mouth. After a slight cough, which caused him to wince and grab for his side, Pāka spoke his first words since the goring. "How is the child?" he whispered.

"The child is all right, just frightened, and the boar has been killed," I whispered, leaning close to his ear.

"How long have I been asleep?"

"For four days. You have lost a lot of blood."

"You look tired, Mauri. You need some rest. I will be all right, thanks to you," Pāka said as he let his eyes shut. He was asleep again.

My eyes moistened with relief. I closed my eyes and mentally expressed gratitude for the divine help I was certain Pāka and I had received. Seemingly in answer, a beam of sunlight streamed through the doorway, focusing its light on the healing Pāka.

Shortly after dawn made its appearance, the village healer came into the room. I directed her to boil some water for an herbal tea. While she was boiling the water, I collected some herbs from the clay jars and placed them into a hollowed out coconut shell.

"Pāka will only be able to consume small amounts of this potent tea at one time, but it can be fed to him whenever he becomes conscious enough to swallow," I instructed the healer.

I knew the tea would be very effective in helping his body strengthen its natural immune system and rejuvenate its injured parts. I also included in the potion an herb known for its ability to dull pain. Along with the herbal remedies, I continued the spiritual healing, channeling the universal energy through my hands, then directing it to my patient. Later, I thought, I would start a regime of color vibration therapy. I would lay pieces of cloth dyed various colors on Pāka's energy centers. As light penetrated them, the vibrations of the different colors would stimulate the chakras, helping Pāka's body to heal more rapidly.

When the village healer returned with the hot water, I mixed the tea and showed her how to give it to him a drop at a time should he wake. I felt confident enough in his survival that I took the opportunity to lay down and take a nap. I had not slept more than minutes at a time during the last four days. I took my mat and spread it out in the opposite corner of the room. I lay there asking sleep to find me. Instead, my mind wandered to the events that had taken place in the secret cave. The whole episode seemed years ago instead of only a few days. As my mind replayed the incidents, I lost consciousness.

Someone nudging at my shoulder awakened me. When I opened my eyes the smiling eyes of the village healer met them. I heard the words, "He wants to tell you something," coming from the mouth of the healer. Coming out of my daze I slowly rose and made my way to my patient. I asked the healer to leave us alone a moment.

I smiled down at him. "How are you feeling?" I could see that color was starting to return to his face, although the circles under his eyes were still as dark as those of a raccoon's. As I talked to him I administered a few more drops of the healing tea, enabling him to only answer my questions with a slight movement of his head.

After he swallowed the last of the potion, he began speaking in a slow breathy voice. "Mauri, I must tell you what I have experienced while I have been in this dream state. Now, don't stop me," he said as he saw me put my finger to my lips as a sign that he should remain quiet and save his strength. "I must tell you while all the details are clear in my head." He then began.

Chapter Twenty-Six

Pãka Tells His Dream

Pãka began:
"Out of a blue mist a tall white being appeared in my dream. He knew me and called me by name. At first, I thought I had crossed over to the land of the dead. He spoke to me as clearly as I am speaking to you. He told me that I had been physically injured but that I would recover. It was what he said next that confused me. He told me that you and I were to be mated as soon as I had recovered."

"Here's the part that made no sense to me. He said that I was to claim the child you are carrying as my own. I was told to raise him as my own son even though it was not my seed that had made him. He said he was a special soul, who would go to another place when he was older. He did not mention at what age he would be when he would do this. You, they said, would see to his spiritual training. They said that he would be born with physical characteristics that were different from us but that you would help him to feel at ease when others shunned him. I am to protect him from any harm from either animals or humans and to teach him to be one with his earthly environment."

"Mauri, it was so real. I have always loved you since the first day we met as children in the Central Building, when the priest was testing us for the schooling. What I'm asking, Mauri, is do you want me as a mate?"

I answered, "Pãka, I *am* with child, but that story is not so simple to tell. Are you up to it or would you like to rest some before I begin?"

I knew his adrenaline was working overtime and would not be able to rest until he knew what all this was about. "I'm anxious to hear it now. I think I'm physically up to it." Then he thought, *But I'm not so certain I am emotionally stable at the moment.*

I began the story of my secret cave. My description of the beings was the same as the one Pãka had seen in his dream. I explained the room where I was taken and the seed that had been implanted. I told him that I, too, was told that he would be my mate and that together we would raise the child growing within me, and that the child would go to another land.

Having said that, I showed him the knobs on my hands and explained what I had been told about them.

I finished my story and silence reined. Neither of us uttered a sound. All the emotional trauma of the last few days since the cave had caught up to me. I knew my lack of sleep had a lot to do with my emotional instability, but even if I had been well rested all of this would have been upsetting.

Pãka didn't know what to think of my story. It sounded unbelievable in the context of his more limited mystical experiences. He was more aware than most of the validity of supernatural happenings, from his schooling as well as his long friendship with me, but to conceive a child without the normal sexual act of penetration and depositing seeds was difficult for him to accept. There again, why did the being come to him in a dream with such specific instructions?

I broke the silence. "Perhaps you should take another dose of the healing tea and get some rest. We can talk again later." I administered the tea and wiped Pãka's head with a cool cloth. He still had a slight fever but was not burning up as before, a good sign that his immune system was working and that healing was still taking place.

When he had fallen asleep, I lifted myself from his side and walked outside the hut. There, I broke down and sobbed. It was as though some dam within me had all of a sudden broken. I sat with my back leaning against a tree to brace me. I don't remember how long I cried before a warning horn blaring abruptly startled me. Everyone in the village was running to the Central Building to find out why the warning horn was blown.

I did not move with the herd of villagers. I would be told the cause of the alarm soon enough. Instead, I walked back into the hut to check on my patient. In my still hazy stupor I thought maybe I had dreamt the whole conversation with Pãka. The thought gave me the extra courage to go inside.

When I arrived at Pãka's side he was awake, also awakened by the loud shrill of the warning horn. In fact, when I walked into the room Pãka was making a feeble attempt to raise himself up from his mat. I bluntly and loudly told him to lie back down or he would start the bleeding again. Startled by the force of my words and his lack of strength, he crashed back down onto the mat, letting out a long painful groan as his jarred body hit the ground.

"Why are they blowing the warning horn? What is happening?" Pãka asked, with urgency in his still feeble voice.

"I don't know, but someone will tell us soon enough. I saw your village healer heading for the gathering. She will come tell us when she finds out. There is nothing we can do to help at this point anyway," I assured him while I checked the open gouge in his side. It was seeping a yellow liquid, which meant there was infection setting in. I needed to prepare a poultice and apply it to the infected area, but I would have to wait for the healer. Her help to hold him in place would be necessary, for the sting of the poultice on the open wound would cause a unbearable pain to my patient. Even so, if the poison were not drawn from him, he would not heal properly and could still possibly die.

As I was pouring some of the grayish white granular from a jar on the shelf, the healer rushed through the door. Her face was flushed, a result of her running. Her breathing was in gasps while she tried to tell me what had happened at the Central Building. The words were disjointed and difficult to understand.

"Take a deep breath," I told her, by now exasperated with trying to interpret her muddled words. After several deep breaths the healer was breathing with an even rhythm again. "Now, tell me what the warning horn was about," I said, holding the healer's hand to ensure she stayed calm.

"The priest has collapsed," she blurted out.

"Where is he?" I asked, now shaken. The old priest had been my mentor and teacher, but he had also been like a father to me.

"He asked that you go to him immediately," the healer said, interrupting my thoughts.

"He is in the Central House, in his room. That is where it happened. He keeps repeating, 'I must tell her. I must tell her,' then he dozes off. I will take care of Pãka. You must leave. Tse Tse will go with you."

"We must get a poultice on Pãka's wound. The infection is growing. I was just starting to prepare it as you burst in. I must have a bird egg or two." I felt myself rambling, distracted by thoughts of the priest. What could possibly have brought on the collapse? The priest was as strong as ever when I had last seen him, though I had noticed that the years had slowed him down.

I was brought back into the moment when I heard the healer speaking. "I have applied many poultices; I can ask Sanlu to help me. She has helped me many times and is very strong. Go now! It is urgent."

Feeling confident the healer was capable, I gathered my healing bag and quickly went through the door. Outside waiting for me was Tse Tse. He took the bag from me and we ran to the Central House. I could feel my heart racing, due to the anxiety of what I would find waiting for me, rather than from the actual exertion of the physical run.

I entered the Central House and went directly to the priest's room, only nodding at Koha, the housekeeper and my surrogate mother, as I ran by her. When I entered his room I was immediately aware of the priest's aura. Expecting to see a rather gray weak aura, I was surprised when I saw a bright white- gold glow surrounding him. I thought maybe he was not as ill as the healer had indicated.

I kneeled down next to the priest's head. His eyes were closed, but opened as my energy touched his. "We must talk, Mauri," he whispered to me.

"You must rest and get your strength, I will stay by your side," I said softly to him as I took his hand in order to channel healing energy to him from All That Is.

144

"I am all right. We must talk now while it is clear in my mind," he insisted.

Without waiting for a reply from me he began. With the first words his voice changed. It took on the strength of a fit young man. "This morning during meditation I was told to go to the cave."

I assumed it was the one they had used close to the Central House for I had not shared the existence or the whereabouts of my secret cave.

"I meditated there as usual when suddenly the entire cave glowed so brilliantly that I was temporarily blinded by its brightness. When my eyes adjusted to the light, I saw standing before me two very tall beings. I was overwhelmed with a warm feeling of love, which made my skin tingle and brought tears of joy to my eyes."

I knew who these beings were for I had seen and talked to them in both caves ever since I was a small child. I knew they were the same beings I had encountered recently in the second secret cave. I had told Pãka about this experience only that morning. It was one of the few secrets I had kept from the priest. I kept my thoughts to myself while I waited for the priest to continue.

The priest's eyes fluttered and his lips quivered. More words whispered from his mouth. "The beings told me that you have been seeded, and from that seeded egg will be born to you a child, who will be the greatest human prophet who has yet walked the earth. He will experience the human duality during his youth. He will know what it is to feel hate as well as love, joy as well as sadness, peace as well as turmoil, all of the opposites felt in human emotion. He will learn and teach the people the meaning of human death, of letting go of their earthly bodies. He will help them to understand that the soul is real and that their incarnations on earth are only an illusion. Through his gifts he will show the people that they have the power to change all matter." The priest paused as though he was gathering more energy so he could continue.

"He will convince the people who are ready to listen that the ultimate goal of living as a human is to join consciousness with the Oneness and at the same time to experience their individual human lives. Mauri, you remember the symbol of the two triangles, one pointing down and the other one on top of it pointing up." I nodded my head in agreement, even though the priest's eyes were still closed. "As the bottom triangle moves up and the top one moves down, that soul has then become totally conscious with the Oneness. That is the six-pointed star symbol that you also were taught. When that happens the star's points are connected and become a circle, the symbol of the One Creator." The priest again stopped.

So intense was the energy in the room that I felt as though my head was going to explode. As I put my hands to my head, a warm feeling engulfed me, and I felt a surge of energy being pushed through the top of my head and back down through my feet into the ground, causing the pressure to dissipate. A peaceful compassion replaced it. I sat silently enjoying the inner calmness as the priest rested.

Moments passed before the priest spoke again. It may have been my imagination but it seemed as though his voice had grown even stronger. "You will have a mate to help you raise this special child. Pāka, who has been your close childhood friend and companion, will now become your life-long mate and earthly lover. You two together will help to comfort and protect this special child. Even though the child is not produced from his seed, he will consider him his own child. He will call Pāka his father." With that the priest fell silent.

I sat waiting, not knowing whether the priest was finished or not. After a while I could tell by his deep even breathing that he was sound asleep. That would be all for now. As his last words rang in my head, I remembered that Pāka was lying in the next village on the brink of death itself.

I rose and rushed to the door. Not far from it sat the old housekeeper, Koha. I instructed her to sit close to the priest and to let me know if he awakened. I called Tse Tse, who was waiting near the Central House. On hearing his name, he came running.

"Tse Tse, I want you to run to your village and take this message to your healer. Tell her that I said to make arrangements to have a carrier built so that as soon as he can be moved without rupturing the wound, Pāka is to be brought here. Tell her to continue to give him the healing tea I made. There is more than enough and I will have more ready when he arrives here. Do you understand all this, Tse Tse?"

"Yes," he said, repeating my instructions back to me.

"Good, now go." Tse Tse was one of the brightest and more reliable boys in all of the villages. On many occasions, I had used him as a messenger between the various tribes.

As I watched him disappear into the woods, I noticed that my hand involuntarily caressed my abdomen. I took a deep breath and blew it out in a sigh. I wondered whether it was fatigue that was urging me to run to the secret cave or my fear of what other insights the priest might reveal to me.

In the Central House I smelled the aroma of cooked grain. I went to the cooking room and saw that the housekeeper had prepared some porridge and hot tea. I filled one coconut shell with the porridge and another with the steaming brew. I took a sip of the tea and felt the warm berry tea, my favorite, relax my frayed nerves. Its sweetness increased my energy almost immediately. I took a spoonful of the porridge and then was surprised how quickly I had consumed the entire bowl without realizing it. I sat back and slowly finished my tea. My stomach was full, and the calming effect of the tea made it easy for sleep to have its way.

Mother's eyes closed as these last words whispered off her lips.

Chapter Twenty-Seven

The Next Morning

Tashi awoke with a feeling of anxiety. Today he was to visit the Abbot. On this visit, he would make the trip alone, for he would be staying at the monastery for three days. He was not expected there until evening, but Mother asked him to gather berries and other herbs along the way. Living on the almost barren tundra of Tibet required the gathering of medicinal herbs and spices on a constant basis. Whenever anyone traveled to the highlands, it was assumed that they would return with a bag of beneficial leaves or berries.

As was the usual custom when he was sent to gather, a satchel was ready and sitting near the door. This time, however, an extra satchel was next to it, filled with extra dried foods for the return home three days later as well as a cake of yak butter as an offering to the monks at the monastery. Tashi shoved his journal into that satchel, after eating a serving of barley porridge laced with berries, a treat he only got on special occasions. He said his good-bye and started up the mountain. The sun was barely poking over the peaks when he reached the outskirts of the village.

His mind wandered as he watched the distant snow-capped mountains turn golden. He wondered if he would ever see what was beyond those magnificent peaks, which created a border to his world. Since he had all day to get to the monastery, he took a less-traveled route even though it was a longer one. He hoped there would be more berries and herbs available since fewer people used it.

As he climbed the path, the sun peeked through the trees and scrubs, which were more abundant at this lower altitude. Even as a boy, he loved his time alone when surrounded by nature. It was as though the birds and vegetation talked to him. He was surprised at the quantity of berries and fruits still available. He congratulated himself for thinking of taking this more obscure path.

As he was breaking through a clump of low growing scrubs in search of herbal bounty, he heard music. At first he thought it only a wind song. Stopping to concentrate on the tones, he was pulled off the trail toward some rocks next to a wall. Walking around a huge boulder in his path, he was amazed to find an opening in the wall, which was the entrance to a cave.

He was drawn into it as though something or someone was compelling him to do so. The actual entrance was no more than two to three meters high and about the same distance wide. Getting down on his knees, he crawled through the opening for about five meters. There seemed to be a glimmer of light toward the back of the cave, which he spotted as he turned the corner, still crawling.

As he crawled toward the light he felt like he was going downhill. The cave became taller and wider until finally he was able to stand and walk. He edged deeper into the mountain, and as he did so the air temperature became warmer. After about a hundred meters, the cave opened up to a bright room. It was so bright in fact that his eyesight was blinded by the sudden transition from semidarkness to a light that was brighter than the sun.

Slowly, his eyes adjusted, revealing to him a room vast in both height and width. In its center was an enormous crystal pointing toward an opening in the ceiling. Around it was a thick bubbling liquid, which was radiating an immense heat. So hot was it that he felt his skin burn, causing him to step back from it until his back was against the wall. As he stood backed up against the wall, he saw movement on the opposite side of the crystal through an opening.

Peering through the holes in the vapors of the hot liquid, he observed a number of short, elf-like beings wearing brown robes. Every two beings were rolling an egg that was a third larger than they were. Almost

149

like machines, they rolled the eggs, never a hesitation in their movement. He knew they had seen him for as they passed him, circumventing the crystal, they nodded their hood-covered heads slightly.

He stood mesmerized by the hypnotic movement of the small beings. So enthralled with their focused circumventing, he failed to notice another tall but narrow opening in the wall of the cave. As he had experienced many times in the past, he saw a mysterious beacon of loving energy. The beacon expanded and wrapped him in a familiar warm blanket of energy. His whole mind, body, and spirit basked in this supernatural force, while from out of the narrow opening appeared two white spirit beings, not unlike the ones he had talked with before in his secret cave. He heard them talking through his thoughts as though they were talking directly to his mind. They directed him to follow them. He did so, feeling absolutely safe in their presence.

The narrow passageway he was led into continued for a great distance, lit only by the glow of the tall beings. For some unexplainable reason, not once did Tashi feel threatened or in danger. As the passage widened slightly, he saw sunlight coming through an opening. A few more meters brought them to the opening. A being stood on each side of him as he gazed in wonder at a large lake, vibrant blue in color. Mountains that had a mystical green hue to them surrounded the lake, and on the edge of it was a small boat, which the beings guided him into.

From his sitting position at the front of the small water vessel, Tashi could see buildings on the lake's far shore nestled halfway up the mountain. Strangely, a slight breeze set the boat in motion, moving it on a course toward the hillside edifices. As they came closer, he saw more clearly that this was like no village he had ever seen. The buildings themselves were all white and reflected whatever colored foliage was near, mixing it with the blue color of the sky, creating a turquoise tint to the entire hillside with hints of violet in the shadows. The roofs of the buildings were dome-like, and the overall shapes of the buildings were round, with the exception of a few rectangular ones interspersed among the beehive-like ones. For a young man who had not been outside his small area of the Himalayas, this was quite an awesome view.

Tashi thought he might be dreaming as he was helped out of the boat by another tall white being, which was waiting when the boat gently nudged itself to a stop on the damp shore. The whole place seemed strange and foreign, and yet he felt as though he had been here before, but how could he have? A fleeting thought crossed his mind, *Maybe I died and this is some sort of afterlife.* As soon as that thought came he negated it. No, he knew he was still a human on earth, but what or where was this place and these people? He decided he would have to wait for a logical explanation, hoping deep down that there was one. He permitted his eyes to absorb all the wonderment that was unfolding before him.

His two original guides joined him on the shore, and through his mind, directed him down a path to a Central Building, which was larger than any of the others. As they approached the entrance, an enchanting scent permeated the air. At first he thought it was sandalwood, but it was sweeter than any sandalwood he had ever smelled. It definitely was not the heavy pungent odor of the juniper incense that was so prevalent in Tibet. Whatever it was, it created a feeling of euphoria within him.

Flute tones came from the surrounding mountains and resonated on the mirror surface of the lake. Everywhere he looked his eyes met vibrant blossoms in a rainbow of colors.

His silent guides led him into the building, through a passage that opened into an all glass room with a fountain at its center. Vibrant cushions were scattered in clusters of three around the room. The light trickle of the fountain relaxed his mind as his eyes jetted from one part of the room to the next. When he gazed toward the corner directly across from him, he froze. Sitting on a dark blue cushion was the most beautiful young woman he had ever laid eyes on.

She looked up as she felt the pierce of his intense stare. Their eyes met, causing him to avert his visual fixation, but only for a moment. He could not take his eyes off of her. She truly was the most beautiful human being he had ever seen. When she smiled at him, he felt a wave of heat starting at the base of his spine and running all the way up through the top of his head. He knew his face must have been the color of the crimson pillows that were scattered throughout the room.

As though beyond his control, his feet took steps in her direction.

The closer he came, the more he felt he was not connected to the floor at all. It felt like he was walking on air and yet moving without deterrent in her direction.

He practically fell over when his feet stopped moving and he stood only a meter from the cushion she was sitting on. She was a magnet, pulling him toward her. As hard as he tried, he could not make any words he was thinking pass through his mouth.

After what seemed an eternity, she spoke, as she pointed to the azure blue cushion opposite hers. "Welcome, Tashi. Please sit down."

Confused by her obvious knowledge of who he was, he let go of the control of his leg muscles and allowed himself to crumble onto the cushion. He made a feeble attempt to regain his physical balance and straighten his position on the large cushion, but overcompensating caused him to roll off the other side. Finally he found his center of gravity and stationed it at the center of the plush cushion. The power that this dream-like woman had on his mind and body was something Tashi had never experienced before.

When she was certain his gymnastics were completed, she spoke in a voice that challenged the melody and sweetness of any songbird he had ever heard. Her hair shone like that of the sun and her eyes, which pierced his very soul, were the color of the sky on a clear day.

"My name is Althea. I was told you would be arriving soon, Tashi. Do not be afraid. This is a very special place, and you are a very special person to be brought here. I, too, am human, and one of my tasks is to help you to understand why you are here." She spoke in the Tibetan language but Tashi knew she was not native to the land.

Her words carried an accent that he thought he remembered from foreign mountain climbers who were occasional visitors of his region of Tibet. "I know you must have many questions, and they will all be answered in time, but first let's get to know each other. Tell me about yourself."

His mind was racing, but he managed to mumble, "My name is Tashi." What was he thinking? She knew his name. She had addressed him with it. "I am not certain where I am. I was on my way to meet with the Abbot at the monastery when I wandered into a cave and followed two tall white beings that brought me here. I thought I had fallen asleep and was dreaming."

She smiled silently as he uttered his words. Then she asked, "Would you like some tea and cakes?"

He nodded as she started to pour tea from the gold pitcher, which was inlaid with colored stones in a design that for some reason seemed familiar to Tashi, although consciously he knew he had never seen it on any other crafted vessels. The cup was a miniature version of the pitcher but without a lid. She handed him a cup filled with the warm liquid and a plate filled with tiny cakes of different sizes, shapes, and colors.

Tashi set the cup on the small table in front of him in order to receive the offered plate of cakes. She poured herself a cup of tea and took a portion of cakes from the large tray. When both were served she lowered her head and her eyes, obviously blessing the food and drink. He followed suit although his mind could not rest long enough to concentrate on any specific blessing. When she looked up, she indicated with her hand for him to start eating.

He picked up the cup of tea and took a sip. How could he eat when his stomach was churning? As the mellow liquid arrived at its destination he heard his stomach respond with a loud gurgle. Involuntarily, his hand went to the source of the sound. His stomach had a mind of its own and he could not make it cease its gurgling. Embarrassed by it, he thought that a bit of cake would help keep it from responding so vocally to the tea. After two bites his stomach stopped its gurgling, and Tashi felt more calm and in control.

"You are hungry," Althea commented in an effort to help him relax.

"Yes, it has been a while since I have eaten anything," Tashi said, feeling slightly self-conscious due to the noisy display of his body's needs.

After a few moments of silence with nothing but the sound of sipping and chewing, Althea spoke. "When you are finished with your tea and cakes would you like me to show you around? It may help you to understand what this place is and why you are here."

"Yes, I would. I would like that very much," Tashi said, as he let the last of his tea slide down his throat.

153

He rose off the cushion. This time his movement had the grace of a swan. He held out his hand to offer assistance to Althea. As her hand was laid in his, he felt his heart skip a beat and then start to race. Why was this woman having such an effect on him? He had seen pretty women before. Maybe not as pretty as this one, but it disturbed him to have someone have that much power over him. When Althea was standing soundly, Tashi quickly dropped her hand as though it was something very hot and would burn him if he held on any longer.

"I will show you the rest of the Central Building first," Althea said, gesturing with her arm. "This room is a gathering room for the students. Here we can gather into small groups to discuss the lessons of the day and have tea."

Tashi followed her to another large room that had a white screen covering nearly one wall. "Here we are shown many things from the past, present, and future on this screen. The teacher stands over there and explains the importance of what we are seeing as it relates to our growth."

Much of what Althea was saying Tashi could not comprehend. His mind raced with questions, but he decided for now he would just listen and observe. How could the future or the past be put on a screen? Was it like the pictures that ran through his head at times?

Althea led him through another opening into a room that was much darker. It reminded him of the rooms where the monks at the monastery did their meditating and chanting. The cushions were arranged in a circle. In the middle of the circle was an empty pedestal.

"This is the room where we come for guided and group meditation," Althea said, answering one of his questions as though she was reading his mind. "They encourage us to come to this silent room at other times as well, and to meditate without the aid or guidance of the teacher. We are to remain quiet here at those times so as not to impede the other students' journeys into the silence."

Tashi heard a loud bell that reverberated through the building. Startled, he found his head jerk from side to side in search of its source.

Althea, seeing his startled reaction, explained, "That's the bell that signals the gathering in the courtyard for our daily breathing and physical centering exercises. Come, let's join them. I think you will enjoy it."

154

Althea led the way through a door, which opened out into a courtyard whose perimeter was filled with flowers of all colors and sculptures of rather stylized forms that resembled the human body posed many ways.

Tashi was overwhelmed with the warmth and friendliness of the area, which helped to ease his anxiety of participating in something he knew nothing about. His nervousness quickly subsided as he took a place next to Althea. Again a feeling of familiarity came over him, although he consciously knew he had never been here before.

A figure dressed in loose-fitting clothing stood before the group. Without speaking a word, she started inhaling, and the group followed suit. Tashi found he was looking at Althea for guidance but was soon in the flow of the exercises being demonstrated. Everyone had his or her eyes closed so he closed his. When he did, he heard music, and his body moved with its rhythm. He was able to hear instructions from the leader through the ears of his mind. As he was told to breathe and release, he did so. As the exercises continued, he became lighter and lighter, as though he could rise off the ground and fly. Yet, he felt a pulse of energy coming through the bottoms of his feet, apparently from the ground, and out through the top of his head. He did not want it to stop. He had never before felt such a feeling of euphoria radiating throughout his body.

Immersed in this exhilarating energy, he barely felt a tap on his shoulder. When he opened his eyes, he saw Althea looking at him, a smile on her face. Everyone else had stopped, and the leader was walking away. His face felt hot and he knew it was probably the color of the crimson flowers, which were so abundant in the courtyard.

Althea broke the silence. "Come, I will show you where you will stay while you are here learning."

They rose, and Tashi silently followed Althea. He was having difficulty believing that walking next to this goddess-like woman was not an illusion. She led him out of the courtyard to smaller beehive-like buildings, which were only a few avenues away. There were no vehicles or animals using the streets, only pedestrians of all shapes and colors.

At the entrance to what was to be his sleeping quarters, Althea stopped. There was no door, only an opening with an invisible shield. To

155

the right of the opening was a flat panel, on which she flatly placed her hand. She directed him to do the same. As he did so a glow of light passed through his hand. Following Althea's lead, they passed through the entry. Tashi had never witnessed as much magic as he had in the few hours that he had spent in this mystical place. He could not even imagine what else was to come.

Inside the entrance she explained that the panel read his DNA, which would then open the entrance to his private pod. Each pod was maintained with a specific atmospheric condition conducive to its individual inhabitant. As a human from the mountains of Tibet, the air in Tashi's pod contained the elements of which he was accustomed to in his homeland. Without this accommodation, his body could react adversely in order to adjust to the different conditions. When his vibrations had risen higher, the physical conditions would not make any difference. His body would be able to adapt instantly because his bodily functions would not be sluggish as they were now.

Tashi's pod was a small room, completely white with a cushioned sleeping mat in one corner. On one wall was a screen that appeared to have a slight blue tint to it. There were no windows and yet the room was warm and bright. In front of him on the floor was a large sitting cushion with a low table in front of it. Another wall had a panel on which were drawn symbols, the same symbols that were on the stones in the game that the Abbot had given him. Laid across the sleeping mat were a robe and a pair of unusual slippers.

"I'll leave you now so that you may rest and meditate. I'll return in a while to direct you to the eating pod. You are to change into the robe and slippers before I return." Without waiting for a response, Althea was gone.

Tashi stood dazed, a bit overwhelmed by all that had happened to him since that morning when he set out from his home to journey to the monastery for his audience and lessons with the Abbot. As he was absorbing all that had happened in the past few hours, he thought of what the Abbot might think when he did not show up. As suddenly as the thought came, it left. He could not be concerned with something he could not change. As this worry left his mind, he realized how very weary he was. He lay down on the sleeping pallet, and within minutes was soundly asleep.

Tashi awoke with a start, sitting up and looking around. At first, he was confused as to where he was. He thought he must have been dreaming until the memory of the morning crept back into his mind. He rose from the pallet and spotted the new robe and slippers. Remembering what Althea had told him, he changed into them. The softness of the cloth on his skin felt very soothing, not like the rough texture of his course native cloth. Around his waist he tied the crimson sash. He slid his feet into the slippers, which felt like dipping his feet into warm, gentle water. Quite a change from the sandals he normally wore, which were made of rough rope woven thickly together so that the rocks of the Himalayas would not cut the soles of his feet.

As his callused hands were caressing his new robe, Althea appeared at the entrance, looking as bright as sunlight. She brought a smile to Tashi's face. If this was all a dream, he hoped he would never awaken. Rarely before had he felt warmth in his heart like he did when he was in her presence.

"It's nearly dinner time. If you are ready, come with me. I'll show you the dining area," Althea said, as she directed him to the outdoors and to another garden where low tables were aligned with cushions on one side of them. On the tables were set pitchers and cups as bright as the sun itself. Loaves of what appeared to be bread were positioned on the tables every couple of place settings. Tashi followed Althea to the place settings that were obviously for them. Others were also walking to their assigned seating. Everyone apparently knew just where to sit. Shortly, every setting had a body situated before it. In front of all the rows of tables stood a very tall man. He looked human, but at this point Tashi was not certain of anything.

A hush came over the garden as the man raised his hand. When he was certain he had everyone's attention, he spoke. "Welcome. We are honored to have a number of new faces. We will introduce them now. Please stand as I introduce you." He called out several names, and Tashi watched as each stood. Then his name was called. He rose. In all, there were twelve new people including Althea.

After all were introduced, people carrying trays of food filed in military-style and put portions on each of the plates. During all this time no talking took place. When each one was served and the liquid in the pitchers was poured into every glass, all the diners started to eat.

Tashi watched Althea and followed her actions. He was about to say something to her when she put her fingers to her lips indicating silence. He took her cue and continued to eat in silence. How different this was from his family's dinner table where sharing of the day's events and laughter were ever present.

Everyone indicated he or she was finished eating by laying their chopsticks across their plates. When every plate had chopsticks on it, Althea and the others rose. She said to Tashi, "We will now go to the teaching center for lessons, where you will meet your teacher."

Tashi rose and followed her asking, "What kind of lessons? Are they like the school we have in the village or like the lessons the Abbot has given me?"

"They are a little of both and more," answered Althea with a knowing smile. "You have special talents as well as a special purpose in this lifetime. That is the reason you have been brought to this place. Your teacher will explain all of this to you. These people are not like the earth people. They have come from a faraway, highly advanced civilization. They were here on Earth long before we humans were ever here, at least in our present form. They have learned and will teach us the mysteries of the universe. We, who have been chosen to come here, will in turn go out and teach these mysteries to the earthlings throughout the world."

"Why do they not teach the world directly?"

"There's so much fear of the unknown on Earth that they would not be accepted nor would their teachings. The present religious and political leaders of the earth would feel threatened, as they, for centuries, have been in control of the beliefs of their followers. Organized religion will not easily give up this control. The tall white beings feel that we, who look and talk like other earthlings, will stand a better chance of breaking down this control in order to help people rid themselves of the fears that are keeping them enslaved to their low vibrations."

158

Seeing his perplexed expression, Althea went on to explain, "Our body's cells move or vibrate at different rates. Fear is a heavy energy, and thus keeps the body's cells vibrating slowly. Love, however, is a light energy so the body's molecules can move or vibrate faster. The tall white beings' vibrations are higher than ours and that's why they appear non-solid to our three-dimensional eyes."

All she was saying was foreign to Tashi. He had lived a rather simple and remote life cut off from most of the world in his small Himalayan village, and yet at some deep level what she said felt familiar to him. "Are you saying we are to go into the world and teach Buddhism?"

"No, it goes beyond the teachings of any religion. I was raised in a family whose religion was Christian, Catholic precisely. The religions of Earth have been used as a tool for control and supremacy. The teachings you will receive and thus teach are not based on any religious dogma, which is basically fear-oriented. The teachings of the tall white beings are those of love and oneness, which are the same teachings that were taught to the people of Lemuria. They are the lessons that recent teachers like Buddha, Jesus, Mohammed, and many others were teaching. Unfortunately, over the centuries their words have been twisted to fit the power needs of greedy and ego-oriented men and women."

"But why would the people of the world listen to what we unknown humans have to say?" Tashi asked, starting to feel a little anxious, if not overwhelmed, with what she was saying. He wondered why anyone would listen to what the son of a yak herder from a remote place in Tibet had to say.

The couple had stopped before the entrance to yet another beehive-like building. Althea turned to him and replied, "Be patient, Tashi. Your teacher will explain in great detail all that you need to know before you are sent out to teach."

With that, Althea, followed by Tashi, entered the building.

The first room they entered was light and bright. The ceiling was high and open to the sky. Diffused rays of sunlight came streaming to the floor of the room, absorbed by the colorful cushions that were scattered throughout the room. Other students wearing the same type of robe that

Tashi had on were mulling around. Tashi noticed that although all the robes were white, there were many different colors of belts, which tied around the waist. He wondered why his belt was crimson while some of the others had belts that were yellow, green, black, and so on. Then the story his mother had told about the priest on the beach came back to him. Could this represent the same degrees of learning as the students of Lemuria? Without much success he searched his mind to remember what each color of belt meant.

With no warning, tones sounded, and like little mice, everyone scurried to find a cushion to sit upon. Althea led him to two cushions that were side-by-side, directing him to take a seat. As everyone settled into their chosen place, the room became silent. All eyes looked forward as a tall being stood austerely in front of the group. Tashi almost gasped when he saw what the being was wearing around his neck. It was an exact duplicate of the necklace that had been given to him in the cave, the one he still wore around his neck under his clothing.

What was this all about? Who were these people and why was he in this place? Lessons? What could he learn from the beings who apparently were not even of this world? He knew he had some special abilities. The Abbot and his mother had made that clear. He could not stay here long enough to learn all that they thought he should know. His family would miss him and be worried. All these thoughts and more ran through Tashi's head.

Althea sensed his anxiety and read his thoughts. She took his hand and squeezed it in a reassuring way. He turned to look at her as she quietly said, "You will soon understand."

Tashi's tension eased a bit, but he was not certain of the truth in her words. Even so, her touch had an immediate calming effect.

The tall being in front of the class began talking, and everyone's attention focused on his words. "Welcome," he started. "Many of you are confused and upset as to why you have been brought to this strange place. Some of you are even experiencing fear of us for we look and act differently than you do. I assure you that we have never nor will we ever harm you or anyone else on this glorious planet. We have been here since the beginning, but because of certain earlier events, have found it

160

necessary to hide our existence for our own safety. There are many on your planet that, through fear and control, try to exterminate and destroy anyone or anything that is not like them. We have lost many of our people in the past because of this.

"Now, as to why you are here. You, too, have your soul origins in a more evolved society where the people live with love as the basis of their actions. It is true that we are a more technologically advanced society according to Earth's standards, but more importantly we are a society that is far more spiritually advanced.

"Duality in our societies is at a minimum, if it exists at all. We understand and live the oneness, unlike most of the human beings on this planet. We have watched the people of this planet attempt to destroy themselves, as well as the planet, for thousands of years. We were instructed by a higher order not to interfere but to only give help and guidance to those who ask for it. Many of you have done just that.

"When you incarnated onto this planet, you chose to do so at this time in order to become human ambassadors for us and the other more advanced societies in this universe. You volunteered to become, at the appropriate time, teachers to help the people of this planet adjust to the inevitable rise in the vibrations of the earth. Unknown to most of you, you have been preparing for this time of teaching since you first incarnated.

"Even who you chose as your earthly mothers and fathers was important in your preparation. You were monitored closely, and many times we even functioned through your human body with you. This was only done when we found it necessary to protect you from being harmed by the lesser-evolved souls with whom you are interacting. Your assignment is too important to let you be harmed in anyway.

"This all took place without you noticing anything out of the ordinary. We felt you needed to experience humanism without prior knowledge of the extent of your soul's true abilities. Many of you, in your brief earth life, have suffered a great deal of ridicule and even persecution from those who did not understand your special abilities. The time has arrived for you to come out and reveal to the world who you really are.

"During your stay with us we will help you to unveil all that you are and all the knowledge with which you came onto this planet. Some of you have already felt the veils being lifted, and because of past persecution by lowly-evolved earth beings, you have kept it a secret. Honorable ones, it is now time for you to share your vast knowledge and energy with the people of this planet during its time of transition. We applaud your courage and offer whatever assistance we are able to give you, for your job is far more difficult to complete while in the human body than our job has ever been in our more ethereal form."

In the silence, Tashi looked around and saw tears lying on the cheeks of the others in the room. Only then was he aware that he, too, felt the tickle of a tear as it made its way down his own cheek. His body felt like a warm blanket had engulfed it. In his mind he was starting to understand why certain things in his life had taken place. Were Mother's nighttime stories planned for his ears from the very beginning? Were all those strange dreams he'd had really dreams? His whole existence in that remote mountain village seemed to be making more sense to him, yet every new revelation brought with it a flood of questions.

Althea spoke, breaking his mental spell and bringing him back into the present.

"Since we have free time, I will show you where all the students go to relax and play games and talk with one another."

Still mentally and emotionally caught up in the maze of questions running through his mind, Tashi, like a robot, followed her from the great hall to the outdoors. They walked down a path to an archway, which led into an open area surrounded by large flowering shrubs. Scattered around its perimeter were low tables and cushions, which seemed to be prevalent everywhere in this strange place.

In one corner of the large park area the ground was marked off and poles stuck out of the soil about fifty meters from each other. The participants in what was obviously a game had sticks in their hands. One person pushed a ball, made of some kind of hard material, with the mallet end of his stick in an attempt to push it toward one of the poles at the end of the marked off field. The others, in turn, used their sticks to try to prevent him from reaching his goal.

The sticks were like no other sticks Tashi had ever seen. They were not made of wood or metal or any other material, for that matter. They were rays of light that magically radiated brighter as the person holding them moved closer to the ball. He saw no handle on the light stick; it seemed to be an extension of the player's hand. The white shimmering ball, sometimes showing a vibrating blue cast, never touched the ground. It was moved through the air by nudging from the light sticks. He had never seen anything like it. *Of course, truthfully,* thought Tashi, *I haven't seen much of anything, sheltered for twenty years in a remote Himalayan village.*

At the thought of his homeland and family, he felt a twang in his chest. He missed them, yet this strange new place seemed more and more familiar to him each minute he was here. He thought, *I would never have met Althea had I not been brought here.* He had never experienced the stirring inside him that she brought on by a mere glance or touch. Even the warm envelopment he felt when the tall white beings were near did not bring on the same exhilaration through every cell in his body that she did.

Tashi realized that his mind was escaping to another world when he took his glazed eyes away from the ball field and met Althea's. On her face was a warm, knowing smile. Could she know what he was thinking? It would not surprise him in this mystical, magical land.

Althea led Tashi to a table where two other people, a man and a woman, were sitting. She introduced the man, who was about Tashi's age, as Jasper. The woman, dark-haired with deep, almond-shaped, black-brown eyes, was called Morning Star. He was told she was an American Indian. Her skin, although light, had a reddish tint to it, not unlike that of the nomads of Tibet. Could there be a connection between the two native people, he thought? She smiled and motioned for them to sit down.

The man spoke first, but in a language that was foreign to Tashi. Althea interrupted his words, translating for Tashi. "You are new here. From where do you come?"

Tashi answered in his native tongue, "I am from a small village in the Himalayans in Tibet."

They both seemed to understand his words. Morning Star then asked, "How do you like being here so far?" Before he could answer she added, "When I first was brought here I was a bit bewildered by it all, and I must admit, a bit frightened. I knew no one, and it is nothing like the desert land I come from in America. On my first visit, I was also concerned that my human family would be worried by my disappearance."

After Althea's interpretation Tashi responded, "I'm still so awed and amazed that I have not had time to wonder about my family. I was on my way to meet with the Abbot at the monastery so my family will not miss me for a while, as they do not know I am missing. The Abbot may be annoyed, however, when I do not keep our appointment."

Althea spoke. "The tall white ones will send someone to speak with the Abbot as well as with your family. They will explain what you are doing, although they will not reveal your whereabouts or the true purpose of your stay here for security reasons. Not that any of them could ever find you here anyway. This place is always hidden from the outside world through the use of an invisible shield. This is to keep any human intruders, or for that matter, any extraterrestrial intruders, from destroying or controlling this place and its inhabitants."

"How long will we be kept here?" Tashi asked whoever would answer.

Jasper answered, "You are free to go whenever you like but you will not want to." A chuckle followed his statement.

Althea added, "Tomorrow morning you will meet with a personal counselor who will explain your individual part in this whole plan and answer any questions you may have on a personal basis. We're all here for specific reasons and to learn specific things in addition to what we're being taught as a group. Tashi, they have told me that you have very special lessons to learn, for you have special tasks after your lessons are completed."

Her words only made Tashi more apprehensive, but he did not reveal this insecurity to the group. At that moment Tashi did not feel very special. Instead he felt like a small child about to take his first step.

The small group continued to talk and laugh. Tashi could only understand part of what was being said before Althea would remember to repeat it in his language. He wondered how they could understand each other so well since to his ears, it sounded as though they were all speaking in a different language.

Evidently, Althea had heard his thought and answered his question. He must be more careful of his thoughts.

"Do not worry about your thoughts, Tashi. They are pure and honest. Most all students who are here have come from a different part of the world and speak a different language. From the very beginning we are taught to tune into the thoughts of the person we are conversing with. In some groups no words are spoken at all. All communication is done through hearing the thoughts of the person who has the floor at that moment. Tashi, you have this ability. It's just that no one has taught you how to access it. With a little practice you will be able to trust the thoughts that you hear as much as you trust the spoken words that you hear."

Tashi pondered. That explains why everyone understood his words but he could not understand theirs. He could not imagine how he would be able to do this, even though he remembered the cave where he could understand the tall white being that spoke no words. He guessed he would wait and see, but the fear of not being able to do this telepathic listening, as Althea had called it, still bothered him.

In the distance Tashi heard the tingle of chimes.

"It's time for group meditation. Come," Althea directed him, rising from her cushion, along with the other two in the group.

Tashi saw that all activity has ceased in the play area as everyone started toward the arched opening of the garden. The parade of students made their way to the Central Building in an orderly fashion. Tashi, with Althea by his side, let himself be swept along with the group.

Inside, everyone sat on a cushion and crossed their legs. Without instruction, they put each of their index fingers to their thumb and closed their eyes. After a moment of silence, a humming sound came from each participant until the whole room was humming on key as though it were one voice. Several minutes of humming passed, and as if on key, silence swept the room. This was not foreign to Tashi for he had seen the monks at the monastery do a similar ritual so he simply followed the group's actions.

165

During the silence Tashi received vivid pictures in his head, not unlike some of the pictures he saw in his dreams. He did not understand what they meant but they were very clear to him as though they were really happening. As the last of the pictures in his mind faded, Tashi became aware of the rustling in the room as people started to get up and make their way toward the door. When he opened his eyes and looked at Althea, he saw that she still had her eyes closed, so he waited in silence. Out of the corner of his eye, he saw her body start to move and her eyes open. She turned and looked at him; he smiled. She smiled back. Every time their eyes met, there was something about this woman that induced an emotion in him like no emotion he had ever experienced.

Without speaking they both rose and walked out into what was now night. A cool breeze washed over them. Feeling much more at ease, Tashi became aware of his weariness. He felt as though he had lived a year in only one day. Hearing his thoughts, Althea broke the silence. "You have had a great many new experiences today. I will walk you to your room so you can rest."

"Yes, it has been somewhat overwhelming. I could use some rest," Tashi responded, feeling a sudden letdown in adrenaline and energy.

They slowly walked toward the building where Tashi's room was located. At the door to his room he turned toward Althea and asked, "Do you also have a room in this building?"

"Yes, all the students from Earth are housed here. These will be your accommodations until this portion of your initiation is completed." Hearing his mental question, she added, "My room is two floors above yours. Have a peaceful rest, Tashi. I will call for you in the morning." He looked at her until she vanished from his sight.

Tashi found a nightshirt lying on his palette. He slipped out of his tunic and into his nightshirt. Next to his bed was a decanter of water and a cup. He poured himself a cup of water and sipped it. It was like no water he had ever tasted. It was cool and clear like water but had a sweetness that made him want to drink the entire cup. He set the empty cup on the table and lay down on the soft palette. Within minutes his body and mind gave way to sleep.

Chapter Twenty-Eight

Another day in the Hidden City

It felt as though he had only just closed his eyes when knocking at the doorway to his pod awakened Tashi. Hearing the melodious voice of Althea calling his name, he thought he was still dreaming. Realizing he was not in a dream state, he answered her call and rose from his bed. The first thing he saw as he approached the doorway was her beaming smile.

"It is time to rise, Tashi. I will wait at the front of the building and walk with you to morning meditation," she said, trying not to stare at his well-formed masculine body, which was more apparent with only a thin nightshirt covering it.

There was something very appealing to her about this young man from the mountains of Tibet. She had had many male suitors, but most had bored of her after a short period. The majority of suitors thought her strange in both her words and actions. Many, she found, would cling to her like a magnet even when she would tell them she did not wish to see them again, while others would leave after one date never to be seen or heard from again.

Her psychic and telepathic abilities often threatened the latter's deeply engraved religious belief systems. Sometimes they sent religious pamphlets warning her about how the devil worked through these forms of psychic and mental acts. This man who was called Tashi was different. When she awoke that morning she found herself anxious to see and be with him. She scolded herself for her human weakness and warned herself not to set herself up for disappointment, which she had done so many times in the past.

Awestruck by her beauty and brightness, Tashi could only nod his head. He watched her as she disappeared down the stairs. Urgent to join her, he turned to see a basin of water and soap on the table, which he was certain had not been there the night before. As he put his hands in the water he discovered it was warm. When had this been brought into his room? Was he that tired that he had not heard someone come and go that close to his bed? Not wanting to take the time to ponder the question, he quickly finished bathing and slipped into the clean robe that was laid next to the basin.

Fully awake now, he scurried down the stairs and to the door of the building. Waiting there for him was Althea, talking to another woman. Hesitant to approach her and interrupt, he stopped a few feet from her and patiently waited.

When she felt him approach she turned to him. "Tashi, I want you to meet Alexandria. She is from the country of Greece."

Tashi said hello to the woman, not really knowing exactly where Greece was but remembering the name from a book he had read in school about the ancient Greek civilization. He remembered he was particularly fascinated with the writings of Plato, which his teacher had brought to him from the vast library in Lhasa. He made a mental note to ask Alexandria about Plato and her homeland at a later date.

"Come, we must go to the big hall for morning meditation and chant," Althea said, noticing the shyness toward each other of the two cohorts by her side.

As they entered the big hall Tashi smelled pungent incense burning. It reminded him of home. It amazed him that he had thought very little of his home in the past day, except for a few random thoughts of his mother and her nightly stories. Would he ever hear her sweet voice again telling the tales of his early ancestors? A feeling of homesickness briefly waved over him. He must not think of this, he told himself. It would only make him sad. His attention was quickly brought back to his alluring guide as she pointed to the cushion next to her, directing him with her hand to sit.

168

There was a hum in the room but no other sounds. Tashi closed his eyes, and unlike the usual thoughts he received when he was going into meditation, this morning he saw a kaleidoscope of colors waving in and out of his intuitive eye and then total blackness.

As soon as the blackness was complete its center opened. In vivid color a man appeared wearing a robe of white. Around his waist was a gold sash. Looking at his head he noticed his hair was long and light brown. As he looked into his clear, brilliant blue eyes he felt magnetized by them. *Who was he,* he wondered. The answer came immediately.

"I have been called many names," Tashi heard him say through his mind. "I have been called Jesus, Sanada, Confuscius, Quatqucoata, Mohammed, Siddhartha Gautama, the founder of Buddhism, to name a few."

Tashi thought, *Why is he in my meditation?*

Again he immediately heard the answer. "I am one of your spiritual guides and advisers. We have worked together on the same council, although in your human form that experience up till now has been veiled. As one of the members of the council of elders, as we are called, you have volunteered to be on Earth to determine its fate."

Tashi thought, *Exactly who or what is the council of elders?* He felt a slight shift in energy as his newly discovered guide sent the answer in a rhymed message through his thoughts.

> The council contains only twelve
> The purpose into which we shall delve
> We review the contracts it does receive
> Wayward souls we do retrieve
> Close to the source we are
> With energy that radiates quite far
> We do exercise much power
> We do not always stay in our tower
> We have used many names through the eons
> Often we are only rayons
> You are familiar of course with our turf

Your vibrations we have raised through the roof
This planet is now under great change
We need to know its ultimate range
A gentler energy will soon come
The intuitive side will not be dumb
Many people will decide not to exist
The changes they have decided to resist
If this all sounds familiar to you
Remember you, too, are one of the crew
Religion has nothing to do
With what we sit around and stew
You are in charge of the earth
We will decide what is its worth
All the talk about positive and negative
Has nothing to do with the relative
There is no way to surmise
What we will send as a big surprise
You will know enough in advance
In order to join in the last dance
The people you will meet at this point
Will be important to the work done in joint
Patience right now is the key
It is the essence of the phrase "to be"

After the final words "to be" rang through Tashi's head, the vision in his meditative mind went black again and the figure disappeared. He could not stay still. He opened his eyes to find the rest of the people were still in meditation.

He sat there contemplating what had just happened, wondering if his mind had just made up all that he saw and heard, yet he knew when he had this type of vision in the past, the vision was in fact accurate. The past visions usually only showed him some event that would take place in his village or some way he would be helping a person in his village. Although he did not fully comprehend the meaning of all the words the guide had just spoken, the last phrase about patience seemed to keep him from fretting, as was his usual reaction to something he did not understand.

Little by little the others in the room came back to consciousness. Out of the corner of his eye he saw that Althea was stirring slightly. He turned toward her, and their eyes met as she opened hers. It was one of the few times she was not smiling when she looked at him. She turned her eyes from him, rose from the cushion, and walked toward the door.

He followed her as they made their way in silence to the eating area. The silence continued even after they sat at one of the tables. Tashi wondered if her odd behavior was a result of something he had said. He at once pushed the thought away, for he really had not talked much with her since she had awakened him earlier that morning. Out of respect, he let the silence continue. Since no talking was permitted during the meal, the quiet did not seem unusual.

After the morning meal Althea broke the silence by telling Tashi that he was to spend the morning and most of the day with his private teacher. Hesitating a moment, she let him know that she would not see him again until the following morning.

"Thank you for being so kind and patient in answering my questions," Tashi responded in an attempt to melt the ice in her tone of voice.

"It is our responsibility to make the new people welcome and feel at ease," Althea retorted in a still chilly tone.

Tashi thought it best not to pursue the conversation any longer for fear of making whatever was bothering her worse.

"This is the building in which you will find your teacher. His name is Master Bashur."

Althea then abruptly turned and walked away.

Bewildered, Tashi gazed long after she had disappeared from his sight. He still had no comprehension of what caused the radical change in Althea's attitude toward him. Pondering this, he entered the building. He stood in a large foyer, the back wall circling around toward the door. The ceiling was very high and was made of something translucent. Diffused light flooded the room from above. Everything was white, but on the wall were mosaic pictures inlaid with various pieces of different metals and gemstones. A circular counter stood in the middle of the room, manned by a tall white being. As Tashi approached, the being addressed him. He heard the being speak even though he saw no lips moving.

"Tashi, we are expecting you. Your teacher will meet with you now. Enter through that doorway."

That was strange, thought Tashi. *I didn't see that doorway when I first entered this room.* As Tashi passed through the door, he was enclosed in a small circular chamber, the back of which opened into a room. There, on a gold cushion, sat a tall being with brilliant blue eyes. He motioned with his hand, which had six fingers, for Tashi to take a seat on the cushion opposite him. Tashi followed the instructions as though he was hypnotized by the very presence of this being.

"I am your teacher, Tashi. We have met before in a cave near your home," The being was saying through his mind. "Today I will give you some tests to determine how to approach our lessons. I want you to become very relaxed and natural. To help you to do this I ask that you meditate a few moments and ask your body and your mind to release any tension that it may be holding."

Tashi did as he was instructed, but it was more difficult than when the Abbot had asked him to do this exercise. He had to admit he found the teacher's presence disconcerting, yet at the same time, almost overwhelmingly loving. It took longer than normal for Tashi to let go and relax.

The being continued, "Open your eyes and tell me what you see sitting on the table between us. Describe it to me with as many details as you can see."

Tashi opened his eyes and to his surprise saw a large chalice. He described it as he was instructed. After a few moments, he saw even more details than when he had first looked at the object. When he thought he had described it completely he fell silent, waiting for further instructions.

"Do you recall ever seeing this before?" asked the being.

"I want to say no but it seems so familiar," Tashi responded.

"Touch the handles of the chalice," instructed the being.

He followed the instructions and soon became extremely warm. The heat started at his tailbone and ran up and down through his body. When his body adjusted to the surge of warm energy, a glow appeared before his eyes. Slowly the glow took a form and he saw himself in strange clothing. The clothing fit tight to his form and had on its front a large image, the same as the image on the necklace, which still hung around his neck. The image of the man in his mind had no hair on his head, but when he looked into his eyes, he knew without a doubt that it was himself. He involuntarily let go of the chalice, and immediately the image and the glow faded.

"Tell me what you experienced," the being coached.

Tashi told him what had happened and what he saw, adding, "But maybe my imagination just made up that it was me."

"No, you did not make up the vision you were shown. That was you at another phase in your soul's life."

"But why was I bald? What lifetime was that? Was it here on Earth?" Tashi asked, a little embarrassed by his impatience.

He thought he heard laughter, but saw no evidence of it in the being's physical form.

"Your questions will be answered in due time. Continue. Describe how you felt while you were having the vision."

"I felt as though I was living the vision that I saw before me, but then I thought maybe I was just remembering one of mother's nightly stories about the ancients and our people's beginning on the earth. Sometimes after her stories I dream about what it was like back then, as though I was there living it," Tashi explained.

"What were you doing in these dreams?" Bashur asked, encouraging Tashi to continue in detail.

"It was like her story but I was a woman." Suddenly as though a light of remembrance went on in his head, Tashi blurted out, more to himself than to his teacher. "Was I the girl and woman in that story? Was I Mauri?" Tashi went silent trying to remember in detail the rest of the story that Mother had been telling right before he had left to visit the Abbot.

He had heard it many times before, but the details were rather fuzzy to him now. What happened to her after the priest was ill? What did he tell her when he called her to his sickbed? Why was he blocking it? He had heard those stories numerous times while he was growing up. Then it became clear to him. She went on to become the spiritual leader, priest of the refugees. In fact, she mated with Pãka and their offspring went on to be an even stronger teacher and leader than his parents. Bits and pieces of the story crept into Tashi's memory, but he didn't recall anyone being bald.

Sensing his frustration, the tall being interjected at that point. "Tashi, you were not Mauri, but the offspring of Mauri and Pãka. Mauri was your present day mother. You were not bald when you were on Earth, but are remembering an experience when you were not an Earthling."

Tashi looked toward the ceiling behind his closed eyes. A vision came into focus. He was in a strange place. As the images become clearer he realized the place looked like where he was right now. The buildings were the same. Everything was the same but he did not look like the tall white beings. He was tall like them but had more of a physical shape. He noticed he also had six fingers like the beings in this place did now.

His culture had taught him that every soul lives many lives. After all, was not their own Dalai Lama a reincarnation of a previous Dalai Lama? But the idea of having lived a lifetime as a being from another planet and another universe was not as easy to grasp. Even the idea of extra-terrestrials was not a strange notion to him for many ships had been reported seen coming and going near his village by numerous residents. The concept of his ever being one of these space travelers never entered his mind. Mulling the thought over, it did not seem wrong. In fact, it actually explained a lot of things that had taken place in his younger years.

His teacher was hearing his questions but did not interrupt them with answers or explanations. The answers would come to Tashi when he was ready to accept who he was. In the meantime, as his teacher Bashur would just help him to open the channels to this knowledge.

"Tashi, you have a special mission in this phase of your soul's life. That mission will become clear when you are ready to see and to accept it. I, as well as the other teachers, will help you dissolve the earthly veils that are preventing you from seeing it clearly."

Tashi listened to the words of his teacher, and tears rolled down his cheeks much like what had happened when the tall one spoke to the group. He did not understand the strange power that these white beings had over him. The more he tried to hold back his tears, the more they flowed. Embarrassed by his lack of emotional control, he covered his face with his hands and mumbled an apology.

"Do not ever apologize for your emotions," his teacher said softly. "It is that emotional part of you that makes you a human earthling. Only as a human will you be able to fully relate to the other humans on this planet. That is why you chose the human body as the vehicle in which to do the work you have contracted to do. Had you chosen to be here in your original evolved body, which is less dense, your work would not be as effective.

"On this planet there is much fear, particularly the fear of the unknown and very little tolerance of those who are different. That is why at this time we have stayed hidden beneath the earth as well as high beyond the sight of most of its inhabitants. There are people here who have seen and met with us, but they were able to accept the existence of life beyond this planet without fear. Many of the earthly astronauts have seen us. In fact one group of them had welcomed our aid when Earth's technology failed while they were on a mission to land on the earth's moon. Without our help the mission would have ended in disaster, and the higher purpose of the universe would not have been met."

The teacher continued. "One space mission by the United States which appeared to end in failure and the loss of human life was actually a success for us. Seeing that it would fail, we snatched the three astronauts from the rocket before it disintegrated. They are with us now acting as human advisers in a much more important mission: helping to prepare the earth for the rise in its vibrations.

"Because of their technically advanced knowledge and the fact that they are in human bodies, we have employed them to help us in determining how much change can take place without stressing the human body and mind to the point that it separates from the soul. I hear your question. Did they volunteer for this mission? Yes, they did. They have all along been one of us but operating in a human body, much like you are, Tashi."

Tashi was speechless. He had always been fascinated with the space program that had taken place in all parts of the world. Visitors from other lands would speak of it. As a boy he often dreamed of flying in space. Because of his interest, many of the visitors to his village sent him books and pictures of the early astronauts. He remembered reading about the mission where the three astronauts, one of them a woman, died when the rocket exploded before leaving the earth's atmosphere.

His village peers looked at him as being odd when he spoke of such things. They did not understand why he worried about such far away things when there were so many more important things to be concerned with, such as food and heat. Only his mother did not laugh at him or put him down when, as a boy, he stated that one day he would fly into space. Tashi remembered her normal response to his boyhood statements: "Never lose your dreams, Tashi, for they are what's real." If his father was present he often reprimanded her for filling his head with crazy ideas. She would look at him and smile adding, "We will see."

"Your earth mother is a very wise and evolved soul. She has worked with us in many soul lifetimes while incarnated on earth. Her job is nearly over and she has performed it well," his teacher said.

This last statement struck a cord in Tashi. "What do you mean? Is she going to die? She is very young," Tashi blurted out at the ever calm being sitting before him.

"No one ever truly dies, Tashi, for the soul is eternal. Your mother incarnated as a human to help prepare you for what is to be your mission. She has completed this job admirably as she has also done in other similar lifetimes on this planet. Did you not wonder about the details of the stories she tells nightly? She is able to do this because she has actually experienced those stories, as have you," Bashur explained, shocking Tashi with this revelation. It now made sense, but yet was hard to believe.

Tashi felt very weary. Sensing this, Bashur said, "That is enough for right now, Tashi. Go, meditate and rest. We will meet again after the

176

evening meal. Althea is waiting for you at the entrance to this building. Talk with her. She will help you understand some of what has been said here today. She is your twin soul."

Tashi's spirit brightened when he heard Althea's name, but then a worry line formed on his brow when he heard she was a twin soul. He had heard the term used but had no idea of its meaning. Perhaps if she was over her mood she could explain it. At any rate, he was happy. He would see her before the following morning contrary to what she had said earlier.

Tashi gathered himself and went to the exit of the building that housed his teacher, Bashur. Althea was exactly where Bashur said she would be, patiently waiting for him. When she saw him, a smile came to her face.

"Hello, Tashi," she greeted him in her melodious voice. "Come, let us have tea while we talk."

Tashi was pleased that Althea was back to her cheerful self. Without a word he followed her to the garden.

They each picked up a cup of tea and a small plate of cakes. They sat on pillows at a round table in the corner of the garden under an overhanging flowering shrub. The scent from the flowers shrouded them, creating a dreamy, relaxing atmosphere. They each sipped their tea before saying a word. When they did speak, it was at the same time. Tashi stopped his words indicating for Althea to continue.

"I will answer any of your questions, Tashi. That is, if I can. How was your session with your teacher? It went well, I hope." Althea asked more to be polite than expecting an answer.

"The session was enlightening, yet I feel more confused now than before in some ways."

Althea smiled, understanding exactly how he was feeling having just had a similar experience. "Would it help to talk about it?" she asked with compassion as well as concern in her voice. "Sometimes that helps to clarify things in your own mind. I'm a good listener."

How easy it was to talk to this woman. Even though he had only known her a day or two, it seemed as though he had known her forever. "My teacher said we are twin souls. I don't know exactly what that means," he explained, getting right to the point that was one of the most perplexing statements made by his teacher.

Before answering or even looking at him, Althea took a sip of her tea, giving her the time she needed to gain composure as well as form the answer in her mind. "First of all, Tashi, I have to tell you that only this morning during meditation did I learn of this myself. It somewhat surprised me. I really didn't have the answer myself, so I, too, went to my teacher. She was waiting for me. We had a long talk so I think I may be able to explain our relationship to you."

Tashi sat in anticipating silence while Althea took another sip of her tea. After a deep breath she began, "Our souls are a small piece of the whole, God. They are eternal. They never die. Sometimes our soul chooses to have certain experiences, such as entering a human body as you and I have at this time.

"Sometimes only a part of our soul wants to have a certain experience, such as incarnating as a human male from Tibet. Another part of our soul may decide to incarnate as someone else, such as a female human from the United States of America. Other times that other part of the soul may decide not to incarnate at all and just live in the spirit world. However, the two parts never lose touch with each other. If they are both in human form, they eventually come together in some human relationship. If one is not in human form, the one in spirit may act as a guide to the incarnate.

"Tashi, you and I are twin souls, and because of the importance of this time on Earth, we have chosen to come together as two humans. Within the customs of this planet at this time we will become mates, husband and wife." A slight flush came over Althea's face as she spoke these words. She quickly picked up her cup again in an attempt to hide it.

"Oh, Althea, that explains my immediate attraction to you. I couldn't take my eyes off of you the first time I spotted you when I entered the room where you were sitting. From that first moment I felt an attachment to you." Although consciously he did not fully understand what she had explained, he knew at some level it was all true.

Althea sensed a feeling of relief run through her. She had been nervous about her ability to explain the whole matter since she had only just received the revelation during her meditation. Her teacher had helped her to put all of it into words. Even so, she harbored a human fear of rejection, probably stemming from her human experience in childhood with her father. No matter what she did, it was never quite good enough for him. All those years of trying to please him in vain had established a deep-rooted fear of not being good enough for any male. This man or twin soul seemed to accept her unconditionally, but she still felt the tinges of that old fear. Maybe with his coming into her life and with the help of her teachers she would finally be able to release the deep-rooted fear of rejection.

Even though she had not seen her father in two years, she still occasionally wondered if he would approve of what she was doing. Her father, being a strict Catholic from the south side of Chicago, would without a doubt be shocked. She could imagine his words to her. "You are no daughter of mine, messing around with all this hocus pocus shit. It's the devil's work." Just thinking about his drunken, abusive words stirred a subconscious anger in her. Would she ever be able to let go of all those years of resentment that had built up in her layer upon layer?

Sensing her agitation, Tashi took her hands in his. "I'm not certain what all this means, but I am certain we are doing what we are supposed to be doing. For the first time since I have been here I am absolutely sure of that."

Both sets of eyes were now filled with tears. A sense of wholeness swept from one to the other. Tashi thought, *If this is what unconditional love feels like, it is even better than what the lamas and monks have preached.*

"Yes, it is," responded Althea, hearing his thought. "This has to be the oneness that they speak of in the lectures. Before I only knew the words. Now I know the feeling."

The rest of the afternoon Tashi and Althea talked and learned of each other's experiences in the human form. They shared their childhoods as well as their spiritual experiences. They were surprised that although their backgrounds were quite different, their thoughts and reactions to certain situations were quite similar. They each had had the same experience in a cave with a tall white being who left them a medallion like the one still hanging around Tashi's neck. When Tashi pulled his out to show her, she pulled out a necklace from behind her robe. They were identical.

So deep were they in conversation and in learning all they could about each other that they neglected to hear the bells, which announced the time for lecture and meditation. They were both so absorbed in their conversation, that when Jasper approached and tapped Althea on the shoulder, her body abruptly jerked as though being awakened from a deep sleep. It was only then that they heard the bells and jumped to their feet. Jasper silently walked off toward the lecture hall. Hand in hand, Tashi and Althea followed.

Most everyone was seated by the time Tashi and Althea entered the room. They found two cushions near the rear of the room and quietly slid onto them just as the lecturer was entering. A tall white being stood before the group. Although he appeared to look the same, Tashi could tell this was not a being he had seen before. His energy looked and felt different. He marveled at his new ability to tell the difference since entering the Hidden City.

Chapter Twenty-Nine

A Unique Movie

Behind the white being a picture began to materialize. Actually, it did not look like a picture at all. It looked like the event on the wall was three-dimensional, taking place right in the room. Tashi was not the only one who was amazed. Nearly everyone was awestruck; their eyes glazed over, and their mouths went slightly agape. The people and the places they were watching on the wall seemed as though they were actually in the room, not like any motion picture on a screen, but more like a play where the actors are on a stage with true to life scenery.

"Some of you will recognize the place that is being shown to you," began the being, ignoring the fact that his audience had never seen a hologram before.

Tashi stared intently at the wall. It was not a place he had ever seen, but, of course, he had seen very little of the world outside the Himalayas in his brief lifetime.

"This is an area in the middle of the United States of America. A very wide river runs through it. Under this river is a fault, a crack, in the earth's crust. It is about to shift, creating a huge hole that will release much molten rock and gas. This shift has been stimulated by a plate shifting far to the north of this area, in a place called the Hudson Bay. The edge of this plate runs from the North Pole down into the Great Lakes, which is the border of the United States and Canada.

"Everything east of the Hudson Bay will go below sea level, allowing the Atlantic Ocean to flow into it. The ocean will flow into the Great

Lakes and overflow the southernmost lake, Lake Michigan. This lake in turn will overflow into the many rivers flowing in that region of the world. The water will stream south into the wide river you saw earlier. This river will become a sea that will split the middle of the United States in two."

Tashi glanced at Althea. There was horror in her face. He could not relate to this area having never seen it before, but he felt the pain in Althea as the being continued.

"Very little in this area will escape the rampage of this deluge of sudden water. The fault, which runs through this wide river, will widen even more, setting off earthquakes and fires. A large portion of the earth's population will be destroyed with this shift. The intensity of this shift will cause other parts of the earth to change and adjust as well. The change in the crust of the earth has happened several other times in its history. Some of you will remember the last time when the continent in the Pacific, now called Lemuria, was lost. Most of you have experienced that major earth change in your earlier lifetimes on Earth. That is partially the reason that you have chosen to be a part of this upcoming one.

"During a time of major turmoil, human fears escalate. When fear dominates human beings they are ripe for the invasion of those who wish to take advantage, such as was the case during the Lemuria disaster. When the survivors of Lemuria found themselves cut off from their neighbors and without homes or leaders, a group of renegades from the Pleiades further infiltrated some of the scattered groups. Filled with fear, the refugees were easy prey for the renegades who brought them under their control.

"Although technically advanced, the Pleiadians were not very spiritually evolved. Through genetic experimentation and biological engineering, many survivors of Lemuria were changed, and veils were placed over the parts of their souls that remembered that the emphasis should be on love in their lives. In other words, earthlings now suffer from spiritual amnesia as a result. The people of the earth, except for a few sects who escaped the Pleiadian rampage, have been in this state of amnesia for hundreds of thousands of years.

182

"We left this planet at that time. However, after the sinking of the continent in the Atlantic Ocean we came back to establish a colony of ambassadors working to rectify the spiritual damage that had taken place during and after the Lemurian and the Atlantic disaster. Many of our ambassadors were sent to walk the earth as teachers, but most of us were attacked or ignored by the majority of the population. Much of our teaching was re-interpreted to strengthen the control and selfish motives of the renegades still in power. When someone or a group did not adhere to the rules of these Pleiadian renegades, they were violently eliminated in one way or another.

"Over the earth years we have increased our forces beneath and beyond the earth's surface. Our number of ambassadors walking the earth is now at an all-time high. They have been operating independently, chiseling away at the veils of ignorance and fear. Dear chosen ones, we are now coming to a time in the earth's history when breaking through this veil of fear-oriented ignorance is essential. As we speak, our evolved human ambassadors are gathering in order to create a united force against those who wish to retain control through fear.

"You have volunteered to incarnate and become the leaders and teachers of these gathered ambassadors. It is time for you to go forward into action. Most of you were master teachers during the days of Lemuria. As you have already been told, the veils over those memory cells have been lifted. Concerning your individual assignments, your personal teachers will prepare you for those.

"This is an exciting and glorious time to be on this planet, for as one of our teacher ambassadors put it, '*No longer will the dark prevail. A Golden Age of Light and Love will again reign on this planet.*'"

The picture faded and the tall white being left, leaving its audience stunned into silence, yet with rays of hope and joy radiating through their bodies. The hologram faded as the being left. From somewhere a series of gongs rang, and everyone closed his or her eyes to meditate.

No great visions or messages came to Tashi during meditation. He just saw waves of vibrant colors come in and out of his third eye. At one point an eye appeared only to then disappear as the various colors had. He had been given more than enough data to digest already so he was happy to just enjoy the relaxed ethereal feeling that the colored light show was giving him.

After what felt like only a few minutes but was probably more like thirty, Tashi opened his eyes. As he did so, Althea's smiling eyes met his. The all-familiar heat wave ran up his body. He smiled back. Together they rose and left the lecture hall.

Outside they stood for a few minutes before either spoke. It was Althea who opened the conversation. "Wasn't that hologram presentation amazing? I had heard about them but had never really seen one."

"I have never even heard of, much less seen, a hologram. How do they do that?" asked Tashi, a little self-conscious about his lack of knowledge.

"Technically, I can't explain it, but it basically is tapping into a timeline or time wave and bringing that energy in so that it overlaps the time wave in which we are present. I wonder if we will ever be able to do that," Althea said with excitement in her voice.

"That might be a good question to ask our teachers," Tashi responded, already having thought that he wanted to ask his teacher to explain in full about the amazing phenomena they had just witnessed.

"I know that region of the United States. I grew up there. Most of my relatives still live in that area, although I have not seen the majority of them in years. I wonder if I should warn them. Today's lecture certainly has created more questions than answers, hasn't it?" Althea asked, talking to herself rather than actually asking for an answer from anyone. She could just imagine what her father would say if she tried to explain any part of her recent experience to him.

"Learning something new always does," Tashi said, remembering something the Abbot had said to him when he was frustrated about his purpose in this lifetime. He had argued with the Abbot about his own knowledge and the ability to do what the Abbot had forecasted that he was supposed to accomplish in life. He had blurted out, "I don't know anything."

The Abbot responded with, "Now you know everything." It had taken Tashi the long walk to the village to fully comprehend the statement, but when he did, it had brought a smile to his face and a peace to his mind. He shared the experience with Althea. He recognized the same perplexed expression on her face that he had had several years before. He knew she was thinking, *How could you know everything when you know nothing?*

"It's near dinnertime. Let's start walking toward the dining area," Althea said, changing the subject.

Outside the dining area they met Jasper and Morning Star. After a brief greeting, Morning Star asked of Althea, "Have you ever been to that area of the United States?"

"Yes, I was born in Chicago. My parents, sister, and other relatives still live there, but I haven't seen any of them for over two years," Althea responded, explaining what she had told Tashi earlier.

"I wonder what other areas of the earth will be dramatically affected by the changes and shifts. The Hopi nation is supposed to have in their possession the prophecies for this time of change, but I have my doubts as to their accuracy," Morning Star said with a bit of sarcasm in the words.

"Why is that?" Althea asked. "I thought they were given special information over and above all other people. That is what I understand they claim."

This sparked an immediate response from Morning Star. "When the Hopis shut themselves off from the rest of the world and considered themselves above all other people, the prophecy gifts were taken away. Along with superiority attitudes always comes the dark side. Their leaders have forgotten the original teachings of the tall white beings. For the most part, they have become greedy and spiritually weak and have chosen the way of separateness. Many of them are addicted to drugs and alcohol, making them susceptible even more to those who wish to control them. They have forgotten the basic universal law that everything and everyone is one. They don't realize that they can't be the 'chosen people' for God does not choose one over another. I am part Hopi and have been considered an outcast for most of my life. I firsthand understand the power of control through bigotry."

A tear or two came to Morning Star's eyes as she remembered the constant ridicule she had been subject to growing up. Althea saw the tear and put her arm around her. "Tell us about it," Althea said, giving her a squeeze. "Did you live on the reservation?"

"I've never lived on the reservation. My father was a Navajo and worked in a nearby Anglo city. My mother was part Hopi but was rejected by her family for marrying out of her tribe. I was very lonely as a child, for the Navajo families would not allow their children to play with me because of my Hopi heritage. The Hopi children avoided me because I was part Navajo. With no one to play with, I often entertained myself by talking with the birds and animals. They knew all my secrets.

"Alone, I roamed the cliffs along the canyon. It was during one of my roaming times that I found the cave and first met the tall white being. Remembering my first encounter with the loving tall one seemed so long ago. The first time I was only about ten years old." She paused, and her hand went to her chest and her fingers felt the familiar shape of the necklace that the beings had given her on one of her cave visits.

"Whenever I was really low I would rub the necklace and immediately know everything was going to be all right, for they had told me in a rhymed message once that peace and joy would soon reign in my life. They said that a gathering of like souls was taking place so that I would no longer feel lonely.

"Before she died, my mother told her stories of a time on the earth when love reigned throughout. A time when a people from afar first taught the earthlings what unconditional love was. My mother died when I was only thirteen. It broke my father's heart, and he closed himself off from everyone including me. A year later he met my stepmother, who was Navajo. She had children of her own and had very little use for a stepdaughter.

"I disappeared to my cave for long segments of time. On my latest visit, a tall white being asked me to follow him, and I ended up in this wonderful place. The moment I entered this valley hidden in the mountains, I felt as though I was home and belonged, a feeling that I've never had before, but have yearned for all my life."

When Morning Star finished her story, Jasper took her shoulders and pulled her to him, then quietly said, "We love you Morning Star. You will never feel lonely or lost again."

Tashi and Althea looked at each other, acknowledging through their look the compassion radiating among them. How absolutely intoxicating it was to witness so much love.

The dinner chime rang, and the group walked as one into the eating area hand in hand.

Chapter Thirty

Tashi Meets with His
Teacher a Second Time

Now knowing his way around the Hidden City, Tashi left the group early to find his teacher on his own. As Tashi entered his teacher's building, there was a young, smiling boy who told him his teacher was waiting even before Tashi had an opportunity to speak. The young boy pointed in the direction of the doorway, which appeared out of nowhere.

Tashi was anxious to meet with his teacher, Bashur. He had so many questions. So much had happened since their last meeting. Was it only that morning? It seemed like a lifetime ago. He certainly was not the same shy man who had left this very building only several hours before. As he entered the room, the tall white being he knew as Bashur indicated with his six-fingered hand to take a seat on the cushion.

"Tashi," the being began, "we will be working together for a long time. You may address me as Bashur. Is that agreeable with you?"

Tashi nodded his head yes. It was nice to have a personal name instead of merely calling him teacher.

"You are filled with questions. Let us discuss those now."

Tashi was so anxious that he could not decide which question to ask first. When he opened his mouth a series of them came blurting out. "How long will I need to stay here? Will I be able to go home ever? Are Althea and I really to become husband and wife? Why was I chosen to come here? I certainly don't feel special like the others who are here learning." Tashi took a breath, giving Bashur an opportunity to stop the run-on of questions.

"Let's start with just these questions. Your length of time here will be somewhat determined by you. As more of the veils are lifted, the illusion of 'time' will be of little importance. You will be aware of it because it is still a significant factor in your third dimensional world. As to how long, I will say this. You have progressed more rapidly than expected. Once you feel comfortable with your mission, you will be leaving here to begin it. At that time, Tashi, you will be taken to your home in Tibet where you will have a brief stay in order to make some closures. Where you will go after that will become clear to you then.

"Yes, Althea and you will have an opportunity to become husband and wife, but of course that will be both of your choices. The institution of marriage has nothing to do with universal law. It is merely a manmade organization, but it is also important at this time that you work within the established human systems in some ways. It will give more credence to the messages that you deliver to the world.

"We did not choose you to do this assignment, Tashi. You chose to do it before you incarnated. You are a very evolved soul; if you weren't, the contract that you agreed to fulfill would not have been accepted. As the veils are lifted, and as you remember more fully your true purpose on this planet, you will understand why you are here. It is because you are so spirituality evolved that you do not feel special. Only an evolved soul would understand that in God's eyes we are all the same but different."

Tashi did not comprehend this answer but decided that probably in time he would, just as he had quickly come to understand some of the previous statements Bashur had made to him.

"Our teaching and help will not stop when you leave here. On occasion we will call you back to this Hidden City or another of our hidden establishments throughout the earth, for particular training as you proceed on your mission. Other times we may come to you as we did in the cave. We will always be connected to you on a level that is a bit difficult for you to conceive at this point but you will understand when your channels are more open."

"How do I open my channels?" asked Tashi, anxious to be able to connect with the mind and energy of all that was around him, as Althea apparently did. He expressed this desire to Bashur.

"You are starting to do this now, Tashi. Did you not understand Morning Star's story even though you are not learned in her language?"

"Wow, yes, I did," Tashi exclaimed.

"You see, you were connecting and you were not even conscious of doing so. As you open more and learn to listen with a nonphysical ear, you will be hearing consciously and able to connect mind to mind at will. Do not try to analyze all this, for that will only impede your ability to open and connect to the higher realms."

At some level Tashi knew that what Bashur was telling him was true, for even during his childhood he found that when he did not try hard to do something and just relaxed, he could accomplish it easily without any conscious effort. When he tried intensely to do something, whatever he was attempting was a struggle.

"Bashur, if I am to teach as you have indicated, will it not be difficult if I do not know how to speak the language in these other places you say I will be going? I can only speak Tibetan fluently. In school we were taught some English and Chinese, but we had very little practice using it."

"You will learn more English from Althea, her native language. She has been schooled in several other languages as well. When you speak to a group, no matter what their language, they will understand because you will be speaking to their mind. They will think they are hearing their own language. Our people lost their vocal cords many eons ago for we find it unnecessary to utter sound to be heard in our race."

"You mean you could not talk even if you wanted to?" Tashi blurted out, a bit shocked at the revelation. "There was a man in our village who had his tongue cut out by the Chinese as punishment for something he said against the state. Is it like that with you?"

"No. Since we found no need to speak in order to communicate, the vocal parts of our body, through generations of our species, withered and finally disappeared. I believe several of your Earth scientists have explained this process as an evolutionary phenomena."

190

"Yes, I remember reading about some of those theories."

"Tashi, tomorrow morning you will be taken to the building that contains what we call the crystal room. You will spend part of the morning with the technicians there. With their help more of your inherent abilities will be unveiled. Tomorrow night we will meet again after dinner."

Tashi only nodded, not really knowing how to respond.

"Althea and her teacher will meet with us. After tomorrow you will be able to begin."

"Already, are you sure? I don't think I know anything."

"Now you know everything, Tashi, for not knowing anything is the first step to knowing everything."

Tashi wondered, *Was Bashur a teacher and a guide for Plato, too?*

"Yes, Tashi, he was one of our human ambassadors during that period in the earth's evolvement. He influenced a great many people and his writing is still widely studied to this day. There have been many such ambassadors as he. You will become familiar with them as your earthly mission progresses. Now go and enjoy some time with your new friends."

Tashi got up and made his way to the entrance of the building where, as before, Althea was waiting.

"Let's go to the park," she said with a lightheartedness in her voice.

Chapter Thirty-One

In the Park

As Tashi and Althea entered the park, Morning Star was waving from the far corner. They walked through the rows of flowering plants and trees, which grew along a field in which a ball game was in full action. Arriving at the place from which Morning Star had waved to them, Tashi spotted several other people seated in a circle on the ground, cushioned only by a thick layer of grass.

In the center of the circle was a cloth. When Tashi came closer, he stopped abruptly. He was looking at a replica of the ancient game that the Abbot had entrusted to him. Could this mean that the game and its mysterious symbols originated from the tall white beings? Before his mind could further ponder the question, Althea pulled him into the circle and to the ground.

A Chinese man was pulling a stone from a bag and placing it on a certain spot on the cloth. He then pulled out three more stones and placed them on other spots. Altogether he had pulled eight stones so that a stone covered each of the points of the star on the cloth. A female with dark hair and blue eyes, who sat next to the Chinese man, started talking.

At first Tashi could not understand what she was saying since he was unfamiliar with her language. Then, a wave came over him, and everything she was telling the Chinese man was clear. She was explaining what each stone meant in relation to where they were placed on the star.

"You will journey to a high place in the country in which you live. There you will set up a healing and learning center and many will pilgrimage to that location." She placed her hand on another stone located on another point of the star. "The field around that center will be abundant with grains and vegetables that will produce year-round." She continued around the star until she had explained the meaning of each of the symbols on the stones and what they meant to the Chinese man. When she had finished everyone closed his or her eyes.

After a few moments, Jasper spoke, adding a further explanation to one of the stones. "You will be visited and aided on occasion by one or two of the people in this circle, who will be revealed to you later. They will give you and the others, who are residing and teaching at your center, guidance in adapting to the numerous earth changes in that area. One such disaster is devastating earthquakes. You and your followers will help many make the transition."

A few of the members of the circle murmured confirmations of what Jasper had predicted.

After a few seconds of silence, the Chinese man collected the stones from the cloth and placed them back in the bag. Turning, he handed the bag to Tashi.

Tashi felt himself flush as his insecurities about not knowing what to do with the game rose in him. The Abbot had shown him only a few times how the game was to be played. Someone in the circle assured him that he would know what to do once he held the bag a while.

Tashi held the bag in both hands and shut his eyes, welcoming the opportunity to quiet the nervousness caused by being in the spotlight. After a few moments he opened his eyes and drew one of the symbol stones from the bag. As the Abbot had shown him, he placed the stone in the center of the star. He continued pulling stones until all the points were covered, working clockwise around the star. Shutting his eyes, he waited.

The man to his left, who was from India, spoke, putting his hand on the first stone Tashi had drawn. "An ambassador to the world you will become." Placing his hand on another symbol stone, he predicted, "This stone tells of your personal relationships. Your mate and you will work as a team. You and she will bear a human child who will be a very evolved soul. This soul will carry on the work you start throughout the upcoming golden age of the earth, long after the two of you have returned to your home planet and universe."

With this prediction a collective "ah" was expressed from the others in the circle. Tashi turned and looked at Althea. There was a smile on her face. *Could this be true?* he thought, letting his human doubts control his mind and emotions. So much information had been given to him in the past few days that he was consumed with questions, but had no idea how to ask them. He decided the easiest thing to do was to just listen and wait and see. He must stay in the moment as Bashur had counseled him. He had to admit, even to his human side, that all that the Indian was saying felt true at an inner level, but the same nagging question queried his conscious mind. *Why me?*

The East Indian man, sensing his question, added, "All will be made clear to you at the proper time. Stay connected to the universal knowledge, and you will remember what you need to remember at the time."

The Indian continued giving predictions and guidance according to the lay of the stones. Tashi listened but found it difficult to concentrate on what was being said. His mind kept sidetracking questions that continued to present themselves to him with every statement the Indian made. Finally, the East Indian man finished explaining each of the stones Tashi had pulled. As before, everyone closed his or her eyes.

After a while, a woman to the right of Althea spoke with a certain amount of awe in her voice. "Tashi, your insights are coming directly from the Counsel of Elders." Almost surprised at the words she was hearing, she added, "You are a member of the counsel and report to it on a regular basis."

Tashi tried to remember where he had heard those words before. Suddenly, it came to him. He had heard this statement from the spirit guide who had come to him during his meditation only yesterday. At the time it made little sense to him. Even now it was difficult to comprehend its meaning. However, he felt that what the woman said was an important message and that its meaning would be made clear to him soon. In response, he just nodded a gratitude to her for the message.

After a brief silence, a large man with blonde hair spoke in a language that Tashi had as yet not heard.

"We have all worked with you before, Tashi, in Lemuria. You were our teacher then as you will be again. We have gathered here to meet and begin our work under your human leadership. Do you remember, Tashi, when we were together before the earth's shift that resulted in the sinking of the Lemurian continent and the scattering of its people? We never saw you again after that, until now, of course. You are our master teacher. Please do not leave us to flounder again."

As almost an involuntary act, Tashi nodded his head yes. Then words came from his mouth. The source of the words came not from his human mind but from a place he could not explain. As he spoke, a white-blue glow surrounded the circle and tentacles of iridescent blue light penetrated each member of the circle.

Tashi began speaking the words of his spirit guides.

"Do not call me master. There are no masters. I am a messenger and an ambassador as each of you is. All thirteen of us have worked together many times on this planet. We have in this lifetime been born and raised in cultures and environments that vary significantly. There is a higher purpose for this, as there is for all occurrences.

"While we do not always remember or understand the incident as it is taking place in our human lives, it never happens without a higher purpose. As you travel throughout the world spreading the message, never forget that your purpose is more than a physical journey. Some of you will occasionally fall prey to the demands of your ego and wander from the original path.

"Do not condemn yourself for this, for this is one of the obstacles of being human. Even when others condemn you and your message, remember it is only their fear that is judging you. Leave them with their doubts and criticisms, for there are many others who are ready to hear your message. Bear in mind that when you try to force feed something into a person's belief system they tend to resist digesting it. When they are ready to hear and perform the message, they will seek you out.

"You will create gathering centers scattered around the planet. Do you now see the greater plan of having each of you come from a different part of this world? Each of you has a different cultural background, yet as we sit in this circle no one is more or less important than the other. On a higher level of understanding, we are all the same. We honor each other's differences and know we are as one with the Source. We are all individual players on the same team.

"Go forth, and do the work you have contracted to do on this planet for this is a glorious moment in its history. And above all else enjoy the journey."

As the last of his words pierced each soul, their heads lowered and their eyes closed. After a while Tashi opened his eyes and was at first surprised to see the group still in meditation. Then he remembered what had taken place. He was somewhat shaken by this spontaneous burst of words that had come through him, but he knew that he had felt so good during his verbal eruption that he had been tempted to stay in that euphoric state, but someone or something had brought him back

The rest of the members of the circle slowly raised their heads and opened their eyes. The atmosphere of the group was filled with love. Each of them turned to the person next to them and embraced. Althea put her arms around Tashi and as she did, he felt safe and secure. In fact he had never felt anything like the ambiance that swept through him at that moment. He yearned to feel like he did at that moment forever.

The first to speak was a man from Brazil. He thanked Tashi for the message and insights. He went on to say, "Up until now I could not fully understand how the problems of my country's people could possibly relate to those of the rest of you. Now, because of Tashi's message, I believe I am starting to see the larger picture of why we have been brought together here. However, I must admit I have more questions than answers at this point, and yet I feel if I can learn to trust in my higher purpose, all my questions will all be answered."

The other eleven responded with silent nods of agreement.

A bell rang, bringing the group back to their present time and location. They stood up and walked to the great hall to meditate. As individuals they each sat in their favorite location. A series of tones sounded, coming from what Tashi recognized to be Tibetan singing bells. The sounds resonated through every part of their bodies and souls. Each felt as though he was sitting on air instead of on the various colored cushions under them.

196

The group of thirteen stayed in a meditative state longer than they had ever before. Tashi was surprised to see that not one member of the group had come back to a conscious state yet. He remained seated, letting all the events of the day parade through his mind. It just did not seem real, but after the last few days, he was no longer certain what real was. In the back of his mind he still had the nagging question of *Why me?* He hoped he would have the answer before he left this paradise like place.

He remembered a visitor to his village talking of a special place in the mountains of the desert where a civilization existed that was like no other. A place where there was no hunger, no fighting, no greed or jealousy. The visitor had said that he had heard the stories from nomads who proclaimed that although they had never been there, the people who lived there never aged and lived forever in peace.

The nomads said that at night they could see large white birds flying into this special place and disappearing into the mountains. As a boy, Tashi wanted to believe that a place like that existed, but as he grew older he rationalized that those were only fantasy stories. Now he was starting to question his previous rationalizations. Instead he started to find some creditability in the nomad's stories. Could this place be the place described in those long ago fables?

Althea's movement interrupted his thoughts. He turned to her, and in unison they rose from the cushions and walked outside. The mild fresh air cloaked them. "Are you tired?" Tashi asked.

"Not at all," Althea responded.

"Let's go somewhere to talk, only the two of us."

"I know a place where we can be alone," she said, as she led him to a bench concealed under an umbrella of trees. A beam of light filtered through the branches and the leaves of the tree, creating dancing patterns of illumination on the ground. They sat quietly for a few moments, enjoying the light show in silence.

Tashi was the first to speak. "Althea, what happened with the game has never happened to me before. All of a sudden everything opened up for me and the words just flowed out. I met with my teacher, Bashur, today. I'm hoping he will help me to understand and adjust to this new energy. But that's not what I wanted to talk to you about. I received another message I did not share with the group. Tomorrow will be our last day here. We will be sent to our homes to complete various things. Some of us will leave our homelands while others will stay near their homes to start centers. Bashur tells me that I will be sent all over the world to give classes and lectures as well as support to those who are teaching the word. From that point on the world will be my home."

He paused for a few seconds as though gathering his courage for what he wanted to say next. "Althea, I don't want to leave you. I have grown very fond of you, almost from the first day I laid eyes on you. What I am trying to say is Althea, I love you and I want you with me always."

He stopped abruptly as though it took all the courage he could muster to say it and now he was depleted. He had never felt more nervous in his life. He had not really had much experience with women. There were none in his village who interested him and he had not taken the time to visit other villages. He had promised a neighbor he would meet his female cousin from the next village but never made the effort to do so.

He took her hands in his and held them, not saying anything. She did not pull away. Finally she broke the silence. "I think I love you too, Tashi. This was all so very quick and I have been hurt so many times in the past. I don't know. I am so certain about other things in my life but anything having to do with relationships always creates doubts within me. Maybe a little time apart will help us to make certain this is not just a feeling brought on by the euphoric atmosphere of this place. Besides, we will always be connected mentally, so wherever we are we can talk to each other mind-to-mind and heart-to-heart. Did you receive a message about how long we will be home before we are to start our work?"

"Yes, but I would like Bashur to confirm it. I was told it would be about three months in most cases, at least in mine. Some will do their work close to their home and will only leave occasionally to meet here or a similar place as a group. Oh, Althea, I will miss you so." He took her in his arms and embraced her. They sat for a long time, wrapped in each other's arms, not wanting to let go of the feeling of being complete.

With the mention of Bashur's name, they both remembered that they were to meet with him that evening. Althea's personal teacher would be present as well.

The two scurried from the park to the entrance to Bashur's residence. Standing outside was Althea's teacher. All three walked to Bashur's room through the doorway, which seemed to appear and disappear.

Bashur began the conversation. "Tashi, you have had a channel open for you today that was of a very high order, your channel to your direct connection to the Council of Elders. Althea, you are present at this meeting so that you, as Tashi's twin soul, may also understand what has taken place. Do either of you have any questions about your destiny or anything else you feel unsure about?"

At first no one spoke. Then Althea softly asked a question. "Bashur, a year ago, I was visiting some Mayan ruins near Mexico City."

"I know them well, Althea. Long ago, I sent you and others there to live and teach."

Althea, surprised at her sudden remembrance, said, "That is why you seemed so familiar and I felt the need to ask you about why I had such a violent reaction to that place in this lifetime. My insight blurred and I never remembered what happened to the priest who climbed to the top of the pyramid."

"I will help you to recall, Althea, for I think it will relieve you to dispel certain fears and anger that have been suppressed by your soul since that unfortunate summer solstice. First explain to Tashi and your teacher your experience."

Althea explained what had happened the year before when she had visited Teotihuacán, near Mexico City. Her story ceased when she was at the top of the pyramid, which is where her memory stopped.

"I will complete the story," Bashur said while Althea's last word still echoed in their heads. "The chief priest, you, Althea, stood at the top of the pyramid awaiting the rise of the sun on that summer solstice dawn. You knew, as did the other priests that this would be the last morning you would be on earth. You had done a magnificent job raising the spiritual evolvement of the people of that rather large community. You were stationed there longer than most of our ambassadors are ever allowed to stay in one location. Over the years you had become very fond of your students, and they of you.

"Power hungry renegades slowly infiltrated Teotihuacán. You were instructed by the alliance not to interfere with their adverse beliefs and teachings. In other words, if you had shown anger or had demonstrated any violence toward them, you would have been contradicting your own principles.

"The leader of the renegades resented your influence, and the only way he could claim that power was to proclaim that you had fallen from the grace of God. You were alone on top of the pyramid, which was the custom at the solstice. One of the renegade's followers had sneaked up the back of the pyramid and was hiding when you took your place before the people. Just as the sun showed, he killed you with a poison dart. With the diversion of the crowd's panic, the assassin quickly retrieved the dart and retreated unseen. In order to keep his secret, the renegade leader later killed the assassin.

"The power hungry renegade played on the intense emotional fear of the people at having just witnessed the strange collapse of their beloved spiritual leader. He took control of the crowd and declared God's intent was to strike down the priest so that he, the anointed one, could be God's servant and lead the people spiritually as well as politically. He went on to explain to them that the priest's connection to God had decayed and that it was time for a new stronger leader. He declared that under his leadership the community would prosper on all levels.

"He told the people that God had spoken to him and that the Teotihuacans were the chosen people. Under his leadership, they would conquer and pillage the villages of their region and eventually the world. All the people of the world would be subservient to Teotihuacán. With excitement in his voice he shouted that they would bring about a golden age such as the world had never before experienced.

"Part of this very well planned takeover included carefully placed supporters among the crowd who would cheer on cue after certain statements, inciting the crowd to follow suit. Needless to say, the civilization deteriorated as one by one the priest's sympathizers were sacrificed in the name of God. You are probably asking why our people who had the ability to stop such a rebellion, did not. Our orders were to let this transition take place for the people of the earth had grown complacent in their attitudes. They no longer took responsibility for their actions or thoughts. The more they acquired, the more they wanted to be given. They were easy prey for a power monger leader who could promise them everything and more. This dramatic event was to be an awakening, the likes of which had not been seen in thousands of years on this planet.

"Does all this help you to understand why you have blocked this memory, Althea, particularly in this lifetime? You see, your father in your present lifetime was that renegade leader and responsible for your body's death."

Althea was crying. Her disgust and anger toward her father at last made sense. Through the tears, she managed to say, "Oh, thank you, Bashur. Although I still feel the pain of that experience, I now feel lighter and so much more at peace with myself."

"That is enough for this evening," Bashur announced. "Tashi, I will meet with you in the morning. Enjoy the remainder of your last night's visit in the Hidden City. It will be a while before you will return."

Althea and Tashi rose and exited the building. Althea's teacher stayed behind to confer with Bashur.

Still stunned by the revelations she had heard, Althea, with Tashi's arm wrapped around her, walked to the door of the building where their rooms were located. There they stood embracing until finally Althea nudged away. "We must go," she said, not really meaning it, but knowing someone had to make the break.

"Yes, it is very late," Tashi whispered in her ear, trying not to break the spell. "We have tomorrow together if my message is correct. You have had quite an emotional trauma tonight. Let's get some sleep. I have a feeling tomorrow will be quite full."

Tashi lay awake in his pod staring at the ceiling. As much as he tried, sleep would not come to him. His mind raced from one subject to another, but eventually always found its way back to Althea. The night dragged on until finally he heard a bell, which announced that a new day was about to begin. In one sense he was relieved, for he would again see Althea, but in another sense it brought on a feeling of anticipated loss. He knew that they would be separated for a long time at the end of this new day.

Chapter Thirty-Two

Another Day in the Hidden City

lthea was waiting at the entrance when Tashi walked into the sun of a new day. Her face did not wear the radiant smile he had learned to expect and love. He could tell by the circles under her eyes that she had not been able to sleep either. They walked to the great hall for meditation, uttering only an occasional comment on the landscape.

During meditation they both had again been given a message that they would be together in the future. It uplifted their spirits. On the way to breakfast they spoke about themselves and shared what their individual homecoming would be like after the extraordinary experiences they had had at this magical place.

Tashi was barely through the door of his teacher's room when Bashur spoke.

"Your messages were completely accurate. However, sometimes in the human world the timing can alter. It really isn't necessary to dwell on the concept of time. Simply remember to live in the moment. Sit down. We will talk.

"I know you are confused right now," continued Bashur. "Opening the third eye as fast and as much as you did in only a few days is a shock to the dualistic human. The human body and mind evolve at a slower rate than that of the spiritual body. Be patient with yourself, for anxiety will only impede the process."

Tashi did not respond.

"You will be taken home tonight. This next statement may come as a bit of a surprise," Bashur said, pausing. "When you arrive home, it will be at the time you were originally expected. We are able to manipulate time and space so you will also remember that you met with the Abbot at the monastery for the same amount of days you were here. It is very important that your stay here be kept secret. Most would not believe you anyway, with the exception of your mother, who of course knows you are here. She has visited the Hidden City many times. It was here that she was impregnated with the seed that produced you. Tashi, I am your father."

Tashi had been quietly listening, striving to keep his mind on Bashur's words instead of Althea. Upon hearing his last statement, his heart skipped a beat and his eyes opened wide, gazing at his mentor with a look of shock.

"Knowing this may help you to understand many things about your childhood years on earth. Tashi, you are very special in many ways. I know it is not easy being in a human body for a being as spiritually evolved as you are. All I can hope is that with this new understanding the experience may become somewhat easier for you."

"You mean my father is not my father? This sounds like one of mother's stories," Tashi said in a louder than normal voice, not able to hide his shock at the news.

"The stories were told to help you prepare for what I have just told you. We gave her those stories. Your mother has known all along that you were to do special work when the time was right and you were ready."

"You said her job was finished. Where will she go? Must she leave? I have so many questions of her. I will miss her."

"She has other tasks she has agreed to perform, which we are not at liberty to discuss and which do not directly affect you at this point. We can tell you that I will be visiting you whenever I feel it necessary or whenever you want to talk. Tashi you are not and never have been alone. For the next few months, when you are confused go to the cave in your mountains and I will come.

"You will have these next few months with your mother so that she can finish the story she has been telling. As you listen, remember the time when you were that small boy whose mother had predicted and experienced the catastrophic events that brought on the end of Lemuria as a continent. It will help you to understand the contract you have agreed to fulfill in this lifetime.

"You may go and meet with your new friends, or should I say your old friends. We will meet one more time before you leave here." Bashur waved him out, preventing him from asking his usual barrage of questions.

Chapter Thirty-Three

The Group of Thirteen

Tashi walked to the game park. Upon entering, he saw the group of twelve people in the same far corner where they all had met the day before. They were sitting in a circle quietly chatting with each other. When he was within a few meters of them, all talking ceased, and they collectively looked up at him as though they had been waiting for him. At first, it made him feel a bit uneasy to have everyone watching.

He waved and sat in the opening that had been provided for him. Althea was on one side of him and Jasper was on the other. All he could think to say was hello, but it seemed to break the silence.

Althea began, "Tashi, since all of us will be working together in one way or another, we thought it might be fun to get to know more about each other. If it's all right with you, each of us will share where he is from on this planet and a little about how he came to be in this place."

Tashi looked at her with a question in his expression. "Of course, but you didn't need to ask me."

"But you are our human leader and teacher," a stately young man, who was sitting directly across from Tashi, piped up.

A shiver came over Tashi as he responded to the young man's comment. "Do I not take up the same amount of space in this circle? Do I not breathe the same amount of air? I am your equal, and yet I humbly accept the position as your teacher, for as your teacher I will be the one learning, far more than I will be teaching. Why do you not start by telling us your earthly name as well as something about yourself?"

The handsome tanned man bowed his head a moment then began to speak. "My name is Mana. I am from New Zealand, on the North Island. I am the medicine man or chieftain of a group of tribes. My Maori name in English means prestige and respect. Since I was a child, I have walked through our rainforest to a cave whenever I needed to be alone and empower myself.

"A few days ago while in the cave a tall white being came to me, as he had done occasionally in the past. He asked me if I wanted to go on a journey with him. I thought he meant a journey of the spirit or mind. I had no idea he meant I would go with him physically as well. The destination of that journey was this magnificent place."

After a pause and an almost inaudible sigh, the Maori continued, "Even during boyhood I knew I had special gifts." He let his cobalt blue eyes roam around the circle of attentive listeners as one or two of them nodded their heads, remembering their own childhood. "Though my powers as a healer and counselor have been growing stronger each year, I have always felt something was missing. I have had the constant feeling that there was something else I was supposed to be doing.

"At times the sensation got so overwhelming that I found it necessary to escape from the company of others to the solitude of my secret cave. It usually was at these times that the white being appeared and gave me a message, often rhymed. When the first rhymed message came, I thought it was a joke, but over the years I began to look forward to them. The cadence of his messages made me feel centered and balanced. I did not always understand what the words meant until later, but I was always left with a new feeling of hope and peace. Being here has explained why certain things happened to me.

"I remember having many dreams of myself as a chief in a past life waiting on a beach in New Zealand. Along with other tribal chiefs, I was waiting for some special godlike person to come ashore."

Prompted by the group he described the dream he had had so many times that he knew every detail. Taking a long breath, he began.

Chapter Thirty-Four

The Dream

The tall white beings that visited me in the cave one day gave me the following rhymed message. It was after this message that I had the dream that I am going to share with you."

The Arrival of the Man-God
A ship with bellowing sails did arrive
To touch the spirit of the people he did strive
His life he showed to get their attention
He showed all that they did depended on their intention
He traveled and traveled many a mile
His magic, to their faces, brought many a smile
They never forgot the one dressed in white
For all around him was a golden light
They remember the fish and the mountain and the trees
They also remember what was under the seas
In his crew the man-god had many from the stars
Many have come again but not from Mars
They come from different places but now join in hand
Some reside beyond and some beneath the land
The man-god was one of many to teach the God within
He was not there to condemn all for their sin
We tell the story for people to hear
That control of the masses is where people got fear

Trust in God and you, are the issues at hand
Give no energy to those who own the land
Beware; the myths have been changed by those of
    the crown
It's a way of keeping your people down
The man-god taught of the one God above
He showed how God had unconditional love
He taught of love sometimes through sound
For at certain tones the spirit is upward bound
He worked with your people and let it be known
That the spirit within, you will always own
He said we must remember that when we fight fire
    with fire
It will grow larger and we soon will tire
He showed us the need to remember how the forces of
    nature work everyday
If you work against them, obstacles will be put in the way
Your needs will be met if you start to believe
That you are worthy of God's treasures, to receive
Let your male negative ego go by the way
It is now the time for your female self to have her say
Remember the tall ones from the sky
For when they speak, they do not lie
Your male ego has been in full force
He has forgotten that he is a part of the source
Your only enemy is that within
He is stronger when love becomes thin
Love is the most powerful weapon there is
Connecting with God is what it is
Once you're consumed with God's love inside
To no angry thoughts will you abide
You will have no enemies, for you are sure
And for all your woes it is a cure
Until you feel this each and every day
Your negative ego will surely have its way

When inspired with love, you will be one
It is only then that life can be fun

With his eyes shut, Mana continued describing his dream as though he was actually experiencing it at that moment.

"Out of the mist, the mast of a ship could be seen. It appeared to be similar to or like the large ship our ancestors had spoken of so often in their stories. Only the slight outline of the tip of it could be seen as we strained our eyes gazing out into the ever-present bank of white fog.

"The mist and the fog rolled toward us as we stood silently on the shore in anticipation. Could this veil of mist be concealing the long awaited deity, for which our people had hoped and prayed for more generations than I have lived? We had never stopped believing that this god who walked like a man would again grace our land with his presence.

"We stood paralyzed by a fear of disappointment, which we had experienced so many times in the past, as had our ancestors. Questions raced through my mind. Was he really larger than life? Did his vibrant blue eyes see right through the flesh and bone to the soul? Were the tales of his miraculous healing only a product of the overactive imagination of our medicine men?

"As we strained to see and hear, our ears detected a sound not unlike that of the sea that sent its never-ending waves rolling onto the shore. It sounded like water lapping against the sides of a small wooden boat, but nothing was as yet visible.

"The fog was particularly thick on the dawn of this cooler-than-usual winter morning. The geysers had been spectacularly active spraying their sulfur water high into the air. It was as though Mother Earth knew in advance that this would not be an ordinary day.

"Our drums beat to the rhythm of the breaking waves and resonated with our heartbeats, keeping them in harmony with the beat of our Mother Earth. I found myself putting my brown hand on my chest to reassure myself that I was still breathing and that my heart was still beating. Everyone was silent. Even the babies strapped to their mother's

210

breasts were silently content. Only the roar of the sea and that faint lapping noise was heard.

"All my life I had listened to stories of a great white ship bringing to our land a light-skinned man with blue eyes who walked and talked like a god, a man-god who spoke only of love for all. He spoke of a larger God in the sky that loved everyone, even our enemies. Our elders spoke of the ancestors witnessing this man-god healing our cripples so that they could stand erect and walk again. They said he did this with the mere touch of his hand on their head. Our ancients spoke of his words that softened the hardest hearts among us.

"As the lapping noise grew louder, even the seagulls and sandpipers froze in place as though hypnotized by an incoming force. The atmosphere was so intense, I wondered if the thicker than normal bank of mist and fog was a coincidence or the result of some god's attempt to set a more dramatic stage for this special arrival. Even my feathered cape and ostrich plumes were still on this windless morning.

"On either side of me my attendants stood holding the welcoming gifts. The carved boxes of gifts included some our finest crafted items as well as many of our exquisitely prepared foods. If the dreams and prophecies were correct, these meager offerings came nowhere close to being worthy of the stature of this special arrival. The tiny parrot eggs boiled and soaked for preservation in fish oil and dill liquid and stored in a finely decorated container would be but a token gift on our part. The small delicate eggs, which were normally only consumed on our most sacred holidays and only by our most elevated leaders, seemed a meager attempt to show our esteem to such a great one.

"Delegations of chiefs and priests had been arriving from outlying tribes all week. The hollow tree drums had been communicating this prophesized day of the arrival for months. The visiting chiefs had traveled great distances in their finely carved boats, heavily laden with gifts. The very powerful and respected priest from Lake Taupo arrived only the day before. He and his entourage stood in humble anticipation twenty feet down shore to my right.

"I swallowed hard as my eyes witnessed the first glimpses of the outline of the boat as it came closer to the shore. It would be only a matter of minutes before the boat's sleek body would slide onto the shore. As head chieftain it was my official duty to welcome the tribal leaders, but I had never had the opportunity to welcome a leader of this magnitude, never one that was at the level of a god. All my years of spiritual study and practice seemed totally inadequate at this moment.

"I stood hypnotically frozen on the beach. My mind raced as I mentally rehearsed my first words and actions as this man-god set foot once again onto our land. The conch horn blowers and the singers were prepared, but was I? I asked the god, Atua, to give me the strength and courage necessary to deliver the welcoming greeting with distinction and honor. The image in the mist was sharper now."

Mana stopped speaking. The group thought they heard a small gasp come from his throat. He opened his eyes and gazed at Tashi through watery eyes. In a shaky voice he said, "Tashi, I think you are that man-god."

He had difficulty finishing his last sentence as his emotions blocked the words from coming forth clearly. He lowered his head as he let the long suppressed emotions release themselves through tears. The group was silent for a long time. Each was relating the Maori's dream to one that they had had with a similar theme.

Tashi broke the silence by encouraging the others to continue to tell a little about themselves and how they had come to arrive at the Hidden City. Strangely enough, although a few of the details were different, the stories were the same. When the last one of the group had finished, a bell sounded meaning it was time for meditation. They chatted along the path to the meditation hall, feeling a deeper connection with each other.

That evening Tashi met with Bashur. It had been a day that Tashi would never forget. So much had happened. It was a day of many joys and many tears. Getting to know his twelve cohorts was very special. He had never been with a group of strangers who were so alike in their thinking. He had never had the feeling of being one with people as much as he had today.

"You had a very enlightening day, Tashi," Bashur commented, as

Tashi settled himself on the cushion. "We feel you are ready to begin to fulfill your contract. Tomorrow morning after meditation you will leave for home."

Tashi felt a wave of remorse as Bashur's words penetrated his soul. In one sense he missed his family and his beloved Himalayan village, but he would miss Althea and his new friends as much. "May I speak to my mother of what has happened to me?" asked Tashi, thinking his mother would help him to understand his feeling for Althea on a human level.

"Yes, she will be the only one who will relate to what you have experienced. Even though she, too, had been here a long time ago, she will only vaguely remember the experience in her soul's memory."

So much else had been on his mind that he had forgotten about the message that his mother was leaving. Could it mean she was going to die or just go away for a while? One part of him wanted to ask more about the fate of his mother but another part was not ready to hear the truth. Maybe he had purposely put it out of his mind, for even though he understood why she was leaving, the thought still brought an emotional pain to his heart. He would miss her.

"Enjoy the day and say your good-byes. We will come for you in the morning. I will visit you soon in your homeland," Bashur instructed him, interrupting the inner battle-taking place within Tashi.

Althea was waiting for Tashi when he exited the building where Bashur was located.

They said nothing but only held each other's hands and stared into each other's eyes. "I love you," Althea said, not breaking the mood.

Tashi embraced her in his arms. "We will be together again. We must just be patient," he told her. But he felt an aura of emptiness after the words were spoken.

They held each other for a long time. With all the courage he could muster, he reluctantly pushed her slightly away. Looking deep into her eyes he whispered, "We must say good-bye to the others."

There were many tears and much well wishing that evening, before everyone reluctantly dispersed to their own space. Tashi and Althea started the group disintegration by excusing themselves. Together, they

213

spent the better part of the night on their bench talking some, but most of the time just simply holding one another. The sky was becoming bright with light when they separated and went to their individual rooms.

The emotional trauma of leaving Althea and the Hidden City hit him as he entered his room. He felt extremely weary. Tashi had no idea when they would come for him. He decided that he probably had time to lie down and take a nap. He had no trouble dozing off to sleep once his head hit the mat.

Chapter Thirty-Five

Back in the Cave

Tashi awoke to find himself in his secret cave. At first he thought he had dreamed all that had happened, but put that thought out of his head immediately. It was all too real to have only been a dream. He sat there in the familiar surroundings of his cave mulling over what he should do: Go home or go to the monastery to meet with the Abbot, as had been the plan before he had been taken to what he could only describe as paradise.

It took him only a moment to decide that going home was the better of the two choices. He needed to talk to his mother. Besides, Bashur had said that because the white beings knew how to manipulate time and space, his meeting with the Abbot had actually taken place. He still didn't understand how he could be in two places at once. If this was true, why couldn't he remember any part of the visit to the Abbot? Finding his questions too frustrating to ponder, he let them go.

As he stood, he spotted a familiar item lying in the shadows of the cave. It was the pack he had brought with him on his journey to the monastery. He picked it up, and inside was everything just as it had been three days prior, or was it four days? He could not remember. As he examined the contents of the bag, he saw that the yak butter and the tea were missing. With this new evidence, he again contemplated the concept of being in two places at one time.

He slung the pack on his back after removing the barley cake that was still inside and in perfect condition. As he munched on it during his trip down the mountain, a thought came to him. If he had been gone three or four days and the pack lay in the cave for three or four days, why didn't the pack rats or some other varmint eat the cake? Could it be that the only answer had to be that he really was in two places at once? Still perplexed, he decided to follow Bashur's advice and live in the moment. When his mind made that decision all worry and questions disappeared. It felt good to trust, Tashi thought.

The familiar trek down the mountain seemed unusually fast. The sun was low in the sky when Tashi saw the outline of his village. He quickened his steps so as to arrive before the mountain had completely swallowed the day's light.

As Tashi entered his house, his mother, who was stirring something on the fire, greeted him. "I have just made yak butter tea, Tashi. Sit. We are alone so we can talk privately of your adventure for a few minutes."

Immediately, Tashi had a feeling of relief. He wanted to tell his mother everything if for no other reason than to convince himself that he had not been dreaming. Bashur said she would understand, yet back in familiar civilization he even doubted whether Bashur was real or merely a dream.

Mother poured two cups of tea and sat next to Tashi at the table. They each silently sipped the tea for a few moments. The tea was warm and sweet and it settled the jitters within Tashi as he tried to figure out in his mind how to begin.

"Just begin at the beginning," said Mother, as though reading his mind.

Tashi took a deep breath and started his story, beginning with the first time he visited his secret cave as a child and met the tall white being. Mother listened without any comment. A smile or an occasional nod was her only response.

When he told her about Althea, Mother took his hand and smiled as though realizing for the first time that her son had grown into a man. "Will I have a chance to meet her?" she asked, not letting go of his hand.

"I don't know. She has gone home to her family in the United States. We made no plans for her to come here. Oh, Mother, I miss her already.

I must practice patience as my teacher and you have advised me since I was a small boy, but I so long to be with her."

Seeing his pain, Mother put her arms around him and kissed his cheek. "Oh, Tashi, you have learned of human love between a man and a woman. My special little boy has become a special man. If you love her, I know that she must be special also. Now, tell me about your teacher, Bashur."

Tashi told her about meeting with Bashur and the ways in which Bashur had helped him to become aware of his multi-dimensional senses. He paused. "Mother," he said, "you are to finish the story of our people from the ancient times. Bashur said that the ending is one I have never heard before and that it will help me understand who I am."

"I know, Tashi. I have been waiting for the right time, and it's now arrived. Tonight we will celebrate your return with the family, but tomorrow you and I will go to my special place where I will tell you the part of the story that no one else can hear. We will leave early and return late."

"You have a special place? Where is it? Why have you never mentioned it?" Tashi blurted out.

Mother laughed, finding it humorous that Tashi had already forgotten his lesson of patience. "It would not have been secret had I told anyone. You will be the only human who will have seen it after tomorrow and I trust it will remain our secret, for it would only upset others to know what happened there."

"You can trust me, and I can wait till the morning."

"Run along and wash the dust from you. There is a new shirt on your sleeping mat that your sister has helped me to make. She is very proud of it. She looks up to you and loves you very much."

Tashi went outside to the well to wash up, although he was not very dirty since his trip home was not by normal means.

Chapter Thirty-Six

The Homecoming and Celebration

After washing, Tashi climbed the ladder to his sleeping mat. Spread out on it was the shirt Mother and his sister Yeshe had made. It was a finely woven cloth made from the soft yak fur, fashioned into a tunic-style shirt. It had been bleached and then dyed red with subtle tones of violet varying the red hue, giving it a shimmering quality. Sewn on it with gold thread were various symbols, creating a magnificent overall texture and design. Many of the symbols were familiar to him from the ancient game the Abbot had given him. They were the same symbols that he had seen when he was in the Hidden City. Lying next to the shirt was a sash that was woven of the same gold thread that was used to sew on the symbols.

Tashi ran his hand gently over the apparel. His hand tingled from the love that had been put into it by its creators. He touched the symbol, which was like the symbol hanging around his neck, and a shot of energy went through him that was so strong it almost knocked him backwards. Tears of joy and remembrance filled his eyes.

As he studied the cause of his emotional outburst, he noticed that the small circles on the points of the upside down triangle were turquoise in color, a color that had not been used anywhere else on the shirt.

Tashi stood there letting its energy penetrate him. He gained his composure just as his mother called to him. Slipping off his rough traveling shirt, he put on the spectacular gift. He called to Mother—after

218

he cleared his throat of the emotions blocking it—that he would be down shortly.

As he climbed down the ladder he saw that the room was filling with people. His father and sister were the first ones he saw. When he took the last step off the ladder, his sister ran and embraced him. *When did she grow up?* he thought as her body met his. Pulling away, she asked, "Do you like it, Tashi?"

"It is the most splendid shirt I have ever seen," he said as he embraced her again.

Neighbors, cousins, aunts, and uncles were still drifting through the door. The room filled so that Tashi thought the walls would likely burst. Each came with a gift of some sort. Many had containers of food, which they placed on the table for everyone to partake. From the folds in their clothing each guest brought forth a cup that they filled with either chang (Tibetan beer) or yak butter tea, which had been brought out in great abundance for the celebration.

Tashi was overwhelmed with the love and appreciation he was receiving from all the people he had known since birth, yet he was a bit confused as to why they were honoring him. This type of affair was usually saved for a visiting lama or a man of a higher spiritual stature.

After all cups were filled, Mother asked for everyone's attention. The room quieted. "We honor you tonight, Tashi, for now you are a special man with a special purpose. We know you will be leaving us in the near future, for you have been sent to the earth for a special purpose. No matter where your path leads you, our love will be with you." Everyone in the room lifted their cups and nodded in agreement with her tribute.

Near the door an opening was made for someone. It was the Abbot. Tashi tensed as the Abbot made his way through the crowd toward him. Would the Abbot be angry that he had failed to make the appointment? Tashi wondered. All his built up anxiety melted as the Abbot embraced him.

"I am honored to have played a small part in your enlightenment," he told Tashi loud enough for everyone to clearly hear. "The last three days we have spent together taught me more than you will ever realize. I thank you for that."

Tashi could tell that a small part of the Abbot was still struggling with humbling himself before a mere peasant. He thought it must have been challenging for a man of his status not to want to take credit for all of Tashi's spiritual knowledge. After all, an Abbot was also a human with a human's ego. Hoping to help him feel more at ease, Tashi thanked him for his excellent guidance during the years.

Mother broke the awkwardness of the moment by inviting everyone to have something to eat. People filed past Tashi, stopping to wish him well and thank him for the times he had helped them in one way or another. Pila and his wife, with a child in their arms, hugged him with thankful tears. Several other villagers showed their gratitude with small gifts. One such gift was a singing bell with an exquisite matching dorje.

Tashi's many supporters gathered various foods from the table and congregated in groups in the courtyard outside the door to leave more space inside the house. As the room started to empty, Mother stood next to her son.

"The shirt suits you, Tashi," she said, smoothing an invisible wrinkle on his sleeve.

"Mother, it is beautiful. Thank you so much," he said, looking deep into her clear loving eyes. "I am overwhelmed by this demonstration of honor."

"I know, Tashi. That is one of the reasons you are so special. You will understand soon enough. Just accept their gratitude tonight. Tomorrow we will talk. I plan for us to leave at dawn. I have already packed our traveling bundle."

"I'll be ready, Mother," Tashi said, squeezing her shoulders and bending over to kiss her forehead. When had he grown so much taller than she? Looking over the crowd of villagers, he noticed for the first time that he was heads taller than most of them.

"Now, mingle with the guests. They each have questions for you. All they know is that you have been chosen to go on a special journey. They are so proud that one of their own has been honored, although they don't understand how you are honored. It doesn't really matter. You have brought some excitement to their otherwise rather mundane lives."

Tashi took a cup of chang and started for a group of men who were about his age. He had played, worked, and wrestled with these men as a boy and yet they felt like strangers to him.

He thought, *I spent only three or four days with the group of twelve in the hidden mountain city and yet I seem closer to them than all these people with whom I have grown up. Have I changed that much in those few days?*

He chatted with his childhood friends without giving much depth to his words, moving from group to group only to duplicate the exercise apathetically. He continued this until he had talked with nearly everyone present and circled back into the house. He felt a sense of relief when he saw that the room was nearly empty except for a few friends of his mother who were helping her to clear the table and store the remnants of the feasts.

After a while the celebration waned, and the guests ambled toward their homes. Only Tashi and his family were left in the house. For the first time since he had come home, Tashi's father approached him. "I'm not sure I fully understand what you are to do, but according to your mother it is very important. No matter what it is, son, I support you. You are a son any father can be proud of. I want you to always remember this no matter where you are or what you are doing. Even when I scolded you for something you had done as a boy, deep in my heart I admired your adventurous and sometimes daring capers, but I could not let you see the joy you were bringing me as I was disciplining you."

Tashi embraced his father and thanked him for all he had taught him while he was growing up. They reminisced a while about the first time his father showed him how to use a slingshot. "I'll never forget how angry Mother was when I killed her prized rooster. I remember that I could not bring myself to eat him. It almost made me sick to see him boiled on a platter," Tashi recalled, chuckling.

Mother broke the spell by announcing that everyone should go to bed for dawn was not far away.

Chapter Thirty-Seven

Dawn of the Next Morning

The morning was brisk, as the disk of the sun had not poked its head above the mountain ridge as yet. Tashi put the pack on his back, and Mother and he walked out the door without saying a word to each other. They were to the edge of the village before Mother spoke. "Did you sleep well?"

"I had a lot of dreams, which woke me several times, but that is not unusual lately. That was a wonderful celebration last night, Mother. My new shirt is the most beautiful shirt I have ever seen," Tashi said, hoping she would not ask him about his dreams. The ones he remembered did not make much sense other than the one in which he was with Althea.

"I'm pleased you like the shirt. My secret place is about an hour's walk from here. Not far."

They walked most of the hour in silence. When Tashi looked at his mother, he could tell her mind was somewhere else. The path to her secret place was overgrown with nettles and vines. It was obvious no one had traveled it recently. He let his mother take the lead. After nearly an hour, she led him through a crack in two large boulders, which opened into a meadow on the other side. They crossed the meadow to a stand of trees, which grew very close together. It was a squeeze to get through them. When they did, they crawled under some thick, large bushes and found themselves at the opening of a cave.

"How did you ever find this place, Mother?"

"At the time, it was as though I was led here. I was much younger then and had a lot of curiosity."

Tashi followed his mother through the cave, which appeared to have a light coming from somewhere toward the back. As they rounded a corner, they stood in a medium-sized room. There was a small table and benches, which were made of stone pieces, fitted together so tightly that you could not even get the thinnest piece of paper through the space where they came together. On the table was a block, which radiated a glowing light and cast a pink luminosity on the room's walls.

"Sit, Tashi, and I will tell the story."

They sat, and Mother pulled two cups from her folds. She took the metal thermos from the pack and poured each of them a cup of yak butter tea. As Tashi sipped it, he felt a warmth flood over him even though the temperature in the cave was quite comfortable. Mother set her cup on the table and closed her eyes.

"Years ago when I was but a young girl, I was sent to gather herbs and roots, much as you were when you were a boy. One day I wandered farther than I should have. I saw a small animal go through those trees and then under the bushes. He disappeared through the crack in the rocks so I followed him. That is how I found this cave. From then on, I visited the cave whenever I went gathering.

"One day while I was sitting in this cave, a tall white being appeared before me. I was surprised, but I never felt frightened. My heart and my mind told me that this being would never harm me. He spoke to me although no sound came from him. The message he gave me was like a song. I have sung that song in my head ever since."

After a slight pause, mother started to sing the song.

A child of the stars, you were here long ago
You've come again to brighten Earth's woe
A son you will bear who to the world will give
A pattern for life, new ways to live
One of our seeds to your egg will bring life
Within you he'll grow without any strife
As he grows, the stories you will tell

Of a time on Earth when all was quite well
As a human he'll learn to live as they do
But other talents he'll have, known by very few
We will protect him and guide him for what is to be
For when he is grown, he must leave thee
Many years in the past this land he did walk
Followed by the twelve, his words they did stalk

"With the last tone of the song still ringing in my ear, the white being disappeared. I must have fallen asleep, because when I awoke it all seemed like a dream, yet the words to the song were clearly in my mind. When I picked up my sack of herbs to leave, this medallion was lying on top of it. I tied it around my neck and told no one how I had gotten it or what had happened. It has remained my secret until now."

In an almost ritualistic manner, Mother pulled out the necklace from beneath her blouse. Tashi felt himself gasp. It was identical to the necklace that had been left for him that memorable day when the white being showed itself and sang to him for the first time in his secret cave. Noting his gasp, Mother smiled and continued.

"After that day, the white being visited me whenever I came to my cave. One day when I was about sixteen, instead of a message in song, he reached out for me to take his hand. It was then that I noticed he had six fingers. Through my mind he told me that on that day I was going to visit a special place. Like magic I found myself in a city hidden in the mountains. I remember the buildings were a brilliant white. There were flowers and green everywhere, not the brown of the tundra around our village. The whole place smelled of a pleasing burning wood like that of sandalwood incense mixed with flower scents.

"I was led to a building that had a large crystal in its center and was open to the sky. Off the central room were smaller ones. I was taken into one of these and laid on a table. Soft music vibrated through the room, and an orange glow covered the ceiling and the walls. Two more white beings came to the side of the table and gently talked to me, putting me at ease and into a hypnotic state. While they were talking, another white being inserted something into me. It never hurt but I could feel a slight warm feeling in my vagina. Within what seemed like minutes, the familiar tall white being was at my side again, helping me to sit up. He guided me to another place where he gave me a strange tasting tea that was rather sweet.

"He talked to me as I sipped the tea. He said that I would bear a son from his seed and that this son would be special. He told me that our son would help to change the minds of men and women throughout the world with his words and deeds. He also promised me that at all times he would be near to guide and protect him. He said that at a certain age he would take our son to the Hidden City and reveal to him his higher purpose in this incarnation on earth. Tashi, your father is your teacher, Bashur."

She watched Tashi's eyes for a reaction. Tashi only smiled. Then he hugged his mother, whispering in her ear. "I know, Mother. Bashur has already told me. I have to ask, though, does my earth father know this?"

"Yes and no. He knows I was with child when we were to be married, but he does not know how you were conceived. When he found out I was with child he changed his mind; he thought I had been with another man and his ego could not stand that. It was one of the most depressing times of my life.

"I loved your father very much, but I couldn't explain how the pregnancy happened; not that he would have believed it anyway. He did not see or talk to me for many months, and you grew larger and larger within me. The only comfort I got was from my father, who kept telling me that all events were happening as they should and to just have patience. Well, he was right, but for a pregnant, young, unmarried woman, to be patient was a colossal task.

"About the eighth month of my pregnancy your earthly father came to me and asked if I would marry him. Of course I said yes. It was on our trip to the monastery to get the blessing of the lama that he told me why he had changed his mind. In the following months after he found out about my being with child, he suffered much anguish. One night he was awakened and was told, by what he thought was a spirit, that he was to marry me and raise you as his son.

"As you know, your father is a very headstrong man and refused to

225

heed the advice of the spirit, thinking the visitation was only a fragment of his imagination. The spirit came to him two more times, more insistent each time. Somewhat frightened by now, he came to me and insisted that we be married. He did love me but had a hard time getting past his stubborn ego.

"It was winter when your father and I started up the mountain to the monastery, and about half way there, we encountered a blizzard-like snowstorm. We took refuge in a cave we finally found on the side of a cliff. Probably because of the emotional strain coupled with the extra physical exertion of climbing a mountain in a snowstorm, you decided to make your entrance into the world. I delivered you that night in that small cave on the side of the mountain.

"To keep you warm your father found a pack rat's old nest and made a bed for you. I covered you with a piece of cloth I tore from my undergarment. I was exhausted and fell sound asleep afterwards. Your father never slept a wink. Sometime during the night the snowstorm stopped and the stars showed themselves.

"As he was staring out the opening of the cave at the sky, a bright white star appeared. It came closer and closer until magically the star transformed into the shape of a tall white being. It told him that he had done well and that mother and child are healthy. It also told him to stay in the cave for three days and three nights before continuing to the monastery. This relieved your father's mind, for you see, he had lost his first wife during the birth of your stepbrother.

"On the fourth morning, three pilgrims on their way to the monastery came upon the cave. They noticed your father at the entrance and called out to him. When they saw a mother and child they offered us food and helped us up the mountain. If it had not been for those three pilgrims, our journey would have been much more difficult. Whenever they sensed I needed to rest they stopped and gave me water. I remember that they always disappeared while I fed you. You never cried. You were the happiest baby. Even at birth you had knowingness in your blue-gray eyes.

"We finally arrived at the monastery and were met by the Abbot, who was then only a lama. He took us in and gave us a room in which to stay until I was stronger. He talked to us many times, saying that he had been told of this birth as well as the part he would play in the life of this child. He told me that when you reached a certain age he would send for you. He had been instructed during meditation that he would be told when that was to happen and what the lessons were he was to give you. You see, Tashi, your birth and your upbringing were very well planned from the beginning."

Tashi could not hold back the tears. He now understood much more about the strange events that had taken place in his life. He also now understood why throughout his boyhood he never quite fit in with the rest of the children or with the rest of the family. He was nothing like his older stepbrother and younger sister. Mother put her arm around him as the tears that had built up over the years poured forth. Finally, Tashi felt he could not cry any longer and opened his eyes to see Bashur standing before him.

"I believe you know your biological father, Tashi," Mother said, looking at the tall white being standing before them.

Tashi only nodded.

"Your mother wished for me to be here to help explain who we are. She has told you the story of the land called Lemuria and our part in teaching the people there. Did not the Hidden City in the mountains look familiar?"

"That's where I remember it," Tashi said, amazed that he had not thought of that sooner.

"Today I will tell you about your paternal ancestry. The planet from which I originated is called the blue planet, just as this planet was called the green planet. Back then the amount of water on Earth was a lot less. Everything was covered with green vegetation. From above it appeared as a green ball.

"Long ago, after several shifts on this planet, we, as part of the alliance, were asked to transport people to Earth from other planets that had become unsuitable to sustain life. Earth at that time was quite stable and had all the attributes necessary to enable these people to start again. Most of the pilgrims were escaping various planets that were dying for one reason or another. In some cases, power-hungry marauders whose only intent was their own gain had infiltrated their home planets.

"I was the ambassador for the alliance assigned to the earth. I directed the settling of the pilgrims, setting up cities as well as initiating educational programs, which focused on spirituality. In addition, we had teams teaching the pilgrims how to become one with this new environment to which they had immigrated.

"The population of the earth grew and grew. Its portals were open to everyone. No one was denied entry, for that would have been contrary to the principles we were teaching. We concentrated our efforts at that time on the continent that is now called Lemuria. We built the Central City as a hub for the outlying communities. It was the center for all teaching. From there we trained the teachers who then were sent back to their original communities to teach their people many of the lessons they had learned.

"Eventually, the continent became so populated that some people migrated to other continents, far from Central City. In order to monitor these outlying areas we established a fleet of small air vehicles, which dropped off a visiting teacher into one of these communities on a regular basis. If there were problems they were available to advise solutions.

"When we originally established the outposts we always included landing ports for our small air vehicles. The ports were located on the highest point of the community. In your studies of the legends of the people on Earth, you may have heard those air vehicles referred to as large white birds. In some of the drawings done by these early immigrants of Earth, the aircrafts are often depicted on walls as strange looking birds. One such group of settlers called us thunderbirds because at that time these vehicles were rather noisy and reminded them of thunder.

"The Central City monitors we sent to the various outlying villages had undergone rigorous training and were of high vibrations spiritually. Even though we discouraged it, the people revered these teachers and looked forward to their visits. Any anger or mistrust they had left over from the deceit and abuse they had suffered on their home planets dissipated after a few generations. Our teachers taught through example and only showed love toward the people, even when in the beginning the people were quite vicious toward one another.

"There was great peace throughout the earth, and its inhabitants

228

were evolving slowly toward a higher, more loving vibration. The work we were doing was much talked about throughout the other universes. Visitors from all over came to study our programs, so that they could incorporate some of the techniques on their own planets and universes. There was a tremendous amount of sharing, technically as well as spiritually, taking place during that period. We held back no information. Nothing was kept secret.

"As you may have guessed, some of these visitors, who did not have a higher intent, ended up using this newfound knowledge against us and the people on Earth. Even though higher intent was always taught as a primary principle to any technical advancement, many of these less spiritually evolved visitors ignored it.

"One area of study we were quite active in was biological or genetic engineering. Our intent was to raise the vibrations of the physical beings on Earth by eliminating genetic malformations and disease, which were out of control when we arrived here. The physical life expectancy of a human being then was only a few earth years. Tashi, at your present age, you would have been considered an old man back then. This aspect of our work interested some of these visitors greatly.

"Unfortunately, once these visitors understood it, they started using it to gain control over certain segments of the earth's human population. The visitors totally disregarded the will of the humans and genetically veiled spiritual aspects of their being by manipulating their DNA. Since the humans had learned to trust all beings, they were easy prey for these manipulators and control mongrels.

"The level of fear and negativity built to such a degree that it started to throw off the delicate balance of the entire planet. This massive negative or heavy energy combined with the natural shifting and adjusting of the Earth planet in the universe, and major physical disasters resulted. Earthquakes, volcanic eruptions, floods, and so on became more and more prevalent, especially in the outlying areas where the renegades had a stronger foothold. We sent many ambassadors from Central City to warn the renegades about what would happen to the entire planet if this continued, but our words landed on deaf ears.

"After many earth generations, the imbalance became so great that an energy shift that normally would only have been a minor adjustment in the earth's magnetic poles resulted in a disastrous planetary shift, causing much death and destruction. The only way it could have been prevented was for us to become as aggressive as the renegades were. Exasperated by this destructive progression, a few of our field representatives took action by themselves. Some of their retaliatory acts were not sanctioned by the board of alliance and those involved were reprimanded and ultimately deported to their original home planets."

Tashi remembered a similar version of this account from a story his mother had told. It was interesting but he wondered how this applied to him today.

"We are coming to that," said Bashur, picking up on Tashi's thoughts. "But first I am going to tell you a story of an outpost with which I was personally involved.

"It was a bright sunny day on Earth when I boarded the craft. One of my duties as a leader, teacher, and priest of Lemuria was to orientate the immigrant arrivals from the other planets. I had just completed a thorough orientation, both physically and spiritually, for a group of about one hundred people. I escorted them to their new settlement.

"The elders of Lemuria had decided that this group be taken to an outpost southeast of the Lemurian center. The outpost was slightly raised above an extremely wide waterway. The ground was fertile and the land was abundant with flora and game.

"The building engineers had preceded us and had nearly completed the construction of the new city. It was a terraced development with buildings constructed of large blocks of granite reinforced by a tempering technique achieved by slightly rearranging the granite's molecular structure. In fact the city was constructed in much the same way as the bench on which you are sitting was constructed."

As Bashur continued, Tashi unconsciously ran his fingers over the barely detectable tight seam where the two pieces of rock met. "They had done a suburb job. Although not the austere look of the congested Central City of Lemuria, it was organized and soundly constructed. The soft blue mist that enveloped the hillside development offered a mystical welcome to its new inhabitants.

"The door of the transfer craft opened and the taller, blonde, blue-eyed immigrants descended to their new homeland. A small crew including one apprentice priest from Central City was to live there until the immigrant's own leaders were trained to take over. Usually these outpost assignments lasted about two years, after which the apprentice priest was required to visit only twice a year.

"A special section of this new city was built to accommodate these representatives from the Central City. These accommodations were located at the top of the terraced city, close to the landing pad. It was from there that much of the spiritual training and exercises were administered.

"Once everyone was settled and oriented, my field job was complete. The spiritual apprentices from Central City reported to me regularly on the progress of the immigrants in their new environment. Only if there was a problem did I need to return. Every year, the immigrant spiritual leaders in training came back to Central City for a six-week training course. The remainder of the year, they performed the duties of the colony's spiritual leader. They taught and guided the people with watchful eyes, as Central City's spiritual ambassadors.

"For the spiritual ambassadors, working at an outpost was a requirement toward completing their own spiritual training, which, after about twenty years, resulted in a degree of mastership as an earthly spiritual leader. Spirituality itself on a soul level never ends and, of course, time is irrelevant, nonexistent, so this estimate of time and degree of mastership is only an approximation.

"After nearly a week of hovering over the new settlement, satisfied with the progress, I gave orders to the pilots to return to Central City of the Motherland.

"Over the centuries this new settlement flourished and grew. The humans' spiritualities grew increasingly stronger. They became one with their new land and its co-inhabitants, the many plants and animals that lived among them.

"Included in the teachings of our ambassadors was the study of the solar system. At night the stars were mapped and charted. The course of the moon and its eliminate on the plants, animals, and humans was studied. During the day, the travel of the sun was measured. By combining all the studies under the supervision of the teachers from Lemuria, the immigrants devised a calendar to fit their new planet. Using the calendar as a guide, the colony was able to determine when and what to plant, as well as when to schedule other events in their daily lives for the best results. By attuning their energies to that of the sky and the earth, they and their lives flowed smoothly and non-constricted, much like the river that flowed beside their settlement.

"Generation after generation, the colony lived in peace and harmony. On my few visits to this settlement, I found the people's spiritual evolvement very gratifying. It seemed to be a successful transition to a new land for a people who were originally many light years away. The size of the settlement grew, but it always maintained a balance with everything else in its environment.

"This outpost was one of many I had the pleasure of helping to build. There were many outposts surrounding the Motherland. At one point the number of people in all colors, shapes, and sizes was awe-inspiring. No one was turned away from the planet Earth, but everyone was required to attend orientation and spiritual training.

"Although their process of settling the new planet was not strictly dictated, their transitional adaptations were closely monitored by the Motherland. We found this advantageous to maintaining unity and harmony in and among the diverse population of the colonies. As a result, the planet Earth was a peaceful paradise, with the hub being the Central City of the Motherland, Lemuria. Spiritual and technical guidance radiated out like the spokes on a wheel from it.

"Once a year, when the leaders of the outposts were brought back to the Motherland for further training, small airships were sent to transport them to a special training center, located just on the outside border of Central City. As we said before, the people in the outposts referred to the small ships as large white birds.

"As time went on and more and more immigrants came to Earth from other universes, the outposts of the Motherland spread further and further beyond Central City. The spokes of the wheel grew longer and longer. For the most part, everyone and everything in this spiritual paradise remained one with each other and the open door policy continued. The earth continued to be a veritable paradise for hundreds of thousands of years. Immigrants from many universes landed on its surface with little or no restrictions.

"One day I noticed the change during the yearly training classes for the outpost spiritual leaders. A nervous, fearful overtone was present in the classes. I knew the magnetic energies of the planet were shifting, but we were teaching the people how to adjust in order to maintain an inner balance that was harmonious with the dramatic changes in the earth's energies. The energy of those attending the classes told me that they were not adjusting fast enough to keep up with the earth's changes.

"In addition, there were a number of new immigrants from the Pleiades who seemed to be at odds with the Oneness concept, which was the essence of the lessons. We had received earlier reports of power struggles between the eliminate and their celestial neighbors. With their malignant efforts being unsuccessful in their homeland, these renegade eliminate immigrated to this new planet called Earth. They found easy prey when these highly technically advanced eliminate used their technical knowledge to biologically alter some of the people and species on Earth in order to control them and thus take over positions of power. The elders in Central City had warned the eliminate, but they ignored the warnings. More and more of the colonies were falling under eliminate influence and control. Violence and separateness were their weapons.

"Because of our intricate studies of this universe, its stars, and its planets, we knew that the earth had been shifting on its orbital axis for quite some time. Already we had lost much landmass from the Motherland to water due to the slippage of one of the earth's plates. This had not proven disastrous, as we had moved the affected sinking colonies to higher grounds.

"The elders had a strong precognition that something, a lot less gradual, was about to happen. These insights were verified when one of our ships returned from another planet in the earth's solar system. They reported that much dissension and great wars were taking place on the planet closest to Earth. That planet we had seeded long before coming to

233

Earth.

"Our own ambassadors, as well as ambassadors from other planets, attempted to negotiate a peaceful resolution, but to no avail. The energy of this other planet was totally out of balance. As a very technically advanced planet, if it did not regain its balance, this turbulent planet posed a definite threat to the other planets in the solar system, and especially to Earth. An interplanetary catastrophe was a probable result if the warfare continued.

"In the meantime, as the gases on the sun continued to explode and implode at an increased rate and the magnetic poles of the earth continued to shift dramatically, Lemuria's landmass continued to decrease in size. At the same time, the lands around the continent continued to rise higher and higher, and as the plates under the water slipped, the water rose. Masses of land were pushing back and buckling up more with each shift.

"I was on an investigating mission when catastrophe struck. Many of the other elders as well as myself had boarded a research spacecraft. Our assignment was to circle the earth, to chart and record any changes to its physical terrain and to its energy flow. We were to record the degree of changes in the magnetic grids and to check each of the portals."

Tashi wanted to ask what a portal was but didn't want to interrupt the flow of the story.

Hearing his thought, Bashur said, "Portals are places where the magnetic energy converges and creates a vortex and an opening to other dimensions. Our craft was hovering outside Earth's atmosphere when a huge shift took place. Our instrument readings went haywire.

"Then we saw it. Coming from the direction of the planet closest to the earth were huge chunks of what appeared to be debris. They were heading straight for Earth. Before our eyes we saw the debris hit the earth. It made an impact somewhere in the vicinity of the Motherland. The force was so great, it reverberated into Earth's orbital space, throwing our craft further from the surface of the earth.

"When we looked back toward the planet all we could see was a gray smoky mist enveloping the entire sphere. We knew we could not safely return to Earth's surface anytime soon, if at all, so we set a course for Uranus.

"Now back to my story about the settlement of the terraced city before the catastrophic events took place. I believe you now call this city Machu Picchu," Bashur said, taking a pause as though changing the dial on a radio.

"At this point in the priest-in-training's studies, it was time for him to return to his people. His intense course of studies in Central City had been completed. My assistant was to do the actual monitoring of this priest, 'medicine man' or 'shaman' as his people called him. The assistant's assignment included helping the new priest to reenter his own tribal culture as well as to help him introduce the new ideas of health and spirituality that he had learned while studying in the Motherland's academy.

"Maintaining high-vibration consciousness in the spiritually antiseptic environment provided at the academy was one thing, but to practice and teach these principles at an outpost created a new challenge and was the ultimate test for a newly graduated priest. Preserving his higher consciousness in an environment where the people's main concern was how to survive the elements always proved to be very difficult challenge.

"During this time, we had chosen the member with the most pure energies from each pod of each tribe to train. Over the years, the number of pods or grouping of each tribe's students had grown considerately."

Tashi wondered why they were called pods. The only pods he knew of were on plants. Again hearing his question, Bashur explained, "Central City was built like a cluster of beehives. Each beehive was divided into pods. In each pod were the students chosen to represent a particular village or community. The priest-in-training I am speaking of came from the pod where the students from Machu Picchu lived and studied. Each student had his own cell within the pod.

"This priest was completing his required twenty years of training. I was not disappointed with his evolvement. Normally I would not have accompanied a graduate on their return, but over the years I had become especially interested in and pleased with the spiritual evolvement of this particular graduate. He was on the verge of receiving his highest-level stones, turquoise. We considered this stone of great symbolic significance because it represented the bringing together of the green earth with the color of the blue planet, the planet of our origin, thus indicative of universal knowledge and love. The symbolic insignia containing the turquoise was rarely presented, for most students usually fell short of the final requirements for this prestigious degree.

"The candidates were put through rigorous tests for many years before any degree was completed, the turquoise degree being the most rigorous and lengthy of all the tests. In our thousands of earth years only three other earth beings had qualified to receive these honored stones for their spiritual achievement. The only remaining requirement that this present graduate priest needed to complete was to choose twelve disciples and to teach them the basic ways of the masters.

"My assistant accompanied the Machu Picchu priest to monitor his progress and report back to me the results of the priest's teaching among his tribe members. I remained in the craft and hovered above his land in the Mothership until the twelve disciples were chosen. The potential master candidate met with me personally on board the craft once a month for the first three months, in order for me to critique and guide his progress. As we had experienced in the past, there was always the chance that he might backslide when he was in his own environment and under the pressure of his new leadership position.

"Of all the assignments I had been given on this planet of duality and free will, the priest-in-training program was by far the most challenging for me. The Supreme Being made it clear to the council that great attention was to be given to this assignment. This universe had had a number of failures in the past. In every previous solar system where I had been assigned, when the vibration level of its energy rose, we lost a number of planets. Even in this present solar system of which Earth is a part, the inhabitants of a planet ultimately blew up their homeland, due to an inadequate vibration level in the spirituality of its people, as I described earlier.

"The council had called on me to intensify the spiritual teaching program on Earth. This was to be a concentrated program so that the people were prepared and in harmony as the planet's vibrations continued to rise. We were now coming close to another phenomenal raise in the vibrations that would surely mean a definite shift of the planet Earth on all levels.

"But let's complete our story of the fate of that Lemurian outpost in the mountains of what you now call South America during and after the shift. We had retrieved several of our ambassadors during the catastrophe by pulling their energy back to the safety of the Mothership. We achieved this by a process similar to the one we used to send you back to the cave after your visit to the Hidden City, Tashi."

Tashi thought, *That explains my being back in the cave with no recognition of how I got there.*

Bashur continued, "This is the report of one of our ambassadors that was located in the terraced city until we pulled him out.

" 'One day the earth rumbled and the air filled with red sparks and gray smoke. Torrential rains came, and many were swept away and drowned in the swollen rivers. The falling boulders that came after each violent shake of the ground killed others. Some escaped to other areas or found refuge in caves. They lit fires with hopes that help would come from the large, shiny white birds that they were so accustomed to seeing coming and going before the catastrophic event. No one came.

" 'After many years, the earth stopped shaking and the water receded somewhat. The blond, blue-eyed beings, once inhabitants of the peaceful colony called Machu Picchu, were found by a dark, rather fierce race of beings. The dark descendants of the Pleiadian renegades coerced the naïve, loving, blond people to their camps where they were used as slaves. They forced them to rebuild the outpost, but without the assistance of the beings from Central City, the building was crude and not of its original quality. The blond women were used for sexual pleasures and often sacrificed in the name of the gods. Eventually all learned to live in fear and none of the original fearless love energy remained. End of report, your loyal disciple, Manir.'

"Hovering above the earth's fiery atmosphere, we watched as though we were watching a July 4th fireworks display in the United States or a New Year celebration display in the Orient. There were continuous explosions and implosions. We retrieved most of our ambassadors and their reports. We returned one more time after the earth had settled down and retrieved the remaining few.

"We felt sadness, for we had a parental concern for the thousands of beings originally from all over the universe, which we had transplanted to this planet that was once a paradise. In the aftermath, the renegades, who were mostly from the Pleiades, had been gaining a greater foothold and were successfully undermining our teachings. More genetic experiments were performed on the immigrants to Earth with very little resistance. Separatism and duality were becoming quite prevalent.

"The concept that everyone and everything was interconnected and could be felt as one, coming from the same source, was fading with each new generation of humans. No longer were the people able to feel, at a primal level, the higher consciousness. The ego and the higher self within the human became two separate and opposing entities. For example, Tashi, when you recklessly killed your mother's rooster without thought that you were also killing a part of yourself, but merely seeing it as an act of power over a weaker living thing would be considered separatism in action.

"The ideology of religious or political sects convinced that their beliefs are the righteous way and therefore qualify them to destroy all others in the name of God is also separatism. On an individual basis the dualistic concept that your spiritual side is separate from your physical side is what created the separatism to take hold and grow like an extremely contagious disease.

"The universal coalition told us not to interfere except where it directly affected us. Most of the infiltration was on the fringes of our Central City in Mu. When the continent of Mu started to shift and sink, and then finally imploded, we were given orders to leave and to take with us only those who believed in the Oneness we had taught.

"Even before the implosion the alliance had begun transferring whole colonies of the more highly evolved people to other locations in the universe. They were to be returned to Earth when the dust settled, and then we were to leave.

"If we had stayed on Earth, it would have meant certain warfare with the renegades. For us to reestablish the Oneness way of life on

Earth, the technically advanced, separatism advocates would have had to be forcibly removed from the planet and the original genetic makeup reinstated. If we forcibly removed the separatists we would then be committing the same offense as the separatists. Our orders were to evacuate without violence or force.

"Many thousands of earth years passed before I received new orders to return to this planet. On a regular basis, we had received reports from our scouts, who lived beneath as well as hovered beyond the Earth's surface. Geologically the planet had basically stabilized, though still a bit wobbly on its axis. Spiritual decay among its inhabitants was prevalent. Through mismanagement of their technical skills, the people led by the Pleiadian renegades had succeeded in sinking another continent in the Atlantic Ocean. It had become the headquarters for most of the renegades. Its philosophy was that of greed and control.

"After that disaster, our ambassadors were sent to Earth as humans to spread the word of Oneness, and they have continued to do so through the centuries right up to the present time. Unfortunately, most of the teaching was rejected. Many times our ambassador's human bodies were destroyed.

"In order to prevent a similar catastrophic incident as what had previously happened on Earth's warring sister planet, we were ordered to establish outposts both on the planet as well as outside its atmosphere. By then, we had a mere five thousand years to infiltrate and dispel advocates of duality (that condition of humanism where intolerance is the optima) before the energies of the earth were ripe for another planetary crisis.

"Before fleeing, after the sinking of Lemuria, we had taken the prophecies and sacred knowledge, which were stored in Central City and hid them at various places in the earth. When the conditions were right, we were to bring the teachings out of hiding and put them into practice again. A headquarters was already established on Uranus with representatives from most of the galaxies who were interested in the wellbeing of this valuable planet.

"When I returned to Earth, I was to direct a group to make every attempt to return the sense of Oneness, but in a peaceful way. My primary assignment was to establish central cities on or within the earth. Our scouts had narrowed down the possible locations for these cities to three. One was below a large lake in the mountains of what is now called the Andes, which is very near to some of the Lemuria outposts I had helped to establish those many thousand of years ago.

"That location could be protected easily and it had a natural source of energy, something like what you know as uranium. From there our ambassadors radiated out to all reaches of the earth. Subterranean as well as surface outposts were established. The earthlings populating the surface area were few; therefore, there was less interference from outside forces. As far as the separatists were concerned, these locations on Earth seemed of little importance compared to the more populated areas. Besides, most of the renegade factions were interested in gaining control of the masses rather than worrying about our apparently non-combatant group. Our ships were free to come and go with little to no intervention.

"The native population of this area in the Andes accepted us and often referred to us as water gods, for our bases were located beneath the surface of the lake they called Lake Titicaca. During our absence, the explosions and implosions had ceased.

"When the landmasses east and north of what was now Lake Titicaca had sunk, the earth buckled up even higher than it had at the time that Mu had disappeared. Volcanic activity caused a bowl-like crater to form in the buckled up mountains, which filled with water and formed Lake Titicaca. Except for those caught in this region during this upheaval, the area was basically uninhabited. The present day natives are distant relatives of the immigrants we had transported to this region many thousands of years before. Because of genetic experimentation and interbreeding, their memory cells had been veiled, but not as extensively as other sects of the Earth's population. As a result, some of the symbols from our teachings show up in their artifacts from time to time.

"Our engineers constructed an efficient complex under the water. Special materials were imported from our homeland planet. The materials we used were not available on the earth, but compatible to it.

240

At first, a relatively small crew inhabited this city under the lake, but as time went on our Mothership bought more inhabitants in order to gear up our force on Earth.

"The new arrivals were trained, and then sent out into the field to undermine the separatists and to bring as many beings as possible back to the Oneness concept. Interbreeding with the Earthlings on the whole was strictly forbidden. However, genetic healing centers were made available to those who were spiritually ready to undergo the transformation.

"Some of your earthly myths and legends tell of our subtle transformations and teachings. Because of a veiled memory, we were often referred to as gods or super-beings or angels. Some of our ambassadors actually took the three-dimensional human form and walked among the earthlings, as they have been doing ever since.

"The separatists constantly challenged our more outspoken ambassadors. Often we found it necessary to rescue them from their earthly three-dimensional bodies, as the separatists sought to destroy them. Unfortunately, this spiritual battle is still going on today.

"The climax to this war may be near, for our orders have changed. We have been instructed to guard the earth's portals and not allow beings from afar who are less spiritually evolved to enter the earth's aura. We have put a stop to their genetic experiments.

"Because of the rise in the vibrational forces of this planet, many souls who are not ready or willing to let go of their slower, denser energies are finding it difficult, if not impossible, to live on this planet. These souls who are leaving their human Earthly bodies are either returning to spirit, as in the case of the native humans, or to their original alien forms and home planets.

"Some of our separatist enemies have migrated to the planet you call Mars, where they have set up a base of operation from which they continue to bombard the earth and its people with the heavier negative energy. Unfortunately, some of our more vulnerable human ambassadors have fallen prey to their attack. Many humans have allowed themselves to be infiltrated by this heavier energy and operate under its influence. Ultimately, this heavier energy destroys the human form. It has crippled many of our Light worker ambassadors.

"From non-interfering, non-aggressive spiritual Light workers, we have now become warriors of the Light. Our most effective and primary weapon is the energy of universal love. Showing humans how to accept and use this invincible energy in the most productive way is our main course of teaching.

"Tashi, you were one of our ambassadors and teachers during those earlier times. After the vast destruction, you volunteered to incarnate as a human to raise the spiritual vibrations of its inhabitants through your teaching on the earth. You have walked the earth under many guises. If it had not been for your work and many others, the people of this planet would have destroyed themselves long ago. We have always been here to support you and the others just as we are now. Your mother has played her part as well. Your mother and I are not strangers. Only two thousand years ago we attempted a feat similar to the one we are attempting now. She, as a human, had agreed to be seeded by us and bear a more evolved human: you. Courageously, you walked the land teaching our higher principles. In order to get the support and attention of the people, you performed what they considered miraculous acts. By then the people on Earth had regressed to a rather primitive state.

"In some areas, the veils were not as thick and you had great success. Places where you were more successful are located in lands surrounding the Central City of Lemuria, where our influence was more deeply rooted. In others areas farther from that influence, the people are heavily veiled, and as a result, negativity and fear are at all-time highs. You might recall in your DNA memory that two thousand years ago, when you were in one of the less-evolved areas, we were forced to snatch you to safety before the people destroyed your human body. You became quite a martyr as a result of that event. Even so, that region and its people have not evolved much since. Your mother continued some of the teachings there after you went elsewhere, but overall the people were simply not ready to listen. As had transpired repeatedly before, your teachings were twisted to suit certain people's greedy desires.

"Tashi, you volunteered again. During this assignment or incarnation on Earth, you will travel and teach throughout the entire planet along with the other ambassadors, some of whom you met recently at the Hidden City. The total universe has raised its vibrational level, the earth as well. If changes in the vibrations of the earth's people do not follow suit, there will no longer be inhabitants on this planet. The planet's people will die, as have other inhabitants on other planets when there were changes in the vibrations of the universal energy. The earth is a key planet in its solar system. If it were destroyed there would be disastrous repercussions far beyond Earth's stratosphere.

"You have already met in the Hidden City the men and women with whom you will be working directly. They are now located all over the earth. This means much traveling for you. We will help in this area, but do not be concerned with those details at this time. Concentrate instead on improving your connection to the universal knowledge and your communication with the spirit guides available to you.

"You have had a tremendous amount of information given to you in the past few weeks. We understand how disturbing this must be for a human to digest, but Tashi, there is a part of you that is not bogged down by earthly limitations. When you feel this inner frustration, call upon your high-vibration spirit, which is half of whom you are. It will help you through those times. Do you have any questions?"

Tashi was not prepared to ask any questions. His entire world as he knew it had just been turned upside down. The new skills, which had surfaced lately, were growing stronger by the day. At times they were even a bit frightening, especially when whatever he was thinking happened almost immediately. His telepathic skills were more accurate and a natural part of him. Distinguishing between what had happened, what is happening, and what will happen was becoming easier and easier. Transporting his physical body from one place to another was still a skill he had not mastered. His ability to channel high-vibration energy to another person, thus healing a defect in that person, was sporadic but improving.

Hearing his thoughts, Bashur said, "Yes, it is more important than ever in the history of the earth for people to be as conscious of what they think as much as what they say. Thoughts are always manifested into action, and now there is no longer a time lag as there was in the past.

The thoughts are becoming apparent in the third-dimensional world almost immediately after the thought is created in the mind.

"Some people will not realize that they are creating the havoc in their lives with their own destructive thoughts. Helping them to become aware of this fact will be a primary goal for you. This will not be an easy task, since they do not understand the importance of becoming one within themselves as well as with the source. They are still deferring the responsibility for their lives to an outside entity, whether it is a leader of a religious organization, a government, or even a fearful God."

Tashi looked at Bashur and his mother. He humbly asked, "Will I ever overcome my self-doubts that I am not qualified to take on this monumental task?"

His mother smiled, and he was certain that Bashur was also smiling. Even though his face did not express it, there was a smile in his cobalt blue eyes as well as in his thoughts, which Tashi found were easier and easier for him to tune into.

"Those doubts are a characteristic of the human lower ego, which will grow less in strength as your higher vibration becomes more dominant. If you did not experience human doubt yourself, it would be more difficult for you to understand and have compassion for those who have given over their lives fully to the lower ego's power, fear, and self-doubt. Embrace that human attitude, doubt, and it can become your friend instead of your enemy. Tashi, it is when you admit that 'you do not know' that the door to knowing or knowledge is open.

"I think that is enough for today. I will leave you with this. Even though your task on Earth will be arduous, do not let the seriousness of the task take precedence over the bigger picture. Enjoy the journey and permit it to be fun. Seriousness itself is a heavy energy, so if you do not mind the pun, lighten up."

With the words "lighten up" still hanging in Tashi's mind, Bashur's image faded out of his sight. Mother took Tashi's hand, and they both just sat looking into each other's eyes. "Let us start for home. We will come here again soon. There is more I need to tell you," Mother said, breaking the almost spell-like atmosphere. She knew her son had had enough surprises for one day, although she thought he took the idea of

Bashur as his father almost too calmly.

"Tashi, feel free to discuss with me any questions or concerns that may arise. It is very important that you feel comfortable with all this new awareness. A major part of my mission in this lifetime is to help prepare you for your upcoming tasks."

"I will, Mother, thank you. You have already made it easier for me to understand. You have always been so patient with me."

They walked in silence the rest of the way home, deeply absorbed in their own thoughts.

Chapter Thirty-Eight

Mother and Tashi Return to the Village

It was late afternoon when they entered the edge of their village. One of the small village boys was running toward them. They hastened their steps to meet him. He barely had enough air in his lungs to tell them what was so urgent.

"You must come quickly," he said, taking a breath before he could continue.

"Something awful has happened," he continued, stopping to take another breath as he walked backward trying to speak at the same time.

Mother stopped and took hold of the lad's shoulders saying, "Take a deep breath and calm down."

He did what she instructed him to do, but not without several gasping attempts. Feeling him relax a bit in her hands, Mother asking, "Now, what has happened?"

"A group of Chinese soldiers . . . came into the village. . . . They were looking for young men . . . to work on the project at the lake. . . . They took three of them by force . . . Waka's father resisted and they beat him with the end of their gun. He is bleeding very badly."

"Are they still here?" Mother asked, more concerned for Tashi's safety than Waka's father at the moment.

"No, they left but will be back tomorrow. Tashi, they know about you and thought we were lying when we told them you were not here. You must hide, Tashi, or they will take you as well. Your father sent me to warn you. No one knew exactly where you were, so I was to wait on

246

the edge of the village," the boy said, finally calm enough to talk without gasping.

Mother looked at Tashi and said in a commanding voice, "Let us hurry and help Waka's father. Then we will pack provisions and you must leave."

"But Mother, if they know of me they will take it out on Father and you when I am not there."

"We will be all right, but you have a more important mission than laboring on a mining project. Come, let us hurry."

They ran to the house of Waka's father. He was lying on a mat. His breathing was very shallow. Mother pulled some herbs from her pack and placed them under the unconscious man's tongue. Tashi took a deep breath and placed his hands gently on the man's chest. Within a few minutes the man's eyes fluttered and then opened a crack. Seeing Tashi, he said in a gravely voice, "You must leave, Tashi. They are coming for you tomorrow." Then he lost consciousness.

Tashi looked at his mother, and he could see the fear in her eyes. "He will recover but it will take a long time," Tashi told her, trying to take her attention away from her concern for him.

"I will minister to his needs, but now you must get ready to leave. You must hide. I think you know where to go. Let us prepare for your departure. Hurry, we must not delay."

They hurried to their house. Father and Tashi's sister were anxiously waiting. Father hugged Mother, and Tashi's sister embraced him not wanting to let go when he tried to back away. They had all been very frightened by the events of the day.

"Thank goodness you were not here today, Tashi, but you must not be here tomorrow either. Where can he go?" Father asked, looking at Mother.

"He has a place he can hide, but I think it best no one knows of it. It will be safer if only Tashi knows it. Now help me get together some of his things and some provisions."

Without hesitation they each went to work preparing for Tashi's departure. Tashi climbed the ladder to gather some of his belongings. He carefully wrapped the new tunic his sister and mother had gifted him.

Something told him he would probably not be back to his beloved village for a long time, if ever.

When he went downstairs, he saw that Mother had packed a bag of provisions, mostly dry foodstuffs. "Tashi, this should sustain you until it is safe for me to bring you more. Make certain you collect an ample supply of water on your way to your hiding place."

"Here is a knife I want you to take, and your slingshot. They will help you to gather more food when this runs out," Father said, not wanting to show the fear in his voice.

"But if I am not here and they know of me, they will take it out on you or Mother. I will not leave and worry about you being hurt or worse," Tashi said, expressing the consequences of his flight.

"We will be fine, Tashi. You know that you have more important things to do in your life than to labor in one of the Chinese camps. You must do this for the good of all," Mother said, trying to hide the tears that were swelling in her eyes. She knew she was right but she also knew that they would indeed suffer some consequences.

"Come now, you must hurry so that you are far away before dawn. I will walk you to the edge of the village. We will talk on the way."

Tashi hugged his father.

"Take care of yourself, son. Our love will always be with you," Father said, patting his son's shoulder with endearment.

Tashi hugged his sister, thanking her again for the beautiful tunic and telling her he would always feel and remember her love whenever he wore it. By this time she was not holding back the tears and as a result could only mumble, "I love you, Brother."

He gathered the satchels of provisions and his meager belongings and followed Mother from the house. By now it was quite dark. Night comes early in the mountains. There was no one present on the streets or in the square. Everyone in the village was cloistered in their houses where they felt safe from any outside invaders. Only occasionally could one see the flicker of a light through a crack in the doorway as the curtain fluttered with an intermittent breeze.

At the edge of town, Mother stopped. "I will leave you here. You know where you must go. Bashur will help you when you need it. When

I feel it is safe, he will take me to you, but not before. Remember always, Tashi, everything happens for a reason and we must accept that it happens for the higher good of all. Keep that higher purpose in mind especially when events in the world upset you."

Then, as though seeing the future and wanting to prepare him for it, she added, "We never die. We just change to a different form. We incarnate to learn and to help others to learn and when our tasks are over we no longer need to remain in our bodies. Go with love, my special son." As her words trailed off, she hugged him for what seemed a long time. She abruptly turned and walked away, fading into the darkness.

Tashi stood there for a long moment feeling as though someone very special had just walked out of his life. He turned and started the climb to his secret cave. He wondered how long he would need to hide, but decided that he would know when he was meant to know. Right now he concentrated on what it would take for him to survive in his new domain. He knew the yogis were adept at surviving for months, even years, on very little food and with very little shelter, but he was no yogi, nor did he desire to be one. What was it Bashur had told him when he departed the hidden mountain city? "Live only in the moment." He hoped he had the fortitude to do that, but at this moment his human doubts were at an all-time high.

The image of Waka's father's bloody body kept appearing in his mind. The thought of his father or mother being beaten made him sick to his stomach. He had heard about the Chinese's brutality, but previously the Chinese had not really been a problem to his village, probably because it was so remotely located. However, since the project near the lake, they had become a bigger threat.

He had heard stories of them entering villages and forcibly recruiting all the young men for their workforce, but he had never before understood the gravity of it. *I guess no one ever does until it affects those close to them,* he thought, talking out loud to himself. He hated the idea of putting his family in jeopardy for his freedom, but his mother had been so emphatic about his leaving.

Chapter Thirty-Nine

Tashi Hides in His Cave

The moon was overhead when he arrived at his secret cave. Even though the moon had lit the path to the cave, traveling had been slower in the mountains at night than during daylight. The path was narrow, and often newly fallen trees or rocks were unexpected obstacles. One such rock, hidden from his view in the shadows, caused him to fall, resulting in a scraped and bruised knee.

He lit one of the nearby plants often used for a lantern and entered the cave. He paused when he heard a small amount of scurrying. Determining that the noise was only coming from the pack rats, he continued. He had no desire to share the cave's space with a bear or a mountain lion. On his trek to the cave, he had gathered some dried sticks and weeds that were lying in his path. For tonight he would use them to build a small fire, but tomorrow he would search for proper fire material. He didn't know how long he would be forced to call this place home. He tried to keep his mind focused on survival rather than on the events that had turned his entire life upside down in this one week.

He laid out a mat, and with the food pack as a pillow, permitted sleep to come. It was a restless sleep. Images of his family in distress awoke him. In his dream, he had seen his mother lying motionless on the floor of their house. His sister was in the corner screaming, and his father was crying over his wife's still body. Tashi calmed himself by rationalizing that the images were only a bad dream.

Primarily because of pure physical and emotional exhaustion, sleep finally came to him again. This time his dreams were filled with images of Althea next to him. He awoke to a beam of sunlight filtering through the cave's entrance with her image still in his mind. Somehow mentally seeing her made everything seem as though it would be all right. Even while he searched his pack for something to eat he held onto this feeling of her.

He opened his food pack and pulled from it a stick of yak jerky. His stomach reminded him he had not eaten in a long while. While nibbling on the jerky, he made plans for the day. The first thing he did was gather fire material and any roots or berries he could find. He knew there was a small spring nearby so he filled a water bag with its fresh water.

The morning passed quickly as he completed his self-assigned chores. That afternoon he climbed to a high rock to view the valley that he had hurriedly departed from the night before. He was actually too far away to see his village, but he could see the general area of where it was located. The high rock was also a good location to spot anyone on the path up the mountain. Even if the Chinese followed him, they would have a difficult time finding the winding narrow path to the cave. It was well concealed by overgrowth.

He sat atop the rock for a long time, gazing across his beloved valley. Opposite him, far away on the other side of the valley, he could see the snow-capped peak of Mount Everest or Qomolangma, meaning snow goddess, as it was called in Tibet. The familiar view and the quiet of the mountain helped him create peace within himself. He must have sat there for a long time, and he only realized the duration when he became aware the sun was beginning to go behind the mountain. In the shadows of the forthcoming darkness, he carefully made his way back to his cave.

He was pleased to see that the pack rats had not bothered his things. He put one of the smaller boiling bags on a tripod and placed it over the fire he had started with the fire fuel he had gathered. Tashi pulled out the tea his mother had packed and placed some of its leaves in the bottom of his cup. When the water was hot, he poured it on top of the leaves. Warming his hands on the outside of the cup, he waited for the tea to brew. The first swallow warmed his insides and caused a gurgling in his stomach. He satisfied its call by taking one of the barley cakes and eating it. He popped a few of the berries he had gathered into his mouth, and their sweetness calmed some of his inner anxieties.

With his hunger satisfied, he lay back on his mat and soon was in a deep sleep. No dreams interrupted his slumber that night, and when he awoke he felt much more hopeful and energetic. His mind was much clearer as he made plans for the day.

He spent the morning gathering more fire material and edible roots. He ate a few of the turnip-like roots, which he had collected, washing them in the spring while he filled another water container. He kept himself so occupied with his survival tasks that only occasionally did the fate of his family enter his mind. When it did, Tashi felt a stabbing pain in his stomach. Several times his mother's last words replayed in his head.

Depositing his gatherings in the cave, he climbed to the high rock again. Looking in the general direction of his village, he spotted a cloud hanging above it. Since the sky was perfectly clear, it was easy to determine that the gray cloud was smoke. He knew that stove fires could not create that large of a smoke cloud. He closed his eyes and astral, or mentally, traveled to his village, a skill Bashur had encouraged him to practice.

Uncontrolled tears came to his eyes when he saw the source of the smoke. His house was burned to the ground and only the charred mud bricks were left in its place. He searched the village for his family and finally found them in a neighbor's house. His father was the first one he spotted. His face was blood-streaked and blackened with smoke. His sister was curled it the corner asleep, her face also blackened with soot, which outlined the tear streaks. He continued to explore, wishing he were better at this remote viewing, when he spotted his mother laying on a mat. Her breathing was shallow, but she was still alive.

His first instinct was to jump up and run down the mountain, but rationality took over. If the Chinese were still there, his family would have suffered in vain if he permitted the Chinese to capture him. He was torn in two by guilt and his promise to his mother to remember the "higher good of all." He closed his eyes and asked for guidance. After a few moments of breathing deeply in an attempt to relax and let any guidance find its way to his conscious mind, the image of his mother appeared before him. She was dressed in a bright white gown and appeared unharmed and younger.

"Tashi, listen closely. It is time for me to leave. You must not go back to the village for any reason. There is a spy within our own village who would deceive you because of his fear for his own safety. Stay in the cave for a while and then make your way to the border. You will be guided to refuge and to a safe place. The Chinese found some of the writings I had from long ago and determined that I was an enemy of the state.

"When I left you at the edge of the village, I had already foreseen this happening, but if I had told you I was afraid, you might not have gone. It is in the bigger plan for you to be free to do the work that you are meant to do. Your sister and your father will physically and emotionally persevere this ordeal. They will help and comfort one another. Killing me has satisfied the Chinese's need to show their strength and power. They will not return to our village. They have taken what they want. In one week Bashur will come to you and give you the guidance needed so you can flee from this country."

Before he could object, she faded from his view. Tashi sat on the rock weeping for most of the afternoon. Why must people be so cruel to one another? Feeling hollow, he climbed down the rock to the sanctuary of his cave. He found it difficult to not go back to his village and take revenge on this traitor of whom his mother spoke, but something within him made him abide by her instructions. The thought of Bashur visiting him helped him to get through the following week. As promised, Bashur appeared at dawn seven days after his mother's visit.

Chapter Forty

Bashur Visits the Cave

Tashi awakened before dawn with a jerk. He opened his eyes and saw Bashur standing before him. Had a week gone by already? He had felt numbness within him since his mother's spirit had visited him. The presence of Bashur gave him a safe feeling that he had not felt since his mother and he had entered the village the night of his flight to the cave.

"It is time to leave, Tashi, but first I must instruct you on the illusion of becoming invisible to others. You must become adept at this by practicing on your way to the border. Clear your mind of all clutter. Ask all the physical particles of your body to raise their vibrations to a speed unable to be detected by a three-dimensional human eye.

"Let me help you with this by adding my energy to yours, so that you may know what it feels like as a human. Every electron in every cell of the human body must be moving at a faster rate. When you have accomplished this, your body matter will be vibrating at a frequency in the magnetic spectrum that is undetectable by the normal human eye. Think of it as changing yourself from a solid state into a gaseous state. In this state only a highly evolved human will be able to detect you; soldiers whose intent is to harm you will be full of heavy low-frequency energy and not able to see you."

Soon Tashi felt a tingling through his body unlike anything he had ever felt before.

"Think only thoughts of love, Tashi, for that is the highest vibration in the universe. The purer your thoughts the more invisible you will be to humans."

Tashi accomplished this by thinking of his mother and her ability to practice unconditional love. He kept her image in his mind and felt his body become lighter and lighter. The air around him felt heavier than he was. Soon he felt himself rising from the floor of the cave. As his head was about to touch the roof of the cave a fear of hitting it came over him. As soon as this fear crossed his mind, he came tumbling to the ground. He could feel laughter in Bashur's thoughts.

"That was a noble attempt, Tashi. Now you understand the effect fear can have. With a little practice you will have mastered this skill. Practice this in this hidden cave for a week. Concentrate on nothing else except this. It will be essential to your later work as well as to your immediate safety."

Everyday Tashi sat for hours going deeper and deeper into an altered state of consciousness, visualizing his vibrations becoming higher and higher. The most difficult task was to not float to the ceiling. Bashur had shown him how to become less dense than air and yet be able to remain connected to the earth. Being shown and doing it on your own were two different phenomena. But with disciplined practice, he was able to become invisible while still walking on Earth about ninety percent of the time. He hoped that would be good enough.

As promised, at the end of the week Bashur was there when Tashi awoke.

"Now is the time for you to leave. Go down into the valley. When the Chinese are near, become invisible to them. Any animosity toward them for what they did in your village will prevent you from raising your vibrations and you will stay in a heavy three-dimensional state."

Tashi felt the anger within him rise at even the mention of the Chinese in his village. He knew Bashur felt his anger too.

"Remember, the overall plan is sometimes hidden by the human veils," Bashur added, encouraging Tashi to overcome his human doubts. "Detach your emotional ties to your family, for now all the people of the earth are your brothers and sisters, even the Chinese and the traitor who brought injury to your family. In the larger realm of things, they are only playing their part in your life's scenario. This event is only one small, yet important, spoke in the large wheel of the universe."

At his deepest core Bashur's words rang true.

"I will do as you have suggested, Bashur. Will I see you before I reach the border?"

"You will, Tashi. We will meet again. Remember to meditate at great depth every day. This will help cleanse you of any residue of anger. Take as much time as you need on this journey for it, too, has a higher purpose in preparing you for what is to come."

Bashur's misty body faded.

Chapter Forty-One

Tashi Walks Toward His Village

Tashi was full of mixed emotions as he descended the mountain into the valley below. He walked toward his village, anxious to witness in three dimensions the results of what he had seen during his astral traveling and remote viewing. As his village came into view he saw a dark aura hanging over it.

Just in case the Chinese or the traitor was still present, he stopped and rested behind a rock before entering the village. Calming himself and taking himself into an altered state, he thought only love thoughts and focused on raising his molecular vibrational frequency. The same feeling he had when he had made himself invisible for Bashur came over him now. When he felt confident enough that he could maintain his invisibility, he walked into the village.

A few people were milling around the square, making an attempt to clean up the debris left by the havoc that had ensued in their village. Tashi walked closer to the group to test his invisibility. No one looked at him; they continued talking among themselves as they stacked the debris on the edge of the square.

He heard one man telling the group, "Where is this special son now? Was it worth the life of his mother and the destruction of the family's home just so he would not have to labor for the Chinese? Why does he think he is above the rest of us? Many of us have lost sons and daughters to the mining camps or the Chinese army."

One of the women added, "She was devoted to that son, and look how he performed in her time of need. She was such a special woman. We shall all miss her. I don't believe I could be civil to that son of hers. Surely he won't have the nerve to show up here again."

Tashi had to concentrate extra hard to not allow negative thoughts to penetrate his mind. He knew that from somewhere he was getting extra strength. He sent his fellow villagers love, and heard from somewhere in his mind, "Discard their words, Tashi; they do not understand." It had felt like his mother's energy, but he could not be certain. This was so new to him. No one noticed him, so he knew he had warded off any anger or fear.

He made up his mind that he must see his sister and father one last time. He had overheard in the square that they were staying with a neighbor while their house was being rebuilt, so he proceeded to the neighbor's house. He found them there.

His sister was sitting in the corner with a blank, dazed look on her face. She did not look well. His father was sitting at the table sipping tea, talking to the man and the woman of the house. "It will take your daughter a long time to get over what they did to her mother, but it will take her even longer to overcome the trauma she suffered from being physically and sexually abused by that evil group of Chinese soldiers. I think it might be best if she stays with me for a while even after your house is rebuilt, at least until she can talk about it. I believe she needs to be near a woman at this time," the woman offered.

Tashi was shocked. He nearly lost his concentration on pure thought, but again some force waved through him and he heard the same sweet voice. "She will survive this, it is part of a karmic lesson. Do not interfere."

Tashi's father, without changing his expression, nodded his head. He could tell his father had lost his vitality, an attribute of his that Tashi had always admired.

Tashi had heard enough. He took one last long look at his sister and his father and left the house.

He saw no need to look at the body of his mother, which was to be taken to the sky burial that very day. He headed out of the village in the direction of the border. The path would take him past the turquoise lake but, fortunately, not near the mining project. He was not sure he could be near it after seeing what had happened to his entire family because he was not a worker there.

By late afternoon he came to the edge of Lake Yamdrok-Tso, the turquoise lake. He had encountered no one on the path, not even a yogi. After a few moments of reflection, Tashi sat down on a rock next to the lake and gazed out into the distance at the snow-capped mountains. His mind wandered back over his years growing up in his small Himalayan village with his well-loved family.

Chapter Forty-Two

Back to the Present

How long have I been daydreaming beside the turquoise lake? he asked himself, as he abruptly jerked back to the present. The reason for the abrupt ending to his reminiscence became apparent when he heard distant voices, speaking in Chinese. He calmed himself and cleared himself of negative thoughts. He failed at his first attempts to raise his energy's vibration to a level where he would be invisible. Hearing the Chinese had conjured an immediate burst of anger in him. After several endeavors he finally felt a release of heavy energy. The anger dissipated, and his spirit became lighter. He became invisible–at least he hoped he had, still battling his own human doubts.

This was not the time to test his skills, so he gathered his belongings and ran at a fast pace for the shelter of some nearby rocks and shrubs. He had hidden himself from view just as a small group of five Chinese stopped at the lake to rest and eat, very near to where he had been daydreaming only minutes before. Tashi watched them eating, laughing, and talking, and wondered if they were the ones who had killed his mother and raped his sister. Those very thoughts caused him to become angry and to lower his vibrations. He was visible again. He thought it was a wise decision to hide physically, although he had a suspicion Bashur would be disappointed.

The sun was only about an hour away from sinking behind the mountain when one in the Chinese group rose and motioned toward a truck that was coming down the road. They gathered their gear and headed for the truck that stopped close to their resting place. After a few minutes that seemed like an eternity the truck became a silhouette on the horizon.

Tashi came out from his hiding place when he was certain he could not be seen and started down the road in the opposite direction toward the border. He must have walked for over an hour when he was unexpectedly overcome with fatigue, either from the physical exertion of the day or from the emotional trauma, or both.

Darkness was closing in so he looked around for a place to camp that was off the road and provided adequate protection from any travelers that might be using the road at night. About fifty meters ahead he spotted an outcropping of rocks with shrubs surrounding them. They were about ten meters off the road opposite the shore of the lake. He climbed the slight incline to them and made a bed in a flat area using his pack as a pillow. He was certain any passersby could not see him, but just to be safe he decided there would be no fire tonight. He ate one of the barley cakes his mother had packed, and it brought back more memories of her and her nightly stories.

Chapter Forty-Three

The End of Mother's Story

Tashi found it strange that the story, as it flooded into his mind, began exactly where Mother had stopped prior to his current life-altering events. As he sat hidden among the rocks he felt like she was present and telling it herself. Had it only been a few weeks since he had sat at her feet listening? A tear rolled down his cheek as he heard in his head the first words of his mother's nightly story, as told through Mauri's voice.

I was not certain how long I had been asleep when Koha, the housekeeper, came rushing to me. "The priest has awakened. He wants to see you," Koha said in an excited voice. Her voice was louder than normal.

By instinct I pulled myself up and followed Koha to the bedside of the priest. I took his hand in mine and whispered that I was there. I had to put my ear very close to his mouth in order to hear the words, which seeped forth slowly.

"I have very little time left, but I must tell you more."

"I am listening, but do not overtire yourself."

"Soon, you must leave this place, for the rumbling will start and the waters will become very high, high enough to cover this place far beneath them. Do not concern yourself if some decide not to follow or only follow part way. Pāka and you must journey west and north. The rumblings will continue but you will be safe. The earth will be pushed up toward the sky and the water will not reach the top of its peaks. Fear will prevail and the climbing will be difficult.

"Do not allow others who are less insightful to sway you from a destination you intuitively are shown. The group who follows you all the way will continue to live the Lemurian spirit for thousands of years. They will be safe even after the next shift of the earth, which will come when another continent sinks into a far away ocean. Your group will remain secluded and will not be affected by the evilness and greed of the technically advanced Pleiadians and their biologically altered followers.

"Secluded and hidden high in the newly formed mountains your people will advance spiritually under the guidance of the tall white ones, who will pass on to your group much universal knowledge. Some of this knowledge includes the ability to keep your bodies functioning for hundreds, if not thousands, of years. Your son will leave this sanctuary and much later will be reborn again as a baby in a place near a river far from here. When he is older he will return to you to learn the Lemurian teaching. Once he is ready, he will leave again to teach in the place of his new birth." The priest paused.

"You must rest now," I said, taking advantage of his pause to caution him.

"No, there is more they want me to tell you," the priest whispered.

Mustering what little strength he had left in his tired body, he continued, "He will fail to sway the majority of the people in the west, but a few will heed his words, although through the years they will twist them to fit their own greedy purposes. The tall white ones will rescue him from their attempt to destroy his body and send him, while still in his human form, to places where other descendants of Lemuria have settled. He will help them remember who they really are and from where their ancestors originally came, namely the Lemurian Motherland. His teachings will continue to live in their stories and legends. Because of the presence of fear in the world outside your hidden mountain city, his body will gradually deteriorate until he returns to you in the Hidden City to dispose of his body.

"Later he will again be born in another physical form. This time it will be in a small mountain village close to the Hidden City. You will again be his mother and his biological father will again be one of the tall white ones. Before the next great shift of the earth, he will be taken to the Hidden City in order to prepare him to be sent to the far reaches of the earth.

"He will spiritually guide the people through the catastrophic events that will transpire again at that time. This time, however, he will have the direct assistance of the tall ones, especially the assistance of the one whom will be his father. Unlike the other shifts in energy on Earth, the tall white beings will be actively involved, for at that time the shift in the planet will directly affect the entire universe. The entire population of the tall white beings on Earth will come forth from their hidden locations, which are both beneath and beyond the earth's surface. Your son will know when his ministry is to begin because he will see three blue stars in the northeast." The priest's voice trailed off. The room was silent.

I sat there stunned by all the information I had just been given. The weight of his words lay heavily on my shoulders. Then the priest began to speak again in a voice stronger than before. I tried to quiet him, but the priest waved off my attempts.

"I must go now, Mauri. Remember these words, for they are sent through me from a very high source. Do not falter from your destined path nor let the weight of the responsibility depress your spirit. Follow your destiny with the joy of the creator of the universe." The priest fell silent for a final time as I saw his spirit leave his human body.

I rested for a long while, holding the hand of my dear mentor. Deep in thought, digesting all that I had been told, I was interrupted by a commotion outside the door. Letting go of the priest's hand, I entered the central room to find that Tse Tse had arrived, leading a group of men carrying Pãka on a stretcher made of bamboo stalks tied together with the sinew of an animal. I was immediately brought back to the reality of the task of helping Pãka back to health.

I instructed the group to take him to a room where I could tend to his wound. After he was settled, I inspected the wound and found it was healing nicely. His coloring was almost normal again, except for the dark circles under his eyes. Feeling secure in leaving him alone, I went to find Koha. I needed her help in preparing the priest for his celebration of passing on.

In his dream state Tashi could feel his mother pausing as though she was waiting to be told what to say next from some invisible source. Then thoughts with a different tone and energy entered his mind and the story continued.

Following the death of the priest, I became the spiritual leader of the Lemurian refugees. Pãka and I became mates after his recovery and I bore a son, named Pa'as. Not long after our son's birth, the ground started to rumble again. With each day that passed, the degree of the tremors increased. Those who had experienced the disastrous quakes resulting in the sinking of their beloved homeland many years prior felt the fear more intensely as a preamble to what assuredly would follow.

One night as I looked toward the sky, I spotted three blue stars forming a triangle. As the priest's dying words had instructed me, I gathered all the refugees and told them to prepare to move on toward the far mountains. There was some grumbling, particularly among the young people, for they had at last established a comfortable home, but the intensity of the rumbling prompted even them to follow my instructions with haste. They saw that the moving water was increasing in strength and swallowing more and more of the shore.

Everything the priest had told me took place, including the fact that some of the tribes decided to travel in a different direction than the one led by me. Some of the blonde, blue-eyed tribes chose to travel farther north, while some of the very dark-skinned tribes chose a more southern route. After a few months of travel, a few of my followers grew tired and stopped journeying all together and formed a settlement, rejecting my urging advice for them to continue on.

The remainder of my followers continued on, until one night a tall white being appeared before me. I had been meditating in a location away from the group as I did every night, when the tall white being materialized. Through my mind he sang a rhymed message.

> Soon the land will rumble and rise
> Dark again will become the skies

Atop a tree a raven will call
Gather your people one and all
Follow his flight, he will lead the way
To a hidden place where in safety you'll stay
In the dark skies three blue stars will show
In their direction you will follow their glow
High and alone, you will climb to a cave in a wall
Inside you will be met by those who are tall
Deep within, you will find a home
No longer then, the need to roam
Your son will grow and leave the rest
For all of mankind he will do his best
Beneath a lake that is turquoise in hue
Are ships that will carry him to teach others from Mu
Dearest one, your honor is great
For never have you detoured from your fate
Soon you will again live in a land filled with peace
    and love
In perfect harmony with the One above

I did as the tall being had advised and my people followed. For many moons the people followed the flight of the raven. On the morning of one of the first moons, the raven perched atop a tree, which on closer examination concealed the entrance to a cave. Every night during the treacherous journey, I looked to the skies and saw the reassuring sign of the three blue stars.

The long climb was arduous, and several of the older members of the group found it almost impossible. A number of them fell and injured themselves, but miraculously by morning they were in perfect physical condition, ready for the new day's climb. When the group was thirsty, out of nowhere would appear a stream bubbling with crystal clear water.Similarly, when the group was hungry, a grove laden with fruits, berries, and edible roots was just beyond the next turn on the path.

Every evening when we trekkers stopped, I led them in a prayer of gratitude for our safe journey. Throughout the difficult journey filled with one small mishap after another, the overall morale of the group was positive and hopeful. When there was a mishap, we banded together and assisted one another. The higher we climbed, the younger and stronger everyone became. By the time we arrived at the entrance to the cave, the group, instead of being road-worn travelers, were a highly spirited group.

A tall white being appeared before the group of adventurers on the second night that we were in the cave. "Follow me, dear ones," he said, speaking through our minds. And the people followed.

We were led deep into the inner core of the cave. We blindly followed the glow of the tall being for quite a distance, even when he unexpectedly led us through an invisible wall. On the other side of the wall was light so bright that we had to shield our unaccustomed eyes. When the group's eyes finally adjusted to the brightness, we gazed upon a valley rich in colorful flowers and emerald green trees.

In the center of the valley was an azure blue lake fed by a waterfall of crystal clear water spraying forth from a crevice in the mountain wall. On one side of the lake were brilliant white, domed-shaped buildings nestled among the patches of emerald trees. We had never seen such beauty, not even on our beloved continent of Mu. Everything in this valley was vibrant. Even the smell released by the flowers and the small pots of burning leaves and wood was like nothing we had ever experienced. Any insecurity we may have been harboring dispersed as the aromas permeated our bodies. A wave of peace and calm enveloped the awe-struck travelers.

I directed the mesmerized group "Continue to follow the tall white being."

They did, and the being led them to one of the dome-shaped buildings. There they were shown to a room with a sunken pool filled with steaming water that smelled as pleasant as the patches of flowers surrounding the exterior of the building.

I instructed them, "Take off your heavy clothing and enter the pool."

They did as they were told without trepidation. They were left alone to soak in the pool and to talk among themselves. While letting the fragrant water wash over them, they felt their bodies and spirits become rejuvenated with the magical effects of the soothing water. Along one wall of the room, neatly laid out, were white tunics, each with a colored sash to tie around their waist.

The travelers dried and dressed. Another being led the new arrivals to a room where mats were spread around the perimeter. In the center of the room was a low table filled with mounds of various foodstuffs and decanters of sweet tasting teas. Filling themselves with the much-appreciated refreshments, they had no difficulty falling into a deep peaceful sleep.

The persevering wanderers led by me felt that they had finally found a home. They lived and learned under the guidance of the many tall white beings in the hidden paradise for thousands of years, never appearing to age a day.

As was professed in the message I had been given, one night, three blue stars appeared, signaling that it was time for my son to leave the Hidden City. One of the tall white beings came for him. He was taken from the city in one of the shiny birds that continually flew in and out of the paradise valley. Although I knew I would miss my son, Pa'as, I accepted his departure, for I knew he was fulfilling his destiny and that eventually he would return to the Hidden City.

Chapter Forty-Four

Pa'as's Mission Begins

Pa'as was led out of the spacecraft into a land foreign to him. After two of the white beings escorted him through an invisible wall, they mystically disappeared. His eyes took in his new surroundings; he saw the walls of a cave. As he looked down at his body, he realized that his soul was now housed in the body of a newborn infant. Lying next to him was a woman whom he had never seen before. Beside her, a man was kneeling, a worried smile on his face as he looked from mother to child.

The poignant smell of animal dung made his nostrils burn. From the large mouth of the cave was a beacon of light, filling the interior of his new environment with a glow. He tried to extend an arm, but it was securely bound with cloth to his body. He tried to speak, but only heard the cry of a baby. He attempted to form words with even more force, but the result was a loud shriek, which startled him as well as the others present. The cry got an immediate response from the lying woman.

She gently picked up Pa'as and laid him on her bare breast, directing his mouth to a firm nipple. His mouth encompassed the damp, hard nipple and involuntarily he started sucking, an act he had seen many animals perform. The sucking action resulted in a sweet liquid running into his mouth. Surprised by this sudden flow, he choked and coughed, projecting the sticky liquid onto both of them. When the liquid was wiped away, his head was directed back to the liquid's source. This time he was prepared for the gush and drank until his small stomach

269

protruded as though he had swallowed a ball. The warm liquid had a hypnotic effect on him and when he was laid on a pile of soft straw, he fell into a deep sleep.

On awakening his surroundings seemed familiar, but he had no memory of a Hidden City or of a mother who lived there. All he could remember was the taste of the sweet sticky substance that was given to him whenever he cried out.

The years passed by and Hasue, as he was known in his new body, grew to be a tall, strong youth who helped with his father's work. He was taught many skills by this man who he addressed as father, but Hasue never quite felt as though he was a part of the family.

As he grew older, the internal uneasiness within him became more intense. He felt estranged from his brothers and sisters. He was different not just in appearance, although his vibrant blue eyes, light brown hair, fair skin, and tall, thin stature, contrasted with his siblings' short stocky builds and their almost-black eyes. His ideas and words were an even bigger contrast than his appearance. If it had not been for his mother's support and protection, the taunting physical and verbal abuse from his brothers and sisters would have made his childhood unbearable.

Local culture prescribed that he follow in his father's career footsteps, but he had no interest in it, and often found his mind somewhere else when he should have been concentrating at the job in hand. His daydreaming brought much criticism from his siblings as well as the peers of his father. One day when he felt he could take no more badgering and criticism, Hasue wandered out of his village instead of going to his father's place of business.

He had no particular destiny. He just had to go into the countryside and be alone. He found an outcropping of rocks, which formed a buttress so those passing by could not see him. Before, when he had tried to recluse himself, his brother, Tamas, always found him and lashed out at him for shucking his family duties. He knew Tamas was jealous of his special relationship with their mother and took every opportunity to demean his place in the family structure.

On this day he had traveled farther from the village than usual, making a greater effort to hide his whereabouts. As he sat among the rocks and let his mind wander, he began to hear thoughts in his head that he knew were not his own. They were so strong and clear that it was almost as though someone was speaking to him but no one was present.

As he listened and gazed into space, before him appeared a tall white being. He heard no voice coming from this being. It was like this being was speaking through his mind's thoughts. Not having experienced anything like this before, he should have been startled and even afraid, but a feeling of love emanated from the being and surrounded him, reassuring him that there was nothing to fear. In fact he had never felt so much peace or calm within him in his lifetime.

"Hello, Hasue. I have come to help you start your work. It is time you understand your purpose in being in this human body and in this place. I will help you understand and remember why you often do not feel a part of this environment."

Hasue thought he must have fallen asleep, that he must be dreaming. He shut his eyes and opened them again, but the tall white being was still standing before him. "I thought I was dreaming, who are you?"

"I come from a place that will be very familiar to you. Come, we will visit it now."

Without hesitation Hasue rose and walked toward the being. When he was within a few inches of him, a cylinder of white light surrounded them. Almost instantaneously Hasue was on board a flying ship. Looking out a window he realized the ship was setting down in a plush green meadow. Across the meadow, he saw the tops of white dome-shaped buildings. Everything seemed familiar, but he could not fathom where he had seen such a sight, except possibly in a dream. This beautiful green place was certainly a contrast to the barren country in which he had grown up.

"Today your stay will be short, but we will send for you again in the near future. Hasue, this is where you came from and these are your original people," the being said, answering questions as they formed in Hasue's mind. "Come, your adviser and teacher will meet with you for a brief time. Many of your questions will be answered by him."

Hasue followed the tall being into one of the white domed buildings and into a chamber that smelled of burning wood.

"Take a seat on the pillow, your teacher will be here momentarily," his leader directed him, both with his thoughts as well as with a wave of his six-fingered hand.

With curiosity, and surprisingly without any flicker of fear, Hasue sat and took in his surroundings.

Chapter Forty-Five

Hasue Meets with a Familiar Teacher

As Hasue sat in the small, pod-like room, another tall white being appeared. He felt an unexplainable familiarity and endearment toward him.

"Hello, Pa'as," the being greeted him through his thoughts.

"Why do you call me Pa'as? That is not my name."

"That is what you were called when your spirit lived here, but of course when you were sent out to experience another body, you were given another name that was more appropriate to your new environment. We in the Hidden City shall always know you as Pa'as, but a name is not important in the larger realms. I am called Bashur by most. I am your teacher. It is time in your current human experience to begin the work that you have incarnated to do."

"Are you saying that I lived here before? Why can't I remember?" Hasue asking, feeling confused as well as frustrated because, try as he might, he could not recall.

"You cannot remember because in order to prepare for the work you are about to begin, we believed it beneficial for you to experience your current environment and its people without any preconceived ideas or learning. Being like them will better enable you to relate to them and they to you."

"But, I have often felt that I was different than most of my brothers and sisters. In fact, as of late, the feeling has been so strong that it has caused me a great deal of anxiety. That is why I was in the hills before I was brought here. Can you explain this special work I am to do? Wouldn't it help me in accepting my current situation?"

"All in due time, my son. You will soon be brought back here for a thorough indoctrination. At that time, memory cells from your past will be activated again. Right now just trust that you are doing exactly what you are supposed to do. About your brothers and sisters, they are showing you a fear, which is that of jealousy. It is very crippling to their greater enlightenment. In this hidden city, we overcame that fear long ago. Be patient, for very soon the reasons for your present situation will become clearer."

Bashur rose to leave the room. Hesitating at the doorway, he said, "Pa'as, you must go back now. We will meet again soon."

As soon as Bashur had left, the white being that had brought Hasue to the Hidden City entered. "Let us go. The craft is waiting," he said, not waiting for a response.

With no more exchange of words (or rather, thoughts), Hasue found himself sitting back among the rocks outside his village. At first disoriented, he thought, *I must have dreamed this whole thing, but it seemed so real.* On the walk back to his village, he replayed what had happened or what he had dreamed in his mind. His confusion was strong, but at the same time he felt much peace within himself, which left him even more confused. He thought maybe if he discussed his feelings with his mother that she would help him to understand. Yes, that is what he would do, he decided during his private conversation with himself. She would help him.

His mother was sewing when he arrived home. Everyone else was gone from the house. His mother made no comment when he entered. In fact she did not even act surprised.

"I left the village today. I did not help Father with work," Hasue confessed.

"Yes, I know. Your brother complained when he came home for the noon meal. Do you wish to tell me where you went?" said Mother, laying down the cloth in her hands, thus giving him her full attention.

"Yes, I went into the hills and secluded myself among the rocks. This may sound crazy, but I was met there by a tall white being and taken to

274

a hidden city. Oh, Mother, it was so peaceful and beautiful. Another white being called Bashur met with me and told me that I was originally from the Hidden City. It was so absurd and yet it felt quite real."

"Then it is time," said Mother, trying to hide the tear that trailed down her cheek.

"You know of this place?" questioned Hasue, surprised at this revelation, and yet annoyed that he seemed to be the last one to know.

"Yes, I know of it. I, too, was taken there when I was but a young girl. They told me I would bear a son who had a special destiny to fulfill once he was a man. I guess the years have gone so quickly that I still think of you as a boy. I was told to treat you as I would treat any of my children. At times that was very difficult, when I saw and felt the pain in you from all the torment you received from the other children and villagers, but I was sworn to secrecy for your own welfare. In some ways I feel relieved that it has started. Trust your heart, my son, and you will be shown your path."

Hasue was ready to make a comment when his brother and father entered the house. His father saw the tear stains on his wife's cheeks and made no comment. However, his brother could not resist taking advantage of pointing out Hasue's laziness in front of his parents in hopes of some praise for his own responsible and dutiful behavior. The expected response never came. Instead, his words were ignored, and he was told to wash for the evening meal.

When Tamas left the house to wash, Hasue told his father that he must leave and that he had greater work to do. Looking at his wife, his father's only comment was, "It is time?"

Mother just nodded her head yes.

Chapter Forty-Six

Hasue Leaves His Home and His Village

Hasue didn't know where he was going. He just knew he had to leave. He felt himself drawn back to the place where all this began, among the rocks. He stayed among the rocks and meditated, hoping that some direction would come. His mother had told him to follow his heart. At that point he was not certain what his heart was saying. Day and night he meditated, stopping only when his body's basic needs interfered with his meditative state for an occasional bit of food and water, which his mother had given him. On the twenty-first sunrise, a glow appeared before his eyes. The bright light took a shape not unlike that of the tall white being who had said he was Hasue's teacher in the Hidden City. It spoke to him.

"Come with me. I will show you the way."

Hasue rose and followed his guide. Again he was back in the Hidden City.

There, he lived and learned of his true purpose in the land from whence he had miraculously been transported. The vibrations in his present body were raised, as his memory cells of who he really was were unveiled. He regained his ability to work with energy and remembered how to use it to help alleviate the suffering that plagued the people of Earth. He was sent out from the Hidden City into the villages of the Himalayans to practice the newfound skills in his present body. He stayed with the various lamas and monks in order to study some of the many ancient manuscripts preserved in monastery libraries. Years passed.

During one of Hasue's visits to the Hidden City, Bashur announced, "You are ready to spread your teachings among the people where you were born into your present body. Today you will be transported back to the rocks in the hills near your village. Let your God spirit prevail."

Chapter Forty-Seven

Hasue Begins His Journey

Hasue awoke and found himself among the same rocks where he had started his journey so many years before. It was as though time had stood still, and yet he reentered his village as a different man. He had left as a frustrated young man without much direction. He came back a man with a purpose: teaching his fellow men the meaning of love for all. He walked into the small village with great hopes.

Those hopes shattered when he found that his fellow villagers were not ready to hear his wisdom. They looked at him as the son who dodged his family duty by leaving. He was met with much ridicule and scorn. The frustration and anger was building in him when his mother privately took him aside.

"You must go beyond this village, for they only remember who you were as a boy. They do not understand the man who has returned."

The next morning Hasue left. He started out for the sea, though he wasn't conscious of why he had chosen that direction. He just knew in his heart that it was the path in which he was to travel. As he journeyed, he talked to anyone and everyone. He told them of God's love and that all people were one, each a brother or sister to all.

In the beginning of his teaching, most of the people he encountered scorned his words, considering him some kind of crackpot who was looking for a handout. However, as he came closer to the sea, he met a few whom wanted to hear more of what he had to say. So enthralled with his message were some that they decided to join him in his mission.

Claudette Cleveland

At some of the stopping places along the way, in order to make his point, Hasue demonstrated his ability to manipulate energy. This resulted in a 'miraculous' healing or some other sort of event. His impressed audience spread the words, and more and more listeners gathered wherever he stopped to speak. However, many still met him with the same skepticism as earlier. Encouraged by his increasing acceptance, he directed his journeys toward his boyhood home, only to be disappointed again when he arrived.

He was met with the same skepticism and ridicule there that he had encountered before. Even the miracles did not impress the people of his boyhood village. They knew about miracles. They were told about them in stories of their ancient ancestors. The people of Hasue's village could not bring themselves to believe that this simple boy could possess the same power to perform miracles as the ancient ancestors had.

Hasue again felt frustrated by the rejection of his own people. Even his brothers and sisters, who considered him a negligent son to leave on his hair-brained journeys without regard for his parents' well beings, scorned him at every opportunity, particularly his brother, Tamas. Tamas felt especially put upon because Hasue contributed neither labor nor money to the family. Tamas felt even more burdened than before since his father had taken ill and he was now carrying the total responsibility of their family's livelihood.

Hasue's visits home became fewer and fewer. The word had spread throughout other parts of the land that this man had a message worth listening to. The sick and the hungry came in groves to receive healing and food. Although the miracles were often slightly exaggerated in the retold stories, the awestruck listeners did not go away disappointed and the word spread.

Those in power in that region, particularly in the established religious sects, became very irritated with the influence that Hasue had with their flock. What Hasue taught nullified a great deal of the fear tactics that most of the religious leaders had been using for centuries. In frustration and desperation, the religious leaders banned together and contrived charges of heresy against him. By paying off a few politicians, they were able to have Hasue arrested and condemned to death as a traitor, which was the regional punishment for such an offense.

When this happened Hasue was very confused. Did Bashur not tell him he was to spread the word? One night as he was meditating in his damp dark cell, Bashur appeared.

"Do not fret, my son. Your words will not be forgotten, and we will be there for you in your time of need," said Bashur, disappearing as mysteriously as he had appeared.

Something inside Hasue told him all would be well, and he faced his death sentence with an inner peace that he had not felt previously during any of his life in this land.

On the day of his execution, the guards brought him to the gathering place where punishment was administered. Hasue was surprised that so many had come to witness the event. Even his earth mother and brother Tamas were present. Many of the spectators were wailing and crying, and calling out his name. The execution was carried out and after his body finally collapsed, he was deposited where most of the executed convicts were taken, which was a cave along the cliffs to the north. As he lay there in the cave semiconscious, a beam of light enveloped him and he was transported up into a spacecraft. Bashur was there to greet him.

"Your work is completed in this region of the earth, but there are many people in other regions who await your words. We are taking you to the Hidden City for some rest. This will allow you an opportunity to assimilate all that has taken place during your stay in this land."

Pa'as, as he was called again, enjoyed his stay in the Hidden City. His last few years of spreading the word had been filled with much anxiety, an emotion that did not exist among the loving people in this paradise land, hidden in these majestic mountains and protected from the struggles of the outside human world.

One day during one of their frequent meetings, Bashur told Pa'as that it was time for him to venture forth and continue his teaching, spreading the word as a human. His body had mended from the abuse that the execution had caused almost immediately once he entered the

Hidden City, but his spirit took longer to cleanse itself of the human feeling of failure. Bashur assured him that on his following missions into the human world, he would not be alone, but would have other ambassadors as assistants. He also guaranteed him that this time, Bashur himself would be in constant contact.

Pa'as's teaching took him to many lands. He visited and lived with people of red skin, brown skin, yellow skin, white skin, and black skin. Sometimes he arrived in their lands on sailing ships, but most of the time one of the spacecrafts used by the tall white beings deposited him in the region of his assigned missions. His missions focused on the areas of the earth where the refugees of Lemuria had scattered when the continent had sunk.

His words opened the memory cells of the descendents of the Motherland, and, as a result, he and his works were always welcomed. He was overjoyed to find a very welcoming reception in most of the new lands. His teaching continued for years and over many generations.

Not long after his so-called execution, Bashur insisted that Pa'as revisit the area near the Tiber Valley where the execution took place. Pa'as found that his closest followers were continuing to spread the word of love. Regretfully, he also discovered that his brother, Tamas, seeking the fame and fortune that Hasue had obtained, made himself a leader of a newly founded ministry in Hasue's name. Evidently Tamas's childhood resentment toward his older brother was still brewing, for he twisted a great many of the original words and teachings in order to gain more power and money. It saddened Pa'as to see this.

When he confronted Bashur with his sadness, Bashur assured him that one day he would return to that region as a teacher and the truth would be known.

Hasue traveled the earth for hundreds of years, and the legends are still told of this god-man sharing words and deeds of hope. Eventually, Hasue returned to the Hidden City where he is still a teacher of a new group of ambassadors of the tall white beings.

Chapter Forty-Eight

Back to the Present

Tashi must have fallen asleep while remembering his mother's story, for he awoke with a start. No one was around, and the sun was only slightly above the tip of the mountain. He gathered his meager belongings and started on his journey toward the border of his beloved Tibet. For several weeks he walked, stopping and hiding only when he heard voices or vehicles. He found edible roots and berries along the way, and filled his skin bag with water whenever possible. He thought he would grow weak with the lack of proper nourishment, but it was as though some kind of force was aiding his every step. Often on his lonely journey he thought about Althea, wondering whether he would ever see her or hold her in his arms again. He fantasized about their being together. It seemed to make the arduous exodus more bearable.

One day while deeply engrossed in one of his fantasies, he was abruptly brought into the present by the sound of laughter and loud voices. He immediately took cover behind some rocks. Peering carefully over them, he saw a cluster of Chinese. The border had to be very near, he thought, for there were too many Chinese in one place in such a remote area not to be close to a military establishment.

He climbed to the top of a cliff, which ran along the road. From that vantage point, he could see that up ahead was a town, which housed the bridge to Nepal. He also saw that it was extremely well guarded. He had never seen so many Chinese soldiers in one place before. If he could safely get past that barrage of soldiers, his clandestine journey would at last end, or so he thought.

He worked his way along the hillside surrounding the town. He made the decision to stay hidden until nightfall. He needed the time to clear his mind of all angry thoughts. What the Chinese had done to his mother was still vivid in his memory. Bashur had told him that only pure thoughts would enable him to become invisible.

He knew the anger was at times overpowering, especially when he was in the vicinity of so many Chinese soldiers. The thoughts of what the Chinese would do to him if he were caught made it even more difficult to concentrate on only love and purity. He knew if he could not dispel his resentful thoughts and angry feelings, his life would come to an abrupt end. The Chinese did not hesitate to shoot traitors, which is what he would be judged as. He could not allow his mother's sacrifice to have been made in vain.

He spent the remainder of the day in deep meditation. At one point, he knew he felt the energy of Bashur, probably when he was so frustrated with his efforts that he mentally yelled for help. Night came, and the twinkle of lights replaced the dirty gloomy buildings of the town. Loud music, that Tashi had never before heard the likes of, filtered toward his hideaway. Singing accompanied the music in a language that Tashi did not recognize, although he knew he had heard it before. It sounded almost like the language Althea spoke but was far harsher.

Thinking of Althea helped him to let in more love energy, and he felt himself getting lighter and lighter, but he didn't know if it was enough to become invisible to the eyes of the numerous Chinese guards. All he could do now was test it. He asked for guidance and protection, and walked toward the town staying in the shadows as much as possible.

When he entered the more populated section of the town, he immediately encountered a man who looked to be a nomad coming directly toward him. The man walked right by him without even looking up. He could not tell if his vibrations were still above those of the three-dimensional human occupants of the town or not. Most nomads kept pretty much to themselves.

He carefully wove his way toward the bridge and freedom. His next encounter was a group of Chinese, but they were more interested in the women who were accompanying them than a ragged looking Tibetan mountain man. They looked quite intoxicated, which was also to his advantage. The whole group, men and women, found their way into the doorway of a dilapidated hotel. He breathed a sigh of relief. He was still safe, for now.

The bridge was in sight and so were the Chinese soldiers guarding it. A huge metal bar stretched across the road to prevent any vehicles or pedestrians from going beyond it. He hid himself in the shadows until he was certain that he had expelled any heavy feelings toward these people who had destroyed his home and family.

He had heard that the Chinese had bribed the Nepalese with road engineering and labor on the mountain pass in exchange for Tibetans who were trying to flee the oppression of the Chinese. When any Tibetans were discovered, the Nepalese returned them to the Chinese, which generally resulted in a death sentence or at the least life in prison for the captives. One of Tashi's cousins had spoken of an uncle who had tried to sneak across the border via the river. He made it to the other side only to be sent back in handcuffs by the Nepalese. He knew this because his uncle was now dying in a Chinese prison for his gallant attempt.

While Tashi hesitated near the crossing, facing the biggest challenge of his young life, he felt a warm cocoon surround him. It brought with it a peaceful feeling of safety. He knew he was getting assistance, although he could not visibly see who or what it was. The source did not matter, for the boost in energy vibration gave him the courage to venture forth. All fear evaporated from him, and he easily strolled across the bridge into Nepal, invisible to all.

Before the Chinese made their pact with the Nepalese, the mountain pass was washed out the majority of the time, delaying travelers for days, sometimes weeks, on their journey into Katmandu. With great concentration, Tashi kept his vibrations high enough so that no one spotted him on either side of the border.

After he had traveled several miles into the interior of Nepal, he let his vibrations return to their normal three-dimensional level. Bashur had told him that maintaining that high of a vibration in a human body for great lengths of time would stress his physical mass. He had explained to Tashi that the human body was not yet evolved enough to hold such a vibration continuously.

Although he did not feel completely safe, and would not until he was in the Tibetan colony in Katmandu, he knew he could now pass as a native Nepalese traveler. Being invisible would no longer be necessary. Yet, with each passerby, he tensed.

He walked most of the night to descend the mountain, using the moon as his light; or at least he thought it to be the light of the moon. For the first few hours his energy level was so high he did not feel the least bit tired, but when his vibrations lowered, he became overwhelmed with the weariness of the physical exertion as well as with the many weeks of mental and emotional strain. It affected him so strongly and quickly that he thought he could not take another step.

He had picked up some fruit during the night outside a house in one of the villages that scattered the mountainsides. He had filled his water bag with water coming out of one of the cracks in the rock wall bordering the road. The only thing left to do was find a secure place where he could sleep in order to rest his body as well as his mind.

He knew there was still a threat, for he had been told that the road into Katmandu was filled during the day with Chinese road crews. Although there was no reason for them to suspect him as an escapee, he did not want to take the chance. He had come too far at too great a price to risk being sent back. He owed it to his mother to succeed in retaining his freedom. He found a break in the rock wall and walked through it to a grassy meadow surrounded by trees. Tashi walked across the meadow to an outcropping of rocks almost hidden by an overgrowth of bushes. He climbed in among the rocks and made a palette on which to sleep. It was the first time in a long time that he felt somewhat secure. Sleep came immediately.

Tashi had slept so soundly that when he awoke, the sun was low in the sky. He was so groggy from such a deep, dreamless sleep that it took him a few moments to realize where he was. Gradually the memories of the past weeks filtered into his conscious mind. Voices from the road reminded him that caution was still necessary.

He sat for a while, nibbling on the procured fruit and drinking more than half of the water in his bag. He needed the time to collect his wits and decide when and how he would continue his trek into the Katmandu valley.

He gathered his few belongings and climbed down to the road, stopping along the way at a small pool of water to fill his bag. He knew from living in the Himalayans all his life that at high altitudes, dehydration came quickly and could be crippling if not deadly.

When he reached the road, he saw only one other human, about fifty meters ahead of him. He could tell by his actions and dress that he was a yogi, genuflecting as he made his way to the city of Katmandu. Because of his belief that sharing would gain him merits and bring him closer to reaching nirvana, he gave the yogi some of his food. The yogi showed his gratitude by bestowing on him the blessing of Buddha.

The loving energy he received from the yogi spurred Tashi on with an increased speed in his step. Getting to Katmandu safely was no longer a hope. He knew he would arrive there without any mishaps. His self-assurance rose even higher as he sat on the crest of a hill overlooking the entire Katmandu valley. He felt like he was sitting on the roof of the world.

Off to his left was an elaborate, stately building with manicured gardens and patios surrounding it. The aroma of cooked food made its way to his nose, something he had not smelled since that fateful day his mother had sent him to hide. Unable to stop them, mournful tears streamed down his cheeks. It was the first time he had let the emotional impact of all that had happened surface.

He was unsure how long he had sat there crying, but when the tears finally ceased, the sun was seeking its hiding place behind the mountains. The sky filled with a pink hue that penetrated him, with a nurturing, comforting feeling reminiscent of the moments when his mother's touch and words had comforted him after some traumatic event in his life.

Tashi walked toward the patio from which the alluring aroma of food was coming. As he approached the edge of the patio, he saw that it was void of people, but on the tables where they had been sitting were the remnants of their meal. Cautiously, he walked to one of the tables and ate the leftovers from each of the abandoned plates. It had been so long since he had had cooked food that he was not certain his stomach knew what to do with it. Filling himself to capacity, he became very sleepy. He collected some of the more portable leftovers and stored them in his bag. Then he sought a place to rest and sleep.

It was much warmer here than in his homeland, although he knew the night would bring the same chill that was inherent in all high mountains. He found a large willow tree whose lower branches touched the ground, creating a tent effect around its trunk, and made it his inn for the night. As he lay on his palette, he listened to the sounds of the night in his beloved mountains. A melody of soft music drifted to him from the direction of the stately hotel. It had a calming effect on him. Its harmonious tones lured him to sleep.

Sometime during the night he awoke and found Bashur standing over him.

"Hello, Tashi," he said, speaking to him mind-to-mind. "Congratulations, you did very well. You have proven to yourself that you have the skills and power to overcome many human adversities. When you arrive in the Tibetan colony in Katmandu in a day or two, ask the whereabouts of a man named Tensin. He will give you food, shelter, and clothing. You will stay with him until you have regained your physical strength. After a while your friend, Althea, will be joining you there. Together the two of you will be given instructions, for your work is about to begin."

"Althea!" Tashi said, louder than he had consciously intended.

Bashur did not respond to Tashi's excitement, but Tashi thought he detected a humorous energy radiating from him.

Chapter Forty-Nine

Althea and Tashi Meet Again

T ashi was more physically and emotionally drained than he had realized. Even at the outskirts of the city, the noise of congestion was evident. Horns and loud engines irritated his innate sense of direction. Since he was a child, he had been able to sense which direction he needed to walk in order to reach his destination. He could not remember ever being lost, but because of the mixture of noise and fumes, he felt immensely disoriented. The farther he walked into the center of the city, the more his head pounded. It was so painful, in fact, that when he saw an open space he took refuge on one of the many benches scattered throughout the area.

He sat for quite an interval, attempting to cleanse and balance his energy. After a spell, his breathing eased and he felt himself becoming more attuned to the environment. He blocked the clutter of the city and its stench of fumes, which burned his nostrils with every breath he drew.

As he was about to set forth again in a direction that he felt fairly certain would lead him to the Tibetan colony in Katmandu, a young man about his own age approached and took a seat next to him on the bench.

"Welcome, I was sent to escort you to the house of Tensin. My name is Lobsang. Let us go now. It is yet a distance."

Tashi observed the familiar Tibetan pattern on his black felt vest. He spoke in Tibetan, but with an accent Tashi had not heard before. Without verbally responding, he gathered his road-worn bags and followed.

288

Lobsang pointed out various highlights of the city along their route. As they crossed the river, Gandak, he directed Tashi's attention to a funeral that was in progress. On a platform, logs were laid, crisscrossing each other, creating a funeral pyre. Layers of small brittle sticks were stuck among the logs. The deceased was wrapped in a beautiful shroud made of silk. A religious leader chanted words over the body as the deceased's family wept.

At one point, the religious guru nodded toward the two boys holding sticks wrapped in cloth, which had been ignited. Large puffs of black smoke trailed off above the flames. The two boys, one on either end of the platform, shoved the burning torches into the logs beneath the body. Creeping from log to log, eventually the entire platform of logs and body were ablaze. Tashi and his guild watched the whole structure become a heap of ashes.

As the fire ate away at the logs and body, mourners tossed wreaths of flowers and petals into the murky Gandak River. Gently, the river's current carried them out of sight.

"These people are Hindu," Lobsang explained, hearing Tashi's mental question.

"The man who died was high in rank in the military. That is why so many uniformed soldiers are present. His lifetime of service is being honored by their presence at the cremation. Let us go now. Tensin is awaiting your arrival."

Tensin welcomed him with open arms. He was the owner of a prosperous Tibetan rug factory in Nepal. Because of their quality and designs, his rugs were greatly sought after by people all over the world. In fact, his export business far outdid the sales he had in Nepal. Because of the duty-free arrangement with the United States and Nepal, his biggest customer base was in the United States.

The first week Tashi stayed in Tensin's rather large prestigious house, he did little else but sleep and eat. He and Tensin talked of their homeland at night and the changes it had undergone when the Chinese invaded. He had lost a son when the Chinese rampaged his village and burned his rug factory to the ground. During his exile to Nepal, his wife had taken ill, and she died soon after they arrived in what was to be their new home. The only family he had left was a nephew and a brother, who were both involved in his rug business.

As he told his story, Tashi noticed the sadness in his voice. Like most families in Tibet during the Chinese invasion, and especially under chairman Mao Zedong, Tensin had suffered great losses on all levels.

After Tashi's week of relaxation, Tensin introduced him to the local lama. He was much more formal than the lamas he had worked with in the monastery near his village. The Katmandu lama had difficulty believing that a peasant boy from a remote village in the Himalayans had the ability to see and heal, especially since Tashi had not gone through the rigorous training of a monk. He was reluctant to give him a private audience until Tensin used his financial influence to convince him. At one of their meetings Tashi brought out the ancient game, one of the few possessions he had carried into exile from his home.

When he showed it to the lama, he exclaimed in an accusing tone, "Where did you get this?"

"It was given to me by the Abbot in the monastery near my village," Tashi responded, trying not to sound defensive or angry, and sensing the lama's accusations.

"And where did he get it?" he asked with the same indignant air.

"It was handed down to him from the previous Abbot. It has been in the region since the ancient ones migrated to the Himalayans from the Motherland," Tashi explained, unable to hide the irritability in his voice. *How dare he question my or the Abbot's integrity?* he thought.

The lama sat in silence for a few minutes, gathering his thoughts and his next words. Tashi's quick answers had surprised him. Pulling together his composure, the lama spoke again in a much softer voice. "Do you know what the symbols mean and how the game is used?"

"Yes, I do. I have been shown by many their meaning and usefulness for my spiritual growth," Tashi explained in a gentler tone of voice.

He hoped the lama would not want to know who had explained the symbols to him. He knew he would never believe the story of the Hidden City and the tall white beings, even if Tashi had not promised to keep its existence a secret. Although he could not see him, he felt Bashur's energy close to him. Feeling his closeness helped Tashi to maintain a more tolerant composure. He knew he was very sensitive when it came to certain aspects of his human life, and his mother and her ancestry were among them.

Surrendering part of his rather inflated ego, the lama asked, "Could you show me how to use this game and explain its symbols?"

"Yes, of course," Tashi replied, hoping it would not be today. He had had enough of this so-called holy man. He vowed at that moment never to let his special gifts inflate his own ego. He promised himself that he would, now more than ever, include exercises on humility in his meditations.

After the confrontation with the lama, Tashi needed time alone to rid himself of any anger he harbored. The lama's lack of compassion was a surprise to him. He had never really been the target of a jealous rage before. It was a new feeling, and he didn't like it much.

Leaving the lama, he found a remote place on the river. Water always helped him to feel better. The way it kept flowing gave him hope. It washed away whatever was bothering him. As he sat on the river's bank, Bashur appeared before him.

"He is one of many religious leaders who has let power seize him. It is an extremely crippling disease. Thank him in meditation for showing you its spiritually crippling effects. Do not, however, take his ego's rage personally. Whatever negative reaction you had to his words was because he showed you a part of yourself that, although dormant at the moment, could raise its ugly head at any time. There is a dark side within every human, no matter how pure and light they may appear. The secret to enlightenment is to be aware of that darkness and shine your light, your love, on it until the shadows flee. Come, Tashi. Althea awaits you at the house of Tensin."

Almost immediately Tashi's spirits lifted. He could feel his heart skip a beat. Any anger he had had toward the lama dissipated immediately with the mere mention of Althea's name. He found it difficult to believe that he would feel her physical closeness again. His human doubts came to the surface. Would she feel the same about him? They had been separated, at least physically, for months. Had she met someone else?

"She is as anxious to see you as you are to see her," Bashur stated in response to Tashi's mental questions. "Now go." Bashur disappeared.

Tashi did not know he could run so fast. It was as though his feet were not touching the ground. He burst into the house, and found his breathing so labored that he could not speak. As he opened the doors to the guest sitting room, he saw her. She was sitting, quietly talking to Tensin. When he burst into the room, their conversation ceased. He felt paralyzed. His feet felt stuck to the floor. He could not move. Althea rose and came to the place where he stood. She put her arms around him. He hugged her back, being careful not to crush her in his excitement.

"I've missed you, Tashi," she said, as she held him tighter.

"I've missed you, too. Your face was always in my mind, especially when things were not going smoothly. Even in your absence you have always been there for me," Tashi whispered, holding her, not wanting to let go for fear that her presence might only be a dream.

Neither had noticed that Tensin had left the room until they both released the grip they had on one another.

"Let's sit in the garden. I want to hear all that has happened with you since we were last together," Tashi proposed, letting go of all but her hand.

Althea followed his lead to the garden. He directed her to a rattan chair under a monkey tree, which shaded them from Katmandu's intense afternoon sun. Still not letting go of his hand, she began.

"After leaving the Hidden City, I was taken back to my hometown where my parents still live. It's a smaller city outside of Chicago. Have you heard of Chicago?"

"I read about it in a book a friend of our teacher sent from India. It's where all the gangsters live, isn't it?" Tashi answered, feeling satisfied that he knew something about where she had grown up.

"Some gangsters, along with millions of other people," Althea said with a laugh in her answer. She found it interesting that the remote areas of the world got their knowledge of the United States from the sensationalism of novel writers and movies.

"Anyway, when I got home, I felt peaceful and full of love. I had dropped all the resentment I had toward my father and my mother and felt the Oneness, just as I did in the Hidden City. I guess I was so high on the energy from the tall ones that I expected a different reaction from them than what I received. It was late in the evening when I arrived there. I let myself in when no one responded to my knocking. My father was drunk on the sofa. My mother was in the den reading. My sister . . . did I tell you I have a younger sister? Anyway, she was still out with her boyfriend.

"I saw my father first. He opened his eyes when I entered. When I greeted him, he started in yelling.

"It's about time you got in," he said. He thought I was my sister. My sister and I look somewhat alike and in his drunken state he thought I was she.

"Dad, I'm Althea," I said.

"He hesitated a while and then started yelling at me. 'What are you doing here? You get no money from me,' he howled.

" 'I don't want any money, Dad. I've come to see you and Mother.' He gave no response, but his shouting brought my mother into the room.

"My mother's response upon seeing me was, 'What are you doing here?' 'I've come to see you and Father,' I told her.

" 'Oh' was her only response. At that point, Tashi, I felt like running out the door and never coming back, but I told myself that I had something to learn from them, although at that moment I had no idea what. As I stood there stuck in my tracks, the front door opened and my sister walked in.

" 'Althea, you're home!' she said, hugging me. She released me while asking me question after question, not bothering to wait for an answer in between. 'Come, you must be hungry. Let's get a snack and go to my room,' she said, looking in the direction of my father, now again passed out on the sofa.

"I followed her into the kitchen, where she gathered some snacks and a juice decanter. We carried it all into her bedroom. She shut the door and locked it. I found this strange but did not make a comment. When I had shared the room with her we had no lock on the door. She must have seen the question on my face because she commented that it was best to lock it when Father was like this. I asked no questions, although at that point I had many.

"We talked until late into the night. Life had not changed in the house since I had left three years prior. If anything, it had gotten worse, but my sister seemed to be coping with it a lot better than I had.

" 'Is Father still drunk every night?' I asked her.

" 'Yes, but some nights are worse than others. Some nights he does not come home at all. Those are the better nights. I want to hear about you, Althea. Where have you been and what have you done? I only have three months left of high school and then I, too, am out of here. I'm trying to talk Mother into going with me, but she just tells me that Father needs her. Althea, he beats her up about once a week.

" 'One night I came in and she was lying on the floor of the bathroom unconscious. I called 911 and they took her to the hospital, and yet she would not press charges against him. When I confronted her on why she didn't, she told me that she was taught to keep the family's dirty laundry hidden. Can you imagine, Tashi, what did she think the neighbors thought when all the shouting was going on?'

"My sister continued, 'In fact, one neighbor called the battered women's center. A lady from there came to talk to us. When the lady asked about the bruises on her body, Mother told her everything was fine and that her body was bruised because she had fallen. I know the lady did not believe her. She told me as I saw her to the door that if things got too bad I should get out and come to the shelter with or without my mother. I told her I would. After she left, Mother called her a busybody.'

" 'Has he hit you?' I asked my sister.

" 'Not anymore. I usually stay out until I am sure he is passed out, or at least so drunk he is too weak to do anything,' she responded.

"Oh, Tashi, I wanted to grab my sister at that moment and get her out of that house forever, but I remembered my teacher talking to me about letting people complete their karma or lessons, so all I did was hug her and tell her I would be there for her if she needed help. She is very smart, and she told me that she had been offered a scholarship to a university in Alaska. She said that soon she would be very far from them.

"I spent three days with them, and I think I could finally look at my parents without getting angry. I looked at them, not as parents who ruined my life, but as teachers who helped me to realize how very strong and loving I really was. I believe I am as close as I have ever been to being at peace with my childhood and looking at it in the larger realm of things. Enough about me. What has happened to you since we were last together? Why are you in Nepal? Is your family here as well?"

"No, they are not, Althea. My mother is dead. The Chinese killed her," he said, trying to hide the anger still within him.

"Oh, Tashi. What happened?"

Tashi told her his story and they wept together.

"Don't you wonder sometimes, Tashi, about all the senseless pain that people inflict on each other? Is there really hope that the world will change? Can we really believe the tall white beings when they tell us that we can be instrumental in that change?"

"We have to believe, Althea. Without the hope of a more loving world, we could not do what we are supposed to do: spread the word of Oneness to all. Not just to the kind and gentle people, but to everyone. Many have done this before us, but Bashur assures me this time there will be a united force assisting. The vibrations of the earth are changing, and its people must change with them or they will cease to exist on its surface."

"I want to believe you, Tashi. If anyone can make an impact, you can. You're the kindest, wisest person that I've ever met."

"Thank you, Althea, but I cannot do it alone. With you and the support of the others from the Hidden City, we can make a difference, and we will. We must believe."

Lobsang came into the garden and announced that it was time for dinner, interrupting their reunion. They ate and spent the rest of the evening talking to Tensin.

The next day Althea and Tashi found a remote place on the river. While they were deep in conversation, Bashur appeared. It was strange that they could see him but apparently no one else on the people-congested street could.

"It is good to see you two together again. There is a powerful force when your energies join. That will help you as you do the work you have taken human bodies to accomplish.

"You will begin very soon, so let us discuss the action you are to take next. You will be presented to the world as a couple. Some societies still think it taboo if a couple is not legally married, so we will give you such legal papers, even though we do not take part in such rituals. To us, a couple is committed in love to each other until the commitment is no longer advantageous to both parties, at which time they may move on and perhaps commit to someone else. In order to be accepted into these earthly societies without arousing fear or suspension, we feel that it is beneficial if they did not have the marriage issue with which to immediately judge you, thus missing the point of your more important teaching.

"Tomorrow, Tensin will see to the proper documentation," Bashur explained, not waiting to ask whether it was agreeable with the two parties involved, which of course it was, for they had known of the arrangement and had agreed to it since their meeting in the Hidden City.

"Now, spend the rest of the day getting to know each other again and we will visit with you two dear ones in a few days. Of course, as always, make every moment meaningful and fun." He disappeared, and Tashi and Althea sat silently for a number of minutes, neither one knowing how to begin the conversation about the major changes happening in their lives. A part of their silence came from the emotional stress of being unsure of the other's true human feelings.

Chapter Fifty

Tashi and Althea Get Married

The following day Tensin was gone from the house when Tashi and Althea awoke. A breakfast of tea and honey, boiled rolls, and fruit awaited them. They chatted nervously during the meal. They knew that today was an important day in their lives and that they were on the threshold of something glorious, the impact of which even their imaginations and psychic insights could not fathom.

After they nibbled on some of the foods, they went to the garden to wait for instructions about what they were to do next. As they sat there, Tashi found the courage to ask Althea the question, which had been nagging him since their meeting with Bashur.

"Althea, I know Bashur said it would be best if we presented ourselves as a married couple, but I want you to know something. I want to be with you always. Althea, I love you. Do you feel the same about me? It's all right if you don't. We can just pretend while in public," Tashi rapidly added, letting his human fear of rejection get the better of him.

Althea smiled. "Oh, Tashi, you were constantly on my mind and in my heart the entire time we were apart from each other. When they came to bring me here I was so fearful that you had found someone else. Even when they assured me you had not, I was still doubtful you felt the same way I did. Tashi, I knew I loved you from the moment I saw you in the Hidden City. I told myself that it must be a silly young girl's crush, that adults don't fall in love at first sight, but the crush never went away. As soon as I saw you again a few days ago, my heart started racing and it hasn't stopped. When I'm with you, I feel like my heart is going to jump out of my body into yours."

Tashi said nothing, but responded by taking her in his arms and kissing her until they felt as though they were two bodies permanently attached. They held each other in silence for a long while. Almost simultaneously, they spoke.

Hearing her, Tashi stopped his question in mid-word.

"There's one thing I don't understand, Tashi. If we are so capable of hearing thoughts, why couldn't either of us hear what the other was feeling about each other?"

"That's what I was wondering myself and was going to ask you," he responded, surprised, and yet not surprised, that they both had the same question at the same time.

Within a second or two of Tashi finishing his statement, Bashur appeared. "Good morning, dear ones."

"Good morning, Bashur," they both said, wondering how long he had really been there.

"We are taught not to interfere or intrude on human situations that are of a personal nature," he said, answering their thought. "Also, to answer your question of why you could not read the feelings or thoughts of each other concerning your human love, it is a complicated answer, which I do not think would be appropriate to answer fully at this time. I will, however, give you a brief answer.

"The human has an emotional veil that most of the thoughts are filtered through. Sometimes in the case of an intense relationship such as yours, that veil is very dense, preventing the thoughts from passing through that are of an emotional nature. Even when a thought does occasionally get through, it may be distorted by the person's own emotional screen.

"Later, when you are in the Hidden City for further study, we will go into this aspect of human behavior in fuller detail. It is important because relationships are creators of many of the human fears and reactions, but for now there are imminent details to complete before you both are sent to do your work." He paused, and there was a slight shift in energy. Both

Tashi and Althea felt it, and looked at each other with questions in their eyes.

Bashur began talking in a voice that Tashi and Althea knew was not the same one that had originally greeted them. "Tensin is on his way with the proper documentation for your legal union or commitment. He is also bringing the proper papers for Tashi so that he may easily pass through any borders without being deterred.

"Tashi, you are now a citizen of Nepal, and Tensin has the proper papers proving it. From this day on, when asked about your citizenship, you will reply that you are a citizen of Nepal and have lived in Katmandu for most of your life. We find it necessary to create this story for your safety. You will have a marriage license with you so that you will be able to easily enter the United States as husband and wife. You will have what they call a green card in your possession that, as Althea's husband, gives you the right to reside in the United States."

Tensin entered the garden holding an envelope of papers containing all the documents Bashur had just explained.

"Yes, I have also been trained in the Hidden City by the tall white beings, but now I work as an ambassador for them, as you two will, but in a different capacity," Tensin, said answering their unvoiced question.

Tashi and Althea looked at each other as Tashi asked the question, "How many ambassadors for the tall white beings are there in the world?"

Bashur answered, "Over the thousands of years we have occupied this planet, we have trained many ambassadors. Since the sinking of the Central City in Lemuria, we have had to establish our training bases in remote secret places for our own safety. The Hidden City, which you visited, is now considered the Central City, similarly operated as it was in the days of Lemuria. However, throughout the world we have built underground outposts for our people as well. Sometimes an outpost is discovered, often because our ambassadors become a bit careless in their movements. When this takes place we find it necessary to dismantle the outpost and move it. One example of this is the outpost we had in your state of New Mexico, Althea. We lost one of our transport ships there, along with three beings from the planet of Uranus."

Althea was shaking her head up and down when she said, "So that's what that incident was all about. It was before my time, but I remember reading about it."

"Yes, that was a regrettable situation. The extraterrestrial beings were not as advanced spiritually as those in the Hidden City and refused to heed to our instructions. We were able to shut down the underground facility immediately. When we did, we saw that they had been doing some genetic experiments that were unauthorized by the Hidden City. We released the products of their experiments into remote places in the mountains of Asia and North and South America. They live there in as much isolation as is possible. I believe the Americans call them Bigfoot or Sasquatch."

Althea and Tashi were astonished by this information. Tashi had heard tales of such large hairy beings from the nomads who had passed through his village. Although a little frightening at first because of their size and grotesque looks, the nomads described them as gentle beings that ran from sight when encountered. Now all the stories made more sense.

"I've always wondered if the Sasquatch were a result of genetic engineering gone astray. What were the experimenters striving for?" Tashi asked, searching his mind for all the tales he had heard from the Tibetan nomads.

"Its purpose was simply the desire for power. The alien experimenters were striving to create a super being, one that was more physically mighty than the current human race," Bashur explained, denoting sadness in the words.

"But where did the experimental being originate from?"

"Briefly, the original specimen was a combination of the altered DNA of a primate animal and a human being. Basically, the experiment was a success except for the fact that the environment in which they could peacefully exist was not available. Even in remote mountain areas, an occasional hunter or hiker felt threatened to the point of shooting when they encountered a Schkanuwan. It is an unfortunate situation."

"Let us get to the business at hand," Tensin said, interrupting the couple's thoughts.

"You have both agreed to this marital arrangement, so let us explain the logistics of what is to take place in the next few days. In three days, you will take a plane to San Francisco, which is in America, Tashi. You will enter the United States through that city. There, you will stay with another of our ambassadors while you are indoctrinated to the American customs," Tensin explained while looking at Tashi. "As we said before, Althea, you are a crucial instrument of this process. When we feel you are ready, we will make arrangements for you to go to the southwest United States to work with Morning Star.

"I have made arrangements for the two of you to spend some time alone at a beautiful inn overlooking the Katmandu valley. On the morning of the third day, you will be picked up and taken to the airport, then onto Singapore. The next morning you will be on your way to San Francisco."

The couple felt overwhelmed by the rapid succession of events being explained to them. "When do we leave, and when will we see you again, Bashur?" Tashi asked, feeling a little anxious about his ability to fulfill his agreed upon work.

"Let go of your human fear and doubts, Tashi. We would not send you forth if we did not feel you were ready," Bashur responded, and then disappeared.

"Gather your belongings. The car is ready to leave as we speak," Tensin said, not giving them time to conjure any more doubts. "The few days alone in the mountains will help you to relax."

Chapter Fifty-One

At the Inn

It was Tashi's first time ever to actually ride in an automobile. He had seen them on a couple of occasions during his childhood when he had traveled on roads that were suitable for such vehicles. The Chinese had trucks running to and from the mine everyday. He saw many during his walk on the road to Katmandu, although when he did see them he hid in fear of discovery by the Chinese.

At first the vibration of the car's engine and its sudden stopping and starting in the city made his stomach a bit queasy, but once they were on the road going up the same mountain that he had walked down, it was quite a pleasant experience. It was fun to see the trees and rocks pass by in a blur as he stared out the window. He found it to be hypnotic.

As the car careened around one of the curves of the mountain, Althea slid into his side. She grabbed his arm to right her, bringing Tashi out of his hypnotic stupor. He turned to her, startled by the sudden pull on his arm. He put his arm around her before the next curve took them both sliding the other way.

"Driving up this mountain is like a ride at an amusement park," Althea commented, forgetting that Tashi had probably never seen an amusement park.

It took less than three hours to reach the inn. To Tashi's surprise, it was the same inn where he had found leftovers on the plates of the guests who had been eating on the patio. How strange it seemed that he was now going to be an actual guest dining on that same patio.

Althea felt as though she was on top of the world as they stood outside gazing at the valley from whence they had just climbed. Other than those of the Hidden City, she had never been in the Himalayan Mountains at this height. Also, she had never been above the clouds except in an airplane. Then, she realized that Tashi had probably never flown on an airplane. She imagined that there would be many firsts for the two of them in the upcoming years.

Her daydreaming was interrupted when Tensin approached them in the garden beside the patio. "It's a breath taking view, is it not?" he commented, as he came up behind them. Not waiting for an answer, for no answer was expected, he announced, "Your room is ready. Come, we will show you the way to it."

The scent of freshly cut flowers and disinfectant filled their nostrils as they walked down a hallway to a door with a number on it that matched the number on a key that Tensin held in his hand. In the hallway, dim lights cast oval shapes on a muted flower carpet.

Once at the proper door, Tensin inserted the key and entered the room, motioning for them to follow. The drapes on the large windows were open, letting the light of the day flood the room and giving everything a warm glow. On the other side of a door with glass panels was a small balcony from which they could see the distant snow-capped mountains. Althea had been in many hotels, mostly motels, but none as quaint and luxurious as this one.

Tensin broke the silence. "You need only to order what you want and tell the desk clerk your room number. We have taken care of the financial obligations. In three days we will come for you. In the meantime, relax and get to know one another." A smile came to his face as he finished the sentence, as though he found humor in what he had said. Any humor was lost on Althea and Tashi. "I have ordered some tea and cakes. I thought you might enjoy them while you unpack and settle in."

Althea and Tashi thanked Tensin as he walked out the door, closing it behind him. For the first time as husband and wife, they were alone. Tashi turned to Althea, took her in his arms, and kissed her long and hard. She returned the passion.

They stood holding each other for a long while, spellbound with the love radiating from each to the other. When they finally did part, Tashi broke the silence by asking Althea if she would like to have some tea and sit on the balcony. She nodded her head yes, not wanting to break the euphoric moment with the sound of her voice.

They took their tea and cakes, which had been delivered by a young man dressed in all white (except for a saffron vest), to the balcony and sat for the rest of the afternoon, sharing tales with one another of their previous experiences. As the sun started to touch the tops of the mountains, Althea suggested that they take a shower and get into warmer clothes since the temperature had suddenly dropped—a normal event, as night was slowly creeping over the mountain inn.

They showered, and when Tashi opened his bag to dress, he found that Tensin had packed many new clothes, some of which were of a western style. As he stood there with a surprised look on his face, Althea came to see what had Tashi so startled. She could tell from the newness of the apparel and Tashi's expression that the contents of the suitcase were unknown to him prior to his opening it.

"What a nice thing for Tensin to do," she commented. "What are you going to wear tonight?"

"I really don't know. What would be appropriate? Can you help me pick something?"

"I think this sweater with these slacks would be nice," she said, pulling the sweater out and holding it up to him. "The flecks in it match the gray of your eyes."

Althea had dressed in a long floral skirt and a deep blue knitted sweater, which made her eyes appear as though they were sparkling pools of water. Around her shoulders was a wrap made of the same fabric as her skirt and lined with a blue silk fabric a few shades lighter than her sweater.

Tashi could not take her eyes off her for the moment, forgetting the perplexity of his newfound clothes. "You are beautiful," he exclaimed to her as he moved to take her in his arms. Althea did not speak, and merely enjoyed the feel of love coming in waves through her from his touch.

Tashi dressed for dinner on the patio, now lighted with lanterns disbursed around its perimeter. Even though the temperature had dropped at least twenty degrees, neither felt cold dressed in wool sweaters and surrounded in a shroud of new love. They sat on the patio talking and drinking wine far into the evening.

When the chilly night air finally penetrated their clothing, they returned to their room. Relaxed by the wine, their first time making love was as though they had done it many times before. They held each other throughout the night, apprehensive that if they let go the dream would end.

The following two days passed swiftly. On the third day they were both sullen, not because of anything that was said or done by the other but because both were unsure of what was in store for them once they left this enchanting place. They packed without speaking and had only a light breakfast of tea, biscuits, and honey, which was sent to their room. They had just finished eating when Tensin knocked at the door. He greeted them and instructed the porter to take their bags to the car.

"I will give you instructions and answer your questions on our ride to the Katmandu airport," Tensin explained in a very business-like tone of voice.

The couple nodded and followed Tensin to the awaiting vehicle. The three of them settled into the backseat of the large car. The driver started the car and steered it down the mountain. Tensin was the first to speak.

"Did you enjoy your stay at the inn?" he asked, smiling with his eyes.

Without waiting for a verbal answer, for he could deduce the answer by the glow around them, he continued, "At the airport I will help you through Customs and onto the plane. The plane will stop in Singapore, where you will spend the night in the airport hotel. You will board another plane the next day, which will take you to San Francisco.

"There, a man named Zopa will take you to his home, where you will spend a few months resting from the long plane ride and orienting yourselves to your upcoming assignment. He will give you further instructions. You see, we do have ambassadors throughout the world, but most of us are clandestine. This will not be the case with both of you. You will be in the public eye and will require protection and a safe house from time to time. Do not worry, for when this is necessary, help will be close at hand. The tall ones have learned from past experience that their messengers are in constant danger from those whose power is threatened by the messages."

"Whom will I give these messages to?" Tashi asked, confused by the gravity of the scene Tensin was portraying. "Why would they want to harm Althea or myself if all we are speaking of is love?"

"Governments and religious organizations will feel threatened. Most of religion is taught through the belief that God is a fearful energy and that if certain actions are taken, God will bring on his wrath. The only way to prevent God's wrath, in these belief-system traps, is to listen and act according to the words of the leader of that particular religion. This kind of human power is intoxicating for those who claim it. If in your message you threaten their cherished supremacy over people, the religious leaders will defend it with their life. Most wars and killing throughout the history of the earth have been the result of just such defensive reactions.

"Governments will feel threatened because you will be teaching responsibility for one's self in thought and action. Most governments rely on people depending on them for their well being."

Every self-doubt within Tashi rose to the surface. How could he, the son of a yak herder from a remote village in the Himalayans, challenge such a strong and ingrained belief system?

Tensin sensed Tashi's anxieties and said, "Never forget that you are more powerful than any of those we warn you of, for unconditional love is the strongest energy. Trust that there are many that are working behind the scenes to assure your safety so that your work of spreading the word can continue, for at this time in the earth's history, it is imperative. Bashur will always be at your side to support you, as he has been since you first incarnated. Now, release the worry and enjoy the journey. America will be full of fun surprises for you. Althea will show you a culture of which you could never have dreamed."

Tensin chatted about the inn and its history in order to bring lightness back into the conversation. At the airport they were led through

Immigration without delay. Tensin said his goodbye, and Althea and Tashi got in line to board the 737, which would take them to Singapore.

As they were slowly proceeding to the stairs of the airplane, Tashi whispered quietly to Althea, "I have never been on an airplane before. I have only seen airplanes as they've flown over my village. They looked so small from the ground. I had no idea they were so large and loud."

Althea smiled and said, "Just wait, Tashi. Our life will be full of new experiences."

Without even speaking the words, they both thought of the Hidden City and the tall white beings in their silent spacecraft. It was strange that an airplane could hold more wonder than a spacecraft and tall white beings, but the latter seemed so much more familiar, as though it had been a part of their lives always.

Soon Tashi and Althea were seated on the plane in row seven, seats A and B. During the five-hour flight to Singapore, they were served food and drink, which Tashi found very different. To him it lacked any taste at all, except perhaps that of salt. The chocolate cookie, he found, was like something he had never tasted, sweet but bitter. Althea enjoyed watching him experience airplane food, something she had never acquired a taste for.

Immigration went smoothly in Singapore, and a woman twice the age of Althea met them, arranging for their room and leading them to it at the airport hotel. It was a small stark cubicle, furnished with two single beds and a bed stand on which sat a simple lamp with a low-voltage bulb. In the corner a television was attached to the concrete block wall on a shelf elevated about five feet above ground. The bath was as austere as the room with only the essentials of a toilet stool with no lid, a sink, and a shower with no tub or door. There was nothing luxurious about the room. It was designed simply as a temporary resting place between long plane flights.

The couple had no luggage except for the few convenience items Tensin had packed for them in a small carry-on bag. Their other luggage was taken to their connecting flight to be put on board closer to flight time.

After washing up, Tashi and Althea explored the city-like terminal.

They found stores of every international persuasion selling goods that were a specialty to that particular country. It was like traveling the markets of the world within the confines of a building. They walked for miles, loosening their stiff plane-cramped muscles.

In one part of the building, there were various restaurants with food and decor indigenous to the origin of the country they were featuring. The aromas from the conglomerate of kitchens drifted into the corridor of the terminal, sometimes creating a nauseating effect for those within its reach. Because of the smell, Tashi and Althea opted to purchase a simple snack of vegetable salads and bottled water, which they took back to their room. They also purchased two Styrofoam cups filled with tea and honey. Tashi had a difficult time getting used to the texture and taste of the strange white cup.

The excitement and physical exertion of the trip had taken its toll on their bodies, and they found that sleep came quickly that night. They were awakened by a voice over an intercom announcing that it was time to rise and that their flight would be boarding in two hours. Evidently the woman who met them had also arranged for a wake-up call.

Disoriented at first, they sat up in bed and just looked around. Althea was the first to speak. "I will take my shower first," she said. "We have plenty of time if you wish to meditate for a while." She knew Tashi meditated every morning before beginning his day.

Tashi's meditation was brought to an end by loud knocking at the door. Standing at the door was a man dressed in a light blue uniform with some printing on it over his left breast. In his arms was a tray with two cups, two tea bags, and a silver pot of steaming water and a plate of various pastries.

"Your room service, sir," the uniformed man said without any expression in his voice.

Tashi took the tray, not knowing quite what else to do since it was more or less shoved into his arms. The man continued to stand there as though waiting for something even after Tashi had set the tray on the nightstand and went to close the door. Tashi said "thank you," a phrase Althea had taught him on the plane ride from Katmandu. He then shut the door. The uniformed man mumbled some words in disgust, loud enough for Tashi to hear but not understand.

Just as he was shutting the door, Althea came out of the bathroom. "Who was at the door?" she asked.

"Someone who brought us a tray of food. He seemed to be angry when he left. Did I do something to cause his anger? I said thank you as you taught me to do."

Althea laughed, which bewildered Tashi.

"I did do something wrong," he said, searching his mind for the action or words that might cause someone to anger.

"No, Tashi. You did nothing wrong. These people who serve others expect a tip in the form of money. You had no way of knowing that."

"A tip? Does he not get pay from an employer as you explained yesterday?"

"Yes, but not very much. They depend on most of their compensation from their tips. I will explain it and other such customs to you later on the long flight over the Pacific. Don't worry. That man will get over it. I'm certain it is not the first time it has happened to him and probably won't be the last in such an international environment as this. Let's drink our tea while it is hot."

They finished the light breakfast. Tashi took a shower and dressed. In the lobby they asked directions to their gate and arrived there just as they called for boarding. Tashi saw the plane they were to take through the window and was dumbstruck with the enormousness of its size. He had never seen anything so big. How could something so large fly? They followed the jet way to the opening in its side. When they entered, he saw rows and rows of seats that seemed to go on and on. Althea led him to the seat that was printed on the tickets she was carrying.

Throughout the flight, except when they napped, she and Tashi talked, mostly about what to expect when they landed in the United States. She tried to prepare him for the speed at which everything, including the people, moved in the States. She knew most foreigners visiting America thought that the people were rude, mostly because they did not understand the American way of rushing to get places.

Although, thinking about it, she herself could not understand why people felt the need to rush to a destination either. Half the time when they arrived, they were not happy to be there and often had to wait anyway.

The trip was long, but it did give them time to talk, for there was very little else to do. They watched some of the television shows on the screen on the back of the seat in front of them. A documentary on San Francisco gave Althea an opportunity to explain to Tashi some of the sights he might expect to see when they arrived there.

They meditated some and made a game out of listening to some of the other passenger's thoughts. One small boy from India who sat across the aisle from them was sending them thought messages. They sent a message back to him, which brought a smile to his round little face. He was definitely connected mind-to-mind with them. Soon the little boy's mother distracted him, and the game ended.

One man, who they connected with mind-to-mind, upset them so much that they looked at each other to be certain that they had heard his thoughts correctly. His energy was heavy and his thoughts were angry.

We will show the world our strength in five hours. I only wish I had been among those chosen to take over the American planes and fly them into buildings on the East Coast, The passenger thought.

They were certain that he was totally unaware that a young couple whose purpose was to teach love, fortified with the ancient spirit of Lemuria, was hearing his thoughts.

His thoughts continued, *My turn will come soon, and I too will be rewarded by Allah. The meeting with our leader and the Chinese delegate has assured me of this.*

Althea and Tashi could listen no more. Their stomachs ached as they felt the rage in this misled man's thoughts permeate them. At the mention of the Chinese, Tashi felt his own rage rise. What had Bashur taught? Look at his demon and send it Light and Love, not an easy task for him with the tragedy of his own family still ripe in his mind. He shut his eyes and focused on his demon. When he felt the universal love fill him, he directed it toward the man whose thoughts he had heard. He felt Althea doing the same. As the couple slowly let their minds and bodies quiet, they gently fell into a deep sleep.

They were suddenly awakened by loud noises. When their eyes

opened, they saw people talking on cell phones and turning white with shock and emotional horror. People in the seats around them shouted, "Oh, my God!" They repeated the phrase over and over.

Just as Tashi and Althea were grasping the gravity of the first disaster, they overheard someone behind them explaining what had happened to the person next to them. Someone across the aisle shouted that a second plane had crashed into another building in the World Trade Center in New York. Althea and Tashi looked at one another in horror. This is the thought that they had overheard from the angry man.

"What should we do?" they asked each other.

When they shut their eyes they heard, "There is nothing you can do to stop this, for it is part of the plan . . . an awakening, if you will. Fill yourselves with light and do not take on the rage of the mass consciousness."

Tashi and Althea closed their eyes and connected with their higher selves. Within minutes they felt the release of the negative energy they had taken on, not only from the angry man, but also from the other passengers who were filled with fear from the event they had just heard about.

Chapter Fifty-Two

Tashi Arrives in America

A stewardess holding a tray of paper cups filled with orange juice brought Tashi and Althea out of their meditative state. "We'll be landing soon," she announced to every row as she came up the aisle. "Would you care for some orange juice? Breakfast will be served shortly," she added after she was certain each person was awake and sitting up.

Tashi and Althea looked at each other. They had talked most of the night. It was so easy to talk with each other. It felt like they had known each other all their lives instead of merely a few months. What adventure lay ahead for them in America? Even with the terror of the current disaster, they knew deep inside of them that for the first time in their young human lives, their purpose was clear.

They heard each other's thoughts and squeezed each other's hands as a sign of love and support. Whatever was to happen, they both knew that insecurities would be minor with each other's support. After eating a light breakfast, Althea helped Tashi gather the proper immigration papers. She hoped entering the United States would be swift, but one never knew. She was sure Tensin had seen to all the proper documentation necessary for Tashi, but Althea had seen immigrants detained at Immigration for no apparent reason many times in the past. She was certain the recent attack would result in more airport security than normal.

On the plane, the fear energy was at a peak. When she looked at the man whose thoughts they had heard earlier in the flight, she thought she saw a smile in his eyes and at the corners of his mouth.

Tashi heard her fearful thoughts and said, "It will go smoothly. We have nothing to be concerned about."

"I know better than to project negative doubts. Of course everything will go smoothly. I just don't want you to think the United States is like Tibet, with the armed Chinese soldiers at its border," she said, looking deep into his eyes.

"Even then, Althea, Bashur showed me a way to overcome that problem. We must keep our faith that we are being helped at every turn. At this point, though, it is important that the tall white beings not interfere with our normal human events. We must appear to be like any other human walking this earth or the creditability of our words could be compromised. People will relate to us much more readily if they think we are entirely human. Our extraterrestrial connections would be difficult for them to accept, and it is not the focus of the messages.

"With the recent attack even more people will be leery and frightened of people from other countries. How do you think they would react to people from other universes? Part of our work is to convince people that we are all one, and that even the extraterrestrials that live beneath and beyond the earth's surface are a part of our Oneness."

Althea knew Tashi was channeling these words. She could feel the shift in his energy.

"Most people are afraid of the unknown. Why else would they fear God, who is the epitome of love? According to Bashur, these fears are why the tall white beings have chosen to continue to stay hidden. It is our job to prepare the path for them to again be visible as spiritual teachers like they were in Lemuria. Althea, the spirit of Lemuria must rise again, or this time the entire planet and its people will be destroyed.

"Let's meditate and clear ourselves of our human fears," Tashi added, taking her hand and closing his eyes. "Our true work is about to begin. Let us prepare by clearing ourselves of our human doubts and fears. Let's focus on channeling the universal love energy and increasing the flow of our Kundalini."

In doing so the couple radiated an energy that spread throughout the plane. Soon babies stopped crying and adults found themselves helping one another prepare for the landing. When the plane landed, its occupants deplaned much more patiently and graciously than usual. People who had sat next to each other for twelve hours without speaking were now hugging each other and wishing each other well. Even in Immigration, no one was shoving or rushing. Everyone was cordial and friendly.

Althea and Tashi looked around and smiled knowingly at one another. "Our work has begun. The spirit of Lemuria is rising again."

CPSIA information can be obtained at www.ICGtesting.com
Printed in the USA
267703BV00002B/3/P

9 781612 042428